The Alphabet Affair

Bill Corbin

Beckett-Highland Publishing

This book is a work of fiction. Names, characters, places and incidents are either the product of author's imagination or are used fictitiously, and any resemblance to actual persons, living or dead, events, or locales is entirely coincidental.

Cover art by Jodi Coyle

Beckett-Highland Publishing
1429 Chase Court
Carmel, Indiana 46032

Visit www.BillCorbin.com

Printed in the United States of America
First Trade Printing: October 2005
10 9 8 7 6 5 4 3 2 1

Library of Congress Control Number: 2005905038
ISBN: 1-893456-14-5

To my wife and the
coaches, advisors, and supporters
who had faith that
I could learn to tell a story.

Also by Bill Corbin

Accidental Soldiers

Players & Pawns

Silent Hero

For information: www.BillCorbin.com

Chapter One

Ted Aldrich sat alone on the front porch of his rustic home, built high on a wooded knoll overlooking the rolling fields and forests of southern Ohio. His sprawling white barn, which he liked to call his personal hangar, sat at meadow's edge below him. Above him, lazy clouds floated in a sky shimmering bluish-white in dry summer heat.

Restless, Aldrich descended the winding stone path that led to the barn, pushed open the massive sliding door, and used a pull-rope to roll his cherry red biplane into the hazy sunlight. Ted Aldrich loved his planes; he loved to fly; but he was battling a feeling of tired old motions as he fired up the bird, lowered his goggles, and taxied toward the narrow blacktop strip that extended into the meadow.

He accelerated for half the length of the runway and lifted off, looking for a corresponding lift in his spirits. He had tried, in a half-assed way, to be a good son. His father had owned a major dry cleaning chain in Tampa, and Ted Sr. died a sad old man. As they sat together on a nursing home veranda, his father said, "Get in your licks while you're young, Teddy. I let life go by, and now my money and I are sitting in a damned rocking chair."

So Ted got in his licks while he was young. He flew jet fighters, drove stock cars, and raced powerboats. He hunted in Africa, climbed in Nepal, and along the way he sampled ladies of every flavor. But he never decided that he wasn't young, and the years sped by and became a deep stack of memories now blurring. Still, he had his toys. He had the game. And one day, he would cash out by going down with all guns blazing.

He lifted the plane's nose to forty-five degrees, aiming toward a listless cloud bank, enjoying the whip of wind on his face. At a deep internal level, Ted Aldrich had committed to going down with all guns blazing. He sure as hell couldn't be a rocking chair guy, tethered to a nose tube, doled soft food by a blue-haired nurse, reading the Bible like a drowning man looking for a life raft. His father lived like that for two God forsaken years. Ted wouldn't survive it for two days.

Prison might be worse, and the thought of gray walls was Ted's only real concern when Daniel added death to their game. Ted didn't mind death, someone else's or his own. Any fighter pilot worth his salt has glared into Death's eye and didn't blink. Ted thought of enemy soldiers he had riddled. He thought of people fleeing and falling in villages he had strafed. He thought of that long-ago morning, of Merri riding her motorcycle beside his, hair streaming behind her, face alive with the joy that filled her. Then the deer, out of nowhere. Merri's frantic swerve. The long grinding slide, sparks flying off Route 40's pavement, until roadside underbrush swallowed his fiancé and her cycle. Finding her. Holding her. Ted Aldrich clenched his teeth, seeing as if yesterday her eyes imploring but knowing, fading slowly to steel gray. If Merri deserved to die, anyone could die.

He leveled at three thousand feet, relishing the throaty growl of the engine. He veered right, roaring counterclockwise around the four vertical fingers of a jutting cloud formation. He lifted the nose to vertical, looped, barrel-rolled, and looped again, this time exploding through the fingers of clouds. He thought about their last game. Ah, sweet Lynn. Lynn Thompson. What a peach! Lynn hadn't handled the biplane well, but even a ghost-white Lynn Thompson was a joy to look at, possibly the most beautiful woman he had ever loved.

He shook his head while pulling the plane's nose back to vertical and starting a five hundred foot climb. Hell, they were all beautiful; he loved them all; the next one is more important than the last, and so it will be with the dearly departed Lynn Thompson. He reached the top of his climb and shut down the engine, playing again his version of Russian roulette. No idea where he was on the map. He would dead-stick to a landing somewhere. Hopefully survive. If not, what the hell? The long glide began. A leisurely study of the terrain under him. Nothing but heavy green forest for now. No problem. Challenging. He banked right, searching. Son of a bitch; nothing but forest. Losing altitude rapidly now. He banked left. Giant trees looming. Needing a break. Only one choice, a farm out further to the left. Dropping faster. Barely clearing a tree line. Close. Heading directly toward the roof of a barn. Not good. Either dead or a police report. Veer right. Missed the barn. More trees. Left this time. Cleared a tractor and wagon by maybe a foot. Bouncing onto the ground between a rusty pickup and a wide-eyed woman holding a bucket. Helluva ride!

Let's charm the lady for a few minutes; probably good for a piece of pie, maybe more; then head home.

Now in full uniform, Captain Ted Aldrich flew his twin-engine Bonanza toward the Columbus, Ohio airport. He would be returning Columbus-to-Chicago for professional reasons, and deadheading on a TransSystem flight would provide another opportunity to fulfill his role as the game's recruitment officer. He thought back over the last several frustrating weeks. As always, meeting attractive women had been no problem. Hell, an airport bubbles with attractive women. Stewardesses have friends; alert buddies on the ticket counters can help. But attractive wasn't enough, and this year's lady still eluded him.

Chapter Two

Jackie Billings had reached the Columbus airport's access road when she pulled her cell phone and called her husband. "Matt, I forgot to pack Jodi's sheet music. You'll need to run it over to your mom's house tonight."

"Okay, no problem," came the distracted reply.

"Don't forget."

"I won't forget, but it would help if you handled the stuff you're supposed to handle. Things are a little crazy here."

She absorbed the shot, knowing that Matt's crew was deep into a complicated remodeling project for a fussy client. But things had been a little crazy in her life, too. "Sorry. Oh, and remind your mom to have Sean at the work project by nine."

She heard his sigh. "Or maybe you could remind her; or maybe you could skip this whole damn trip thing and give me a little help."

"C'mon, Matt, it's only once a year." The bank had downsized and her department was doing more work with three fewer people. She was an assistant den mother, a PTO treasurer, a Heart Association fundraiser, and the kids' primary taxi driver. Matt worked twelve hours most days. And Sean had turned thirteen and discovered his own brand of maddening moodiness. She needed this break.

"It would help my attitude," he grumbled, "if your damn get-away didn't include the sister-slut."

Jackie decided to ignore Matt's latest sister-shot, a theme grown tiresome. "Okay, honey, I'm at long-term parking. See you Sunday."

With time to spare, Jackie Billings stopped by an airport newsstand and browsed the magazine rack. She hadn't opened a *Cosmopolitan* for ten years, but she thumbed through a copy and decided to buy it. It felt like a gloriously free-spirited thing to do.

Jackie boarded TransSystem Airways Flight 223 and made her way toward seat 36B. She found her row completely filled, with a man of Asian ancestry firmly planted in her intended spot. "Ah, nah, B, B, B for use of my body," he insisted.

An alert stewardess hurried toward them, while scanning some kind of computer report. "I'm so sorry for the inconvenience," she said to Jackie. "There's a seat available in first class. Let's move you up there." Pleasantly amazed, Jackie followed the stewardess through the blue veil of separation. "This window seat is empty," said the young woman, gesturing toward the second row.

Jackie hoisted her carry-on into a roomy overhead compartment, glanced briefly at the maze of dials visible through the open cockpit door, exchanged greetings with a steward who looked to be about Sean's age, and nestled into soft brown leather. After another minute or two surveying the trappings of the upper crust, Jackie slid *Cosmo* out of her shopping bag and began perusing. Someone settled in beside her, but she didn't look up. A few minutes before take-off, the steward stopped beside their row. "Champagne for either of you?"

"Just coffee, please," said the man next to her, his voice deep with just a hint of drawl.

"Ma'am?"

Jackie decided to fully enjoy her unexpected collision with luxury. "Sure, I'd love some champagne."

She had sipped half the glass and was feeling pleasantly light-headed when the man said, "Learning anything useful?" She clenched her teeth and closed her eyes, feeling like a schoolgirl caught by the study-hall teacher. A two-page spread blared, *Ten Ways to Titillate that Man of Yours.*

She turned and looked into striking blue eyes. His hair was silver-gray, but the face was strong and an odd blend of weathered and youthful. She considered ignoring the question then searched for a clever reply. Nothing came to mind. "No. I mean nothing I care to—"

He chuckled, forming creases at his eyes and mouth that suggested habitual laughter. "No offense, but your cheeks are clashing with your blouse. It might help if you just wore white."

Jackie smiled, but uneasily, not doubting a clash with her pink blouse. But she felt a twinge of anger. "I guess I'm just not used to sitting beside nosy men, but thanks for the fashion tip." She looked away, realizing the comment was a conversational train wreck. The adult in Jackie Billings would happily return to her magazine, although she would flip to a new page. But she missed the part of her that could have chatted easily with an interesting man. She thought back to sorority parties where her sisters actually envied her sense of humor and quick one-liners. It had been a long time ago.

"My name's Ted Aldrich. Sorry for the comment; I couldn't resist."

She turned toward him. His smile was friendly, showing strong white teeth. "I'm Jackie Billings, usually I'm…" She glanced toward her lap and closed the magazine. "I'm usually reading about something like wallpaper or petunias."

"Titillation sounds more interesting than petunias, Jackie Billings."

She nodded, ready for a halt. "*Cosmo* thinks so, anyway."

She turned away, again assuming the conversation would end, but Ted Aldrich apparently wanted to chat. He began by asking whether she worked. They discussed her job at the bank and Matt's job as head of Billings Construction. Soon she had shown him pictures of Jodi and Sean.

He said, “You sparkle when you talk about your kids.”

“I sparkle?”

“Yep, sparkle, and maybe glow a little.”

“Gosh, is that safe at thirty thousand feet?”

He smiled, laugh lines at full crinkle. “That was a good one, Mrs. Billings.”

“Thank you. I’m a little out of practice in the art of repartee.”

“Why’s that?”

She hesitated, but realized that she felt amazingly comfortable. “You might say my hubby keeps me on a pretty short leash, you know, socially.”

“Leashes don’t sound good.”

“I’m pretty well used to it.”

His expression turned quizzical, and doubtful. “But how do you *feel* about it?”

She leaned back for a moment, her mind a revolving slide show of Matt’s jealousy moments: some disappointing, some infuriating, and some absurd. But none felt shareable with Ted Aldrich. “I’m okay with it.”

He gave her a compassionate smile as if somehow he had seen her slide show. “I don’t know if this will help, but as a fellow male, I can understand why he’d be possessive. He married a real winner.”

She felt new warmth on her cheeks, appreciating the thought—at least the last part of it—but ready to duck. “How did you become a pilot?”

She learned that Ted was fifty-two, a Vietnam veteran who became a commercial pilot and now flew world routes. He had dreamed of flying since boyhood, and still loved the sense of freedom that soaring through the clouds gave him. He was deadheading, which he explained meant returning to Chicago to connect with his crew. He steered the conversation to her feelings about the joys and challenges of parenting. And she returned to a feeling of being energized, amazed to be so openly sharing her feelings.

The plane entered final descent into O'Hare, and Jackie found herself wishing that time hadn't passed so quickly. While she gathered belongings, a stewardess hand-delivered a gold-striped jacket and cap. "See you around town, Captain Aldrich."

He slipped into uniform, and they walked together through the long jet way and into the crowded concourse. He turned toward her and extended his hand. "It was wonderful meeting you, Jackie. Have a great life."

She took his hand and shook formally, although aware that their eye contact didn't exactly feel formal. She said, "Thanks for making my trip enjoyable," and turned toward a flight information monitor. When she glanced over her shoulder, he had disappeared into the throng of passengers.

She meandered toward her gate, window-shopping absently, still thinking about unlikely conversations. "Jackie Billings. Jackie Billings. Please pick up the nearest white courtesy phone." Her stomach jumped instantly as she visualized possible family emergencies. An accident at summer camp? Something at Matt's work site? She stopped at the nearest ticket counter, asked where she could find a white phone, and rushed toward it. "This is Jackie Billings," she said breathlessly.

"One moment, please. I'll connect you."

"Hello, Jackie, the ever-alert Ted Aldrich has noticed you have a long layover. Might we do lunch?"

Although vastly relieved, she blurted, "Why?" instantly aware that all conversational glibness had vanished again.

"I enjoyed talking with you. I didn't want it to be over."

The two sides of Jackie Billings debated briefly, but intensely. The conservative side insisted on more information. "Where would we have lunch?"

"In the crew lounge."

She smiled, realizing that this story might earn more than a casual eyebrow lift from her worldly sister. And the crew lounge felt safe enough, although Matt wouldn't have thought so. She ignored her flip-flopping stomach and said, "Okay, lunch would be nice."

He arranged for an electric cart pickup, and she was soon riding behind a uniformed driver, weaving through a crowded concourse before stopping at a hallway marked *Airline Personnel Only*. Ted stood waiting, looking crisp and professional in his blue uniform. He handed her a plastic ID necklace, guided her through a security check and on into an ultra-modern lounge where their window table looked out onto the massive O'Hare complex. As they settled in, he briefly explained the reasons for the maze of crisscrossed runways, and the interplay between pilot and control tower.

While they lunched on baked halibut, they talked about her colorful family, about her dad's death, and about her volunteer activities. He asked probing questions; he listened; his eyes said he cared. And they shared easy laughter. But as they worked on a pudding dessert, he leaned forward and asked, "Why the *Cosmo*, Jackie?"

She looked for a quip. She looked for indignation that he had suddenly violated her comfort zone, but his eyes remained warm and sincere and caring, and she had apparently allowed a barrier or two to fall. "I'm not sure," she answered honestly, "maybe just to spice up the weekend a little."

"I'm not surprised by that, Jackie. I think your husband is making a serious mistake."

She looked again for anger but failed to find it, maybe because Ted's tone was so sincere, maybe because she knew, deep down, that Matt had made some mistakes. "What kind of mistake?"

"He's trying to keep a wildflower from blooming."

Her feelings began tripping all over each other. His words sounded heavy, silly, true, debatable, but way too personal. "I'm sorry, Ted, but I'm really not comfortable with this."

"I meant no offense, Jackie. But I truly believe each of us needs to be challenged now and then—or life goes by and you spend the last part regretting all the things you missed."

She studied him carefully, still finding nothing but sincerity. For a crazy moment, she considered diving in. Ted's blend of maturity, wisdom, openness, and good humor made deep conversation feel possible. But this water felt too deep. "Maybe so," she said, "but that's plenty of challenge for today. Where are your favorite places to fly?"

"I just like to fly: New Orleans tonight; then Mexico City. Both good ones."

"Do you need to speak Spanish in Mexico City?"

They finished desert, talking about the airline industry's universal use of English, but her feelings were crazily ambivalent: wishing they could have talked at a deeper level; relieved that they hadn't. He walked with her through the corridor to the waiting cart. As they shook hands for the second time, he said, "You are a special lady."

She smiled, stepped back, and lifted a mock salute. "Thank you, Captain Aldrich. It really has been fun to meet you."

***

Ted Aldrich strolled to the pilots' lounge, found an isolated couch, pulled his cell phone, and dialed. "Let the game begin."

"Target?"

"Jackie Billings; Dublin, Ohio, a northwest suburb of Columbus; the bucks will come from Third Ohio National."

"Vitals?"

"Mid-thirties. Slender, but nice tits. Long legs. Long brown hair. Sweet, vulnerable, a suffocating husband. Perfect."

As it did annually, the voice darkened. "Bright enough to be challenging, Theodore?"

"Without a doubt."

"We'll see."

As he did at least once annually, Ted Aldrich asked, "Do we need to hurt this one?"

"Not your department, Mr. A. Just enjoy."

Chapter Three

Jackie's seatmate for the Chicago-Omaha leg of her flight turned out to be an elderly lady deep into a Nora Roberts novel. The change would have been more relaxing, Jackie decided, if Ted Aldrich would leave her alone. For a few minutes, discomfort had lingered, but her unease lifted like a thin morning fog, letting her spirit soar. An attractive man hadn't engaged her or challenged her for a very long time. Being honest, even the small bit of titillation had been fun, although *blooming wildflower* might have been a little over the top. She found herself daydreaming, and she could barely believe her own daydream. She chuckled out loud.

"What's so funny?" asked her seatmate, looking up from Nora.

Jackie decided against candor. "Oh, nothing. I was just thinking about a joke my husband told me." In fact, she had visualized two shopping trips. During the first, Matt helped her select a high-necked granny dress. During the second, Ted Aldrich helped her pick little scanties to wear under it.

"It must have been a good joke. You're blushing, dearie."

Jackie told Ted Aldrich to exit her mind, immediately.

As Jackie approached the baggage carousel at Omaha's Epply Airfield, she spotted Mia Marie Morris Bowman Grant, busily engaged in a cell phone conversation. Mia waved from afar, pointing toward her watch and flashing an open-mouthed *surprise, I'm here on time* expression. Punctuality was not one of Mia's strong suits.

Jackie marveled again that two small-town Ohio girls would be gathering in Nebraska for a reunion. After graduating from Greenville High, Jackie had entered Ohio State's business school—boring as dirt in Mia's opinion. Mia roared onto campus two years later and attacked the drama school with her eyes on New York. She never hit it big, but managed a career as a touring actress, mostly musicals. Jackie married Matt Billings, also boring as dirt in Mia's opinion, and stayed in Columbus. While in New York, Mia married an intense young character actor named David Bowman—a brief, fiery disaster. She was twenty-eight, touring in Chicago, when Omaha meat baron Julian Grant sent his flowers backstage. He promised her career freedom, but tried to lasso her almost immediately. Two stormy years later, Mia used her settlement money to buy her wooded mini-estate and her Jaguar. Jackie had expected her to leave Omaha, but Mia called it a great retreat as long as planes flew to Chicago and New York.

Jackie decided that a few more pounds of the good life had settled onto her sister's always somewhat stocky frame—a look that Mia called "bursting with ripe womanhood." But Mia had found another great style for her short reddish hair, the smile and blue eyes bubbled mischievously, and her summer dress, swirling mint and white, shouted *Vogue.* They embraced and Mia stepped back to conduct an annual survey, no doubt deciding that khaki slacks and a pink blouse did not shout *Vogue*. "Welcome to Omaha, big sister, I hope your ass gets as big as a barn one of these years."

Jackie greeted her sister warmly, but skipped bantering about the size of fannies. They both understood part of the reason. Jackie still worked out four times a week, although she sometimes wondered why. Mia hated to sweat. And they knew that a second possibility had fascinated the Greenville rumor mill for years. Jackie had inherited their father's height, slender frame, and dark hair and complexion. Mia had inherited their mother's brimming personality, even her passion for theater. But Mia's hair, eyes, and robust shape could not be easily located on the family tree.

They found Jackie's suitcase, stuffed it into Mia's dark green Jaguar convertible, and roared out of short-term parking. As they rocketed along I-680, Jackie shouted above the roaring wind, "You'd never guess what I want to do this weekend."

Mia glanced toward her, grinning. "Roast marshmallows and sing campfire songs, right?"

"Nope. This weekend I want to, you know, have some fun."

Mia's glance became an exaggerated curious squint, one eye closed. "What the hell, pray tell, might that mean?"

"I don't know. Something a little wild and crazy."

"Seriously?"

"Yes. Seriously."

Mia grinned again. "I'll see if the Chippendales are in town."

"We don't need the Chippendales. Just something, I don't know, a little different."

"Are you and Mr. Jerkwad okay?" asked Mia, her expression actually serious.

"Yes. I mean things are fine, but too busy and too serious and…"

"Want to know something?" said Mia.

"Sure. What?"

"I've been waiting for years for this moment."

Mia parked the Jaguar in the circular drive in front of her rambling brick and cedar ranch. Soaring oak protected the triple lot. Eye-level rows of shrub enclosed the front lawn. Stockade fencing guarded the pool and gardens behind the house. As she pulled her suitcase toward the bedroom wing, Jackie marveled again at her sister's stunningly eclectic interior decoration. The feel was open and breezy, mostly yellows and oranges. But furniture ranged from

Scandinavian to antique, with textures ranging from metallic to tweed. Artwork included a chaotic variety of wall paintings, sculptures, and twisted metal oddities clawing toward the ceiling. Mia confessed to buying things based on the mood she was in.

They settled Jackie into the Picasso room, one of four bedrooms larger than the Billings' master bedroom in Columbus. "Come with me to the dressing room," Mia commanded playfully.

"Where's that?"

"My closet, silly."

Jackie followed her sister into a master bedroom decorated in something like tropical chic, including soaring plants surrounding a yellow-topped canopy bed that appeared to be forty feet wide. They entered an enormous walk-in closet, and Jackie simply shook her head. The place was a loosely organized riot of shoes and outfits ranging from tennis dresses to formal gowns. Mia glided to her left, stood for a moment of perusal, pulled a short, snow-white cocktail dress, and said, "Let's try this."

Jackie analyzed and wished she could quit analyzing. But she said, "Where will we be going?"

Mia grinned. "To find the wild life in Omaha."

Jackie laughed. "That sounds safe enough." She slipped out of shoes, slacks, and blouse, and took the dress from Mia.

"Sexy," Mia observed, but saltily.

"Why thank you," replied Jackie, knowing they were talking about Jockey for Her white cotton. She slipped into the dress.

Mia stepped toward her, helped zip, then stepped back to inspect. "I would kill for those legs."

Jackie walked to the full-length door mirror, turned slowly, and the years fell away. She smiled and turned back toward Mia. "Remember Tommy Kerrigan?"

"Sure I remember Tommy Kerrigan. I'm glad you do."

Jackie drifted into memory. Tommy was her only serious boyfriend in high school, a football player and a reward of sorts for emerging—with the help of a wonderful P.E. teacher named Miss Felding—from her long period of weight and complexion problems. Jackie had been clueless about male obsession, but she quickly learned about Tommy's. She caught his eye, he admitted, as she cavorted in her cheerleading skirt. After they started dating, she wore miniskirts for him and, later, Mia's shorter miniskirts. He eventually confessed that the idea that her legs and panties were available to him—to see and to touch—turned him on beyond belief. At first, the idea embarrassed her, but she learned to be okay with it. Later, as she gained confidence and at least a smidgen of sexual experience, she decided that being able to turn Tommy on was something like reassuring fun.

Jackie winced, as her memories grew darker. Tommy wouldn't have tolerated Jockey for Her cotton, so she wore the skimpy bikini panties he liked. But she balked when he demanded no underwear at all, and by late-senior year, he had apparently talked a cheerleader named Penny Beck into playing his games. But the split hurt, a lot. Jackie had thought they were in love. She had gone to bed with him, although she later realized that Tommy as a lover had been a bad joke—three times for a grand total of maybe forty-five seconds. She escaped to college, and she spent a year or so healing, becoming one of the funny-but-nice girls at the sorority. Soon she met Matt—solid, steady, and quickly oh so possessive. So she decided to reveal forty-five seconds less than full truth about her sexual experience, although it felt a bit 1950ish to fib. And Tommy Kerrigan disappeared into a stack of old photographs stored in a Greenville, Ohio attic.

Mia said, "Earth to Jackie. Earth to Jackie."

"Sorry. Just thinking about Quick-Draw Kerrigan."

They laughed their way through four different outfits, eventually settling on a peach spaghetti-strapped sundress with the kind of hem the fashion catalogs call flirty. Mia said, "Give it a spin." So Jackie spun, the hem flew, and she loved the feeling.

The evening's restaurant choice was Henrico's, mauve-and-brass modern, softened by wispy asparagus fern, with light provided by crystal-enclosed wall and table candles. While ordering wine, Mia flirted shamelessly with their white-jacketed young waiter, a boyishly dark and handsome guy named Georgio. After approving their selection and toasting their weekend, Mia teased, "Should I ask Georgio whether he wants to do something wild and crazy tonight?"

Jackie spent a silly moment trying to form a fantasy. The only thing that came to mind was *The Graduate's* Mrs. Robinson making a fool of herself with Benjamin. "I'm not quite ready for Georgio."

Almost as if forced by an unseen director, they fell into conversation about their mother, refusing by unspoken agreement to revisit pain they had discussed two years before: Two little girls, nine and seven, with no idea where to find their mom. Mia finding their father on the floor of his workshop and running into the house, screaming in uncontrollable terror for her big sister. Jackie terrified, too, but able to call for help. Riding in the back of the emergency van because the paramedics decided they shouldn't be left alone. Listening to the wailing siren. Feeling the sway and lurch as the van careened toward the hospital. Watching, barely able to breathe themselves, as their father struggled for each breath. Looking at each other in wide-eyed horror when the breathing stopped. Jackie held Mia in her arms that night, but their lives began to diverge in every possible way, almost from the instant he died.

"Mom's been in and out of AA again," said Mia. "She doesn't think she has a problem, even though the country club has a cot set up for her."

"A cot?"

"It was Bernie's idea. He's on the club's board or something. When she gets hammered, they drag her to her own spot in the ladies' locker room."

Jackie closed her eyes, but decided the news didn't really surprise her, nor could it embarrass her or hurt her anymore. "So our mother has her own official sot cot."

Mia's face twisted into a wry grin. "Makes you proud, doesn't it?"

Jackie changed the subject, at least slightly. "So ol' Bernie's still hanging in there. I wonder what he sees in her."

"An easy lay, probably."

"God, Mia, you are truly appalling."

A glass of wine and the antipasto later, the conversation shifted to Mia's love life. "I'm between men at the moment. Come to think of it, I may stay between men for the next hundred years or so."

"What's the problem now?"

"There is no problem now. I dumped the whole damn bunch of them, except for Michael, of course. So life is fine with my roomie, Ashley."

Jackie decided not to probe deeply into Mia's relationship with Ashley. She vaguely recalled Michael from discussions of the previous year, and she suddenly recalled a detail that might possibly be fun. "How is your wandering poet?"

"Michael's great. No muss. No fuss. And, unlike the male populace in general, no bullshit."

"Is he still your massage buddy?"

Mia raised one eyebrow in mock curiosity. "My, my. Good memory, sister. Why ever would you ask?"

Jackie felt a flutter in her stomach that told her she wasn't quite ready for this fantasy to become reality, although Michael Ledereaux, renaissance man, was supposedly a trained massage therapist in addition to being a writer, actor, musician and junior college professor. She looked down and poked at her salad. "Just curious."

Mia retrieved her cell phone from her purse. Jackie watched almost fearfully, but didn't protest. "Michael. Mia. Could you join us for brunch tomorrow? … About ten-thirty … Wonderful. See you then."

"I don't know, Mia…"

"God, Jackie, just chill. If it sounds like fun at the time, do it. If not, just relax and enjoy the day."

After dinner, Mia drove directly to The Den in downtown Omaha, a black and chrome kind of place with thundering music and ricocheting beams of laser light. They made their way through the crowd, while Mia nodded to friends and Jackie wondered whether eardrums get out of shape—sound seemed to be beating on her physically. An empty table awaited them; surprising in a place so crowded, Jackie thought. The waiter shouted for their drink order. Mia shouted back that they would order in a minute. Despite her anti-male rhetoric, she walked directly to a guy-table-for six and returned with two men. "This is Frank and Kevin," she shouted. "You can have Kevin. He's taller."

Jackie shook Kevin's hand. He sat to her left. They shouted drink orders and began shouting at each other to get acquainted. Kevin turned out to be a fortyish employment counselor who loved helping the downtrodden and loved community theater and loved Mia's verve. Within a few minutes, he had decided that he loved Jackie's dimples and loved Jackie's dress, and he kept spraying breath freshener in his mouth before leading her to the dance floor where she quickly, awkwardly remembered that she hadn't danced anything but the Matt shuffle since college days. She drank a Tom Collins and two sips of another one. But she began worrying about how much Mia was drinking, and she tugged repeatedly at the hem of her dress, unable to forget that Matt would have killed her for wearing it. And her world began feeling like a blinding, spinning, 140-decibel nightmare.

Mia kept drinking and dancing, although she shot Jackie several annoyed looks. And Jackie soon realized that Kevin would rather be back at the guy-table, which would have been just fine with her. Finally, mercifully, Mia decided to go home. She fought Jackie about who would drive, but Jackie held firm, and she decided that the purr and power of a Jaguar had been the highlight of her evening. Mia mostly sang along with CD music, but as they pulled into the driveway, she slurred, "You're a wild and crazy guy, all right."

As she waited for sleep, Jackie tried to understand what had happened. How could it be so much fun to pick a dress and so little fun to wear it? She tried for the high road. I'm a married woman with two kids. What was I even thinking? But she knew the truth and she couldn't avoid some resentment about her thirteen years in social bondage. She couldn't even remember how to relax and have fun, much less actually do it. But by 1:15 on the digital alarm clock, she had decided to try for the high road, focusing on two great kids and a nice house and an okay job and a husband who has a lot of good qualities.

Chapter Four

On Saturday morning, Jackie slipped into her full-length terry robe and headed for coffee, guessing that Mia would be slow to rise this AM. She found Ashley Trent bustling around the kitchen, arranging cups and saucers on the kitchen bar, and preparing the makings of omelets. Ashley wore fluffy yellow slippers and a short cover-up painted, front and back, in well-rounded cartoon nude. She smiled brightly. “Welcome to Omaha, sane half of the sisters Morris. I’m Ashley.”

Jackie returned the smile. “Thank you. Great outfit.”

Ashley put her hands behind her head and shimmied a bit. “A costume selected by our director, Mia Marie. How did last night go?”

Jackie grinned wryly. “I bombed.”

“I kind of gathered that, although Mia wasn’t exactly coherent when you two got home. What happened?”

“I felt something like the fish on a bicycle, I guess.”

Ashley pondered for a moment. “I think life’s all about finding scenes you like and getting comfortable. Right?”

Jackie smiled, wondering if by any remote chance, the entire secret to life had been revealed before her first sip of coffee. “Right.”

The two women chatted on. Jackie learned that Ashley was thirty-two and had known Mia for just over nine months. She was slender. Her hair was coal black, short and tightly curled. Her eyes were olive green and seemed almost too large for her face. She was a now-and-then concert violinist and a practicing nudist. As the better cook, Ashley traded kitchen-time for Mia's contribution to housing costs.

Mia dragged into the kitchen, pulled herself onto the counter stool beside Jackie, and used her eyes to beg for caffeine. "I see you've met my roomie," she said, after Ashley delivered a steaming cup.

"Yes, we've been chatting about my becoming a nudist," said Jackie, deciding to attack rather than defend.

Mia rolled her eyes dramatically and sipped her coffee.

Ashley was arranging four place settings on a table by poolside when they heard the front door open and the man named Michael bustled into the kitchen. He pecked Mia on the cheek and said, "Good morning, darling." He walked around Mia's chair to Jackie. "And good morning, darling's sister. I'm Michael Ledereaux."

She extended her hand, which he turned theatrically and grazed with his lips. "Hello, Michael. Mia told me a little about you."

He met her eyes, warm but somehow challenging. "A little is enough, I'm sure."

Jackie guessed Michael's age as late-forties. His brown hair was full, though receding slightly and flecked with gray. It was pulled back and tied into a ponytail that reached nearly to his shoulders. His beard and mustache were thick, close-cropped, also flecked gray. He was medium height with a stocky build and a ruddy complexion. Jackie decided he looked more like an outdoorsman than a professor, although his hands had a more professorial feel, very smooth to her touch.

They shared a light and lively poolside brunch, mercifully absent teasing about Jackie's social life or her performance of the previous evening. Jackie mostly listened, but enjoyed, as Michael dissected a Phillip Roth novel, recited some Edgar Allen Poe, improvised a scathing attack on Republican Party social policy, easily clobbering Jackie in light-hearted debate, and credibly performed his half of a hate scene from *Who's Afraid of Virginia Woolf,* with Mia playing Virginia.

Michael and Ashley announced that they were departing for a matinee performance of a play written by one of Michael's friends. Jackie said her goodbyes with an odd sense of disappointment. She couldn't be surprised that the possibility of a massage session hadn't been discussed. But it had been exciting to fly around in the air of Michael's energy and intelligence.

On Saturday afternoon, Jackie and Mia slipped into swimsuits and carried a pitcher of Bloody Marys to poolside. Their spot was wonderfully secluded, guarded by an eight-foot redwood fence and a lush tangle of trees and plants as tropical as Omaha weather would support. The sisters had pointed two lounge chairs in the direction of the sun and were fully reclined, eyes closed. Mia was spilling in all directions from a green print bikini. Jackie wore a blue one-piece that would have worked nicely at a Catholic girls' schools swim meet.

"Okay, I figured it out," said Mia, while sucking her Bloody Mary through a straw.

"Figured out what?"

"That Tommy Kerrigan—boy voyeur—crapped all over you, so you ran into the arms of Matt Billings so you can wear pitiful swimsuits like that."

Jackie had puzzled over the possibility many times. "It wasn't like that, Mia. When Matt and I were dating, I wore sexy stuff sometimes. Remember my topless on the non-topless beach story?"

Mia frowned, closing one eye, her signal of memory search. "Oh, yes, Jackie and the sombrero. I had a little trouble believing that one."

"Well it really did happen..." Jackie sat back, sipping from her glass, revisiting their Club Med honeymoon and the afternoon that planted the seed of her favorite fantasy. They had spread a blanket on the ocean side of a long row of palm trees—an isolated spot, but vacationers strolled by now and then, so her moment had been wonderfully daring for a girl from Greenville. She was lying on her stomach, wearing a little white bikini,. She reached back to unfasten her top and asked Matt to put suntan lotion on her back. He went along, but also carefully snuggled her top up against her breasts, as if nervous someone would see something. A few sun-soaked minutes later, she watched him become open-mouth distracted by two bikinis wiggling their way toward the ocean. She thought, *Okay, buddy*, and turned onto her back, hands behind her head. "Hey, Matt, I need some more lotion." Matt turned toward her, and his mouth fell open another inch or so. He asked what the hell she was doing and quickly covered her with a huge sombrero he'd been wearing. But she talked him into applying some lotion, under the sombrero. She was soon wildly turned on. Matt at least survived it. And back at the cabin, she got her first clue of what all-out sexual passion might be like, although it didn't last very long.

"So what the hell happened to you guys?" Mia asked.

"I'm not sure what happened, but I think I knew when. Haven't I told you about my windy day in Chicago?"

"I don't remember that one."

"We were with Matt's mom and dad at a construction trade show, maybe three months into our marriage. I was wearing this little white skirt. Tommy would have loved it, and Matt seemed okay with it, which made sense because we had decided to get pregnant so why not be a little wild and crazy? Anyway, the four of us were walking toward McCormick Place and the wind flipped the back of my skirt clear to my shoulders. Some guys behind us whistled. I turned around and smiled at them, you know, while I was trying to get my buns covered. I think the smile was where I went wrong."

"What the hell? You were wearing undies weren't you?"

"Yes, I was wearing undies, although there wasn't much to them. Anyway, it started that night. Matt called me 'damn near slutty,' and I wore slacks for the rest of the weekend."

"And the rest of your life, it would appear."

"Pretty much."

"Even though you thought it was fun to wave your fanny in the breeze."

Jackie smiled slightly as she thought back to some moments that were admittedly fun, before the clamp came down. But she said, "I'm okay with it, you know, at this point in life."

"That's bullshit, Jackie. I don't see why you put up with it."

"We fought for a while, but I guess he just cared more than I did; with my job and the kids and everything."

They sat back, sipping in silence. Jackie assumed the conversation would veer to some of Mia's adventures while touring, several of which made topless beaches and wind-flipped skirts sound like kindergarten. But Mia said, "Know what?"

"What?"

"I hate him for what he's done to you."

"That seems a little harsh."

"I know things were hard for you—I mean when we were kids. You're a great person who deserves the best, and Mr. Asshole has thrown a giant wet blanket on your entire life."

Jackie smiled as she connected dots. "That's a lot like a thing Ted Aldrich said."

"Who's Ted Aldrich?"

"Oh, just a pilot I talked to yesterday," Jackie said, trying for coy and casual.

Mia sat up abruptly, sloshing Bloody Mary onto her right thigh. "The hell you say! You met a pilot?"

"Yes, believe it or not: Captain Ted Aldrich. I met him when I got bumped to the first class section."

"I'll be damned. So I gather this Ted was a gorgeous guy."

Jackie reflected briefly. "I guess so. Older, but really distinguished, like the guys they always have in airline commercials. But he was mostly just nice."

"So how'd Captain Nice Guy get your motor running?" Mia asked with eyes dancing.

Jackie thought back. "It really wasn't like that. He didn't hit on me at all. He didn't even touch me, except for shaking my hand after lunch."

"Lunch?" Mia practically gasped. "My sister went to lunch?"

"Yes. In the pilots' lounge."

Mia sat upright and swiveled her feet to the ground. She eyed Jackie as if getting to know a new person. "So, one more time, what got you all revved up?"

Jackie closed her eyes to ponder. "I think it was just the adventure. Meeting this guy. Kind of, you know, sharing feelings with him." She frowned. "So we were sharing. And it was like he really cared. And I knew it was wrong in a way. Yet it was completely safe. And… Okay, Mia, I really loved it that he listened to me."

Mia filled their glasses and sat back, her tone road-weary. "Guys have been getting in girls' pants for centuries by acting like they care."

"But he didn't even ask for my phone number. "

"Do you wish he had?"

"No! Not at all. I just loved the experience. He did talk to me about my lame adventure life, but I think it was the adventure itself that got me thinking, more than what he said. Does that make sense?"

Mia chuckled. "Just barely. So what happened last night?"

"I was a mess, huh? I really am sorry." Jackie took a long sip while contemplating. "I guess it was just too much, too soon."

"Do you even want to talk about tonight's wild and crazy event?"

Jackie turned to study her sister. "Do you mean with Michael?"

Mia nodded but said, "I told him the odds are about zip."

Jackie took a deep breath and another sip of her Bloody Mary, her mind a whir of pros and cons. "Would it just be a massage?"

Mia's brow wrinkled. "What does that mean?"

"You know…last year when you told me about Michael, it sounded like…"

"It'll be whatever you want it to be," Mia said edgily. "I wouldn't send you helpless through the gates of hell, would I?"

"I'm sorry. It's just that I've never even had a massage, and—"

"Good grief! Never?"

"We don't spend money on stuff like that."

"Well it's about time. Okay, here's the deal: Your limits, for sure. Meet Michael at seven in the playroom. We'll grill steaks afterward."

Jackie thought about the ads she had seen in cruise magazines, and the sun began feeling warmer on her skin, but there was a hole in her knowledge. "What do I wear?"

Mia chuckled. "Long johns, probably."

"Seriously. What do I wear?"

"Well, Ashley and I wear zip. But you'll probably be more comfortable in panties."

"Does he…? Do I…"

Mia's chuckle erupted into laughter. "Good God, Jackie. He'll avert his gaze. He'll leave the room. He'll poke his eyes out with sticks. Give me a break."

Jackie hesitated. "Want to hear a true thing."

"Sure."

"Since I've been married, all my doctors have been women."

Mia exhaled and shook her head. "Pitiful."

At 6:30, Jackie sat in the bathtub, shaving her legs. Smooth legs were important to her, although she was battling a small voice that said it shouldn't matter. She finished her legs and took a long sip from the plastic wine goblet Mia had brought her. She added more hot water and bubbles, reclined with her eyes shut, and prepared for a bit of fantasy time inspired, if accidentally, by the ever-helpful Mia. When Jackie awoke after a short afternoon nap, she found a Victoria's Secret bag with choice of black or white bikini panties—not scandalous, not thongs, but also not Jockey for Her briefs. And now Jackie made her way, vividly, into her beach fantasy:

She turns onto her back, topless, hoping to rivet Matt's attention. He reacts angrily and stomps off, leaving her alone in the warm sun. She falls asleep. A stranger watches from a distance then approaches and kneels beside her on the blanket. He waits, watching her stretch and murmur in her sleep. He reaches toward her... Usually her stranger was gentle; sometimes he was forceful; but tonight Matt exploded into her fantasy and the stranger evaporated.

She stepped out of the tub, dried off, and slipped into her terry robe. She drank the last of her wine, walked into the bedroom, listened to the little voice tell her that Jockey for Her would be fine, but boldly opened the Victoria's Secret sack and decided on white. She returned to the bathroom vanity where she brushed her hair, applied makeup, and listened to the slow-tick of a modernistic wall clock with hands that ran backward. She moisturized her hands, arms, and legs. The wall clock ticked even slower. She flipped on the small TV in her room and restlessly watched the end of the evening news.

She walked barefoot down a stairway lined with Broadway musical playbills. Mia's entertainment room with its big-screen theater sprawled to her left. She pushed open the purple door to her right, entered tentatively, and waited for her eyes to adjust. Multiple candles generated a potpourri of fragrances, their dancing flames providing the room's only light. She heard gentle music: sounds of nature interspersed with Irish-sounding instruments. Michael, wearing tennis shorts and a black pullover, sat on a deep-cushioned love seat in the corner, sipping pink wine from a large rounded glass. "Join me, Jackie."

As she sat down beside him, Jackie unconsciously reached down to hold her robe closed at her knees. She winced, hopefully imperceptibly, reminded again that the winds of Chicago had been a long time ago. Michael handed her a glass of wine, already poured. He smiled slightly; his voice quiet, very gentle. "Are we a bit nervous?"

Jackie nodded as she lifted her wine glass and sipped. "Silly, huh?" She sipped again, longer this time, feeling the wine calm her, at least a little. She studied his face, surprisingly attractive in the soft glow of three candles on the coffee table in front of them. His brown eyes sparkled inside the frame of his hair and beard; his nose was strong, although at lunch she had noticed the bends: a shallow *S*. She asked, "Who bent your nose?" hoping she sounded friendly and playful.

He chuckled. "Believe it or not, a hockey stick. I played semi-pro in my twenties; not very well, but it was part of my *experience life* philosophy." Her mind blanked, wondering why she had taken them on a silly diversion into hockey sticks. She emptied the wine glass in embarrassingly audible gulps.

He smiled as if aware and refilled her glass. “Our session will begin right here. We’ll work on some in-the-moment relaxation.”

She gulped once more and laughed, almost comfortably. “What makes you think I need to relax?”

“I’m just a perceptive guy.”

He took her on a leisurely tour through the senses: aromas, dancing candlelight, gentle music, the taste of slowly savored wine, even the feel of carpeting on her bare feet. Five minutes later, she found herself with eyes closed, head reclined on the couch, wondering whether being hypnotized felt something like this. But as he gently repeated the tour, Jackie decided that she hated small inner voices. She had come wonderfully close to being soothed into the relaxation that Michael had called their goal. But a man’s voice had done the soothing, and a man’s voice hadn’t soothed her since she was nine years old.

She heard Michael rise and felt his hand at her wrist, lifting. As they stood face to face, he said, “Ready?” She met his eyes and simply nodded, knowing that her mind was far more muddled than it was supposed to be. He gestured toward the far corner of the room, and a linen-covered professional-looking massage table. “I’ll step outside while you make yourself comfortable. On your stomach, please.” She took a few steps toward the table, but returned to empty her second glass of wine, or maybe her third; she had kind of lost track amidst all the soothing.

Although vaguely aware that Matt’s veins would be bulging if he could see the scene, Jackie unfolded the mega-towel that waited at table’s edge, slipped out of her robe, climbed aboard, and reached back to arrange the towel from knees to mid-back. She called out a wobbly, “Okay, ready,” and buried her head in folded arms.

The door opened and closed. As Michael approached, he said, "Let's assure no distraction; lift your head just a bit, please." He slid a black blindfold over her head and carefully positioned it over both eyes. "And now we begin. Just say stop if you're uncomfortable in any way. Otherwise, we'll not talk."

She heard the gentle burp of a plastic bottle, and felt a line of lotion being poured directly onto her upper back. The liquid was marvelously warm, apparently pre-heated. He began a long, slow process that deep massaged her neck, shoulders, and upper back. She decided that inner voices were being quieted nicely, at least for the moment, by wine and hands and gentle music in blindfolded darkness. After several exquisite minutes during which tight muscles began relaxing wonderfully, she felt him slowly lower the towel and slip the edge inside the waistband of her panties. She drew in a long but quiet breath, her stomach again alive as she absorbed the new familiarity. She tried to focus on his hands as he kneaded, deeply and powerfully, the small of her back and her upper buttocks—a sumptuous feeling—but Matt and the voice were doing their best to shout at her.

Michael shifted to the end of the table, lifting her right foot toward him, pressing and caressing, sometimes with fingers and thumbs, sometimes the palm of his hands. As she bent one knee then the other to receive new attention, Jackie began to believe the magazine articles she had read about foot massage. Heavenly, she decided, as she came ever closer to focusing purely on this place and this moment.

He applied fresh, still warm lotion to her calves and began kneading her lower leg muscles. He worked slowly from calves to knees to thighs, and she felt, keenly, the texture of the protective towel as it slid upward. When he brought lotion and strong hands to her upper thighs and the curve above them, she became aware of her thudding heartbeat, of her breath coming in short bursts. The voice tried to tell her to stop him, to cover herself. But she felt sexy, and she loved the feeling. And the sensation of a man's slow, patient caress—with Jackie Morris Billings as center of the universe—was brand new and wonderful.

Michael returned the towel to full coverage. "Turn over, Jackie."

She thought about turning over, and her beach fantasy flickered through her mind, and her heart pounded harder. "Could I have a little more wine first?"

"Of course," he said softly.

She heard wine pouring and footsteps returning. She lifted her shoulders to accept the wine glass, keenly aware of the caress of the table linen under her. She drank slowly, thinking of the honey-mooning Matt, worried, snuggling bikini straps against her breasts. And through the wine's warm haze, she finally told Matt to give her at least a few minutes of freedom.

After returning the wine glass to Michael's invisible hand, she shifted toward the edge of the table and turned, now holding the towel to her breasts, but aware it had fallen away from her hips and legs. Michael smoothly retrieved the wayward hem, positioned it just above her knees, and began again. Tantalizing minutes passed as the towel inched upward. She felt both his hands on her right thigh, thumbs and fingers spread around her leg, probing deeply to find and almost painfully relax each long muscle. She loved the feeling. She marveled that the fingers on her inner thigh could work so powerfully, and be so close, yet avoid making intimate contact. He began working her left thigh, just above the knee, slow, firm, strong; then higher and eventually so close that she wondered, but faintly, whether he was torturing her intentionally. Her eyes closed tightly behind the blindfold. Her body began to move as if on its own, her teeth clenching and unclenching, her breathing coming in shallow gasps. She felt her hips reach up to him. She heard herself whisper, "Please, Michael…" And she disappeared into her beach fantasy; soon writhing helplessly under the control of the first expert hands she had ever known.

She lay still, gasping for breath, her fingers gradually releasing the sides of the table and searching for the towel. She felt Michael snug it under her chin and smooth it around her knees. She reached for the blindfold and slid it up her forehead, her eyes finding his face, her mind partly embarrassed by the loss of control, but feeling a warmth and affinity that she understood and found embarrassing in its own way. "Oh man. I kind of lost it."

He smiled, his expression warm. "You certainly experienced the moment."

"Did you plan that?" she asked softy.

He frowned, perhaps playfully, shaking his head. "Of course not. Did you?"

She smiled lazily, still glowing, "I don't think so, but…" And suddenly the voices began clamoring. "Can this, you know, be our little secret?"

This grin included some mischief. "I won't tell if you haven't already told."

She knew he meant a barely stifled scream and furnace duct-work. And suddenly the idea that Matt would somehow learn of this evening gripped at her stomach. "How about leaving me alone so I can get myself together?"

He said, "Sure," and exited. Only then did she wonder whether she had been anything to him beyond a favor that Mia had asked, and tawdry joined guilty. Then, belatedly, she considered the possibility that he had been turned on, and she wondered vaguely whether she had been totally self-centered, whether she should have offered to help him out. And the inner voice screamed that she was now officially insane.

When she returned to the party, Mia and Ashley were sipping wine in the music room. Michael was busily grilling on the patio. Mia raised her glass. "Here's to adventure."

Jackie exhaled slowly. "I don't want to talk about it right now."

"C'mon, lighten up," smiled Ashley. "You were in good hands with Michael, right?"

Jackie winced. "I'm still processing."

"Good grief, Jackie. Have some wine," Mia scolded. "We'll talk later."

"I sure don't need any more wine."

After dinner, they moved to Mia's entertainment room to watch a subtitled French film having a complex plot and several complex subplots. Jackie couldn't concentrate, said subdued goodnights, and left the party.

Jackie lay in an oversized daybed, covered to the waist by a single sheet. She wore a yellow Tweety-Bird nightshirt that Jodi, via Matt, had given her for Christmas. The only light came from a garden pole lamp, reflecting through pulled blinds in the window above her. She stared toward the ceiling, the tape recorder of her mind hitting *rewind* and *play*, giving her more reasons for conflict, guilt, embarrassment, and more than an occasional flicker of exhilaration. Tonight—unbeknownst to anyone in her life, most especially Matt for whom she acted on a regular basis—she had experienced her first non-solo orgasm.

She heard Mia's grandfather clock chime twelve. After the clock chimed the half hour, she heard Ashley and Mia laugh their way into bed. Sometime after that, she heard a light knock on her door. She didn't speak, but the door opened slightly without permission. "Jackie, are you awake?" His voice was just above a whisper.

She replied softly. “Yes, Michael. I’m definitely awake.”

He entered and closed the door quietly, walked to the edge of the daybed, and sat down. “I’ve been thinking about you.”

“I’ll bet you have.” She hadn’t intended a joke but his try at stifling a chuckle failed completely. She managed no more than half a smile.

“I mean I’ve been thinking I should say I’m sorry.”

She studied his face, partially illuminated by shafts of light filtering through the blinds. His expression was solemn. “What are you sorry about?”

“For any part of tonight that made you unhappy.”

“Anything that happened was my own doing, Michael. I’m a grown woman.”

He hesitated then smiled. “You definitely are that.” This time she tried to stop a light chuckle but failed.

She shook her head. “Surely, that woman down there wasn’t me.”

“I’m pretty sure it was you. But don’t let tonight drown in an ocean of guilt.”

“I can tell you’ve never been married to Matt Billings.”

“This was about you, Jackie. No harm was done to your husband.”

“I’ve been lying here for two hours trying to convince myself of that.”

“How did you do?”

“Better than I should have.”

She felt his hand on her right thigh, stroking gently, just below the hem of her nightshirt. “I have a two-for-the-price-of-one special tonight, if you like.”

Feelings suddenly began revolving like a carnival kaleidoscope. Part of her called for an instant halt, a return to sanity, even a verbal slap to tell him that this visit was out of line. But she now wondered, actively, whether he had visited because he wanted more. And his touch was sending powerful currents through a body that suddenly had a mind of its own, as if instantly ready for an encore. She inhaled sharply, exhaled slowly, and reached to arrest his wrist. "No, Michael; no more. Please, no more." But her voice sounded pleading, not commanding.

The hand lifted, although not before a few final strokes that caused her to close her eyes, tighten her grip on his wrist, and actually consider yielding. He said, "No problem," as he stood and walked to the door, and turned toward her. "I hope we'll meet again one day."

She searched for the right reply and couldn't find it. She worked through another temptation that she didn't understand—to ask him to stay longer, just to talk. "Good night, Michael."

Sunday was a quiet day of newspapers, eggs benedict, and conversation among the three women. As Mia drove toward the airport, she said, "Well, did we succeed or did we fail?"

"Did Michael tell you what happened?"

"Not exactly," Mia lied.

"I absolutely made a fool of myself; sexually, I mean."

Mia turned to meet her eyes. "Okay, sister, tell me the truth about something."

"What?"

"Did you like it?"

Jackie pondered, suddenly feeling warm. "I guess, honestly, I would have to say yes."

"Then give yourself a break. You deserve to have some fun."

As she flew east, Jackie leaned back in seat 22A, closed her eyes and tried to process the whole incredible experience. Amazingly, Michael had nearly washed Ted Aldrich out of her mind. Ted felt like a month ago. But guilt wouldn't leave her alone, mostly because she knew that Mia's simple "you deserve to have fun" was far too simple. Complicated things had happened in her head, and she knew it's risky to get involved in situations that you don't fully understand.

But, most of all, she found hope that she had learned something about living life. She had made a decision to find adventure. She might have stumbled and bumbled some, but she found adventure. She made a decision, and she acted, and things happened.

Surely, she decided, the same idea can work in my marriage. Obviously, I have needs that I haven't been dealing with honestly. I shouldn't have to feel afraid of those feelings, or afraid of telling Matt how I feel. I don't want to be like *Thelma and Louise* running away from their controlling men. Matt is my husband. I want it to work. And I don't want to be like me in my own beach fantasy. Asleep and waiting for something to happen. So I'll be more assertive, and I'll find ways to make our marriage more exciting and more fulfilling.

She laughed out loud, but softly, there in seat 22A. Brace up, Matt Billings; you're about to become a much luckier guy. The new Jackie is heading back to town.

Chapter Five

Daniel Andrew Berringer hung up the phone, smiling at the youth-like horniness that Ted Aldrich managed to muster after all these years. Once upon a time, Daniel could match him lay for lay, but that was a long time ago. Now Daniel viewed their annual adventure as something like a Viagra tablet of intrigue.

Daniel walked to the patio door of his soundproofed lower level study. His wife—more relevantly, his partner in a lucrative drug business and the woman who screwed him now and then, though indifferently—was upstairs likely Internet chatting about her next rendezvous with Len Castle, a guy Daniel tolerated indifferently. Daniel had had a life partner once, and their lives might have been something like normal. But from the night they found Paula's body, raped and tortured, he hadn't worried much about bullshit like deep bonds of matrimony.

He watched night descend on the Pennsylvania forest in the valley below him, turning summer trees to dark green headed for black. And he thought about the project called Jackie Billings, hoping with a lust of its own that he would find some intrigue. Daniel's father had been an FBI agent, a guy who told incredible stories to a lad who loved the stories. His dad died—literally out of uniform—in an L.A brothel, but not before planting the seeds of adventure in his son.

A lifetime ago, Daniel was a CIA agent, and he relished every minute of covert operations with their night meetings in back alley apartments, not to mention the thrill of gunfire and the joy of delivering deserved death. But it didn't last. Paula's death fucked him up, bad, because a security breach by a CIA supervisor—a guy who sure as hell should have known better—brought the enemy directly to her door. Later, the CIA screwed him over for two promotions before sacking him without pension on suspicion of involvement in the drug trade. Fortunately, he had managed to squirrel away four million dollars in cocaine-cash before the hammer fell, and his life on the other side of the law had provided a decade or so of intrigue. But things went stale steadily, and he grasped that he would pick dead over stale.

He reconnected with Ted Aldrich at a reunion of their Vietnam unit—what, twelve years, thirteen years ago now? They drank together and ventured deep into a discussion of the enemy named *Stale*, although Ted called his enemy a rocking chair. The next day, they drank with good buddy Mark Coffey, and they cobbled up the annual project—exhilarating for a while, growing stale for a while, exhilarating again when the fourth player became *Death*—what, six, seven years ago? But now growing stale again. Of course, Ted assured him that their latest target was world-class, but Ted thought they were all world class.

Daniel didn't pretend to understand Ted Aldrich. A jovial ladies' man, carrying enough anger to ignore that he was signing a woman's death warrant for sport. But the scars of Vietnam and prison camps and lives visited too often by death—scars that bound the three of them—had screwed them up in all kinds of ways. So they created their game, partly for fun, partly for intrigue, partly as an outlet for fury, and mostly as a giant fuck-you to a world that had screwed them since they were nineteen years old.

Daniel began to focus. His role had been defined correctly: mastermind of the master plan and collector and analyst of information about the target. His CIA experience gave him the credentials. Aldrich was a piss poor detail man. Over the years, Coffey had become a borderline flake.

So he opened three database files: *Jackie Billings Life Events, Jackie Billings Physiology, Jackie Billings Psychology.* And he began entering the data that Aldrich had dutifully provided, per the rules of engagement.

Chapter Six

Matt Billings waited in the family room, his lanky six-two frame sprawled backward in full La-Z-Boy recline. He was wearing jeans and a Cincinnati Reds t-shirt and cap, sipping a cold Bud, and watching a British soccer match on DirecTV. Sean had disappeared into his basement nook, hopefully doing his summer reading, likelier web surfing or playing video games. The Jamesons had driven Jodi to her Methodist Youth Group meeting and would bring her back at about eight, so Matt had an R&R night. Some rest and relaxation felt good; he had been working too hard since his father died, and that was four years ago. The perpetual circles under his eyes, along with several permanent creases by his mouth and on his brow, bore silent testimony. Fortunately, the hairline had held, still cut military short as it had been since junior high, only a few flecks of gray.

He heard the overhead door go up and swiveled in his lounger as his wife came through the interior garage door. She looked damn good, and Matt appreciated her looks. She stayed in great shape, her body nicely curved but not voluptuous. Matt thought of her as sweetly beautiful rather than seductively beautiful like Sherry Jameson. He couldn't have handled seductively beautiful. She walked toward him and leaned for a kiss. At least fifteen seconds and a couple tongue thrusts later, he said, "Well, hello. What was that about?"

"Hello yourself, big guy."

Her tone had been Mae West comical, but French kisses early on Sunday evening struck him as an ominous clue. She sat in the chair across from him, and he flipped off the TV, a decision that earned a big smile. He loved her smile: nice teeth, great dimples. They caught up on Jodi and Sean's activities. Next, Matt pretended to be interested in her Omaha trip. After that, Jackie walked to his chair, gave him another long smooch, told him to be ready tonight, and carried her suitcase upstairs. He got back to his soccer game but couldn't concentrate—partly because he didn't much give a damn whether Manchester beat Liverpool, mostly because he feared that *Mia Marie whatever the hell her name is now* had influenced Jackie big-time this year. It's a problem when your sister-in-law is a slut, especially when your wife views an annual visit as an important part of life.

At about 9:30, after she had scooted Jodi off to bed, Jackie glided back into the family room wearing a short nightshirt, a *very* short nightshirt. She leaned over the back of his chair, nuzzled his neck, and whispered, "I want you tonight, Matt. Really bad." It was good that she whispered. Sean emerged from his basement hideaway at mid-nuzzle and said an embarrassed hello.

Of course, Matt had no problem with the idea of romp, as long as they could stay awake until Sean was asleep. But she damn well knew that he initiated their romps. He had friends who griped that their wives were never aggressive. Matt didn't like aggressive and never had. At 11:30, he finished watching the news and climbed the stairs to their bedroom. He opened the door to find her standing beside the bed, her hair brushed out full, shining in the light of candles on both bed stands. He could smell perfume.

"Where did that come from?" he demanded. She had changed outfits again, now wearing a short, absolutely sheer pink top that he had never seen. Nothing else.

"Don't you like it?" She put her hands behind her head and turned in a full circle.

Matt liked to peel layers, forcefully sometimes. This outfit seriously lacked layers. “If my immediate goal was seeing every inch of your body, I’d like it.”

“Don’t you like seeing my body?” she purred.

“What the hell is going on, Jackie?”

“I missed you. And maybe I read a little *Cosmo* over the weekend.”

“Good ol’ Mia. You stick with her and you'll be standing under a street light.”

“This is kind of on my own. Why don’t you get undressed?”

He had to admit that it was a helluva romp, maybe five times hotter than normal. Okay for an evening, but he hoped things would return to normal, quickly.

They spent a normal week, running by each other while heading for jobs, meetings, and kids’ events. Matt considered Jackie a wonderful wife and mother. He admired the way she could juggle the balls of their lives. But on Friday night she said, “I’ll give you a great massage if you’ll give me one.”

He looked at her, amazed. There had been no need for massages since deep into her last pregnancy. “More *Cosmo* crap?” he asked bluntly.

“Maybe. C’mon, Matt, loosen up, it’ll be fun.”

If he hadn’t agreed, a great deal of planning would have gone down the chute. She had arranged sleepovers for both kids, turned the bedroom into a candlelit parlor, and covered the bed with oversized bath towels. She told him to strip and lie face down on the bed, and she covered his bare buns with a towel. She pulled a little jersey dress over her head, leaving her in nothing but the first bikinis he had seen in years. He tried, but he couldn’t get into her program. Jackie Billings, bank employee and soccer mom, becoming a topless massage parlor queen just didn’t work. God knows he didn't handle it well. She caressed him for a while; Mr. Big got a mind of his own; and Matt wound up taking matters into his own hands. Afterward, he had been too tired to give a massage, so he promised to make it up to her someday.

***

Michael Ledereaux had retreated to his cozy office at Lincoln Junior College where a ringing telephone intruded on his preparation for a summer-school English Lit class, one of his favorites.

"Hello, Michael, it's Jackie Billings. Mia gave me your number."

He said, "I'm a bit surprised to hear from you," a minor masterpiece of understatement, he decided. He had willingly—all right, enthusiastically—agreed to participate in a carefully orchestrated *adventure*, as Mia called it, for a surprisingly complicated woman. But he had assessed Jackie Billings as virtually overwhelmed by the complexity, likely to slink back to the safety of Columbus, Ohio.

"I'm a bit surprised to be calling," she said. "Can we be, you know, friends?"

He laughed. "As opposed to what?"

"You know…"

"I'd be honored to be your friend, Jackie. Nothing else even occurred to me." Michael liked the ring of nobility, although a lie detector stylus might have squiggled feverishly. He hoped that Jackie liked it, too. Early in life, he had been an admitted loser with women, primarily because he pressed too hard to be a winner. After he learned the magic of being a supportive confidant, his love life began to soar. He liked the tone of this call.

She said, "I hoped you'd say that, Michael. I need a friend."

"Aren't there friends in Ohio?"

"Not for this subject. I think I need a man's perspective."

"What's happening?"

"It's not happening. When I left Omaha, I decided to work on my marriage. My weekend helped me see the need, if you know what I mean. So I'm trying to help Matt understand how important it is to me, and to be exciting for him. It's just not happening."

Michael smiled inwardly as he launched a marriage counseling effort unaided by the slightest personal success in marriage. His only try had been an early-twenties debacle. They talked about the need for gradual change in a relationship with long-standing issues. She said her attempts thus far didn't seem radical. He agreed, but admitted that it's difficult to see inside another man's head. He said, "Perhaps you're trying to superimpose your fantasies rather than discovering his. Surely he would enjoy acting out his own fantasies." She said she'd give that a try.

Michael hung up, confident that he had scored points, already looking forward to next year's Jackie-visit when he would more actively seek repayment. Who knows; there might even be a rendezvous before that, if the fates were kind.

***

Daniel Berringer had told him enough to make finding her house simple. Tailing her downtown turned out to be tougher. The woman drove like a lady in a hurry, but she was far too innocent to notice a tail, even a Lincoln Town Car tail. Now he knew she worked at the headquarters building of Third Ohio National Bank. By tomorrow he would know her department and phone number. Their cell phones would take a little longer, but he had plenty of time, a full week according to the rules. Then off to Greenville for background details.

Aldrich had done it again, he decided. Definitely a looker, but without being hard or brassy. That son of a bitch can pick 'em.

Mark Coffey called Daniel Berringer, per their detail man's firm policy. As he spit information, he could hear the clatter of the keyboard as Berringer logged facts and figures. "Keep it coming," said Berringer.

***

Matt Billings had hoped for the return of normalcy in their busy lives, but she refused to let it happen. On Wednesday morning, his leaving-for-work kiss included a blatant grope and a joke about saying good morning to Mr. Big. On Thursday night, a braless sweatshirt suddenly descended over his head while he watched an Arena football game.

On Friday, one week after the massage fiasco, she said, "Matt, tell me about your fantasies. I'd be willing to play some games that you think would be fun." He knew this kind of thing came from magazines like *Cosmopolitan* or maybe *Redbook* trying to pretend it was *Cosmopolitan.* He knew that some couples played around with leather and lace or whatever, but he just wasn't into cheapo stuff like that.

"Jackie, what's with the massages and fantasies? I think things are just fine."

"There can be more, Matt. Lots more. I'd like to be with you more, and—"

"What the hell is this? A female mid-life crisis or something?"

She paused, apparently to analyze. "I don't know; maybe so. But what's wrong with acting younger, being a little crazy. We can make each other happy in ways we haven't even thought of yet."

He snapped, "I think this is all bullshit. Three weeks ago you visit the woman with the roundest heels in Omaha and you've been screwed up ever since."

"It doesn't help when you attack my sister."

"Okay, I'm sorry; the second roundest heels in Omaha. You know she's nothing but a bi-sexual, hedonistic, God knows what."

The argument sputtered on. He could tell that she didn't understand.

Later, after chilling with a couple brews, Matt regretted exploding at her. He had inherited his father's temper and sometimes lost it. But this whole deal was damned irritating. He had been struggling to make the business work from the minute he took over from his dad. Clancy Billings was a huge, rawboned man who had motivated by intimidation; but he had an uncanny ability to price jobs right and bring them in under budget. Under Matt's leadership, despite his degree from Ohio State, job costs often came in too high. He needed to focus. He sure as hell didn't need Omaha crap to complicate his life.

***

Michael received her second call on a Monday morning, reporting the failure of the Ledereaux fantasy theory. He hadn't formulated a personal strategy for time spent talking with Jackie, but concerned friendship felt right for now. They talked for fifteen minutes, primarily about men and their thought processes. He again advised persistence. "Change takes time, Jackie. Remember that."

Michael did not begin to understand the man named Matt Billings. Surely there was more to him than Mia's one-word assessment; a purebred asshole couldn't have remained married for so long to a woman like Jackie. But what in the name of heaven is he thinking? He might be the only man in America with a hot new lover who happens to be his wife of fourteen years: beautiful, passionate, willing; and the dumb bastard gyrates between indifferent and angry. Maybe I'll call Matt for her and try to straighten him out. Michael chuckled out loud as he spoke toward his own ceiling, "Maybe not."

***

The phone tap had been a simple matter. Of course, the microphone plants required some ballsy intrusion, but no problem. Now Mark Coffey sat outside their suburban two-story, taping another Billings' argument, declaring Matthew Billings every bit the dipshit that Aldrich had initially reported. He loaded the conversation into a digital file and downloaded to Berringer. He knew that Aldrich would love this broad with her gentle beauty and bubbling passion. Berringer, though, would likely declare her too soft. Of course, Mark Coffey simply appreciated the chance to play, because nowadays he had some good days and some bad days.

Chapter Seven

She had connected with Michael for a man's point of view, but Jackie was bubbling with issues to be shared with a woman. She had two close friends at work, but she didn't want to mix work with personal problems. That left Sherry Jameson and Joy Phillips. But Joy was the volunteer head of their church's adult Bible school department. Jackie couldn't imagine that discussion.

Sherry Jameson wouldn't be shocked or judgmental. They had become close friends despite a competition that traced to their days as college sorority sisters. Sherry was a dazzling, head-turning blonde whose exploits inspired both gossip and envy. Jackie had inspired more friendship than envy, and Sherry envied that. But as wives and mothers, their similarities began to outweigh their differences. Their husbands were even good buddies, although that could be a problem when sharing secrets.

The women connected for coffee in Jackie's kitchen on a Saturday morning when Matt and Ty were golfing. Sherry's blue eyes were bright. Fresh make-up accented perfect cheekbones. She wore a perfect lilac cotton romper. Even now, Sherry's appearance could be really annoying.

After discussing Sherry's fear that Ty's company might be acquired by a German firm, Jackie said, "Okay my turn. I'm about to pop. But Matt can't hear about any of this, okay?"

"Sure. I can keep secrets," Sherry pouted, although curiosity brimmed in her eyes.

"Well, I have one. While I was in Omaha, I had a real-live sexual adventure."

"You mean an affair?" Sherry asked, wide-eyed.

"No, nothing like that, but my sister set up a massage session that turned out to be really erotic."

Sherry lifted her eyebrows mischievously. "I've done that."

"You have?" Although surprised, Jackie found herself instantly less concerned about Sherry spilling any beans.

Sherry said, "Can you keep a secret that's probably bigger than yours?"

"Sure."

"Ty hired a massage guy from the *Columbus Other* newspaper. He came to our house and the two of them massaged me at the same time—all over, if you know what I mean."

"Are you kidding me?"

"Would I make that up?"

"I just can't imagine it, not in my wildest dreams."

"Ty likes stuff like that. Remember my lost bikini top at Blakely's pool party last year? That was his idea, too."

Jackie shook her head. "Go figure. I'm here partly because Matt would keep me in several layers of burlap if he could."

"I know. Matt has made it clear that no one is to touch, or look at, the ice maiden."

"He has?"

"From that night at Snowbird on."

Jackie recalled the night, maybe three years into their marriage. The foursome had partied after a day of Utah skiing. Late in a wine-enhanced evening, Ty suggested a game of strip poker. Sherry and Jackie said they were willing. Matt went nuts at the thought. "Who called me the ice maiden?"

"Ty came up with that."

"That is funny. There was sure no ice in Omaha."

"You liked it?"

"Oh my, yes. But I felt…feel…guilty. It was a guy I hardly knew. Matt would—"

"Did you have sex?"

"No. Not sex. But about everything else."

"Oral?"

"Hmm. Okay, not quite everything else. Matt isn't into oral. Michael just used his hands, like I didn't know hands could be used."

"Good grief, Jackie, that doesn't sound like the sin of the century."

"I'm about over the guilt. But it taught me something."

"What?"

"That I really like screaming orgasms."

Sherry laughed, nearly spewing her coffee. "I'm sorry. I wasn't expecting that."

Jackie remained serious. "I mean I *really* liked it. I want to fly, and I want to fly with Matt. Nothing as wild as you've done. Just wear sexy stuff. Get turned on in a restaurant. Make love on a riverbank. Is that so bad?"

Sherry smiled complete agreement. "So just do it. What's he going to do if you take charge?"

"It's unreal. He goes negative, almost mean."

"That's baloney. He wouldn't hurt you, would he?"

"No. I can't imagine that."

"Then you need to do it. If you don't do it with him, you'll do it, someday, without him. And your marriage will come apart."

Jackie paused to contemplate analysis that felt extreme. "I am planning to do it. I just haven't figured out what *it* is."

Sherry drummed her fingers on the table, her brow furrowed. "Let's go shopping together for the Gala. We can begin the enlightenment of Matt Billings."

"Okay. But Matt never knows about Omaha, right?"

"My lips are sealed."

***

The Lincoln Town Car tailed them, first to a strip mall where they visited a shop called Rhonda's Intimates & More. Mark Coffey was exceeding regulations in terms of proximity to the target, but he loved to build anticipation. Watching the appealing Mrs. Billings—not to mention her friend, a kick-ass blonde honey-pot—damn sure built anticipation. He stood at the store window then sauntered in to browse.

Apparently the girls had made this stop mostly for fun. A little redhead, who Coffey guessed to be Rhonda, appeared to be a friend of theirs. She showed them some knock-a-guy-on-his-ass outfits, and the two broads tried things on and vamped and laughed themselves half silly. Damn good shopping trip, he decided, although they only bought a couple frillies. By tipping the rim of his safari hat when necessary, he got an eyeful without fear of detection. Matt-Baby sure wouldn't have liked that.

He followed them to Nordstrom's and watched a serious shopping session. Party dresses, it appeared. Nice thigh slits. Good luck, Jackie-Baby.

***

As they dressed the next morning, Jackie said, "You're going to have the prettiest date at the Gala, Friday."

"I am?" Matt asked uneasily, as he studied her reflection in the mirror in front of him.

"You'll be so dazzled you'll throw me onto your white horse and we'll gallop off to your castle."

"I will?" He had no idea what she might mean, but it sounded ominous.

"Guaranteed."

Two days later, Matt waited uncomfortably in the family room. With a little luck, the Soccer Club's annual fund-raising gala would be the only reason he would wear a tuxedo until the next gala. He watched in amazement as Jackie sashayed through the entryway. Her necklace and earrings sparkled brightly. Her hair was swirled into a French knot. Her eyes were lined in blue that accented her outfit: a clingy, low-cut, shimmering party dress slit halfway up her right thigh. He exploded instantly. "What the hell are you doing? My wife is not going to the Windsor Country Club looking like a street whore."

She stepped backward, almost as if he had hit her. "C'mon, Matt, Sherry's dress is at least this revealing. We had the best time finding things you guys would like."

His anger erupted from an almost forgotten source. "If Ty Jameson doesn't mind having a harlot wife, that's his business. Now haul your ass back upstairs and find something decent."

She crossed her arms. "We need to talk about this, really bad."

He could easily see her hurt and anger, but at the moment he didn't care. "We *will* talk about this, tomorrow morning. I want to get to the bottom of all this bullshit. For now, get out of that outfit."

She stepped toward him as if preparing to fight back, but wheeled, walked out of the room, and stomped upstairs. He continued to seethe, but less so when she returned in a tolerable black dress. They went through the motions of a tolerable evening, mostly because Ty and Sherry Jameson worked heroically to lighten the mood.

They carried coffee and bagels to their back patio and sat opposite each other at the umbrella-topped glass table. Matt spent a moment stirring coffee while he studied her. Her eyes were looking somewhere else, somewhere out to his right, but not really focused. He couldn't read her expression—not angry, not sad; maybe just hard. Matt had lost some sleep thinking about her reaction to his *whore* comment—a spectacularly poor choice of words, without a doubt. He loved her; she was the most important part of his life. So it was important to nip this bullshit in the bud before things got out of hand.

"I don't know what happened in Omaha, but I'll not have my wife behaving like a slut. You won't dress like a slut and you won't act like a slut. Is that clear?"

She continued to look past him, her voice flat, strange, almost indifferent. "How in the world does a Nordstrom party dress make me a slut?"

"If you know I hate it, why would you show the world your body?"

She turned toward him, her eyes flashing anger. "God, Matt, it was a party dress, not pasties and a g-string."

"Why do you need to flaunt yourself?"

"If you can possibly call that flaunting, it was for you. For us."

He focused on her eyes. "Listen carefully: I don't need it. I don't like it. Stop it."

Her return gaze changed again—not angry, more like coldly hostile. She pushed back from the table. "Anything else?"

He scrambled to adjust. "Damn it, Jackie. Try to understand how I feel about this, okay? I really thought we had an understanding."

She stood. "Do you know what you were last night?"

"What?"

"You were an asshole. And I don't need it. I don't like it. And I wish you would stop it." She wheeled and walked into the house, slamming the sliding door behind her.

At church on Sunday, Jackie spent some meditation time on her suddenly complicated life. She was ridiculously busy, both at work and at home. Her venture into sexuality had yielded maybe two bedroom moments and a thousand conflicts. Should she just give it up? Was it worth the battle? Was there even any hope?

The answer came surprisingly easily. Matthew needs to get with the program. It is surely reasonable that a married woman wants to enjoy the pleasures of sex with her own husband. Sex is the spice of marriage and our marriage surely needs some spice. She looked deeper and she saw more. She would not tolerate treatment like his outburst over a perfectly acceptable party dress. Matthew had choices to make.

***

Mark Coffey wound up his reconnaissance role. The rules of engagement provided Aldrich no details; only a clue that the time was right. Coffey removed the phone tap and bugs, one of Daniel's many rules designed to make the game more sporting. He called Berringer. Berringer received and entered the new data batch. And Berringer called Aldrich.

Chapter Eight

Jackie sat at her desk working through a set of loan application forms. Six days had passed since the dinner-dance debacle. She and Matt were co-existing, though coolly, without having revisited the incident. She knew they were not good at the art of marital fighting. After intense confrontations, the cool mode could last for days. Eventually one stubborn streak would declare the battle unworthy of the pain and yield to the other stubborn streak. No such declaration yet, but they always worked things out. And just last night, Jackie had spent some time in her favorite place, visualizing a different kind of beach scene; and her husband was the star of the show.

She picked up her ringing phone. "Jackie Billings, may I help you?"

"If you'll have lunch with me again, that'll help me."

She remembered the voice, but didn't connect it with a face, "Who is this?"

"Ted Aldrich of the world famous flying Aldriches."

She felt an immediate quiver in her stomach. "Ted? How in the world did you find me?"

"I have my ways. How have you been?"

That is a better question than you would ever imagine. She said, "Just a minute, let me close my door." She hurried to the door, closed it quietly, and returned to her desk, oddly aware of the family picture on the credenza behind her. But she said, "I've been fine, how have you been?"

"Things are good. The planes are flying; the air traffic guys are keeping us separated. By the way, I'm flying to Columbus next Wednesday."

"Why?"

"To take you to lunch."

"How do you fly one of those big birds somewhere for lunch?"

"This is just a little bird. I'm off duty. What time shall we meet?"

"I need to pass, Ted. I'm in kind of a crazy time."

"So let's have lunch and talk about your crazy time."

"I'm sorry, I.... It's just a really bad time for me right now."

He asked what was troubling her. She talked a little, because she needed to talk. He asked again about lunch, arguing that she clearly needed to work through some things, and he would be happy to help. She said no. And she said no again when he called the following day.

He said, "I'll call you Tuesday afternoon. Be sure to change your mind."

"Not likely. Bye, Ted."

The weekend included a Sean soccer game and Matt's mother's birthday party. Matt remained distant, and Jackie tried not to focus on her Ted Aldrich lunch offer, partly because it felt too much like an oasis. But for most of her weekend, she understood that lunch with Ted Aldrich would complicate the already complicated.

On Monday morning, she used her cell phone to call Michael. She had made several unauthorized long-distance calls on the bank's phone lines, so decided not to risk getting fired.

***

Michael Ledereaux began the conversation unsurprised that she had called—today was Monday, after all, and the idiot husband tended to screw things up on weekends. But he decided, quickly, that he didn't like this call's content, or the fact that she was upbeat following several weeks of increasing gloom.

"Michael, you'd never guess who called me at the bank: Ted Aldrich, the pilot I met on the way to Omaha. He wants me to do lunch with him again. Of course I said no."

"How did he find you?"

"I have no idea."

"Doesn't that seem strange?"

"Well, I don't know. My name was probably in the airline records."

"You're wise to stay away from Ted Aldrich."

"Why do you say that?"

"The same reason you said no, I imagine. You've got a full plate right now."

"I know. It was a nice surprise, though."

After his last class, Michael drove to Mia's place, where they mixed martinis and adjourned to the sunroom. Michael related the reappearance of Ted Aldrich. "So why are you upset?" asked Mia.

"Your sister is a totally vulnerable woman right now. Believe me."

"She's an adult, Michael. Even if she fell ass over tea kettle for Ted Aldrich, it's the prick's fault."

"I can't avoid feeling it's partly our fault."

"What the hell are you talking about? We didn't introduce her to Ted Aldrich."

"You know what I mean. We helped generate the adventure that began all this."

"That's bullshit, Michael. She wanted to have her adventure. This whole thing is as inevitable as night and day."

"Still, your sister needs to stay away from Ted Aldrich until she gets herself together."

"Playing God, are we?" Mia asked, curious about Michael's level of interest in her sister.

"I'm concerned about vulnerability. Nothing more."

"She's been vulnerable since she was nine years old."

"If that's true, shouldn't you be involved; helping her figure things out?"

"It's not that I don't care, Michael, but I can't be her frigging therapist. It's a giant sinkhole, and you know it. So I'd suggest you stay the hell out of it."

***

Jackie's afternoon dragged interminably. She forced herself to concentrate on work, but the Ted Aldrich call wouldn't leave her alone. Later she drove carpool to Jodi's soccer game, where she would be the only Billings parent in attendance. Matt had asked for a night out with the boys, usually meaning a few beers with Ty Jameson.

Watching Jodi run the soccer field—brown ponytail flying, happily unconcerned about the loss of two front teeth—triggered a flood of thoughts. Jodi had been a happy, chubby baby with cheeks too wide, and huge brown eyes. By age two, she was sleek and cute as a button. She remained nearly lovable through the terrible twos and threes, and had been a delight ever since, curious, eager to learn, a delight to nurture. She bubbled with a rare kind of inner joy, laughing more than either of her parents laughed. And when she laughed, she had her mother's dimples. Jackie liked that, but she couldn't avoid some sadness. Why can't life keep this kind of pure, wide-eyed joy?

***

On Monday evening, Matt Billings sipped on a Killian Red, waiting for Ty Jameson to show up at O'Hannahan's Pub. Without doubt, Ty was his only friend close enough for an honest discussion about marriage. Matt had known Ty since fraternity days, and served as a groomsman in the Ty-Sherry wedding. The Jameson children, Brett and Brittany, were nearly the same ages as Sean and Jodi. Over the years, the Billings and Jamesons became a social foursome and eventually good friends. Of course, Matt kept an eye on the notorious lover when he hovered at all close to Jackie. The guy had captain-of-the-team good looks: black curly hair, chiseled jaw, and a smile that showed several more teeth than the average smile. But they had an understanding.

Ty sauntered in, shouted greetings to several friends, gave a bear hug to a smiling waitress named Talley, and sat down across from Matt. They began with baseball talk and moved to the upcoming Bengals season. They shared two jokes inspired by the size of Talley's hooters, followed by intense discussion of the Hooters restaurant chain's marketing strategy. After two more Killian Reds, Matt dove into his dilemma.

"Jackie and Sherry went shopping together for the Gala."

"I know."

"I wound up in deep shit with Jackie, when I made her change outfits."

Ty knew that, too, but decided not to mention his foreknowledge. "Were both tits hanging out or something?"

"It was about like Sherry's dress. Some cleavage. A thigh slit."

"So what's the problem, Matthew? You certainly stole a glance or two at Sherry's thigh and cleavage."

Matt forced a laugh, "I totally deny that." But he quickly returned to serious, "I don't know how the hell you do it. The idea of

Jackie intentionally showing herself to you, or anyone else, makes me crazy."

"Buddy! Fellow member of the Buddy Club; let's talk double standard here. It's okay for you to check out Sherry. Hell, it's worse than that. If I remember right, you and I were down at the Golden Garter with legs wrapped around our shoulders, not more than two months ago."

"It's different, Ty. I'm telling you it's different."

Ty thought back to the aborted strip poker game at Snowbird. Matt had made a major ass of himself that night. "I thought you had the jealousy thing in a box somewhere. We haven't had this talk for years."

"It's been in a box because she started behaving like she should; after two solid years of fierce debate. Now she's changed, big time."

"You're overreacting, man."

Matt's brow knitted as if he were struggling to make his mind and memory work. "Let me tell you what my dad said, okay?"

"What did ol' Clancy say?" Ty asked, now more concerned about Matt's beer consumption than his father's wisdom.

"He said, 'There's a place in life for trashy women; and there's a place in life for a wife; but cursed is the man who has a trashy wife'."

Ty chuckled. "Cute; but it sure as hell doesn't apply to you. Jackie is the least trashy woman I've ever known."

"Okay, listen to what's been happening and see what you think." Matt recounted the multiple encounters and their sexual themes, pounding Killian as he described Jackie's antics.

Ty shook his head "Well you poor bastard. The second foxiest lady in White Oak Estates wants to massage you and play fantasy games with you and dress up for you. I can see why you're so pissed."

"Kiss my ass, Ty. I'm telling you this is different. It's coming from crap her sister fed her."

"If I were you, I'd go with the flow. In fact, if you don't want to help her out, I'd be happy to."

Matt struggled to accept the joke lightly but failed completely. Even the thought of Jackie with Ty sent tidal waves of anxiety crashing through his chest and stomach. He hated the feeling, and he hated having it back in his life. He swilled a full half of a Killian. "This just isn't funny, Ty. My dad also told me a man can see his future by looking at his wife's mother. He warned me about marrying Jackie."

Ty shot a knowing glance. "The famous Madeline, huh?"

"I kid you not; if you got to Greenville by four o'clock with a fifth of rum and enough money for a cheap room, you could be bagging that woman by sunset."

"Even if that's true, it's not fair to Jackie. She's her own woman." Ty paused, but fired away. "Let me share an old saying with you, Matthew."

"Share away."

"That which you fear will come upon you."

"Meaning?"

"Christ, Matt. Figure it out."

Matt had two more beers, becoming increasingly sullen, more obviously drunk. Ty insisted on driving him home, but Matt refused and stumbled into the parking lot.

***

Jackie and Jodi had stopped at Pizza Hut before diving into one of Jodi's summer reading books. Jodi fell into the sleep of the innocent before 9:30. Jackie coerced Sean into his room just after 11:00. At 11:15, she drew a hot bath and found her paperback murder mystery, determined to clear her mind for a while. She leaned back against the smooth side of her tub, its whirlpool jets pulsating on the light setting; twin candles burning peach blossom on the ledge beside her. Several soothing minutes later, she heard Matt's heavy stomp on the stairs.

"Jackie, where the hell are you?"

She sensed the anger. "I'm in the tub, honey."

He lurched into the bathroom, unsteady on his feet. She was surprised at his condition; he and Ty were usually sensible. "I've been with *your* friend Ty."

"I know, but he's your friend, Matt. How many beers each?"

He ignored her. "I'm going to ask you a straight question, Jackie. I want a straight answer."

Now she knew he was drunk, struggling to focus his eyes, his usually strong facial features disjointed. She hated feeling so vulnerable in her shrinking mound of bubbles, but she said, "Okay what's the question?"

"How often have you played prick-teaser with Ty Jameson?"

She winced and put fingers to her lips. "Not so loud, Matt. I'm not sure Sean's asleep. What in the world are you talking about?"

His voice grew louder, angrier. "How often have you teased him? Showed him your—"

"I haven't shown him my anything," she shot back, with anger of her own brewing, "unless he has X-ray vision."

"Don't joke with me, Jackie. I'm in no mood for your goddam jokes. "

"Matt, please go to bed. We'll talk in the morning."

He shouted, "No, we'll talk right this goddam minute. I will not have a prick-teaser for a wife."

She tried to stay calm, to keep her voice low. "I'm not teasing anybody, except maybe you once in a while."

Now he glared, weaving unsteadily. "You love it, don't you? Wearing your damned dress slit clear up to your… Do you have any idea how I feel knowing you—"

"No more, Matt," she said as firmly as a naked woman can speak from a bathtub. "Go to bed."

His eyes narrowed to furious slits. "Just get a towel and cover yourself for a change." He pulled two towels off the wall rack, hurled them into her bath water, turned and slammed the door violently.

The four sat together for a brief, tense breakfast. Jackie was battling exhaustion after a fitful night's sleep. Matt and his hang-over drank coffee in grim silence. A sullen Sean hurried through orange juice and Pop-Tarts and headed for the door. Jackie feared that their house's sound insulation hadn't concealed the words of a screaming drunk. Jodi happily reported the latest events in the lives of her hamsters, Ollie and Olivet.

During her drive to the bank, Jackie called Sherry Jameson. "I'm not letting my husband party with yours anymore. Last night was bad."

"Ty was afraid of that. He said Matt was really struggling."

"The worst ever, I'd say. He's not much of a drinker. It was bad, Sherry. I don't see how women live with drunks."

"All guys get clobbered now and then, right?"

"I guess so, but damn, that was ugly."

Jackie spent the morning hoping the phone wouldn't ring. She couldn't decide whether to lunch with Ted Aldrich, and she couldn't decide why she couldn't decide. But her mind wouldn't work, as if mired in a bog of exhaustion. She told her boss she needed a think break and walked to the city park half a block south of the bank building. It was a peaceful spot compared to the bustle of Broad Street, a spot she visited often, sometimes with her lunch, sometimes just to be alone. She bought a Frito snack bag from Hans the ever-friendly street vendor, found an isolated bench, and tried to figure it all out.

For reasons she couldn't explain, she began by asking herself whether she might be a closet nymphomaniac. She thought back, for maybe the twentieth time, to her physical reaction to Michael on the Picasso room daybed. She had come too close to an encore, and she couldn't explain what had happened inside her, and she couldn't honestly say that she could have stopped him if there had been an encore. But surely nymphomania didn't make sense. She had survived for fourteen years on a starvation diet. She didn't have a drawer full of plastic friends like some women kept. And she had managed to resist Michael, even if it was close.

She asked herself whether she was restless because she had married America's premier jerk. Surely not, she decided. He has good qualities. He cares about his family. She believed that, in his hardheaded chauvinistic way, Matt loved her. And if he loved her, they could find ways to make it work. But the fury had to stop. She hated the fury.

She asked herself whether she was concentrating too much on the sexual side. Maybe she and Matt could do something like skiing or mountain climbing together, or learning to fly a plane. But that felt like letting him off the hook. There were sexual problems in their marriage that needed to be resolved. She didn't make love, for God's sake; she romped. She wondered whether she should be communicating better. Maybe so, but she had surely tried.

She thought about why she might have lunch with Ted Aldrich. And the answer suddenly rang clearly in her mind, although she knew the answer failed to address the real questions. My life feels heavy. It's weighing down my spirit. It's weighing down my marriage. I need a friend, someone to share with and to laugh with. I want to feel like Jodi looked that day on the soccer field, even if just for a little while. She had felt that way with Ted Aldrich, even if just for a little while.

At 2:00, Jackie gave herself one more chance to reconsider. She called Mia, a twice-weekly employee of the rarely busy Panache Art Gallery in downtown Omaha. After a few minutes of apology about using Michael as her confidant, Jackie dived in. "You know that Ted Aldrich got in touch, right?"

"Yes. Michael is concerned about you and your pilot."

"What's that about? I thought you guys were okay with me stretching my wings."

"Hell, I'm okay with you stretching your legs."

Jackie laughed at her irrepressibly disgusting sister. "So what's Michael's problem?"

"He says you're vulnerable. That you shouldn't do anything while your head's not on straight?"

"What do you think?"

"I told him he's overreacting, big time."

"I might be confused a little. But I'm not talking about forever with Ted Aldrich, right? Just having lunch."

"If I were you, I'd think about a lot more than lunch."

"It's just a lunch, Mia. Really."

"Whatever," said Mia lightly. "Enjoy your pilot."

At 3:30, he called.

"How about that lunch, Mrs. Billings?"

"Okay, Ted, let's do lunch."

"Can you take a few hours off work?"

"How few?"

"Maybe four."

"Four hours for lunch?"

"I've got a nice surprise for you. You'll love it."

"I'll see."

He gave her detailed instructions for their rendezvous. She took careful notes, and she struggled to find a safe place to keep the notes.

The Billings home included a Matt-built screened porch that led to the patio and a kid-friendly back yard. Sean and Jodi viewed the screened porch as a dreaded spot where discipline problems were discussed and punishment dispensed. On this night, Matt invited Jackie to the porch. Kids played raucously in the back yards adjacent to theirs. The rich aroma of fish wafted from the grill on Carl Handley's deck to their left.

Matt said, "I'm sorry I was so rough on you last night. I was pretty well hammered, and I've had a lot on my mind."

She eyed him, somewhat surprised but wearily so. "We need to work through all that. But I don't feel up to a big discussion tonight."

"Okay, but I won't do that again. I drank way too much. My dad was a mean drunk and I hated it."

His pain appeared sincere, but she again focused on his drunken rage, trying to ignore the side issue that his tantrum had helped push her toward a secret luncheon date. "Let me tell you something important."

"I'm listening."

"The anger doesn't work. Something happens inside me. I didn't like bullying when I was a little girl and I don't like it now. Surely you remember Bruiser the Dog."

Matt nodded glumly, as she knew he would. Bruiser was a favorite Morris family story. Jackie was eight, Mia, six. Mia had managed to inflame a ten-year-old kid named Carl Rollins by saying he looked like the Goodyear Blimp, about a hundred times in one summer afternoon. Jackie came home from the library to find Carl's unleashed Doberman snarling at Mia, who had managed to back halfway up a backyard slide. Mia was hanging on for dear life. Carl was standing just behind the dog, arms crossed, demanding an apology. Jackie told Carl to take his dog and get out of their yard. Carl said, *no way,* and told Mia to apologize or *you'll be gobbled up to your knees, you little shit.* Jackie told Mia to hang on a little longer, hurried into their garage, found their father's golf clubs, pulled out the five iron, returned to the scene, and delivered a mighty wallop that broke three of Bruiser's ribs and sent him gimping home. The episode cost Jackie a lengthy grounding and thirteen weeks of allowance to help cover Bruiser's medical bills; but it established Jackie Morris as a pretty tough customer in her neighborhood.

"Something happens inside me, too," Matt said. "When I think about—"

She sighed. "No more, Matt. And no more screaming matches."

Matt headed for his TV room. Jackie tried to concentrate on her book. Later, as if on autopilot, she put two kids through their evening ritual. She had retreated to their bed, pretending to sleep, when Matt came up the stairs. He soon began snoring loudly, but the snoring didn't explain a long, sleepless hour. She had decided to have lunch with Ted Aldrich, but she hadn't been decisive. She felt adrift. Trying to improve her marriage. Failing dismally. Reaching out like a drowning woman to the life rafts of Mia and Michael and Sherry and now Ted Aldrich.

She thought again about Bruiser the Dog. She had felt brave and strong and decisive that day. What happened to brave and strong and decisive Jackie? That day was just one year before the most horrible day of her life. *Did my strength come from Daddy, and then he was gone?* She really didn't know.

***

Daniel Berringer received the Aldrich call that formally launched the physical portion of their project. "JB rendezvous number one, tomorrow."

"Prediction?" asked Daniel Berringer.

"Three, four maximum."

"That does not sound intriguing, my friend."

Aldrich chuckled. "I'm on top of my game, Mr. B. But you will have all the intrigue you can handle, guaranteed."

Chapter Nine

Jackie drove northwest on Route 37, following Ted Aldrich's complex set of instructions. The two-lane road wound through vintage Ohio countryside: phone and power lines spanned poles that lined both sides of the highway; livestock grazed in gently rolling pastures; corn and soybean fields surrounded farm homes, barns and outbuildings, some immaculate, some near collapse. She could always see a tree line on the horizon.

She turned onto the first of four county roads that Aldrich had specified, drove six miles, and turned again. She became increasingly aware of immense isolation—of fields, forests, and pastures, but remarkably few dwellings. On some days, she would have relaxed and enjoyed this kind of drive. Today, she struggled with a sense of disconnect.

Her day had begun conservatively in every respect. She had certainly dressed conservatively: a lightweight ankle-length mint skirt with matching jacket over a white silk blouse, simple jewelry, and pantyhose closer to support than sheer. She had consciously adopted a *no sexual agenda* attitude for her day, and the outfit felt just right. She had fixed breakfast, arranged the children's schedules, and assured that her department was running smoothly before her pre-arranged early departure.

But nothing else felt conservative. She didn't like deceiving Matt, although the only deception was omission. The countryside reminded her of her hometown, causing her to think of her father, adding more weight to guilt she already felt. And she had little idea where she was going, in any sense of the word.

She turned onto the third then the fourth specified roads, putting her more than thirty miles northwest of Dublin and forty-five miles from downtown Columbus. Now she saw fields and heavy tree stands but no farmhouses at all. She drove north for exactly six-tenths of a mile and stopped abruptly before turning into the farm lane that he had described. Her stomach had been on edge during the whole trip; now it quivered fiercely. What am I doing? Who is this man? But she had okay answers. He's a pilot for a major airline. He's a gentleman and a great guy to talk to. I'm sure I'll be fine.

She turned onto a lane that took her through an open metal gate. With tires crunching loudly on gravel, she followed the lane past a well-worn two-story white farmhouse. An immense barn loomed just beyond the house, painted the traditional red, but of vintage far more recent than the house. White letters above massive double doors shouted *XYZ Farm.* She continued along a narrower version of the gravel lane running to the right of the barn, made a sharp left turn, and she found him.

Ted Aldrich sat casually on the right wing of a sleek white twin-engine plane parked near the rear of the structure. He smiled broadly as she drove to within a few yards of the plane's tail, slid gracefully off the wing, and approached her car. He wore a dark blue jump suit with a gold emblem that looked like eagle wings. She noticed a tan darker than when they first met. The sun highlighted his silver hair. As she stepped out of her car, he said, "This moment feels strange to me; do we embrace like old friends, or just shake hands?"

"How about a nice handshake, Mr. Aldrich." She extended her right hand, smiling warmly, but grateful for a chance to set the right tone.

"Good enough," he said, accepting her hand.

"Talk about strange… Everything in my life has been strange lately."

"We'll have plenty of time to discuss all that. Let's fire up the Beechcraft and go to lunch. Do you have four hours or so?"

"Yes, but where are we going?"

"That will be revealed shortly. Right this way, young lady."

She experienced another moment's anxiety, visualizing that she might fly off and simply vanish. But it didn't make sense to come this far and chicken out. Ted held out his hand, guided her up the short steps into the plane, and helped her strap into the right cockpit seat. He sealed the door, ran through his take-off checklist, and taxied down a narrow blacktop runway that extended into a field that appeared to be an ungrazed pasture. They raced by trees, fencerows, and a small creek, and lifted off. As the plane angled into a bright blue sky broken only by fluffy white clouds, Jackie's father visited her thoughts for the second time. She remembered lying with him in their backyard or at the city park, searching the sky, making up stories about the cloud-shapes they could see. She decided to focus on something else.

She lifted her voice above the drone of the twin engines. "That sure is a complicated dashboard."

He turned toward her, frowning and shaking his head. "My co-pilot damn well needs to know more about a plane than that." Although he had clearly been teasing, the comment led to a more serious than she expected discussion of the Bonanza's instrument panel and other major cockpit components.

She asked about the XYZ Farm and learned that Ted had found it by accident, almost literally. Mechanical trouble necessitated an emergency landing. He spotted a clearing and landed safely on the farm of a family that turned out to be eager to wrap up a long-standing inheritance battle. Ted and several associates put together the money needed to do a deal, and the XYZ Farm was theirs. They remodeled the barn and poured the runway. Ted didn't visit central Ohio often, he said, but the farm was a perfect stop-off point for some of his personal trips.

She could tell they were flying southwest, initially following Interstate 71 toward Cincinnati. She could also tell that small planes provide a much bumpier ride than flying hotels like she flew to Omaha. She appreciated her iron stomach; Mia would have been heading for the barf bag within ten minutes. "So, where are we going?" she asked again.

"We're zipping over to Indiana, a little town called Madison."

"Indiana for lunch?"

"To a great spot on a hill overlooking the Ohio River. You'll love it."

Jackie couldn't avoid a surge of childlike excitement as she contemplated a new adventure that would rival some of Mia's stories. She again studied Ted Aldrich's face, now in profile as he checked instrument settings. She saw creases that a Hollywood actor would pay a plastic surgeon to eliminate, but the look fit him like a weathered duffel bag fits a veteran seaman. His eyes were alert, intelligent, and focused on flight details most of the time, on her some of the time.

As the wooded hills and valleys of southern Ohio glided under them, he asked, "Is it exciting or frightening to be mother to a little girl?"

"More exciting now. She's a dreamer and a hard worker. It's fun to help make her dreams come true. Frightening is a few years off."

"The dreaded teenage years?"

"Yes. Sean just arrived. I think boys are easier, though."

"Why do you think that?"

"Because Sean is Matt's job."

She delivered the line with only a slight smile. Ted looked at her as if gauging a person he didn't yet know well. "Joke, right?"

"Yes. We're struggling together with Sean."

The conversation bounced along easily. They talked about Matt's potential jealousy when Jodi began dating. She narrated a review of a new set of photographs she had brought with her.

Ted said, " I can tell you really care about your family. That's got to be the key."

"I really do care."

"Your husband looks like a solid customer."

"He's a good man. We have our moments, but who doesn't?"

She watched Ted working both the instrument panel and the radio as he secured clearance from Madison Municipal Airport and prepped for arrival. As the distant runway rose to meet them, Jackie struggled against a too pleasant feeling that she had escaped to a whole new world. Ted had pre-arranged the taxi that took them to the Clifty Inn, a restaurant as good as advertised. They watched boats ranging from kayaks to coal barges maneuver the Ohio River, far below them. He explained the Regatta hosted annually by a town that might otherwise enjoy the quiet anonymity of most Midwestern communities. Ted mentioned that he had raced power-boats at an earlier point in his life—not surprising, she decided.

They ate the restaurant's shrimp specialty; she drank a glass of chardonnay; he drank iced tea, explaining that drinking alcohol while flying was a shortcut to heaven.

"This is a nice break in my crazy life, Ted."

"I thought you'd like it. I've been hoping Chicago wasn't our last lunch together."

She smiled, but couldn't come up with a reply that felt appropriate.

He looked at her with blue eyes now probing. "What's that smile about?"

"Nothing. I'm just having fun; you know, good wine, good food."

"Good company?"

The question brought her up short again. The answer was an obvious yes, but she couldn't bring herself to say it. Aldrich said, "A minute ago, a sparkling smile and now it's gone. What happened, Jackie?"

"I'm still adjusting to all this, and sometimes I'm too serious, I think."

"Why so serious?"

"I don't know. Things just get serious. Why does that happen?"

"It doesn't happen to me. I refuse."

During the return flight to Columbus, the discussion concentrated on Sean. Again, Ted asked the kind of questions that allowed Jackie to discuss both her pride and her fears. About twenty minutes out, he said, "Okay, co-pilot, take over the controls."

"Get a grip, Ted, There's no way."

"Pretend you're in one of those movies where the pilot gets food poisoning. Those women always figure out how to do it." He put both hands on the back of his neck. "Go gettum, tiger." The plane fell into an immediate shallow dive.

"Don't, Ted, we're going to crash."

"Pull back on your wheel." She yanked the wheel. The plane began rising sharply.

"Now down." They began diving, more sharply than the first dive.

"Up!" They shot up, but also banked right.

Ted laughed, almost uncontrollably. "I hate to say this, Jackie, but you are one piss poor pilot."

She laughed, too, although her stomach had jumped somewhere near her throat. "That's it. You hurt my feelings. I quit." She took her hands off the wheel and crossed her arms.

He took his wheel and stabilized the bouncing plane. Later, he explained more about the navigational system and how he could zero in on the XYZ Farm. He brought the plane in smoothly and taxied slowly toward the barn. As they walked toward her car, he said, "Jackie, this has been a wonderful day for me. Thanks for sharing it."

"Thank you. I had a great time."

He raised his right hand to her cheek and said, "You're a treasure. I hope we will meet again."

She hesitated, stymied again. "Take care, Ted."

He turned and walked toward one of the small side doors of the XYZ barn. She checked her voicemail from the car, relieved to learn that Matt hadn't called. Her planned explanation for the afternoon was a long lunch and an impromptu drive and shopping trip to get away, but she hated the idea of out-and-out deception. She drove toward Columbus, bouncing between elation and guilt. She picked up Jodi, and returned to her world.

Later that night, Jackie Billings belatedly accepted her husband's apology and set about seducing him. She could feel her spirit soaring. She wished that Matt could soar with her, to connect with her feelings before they made love, but she understood how things needed to work, at least for now. She said, "I'll bet you can't turn me on." She resisted him playfully and she realized that their foreplay was truly exciting as he peeled away her nightie and fondled breasts that had always been unbelievably sensitive. She fought him for her panties, playfully, and when they slid off her feet she said, "Make love to me hard, Matt. Own me. Make me crazy." And he responded and she responded, and she came closer to real than ever in her married life.

Michael Ledereaux received her call the following day. "It was a great day," she bubbled. "It helped me feel better about myself at a point when I really needed to."

Michael participated graciously in her enthusiasm, hearing about Ted Aldrich the perfect gentleman and Matt Billings' rise from the ashes. But this conversation, he decided, was a crock of crap. How could she not see that Ted Aldrich's gallantry was aimed directly at her crotch? How could she not know that her idiot husband would fall flat on his ass again, and soon, because that's what idiots do. Good God, he thought, being Jackie Billings' friend is hard work.

***

Two high-flying weeks later, Ted Aldrich contacted her, and she again drove toward the rural barn, this time finding a reason to be out of the office from 10:45 to 2:45. There had been less mental struggle this time; in fact, she told herself at one point that the trip would be like getting a booster shot. But she wore black slacks and a cream boat-neck pullover, conservative enough for continuation of her *no sexual agenda* policy. She had even spent some time analyzing her motives and Ted Aldrich's motives. She knew she wasn't worldly, but she didn't want to be stupid.

She decided her motives were clear. Time with Ted Aldrich was reassuring and uplifting. There was an easy comfort that she had never experienced. But what about Ted? Jackie's mother would say that men are always motivated by sex. Mia would probably agree. Michael sounded worried, for some reason. But Ted was older; surely not some kind of horny toad; and if he was a horny toad he could likely choose from any number of airline stewardesses or customers. So, for whatever reason, he apparently enjoyed spending time with *no sexual agenda* Jackie Billings. Of course, she would be careful. She didn't know Ted well enough to be completely sure of anything. And she reminded herself that she was a mother, not Ted Aldrich's footloose co-pilot.

This time, the plane parked behind the barn was a cherry-red two-seat biplane, its slide emblazoned with a black and gold eagle above the words *Fight On*. Ted walked toward her car, wearing tan slacks and a dark brown bomber jacket, and carrying two sets of goggles. He told her she would have to dress the part, and led her inside the barn and up a narrow wood ladder. He unlocked a weathered door revealing a complete studio apartment built into the loft section of what had looked like a typical, if oversized, Ohio farm barn.

"This is quite a setup. Do you live here?"

"No. It's for guests mostly; the farmhouse is very small." He opened a closet and pulled out an orange jumpsuit. "This should fit you. Suit up."

He closed the door behind him. She changed into the jumpsuit, climbed carefully down the ladder, and met him at the biplane. As he helped her onto the wing, he said, "I imagine you'll want me in the pilot seat, right?"

"Yes, funny man."

"Okay, hop into the front. I'll help you get strapped in."

He handed her the goggles and strapped her in, carefully avoiding, she decided, a chance to make major physical contact. That seemed reassuring somehow. He settled into the rear cockpit while she worked on getting curls and stray wisps of hair out from under her goggles. After firing up, he shouted, "You should feel honored, Jackie. This is the very plane that brought down the Red Baron during World War One."

She turned, smiling. "You wouldn't tease a girl would you?"

"Maybe not the exact same plane. But it was something like this."

Ted pulled down his goggles and they headed skyward, cruising for twenty minutes over lush Ohio countryside. Forests and farms zipped under them while the wind whipped Jackie's face, generating a sense of being part of nature unlike anything she had ever experienced. Ted shouted, "Brace up," and raised the nose sharply. Suddenly they were flying at vertical and in a breathtaking moment, they were upside down. He finished the loop and shouted, "What did you think of that?"

Jackie's insides still felt upside down, but she shouted back, "It was great!" The feeling reminded her of the *Son of Beast* at Kings Island without the tracks, and Jackie was always designated parent on roller coaster rides. Ted put the plane through a series of loops, barrel rolls, figure eights, and a few maneuvers that might have been Aldrich originals. Jackie hung on for dear life.

When they landed at the barn, he exited first and helped her off the wing. She stepped off by holding onto his shoulders, sliding into an almost automatic embrace, though brief. She looked up at him, smiling. "That was incredible. Thanks."

He stepped back and put both hands on her shoulders. "I really enjoy being with you. You are special."

She again searched for an appropriate reply. "Take care, Ted; I've got to run." She turned toward her car.

"Jackie…"

She turned back toward him. "Yes?"

"My jumpsuit."

She felt her cheeks go warm. "Oops."

"Just pull the east door shut after you change. It locks automatically."

He returned to the biplane and climbed aboard. Jackie changed clothes and hurried back to the office.

She looked forward to another great night. Sean would be at the Jamesons' for an overnight. She dispatched Jodi at 9:30 and walked boldly into Matt's TV nook, wearing nothing but one of his t-shirts and the tiniest panties she could find. He protested briefly when she pulled his remote away and flicked off a soccer match in overtime; but she found his zipper, changed his mind about soccer matches, pushed him backward in his recliner and climbed on top of him.

"Whoa!" he protested. "Remember that Mr. Big calls the shots."

She decided that only a buoyant mood could allow a comment so pitiful to be tolerated, but she thrust herself against him several times and whispered, "Then tell Mr. Big to get busy."

He grinned and said, "Upstairs, wench."

She forgave him again and led him toward their bedroom.

The next morning, she wore sheer lingerie to work, for the first time in years. And she thought about her husband and they made love that night and the following night.

At midnight on Thursday, Matt said, "Do you realize this is our first triple play in about a hundred years."

"Triple play?"

"Remember how we used to keep score? Three nights, three romps. Not bad for an old married couple."

She laughed, deciding that being closer to him was worth the guy moments. But she didn't like his next question.

"So what's going on, lady?"

"I'm just showing you there can be life after thirty-five, Matthew."

***

Michael Ledereaux received another phone call reporting dramatic improvement in her sex life. He didn't like any part of the pattern that was developing: Matt's newfound good fortune, or the immense risk of Ted Aldrich's impending good fortune. He decided to go on the offensive.

"Jackie, may I speak candidly?"

"Of course. It's why I call."

"Ted Aldrich is a dreadful mistake."

"Explain."

"While your focus is so single-mindedly sexual, having a man like Aldrich in your life is like playing with fire."

"I don't think it's about sex, Michael. It's about living, freeing my spirit, flying. And I'm learning to fly with Matt."

"Jackie, listen carefully. You are a remarkably passionate woman. Perhaps more so than you even understand. This isn't about flying. It's about playing with fire."

"If anyone gets set on fire, it's going to be Matt Billings. I'm making progress."

***

Daniel Berringer enjoyed the phone call.

"I'll use the database now," said Ted Aldrich.

"Struggling some, I gather," gloated Berringer.

"She's a bit more complicated than I thought."

"How so?"

"Very strange lady. She's so innocent you want to laugh at her. But she's a fighter."

"I'm not following. Is she fighting you?"

"Negative. We're best of friends. She's fighting for her husband."

Berringer laughed. "I wish you the worst of luck, my friend." Berringer uploaded the Jackie Billings Life Events database, the only one of the three available to Aldrich according to the rules. He opened the ledger spreadsheet and entered A's first penalty points in four years. Berringer nodded toward the valley outside his window. The odds of intrigue had just skyrocketed.

Chapter Ten

Ty Jameson agreed to meet Matt at O'Hannahan's Pub, although he greatly feared a repeat of their night from drunken hell. His friend had been somewhere between upset and furious this afternoon when he called about getting together.

Ty entered the pub, gave Talley the hug that always allowed a moment of contact with the incredible pillows of her chest, and weaved his way toward Matt, sitting alone at a table for two against the back wall. The Killian appeared to be half empty, but no sign of a row of empties. Ty slid onto the chair. "What's happenin', man?"

Matt reached into the breast pocket of a tan *Billings Construction* work shirt, extracted a quad-folded sheet of paper, opened it, and handed it to Ty. Matt waited silently. Ty noted that Matt's face was actually pale. He read:

To: MBillings@BillingsConstruction.com
From: anon123@specmail.net
Subject: Twenty Bucks

Hi, Matt,

Sorry to be mysterious but my wife can't know about this for several reasons. I'm old buddies with a guy named Tom Kerrigan who has bet me twenty bucks that he popped Jackie Morris's cherry. I say there's no fuckin' way (so to speak).

Please settle the bet. Thanks.

A believer in Jackie's virginity

Ty swiftly put two and two together. He also recalled their previous session when even minor jokes about Jackie's sexuality had created a run on the Killian Red inventory. But this moment was too absurd to handle. "So?"

"She was supposed to have been a virgin," said Matt grimly.

Ty put fingers to both temples and shook his head incredulously. "Holy shit, man. If she says she was, let it go." He blew out his breath through pursed lips and signaled to Talley, the clenched fist that meant double manhattan. "Son of a bitch, Matt. What difference can it possibly make eighteen years later?"

"If it doesn't make a difference, why do I wonder if I might have a heart attack?"

"If you have a heart attack over this, you are the dumbest ass in Columbus. Son…of…a…bitch!"

Matt swilled from his bottle. "Was Sherry a virgin?"

"Are you shitting me? I just hoped she hadn't done the whole Ohio State offensive line."

"How can you stand it? How can you even think about another guy…?" Now Matt exhaled hard. He appeared to be struggling for breath.

"Jesus, man. Take it easy."

This time Matt stopped at four beers, but he grew steadily more sullen and Ty grew steadily more impatient. When they said their goodbyes, Ty simply said, "Be careful driving home, and wait until at least tomorrow before you talk about this."

Matt's glare carried real fury. "Never tell me how to handle Jackie. Got it?"

Ty glared back. "Then what the hell was I doing here tonight?"

"Damn good question," Matt growled, as he turned toward his car.

***

Jackie sat in the small room off the kitchen where she usually ironed. But tonight she had wheeled out her sewing machine and tackled her first alteration project in months. She smiled happily as she finished the last row of stitches and held up the dress—formerly a yellow sundress she rarely wore, now a yellow mini-dress she would likely never wear outdoors, unless Matt someday agreed to public adventure. But it was absolutely positively perfect for fun at home.

She carried the dress upstairs, slipped out of her jeans and top, suited up, and checked herself in the mirror. Oh my! As short as the crazy things people wore in the '70s. Deliciously dangerous if she sat, or leaned, or reached, or even breathed hard. Exciting memories flooded into her mind, but she turned them into fantasy: She would show up in the bedroom in the little dress. She would admit to Matt that the outfit made her a bit vulnerable, but she would pull the hem down as far as possible and tell him she could easily keep him from getting her turned on. He would love it. She would love it. She loved thinking about it.

She heard the garage door go up. She heard his shout. "Jackie, meet me on the porch. Right now." He might have sounded gruff; she couldn't tell for sure. Maybe he had a game of his own in mind. She thought about just rushing downstairs and popping onto the porch, but realized she didn't know whether Sean might come home unexpectedly. So she put on her robe, hoping she wouldn't need it.

She reached the doorway to the screened porch, checked for Sean, and boldly slipped off the robe. She opened the door and sashayed onto the porch. "Surprise."

Matt was sitting with his back to the yard, as if waiting for her. He actually closed his eyes and shook his head, angrily as best she could determine. "Cover yourself and come back," he demanded flatly.

"Matt…? What is it?"

"Cover yourself and come back."

She turned, retrieved the robe, and returned to the porch. She sat silently in a chair that faced him.

He breathed deeply, his face almost white, his voice hoarse. "I just learned that you…that you screwed a guy named Tom Kerrigan."

Her mind spun. How could he possibly know? Why would it possibly matter? But his expression mixed anger and grim anxiety in a way she had never seen. She felt her throat go dry. Could she just deny it? Guys like Tommy lied about conquests all the time. It would be her word against his. Oh, God. Mia! Mia knew even back then. And… Maybe…

"Why would you think that?" she asked in a voice even weaker than his.

"I think it because you just admitted it, by…by…" He stood, veins visible in his neck, his breath coming in gasps. "My dad warned me… Shit…"

"God, Matt, get a drink of water or something."

He stormed past her. She followed him into the kitchen where he drew a glass of water and gulped loudly. She spoke softly. "I know it's the wrong time to talk about this, but it can't matter anymore. It was a long time—"

He held up his left hand and shook his head, his face drawn into a ghastly gray mask. "I can't do this. I'm going to sleep at the office tonight."

She slept alone that night, wondering how so much progress could come crashing down so fast, especially over a laughable physical relationship. She told herself that Matt couldn't reasonably expect a twenty-three year old virgin bride. But deep down she knew the problem, and it went deeper than a lie she shouldn't have told. She knew all about visualization. And she knew that Matt visualized constantly—for negative reasons more than positive. And Matt could see her in a car or on a bed with another guy's... And he couldn't stand it at all. She understood that, too well.

Matt slept at home the next night, but he put her in a sullen deep freeze that showed no sign of ending. She talked once to Michael, but she was beginning to lose patience with Michael. Too often, Michael was negative when she was positive, and positive when she was negative.

On Wednesday afternoon, Ted Aldrich called to invite her to "an old-fashioned picnic" on Friday.

She began, "I really can't, Ted. My life right now is..."

But she stopped in mid-thought and decided that nothing in the whole world sounded better than an old-fashioned picnic with Ted Aldrich. She had tried twice to talk with Matt. The first time he failed to get over the lie about Tommy Kerrigan. The second time, he called the entire period since Omaha a perfect example of his father's warning about Morris women being sluts. He had even demanded that she burn her yellow mini-dress. She decided not to be controlled by a man being so unreasonable, but even the need to hide the dress felt like unreasonable control.

"Now that I think about it," she said, "I'd like that, Ted."

"Great. Wear something cool."

Chapter Eleven

On Thursday evening, Jackie shopped at the Dress Barn and picked a snow-white sundress, an outfit perfect for the picnic she visualized, but on Friday morning, guilt felt like a physical presence in their bedroom as she dressed for work, aware she would change clothes later for another man. She had to jockey Sean's carpool arrangements because Sue Morton was sick. At the office, she absorbed a mild lecture from her boss about an attendance record being marred by a pattern of half-day vacations. She could list twenty good reasons not to head out for XYZ, but she failed to resist the vision of Ted's picnic.

She found an abandoned lane and retrieved her new outfit from a bag stashed in her trunk. As she twisted and turned behind the wheel, struggling with pantyhose and zippers, she battled one more wave of doubt and misgiving. But she finished changing, freshened her make-up, and drove the last few miles to meet him.

She quickly gave Ted credit for doing everything possible to make her vision reality. They camped on a huge blanket on the pasture side of the barn, allowing them to see for miles across rolling countryside; yet they had wonderful privacy. Music surrounded them, floating down from speakers tucked under the eaves of the barn.

As they sipped wine, Jackie sat with her back against the trunk of an oak tree that towered above them. Ted sat across from her, smiling as always, blue eyes twinkling.

"Pretty dress."

She smiled but unconsciously tugged at her hem. During one moment of mental rebellion, she had actually thought of bringing her yellow mini. But today, her head was a million miles from that kind of fun.

He reached toward her and passed his hand over her wine glass. "Just adding some happy powder."

Her brief laugh was the last she would enjoy for the next hour, despite the setting. The music was light rock: Chicago, The Eagles, Rod Stewart. Ted's bottomless picnic basket began with smoked salmon appetizers, proceeded through salad, baked ham, and an assortment of vegetables, and ended with blueberry cheesecake, still chilled. She tried for upbeat, especially during a talk about Sean and Jodi's new school year, but she couldn't rise above the turmoil she had tried to escape. As they finished the cheesecake, Ted said, "Let's talk about what's wrong."

She studied fences and trees on the distant horizon. "I'm sorry to be so down. It's just that my life's kind of a mess right now."

"Is it my fault in any way?"

She sensed that the question deserved real consideration, but she didn't want to face it. "I don't think so. In a lot of ways you've been good for me."

"I mean this, Jackie. Say the word, and I'll disappear."

She stopped herself before admitting that his disappearing would create another hole in her life, but pyramiding anxieties suddenly included Ted Aldrich.

"I need to know something, Ted."

He smiled. "What we're doing here, right?"

"Yes."

"Do you remember my telling you I refuse to be unhappy?"

She thought back to the restaurant in Madison. "Yes, I remember."

"People get all screwed up about happiness. It's something that happens today; right now. So I spend my life accumulating daily treasures."

"Why am I…I mean why is this a treasure?"

"You don't sound very confident."

"I guess not. I really need to know."

"Tell me why you enjoy time with a good friend."

She paused, realizing she had never really thought about it. "It's comfortable. I can relax and laugh. I can care, and know that my friend cares."

"I couldn't have said it better. That's all there is to it."

"Is that really all?"

"Are we talking about sex?"

"Yes."

He frowned, but the eyes twinkled. "We've known each other long enough to speak honestly. If you want sex from me, Jackie, just come right out and say it."

Laughter welled up in her, washing away her instinctive protest. She welcomed the feeling. "Not today, Theodore."

"Well, damn. Okay, finish your wine and we'll go for a walk."

They walked side-by-side through the meadow beside the landing strip, and into a wooded area at the edge of the property. He said, "Do you want to know what I really think about physical stuff, especially at my age?"

"What do you think?"

"It's spice. Allow me to illustrate." He took her hand and they walked for several seconds without speaking. "Isn't that better?"

Yes, better, she decided, but that didn't make it smart. She tried for a self-assured laugh. "Where would the logical extension of the spice theory lead, Mr. Aldrich?"

To her surprise, he stopped on the path, turned toward her, and took both her hands. His eyes were kind but newly intense. "With one exception, it will lead wherever you want it to lead, no more, no less."

"What's the exception?"

"Close your eyes."

She closed her eyes and waited, feeling his hands release her hands and gently cup her face, surprised but not really surprised when she felt a gentle kiss on her lips, brief but tender. He stepped back, put his forefinger to his lips, brought it to the tip of her nose, and smiled gently.

Jackie returned the smile, her eyes shining. She felt close to him. She was filled with appreciation that he was in this place with her, strong and solid. "Hold me for a minute, okay?"

He took her in his arms. "For as long as you like."

They walked to the far edge of the forest and wound back toward the barn. When Ted helped her over a fallen log, he took her hand and held it during the return walk. Back at the blanket, they talked and laughed and listened to music for another hour. Jackie was aware of relishing each minute, as if already learning to adopt his happiness-is-now philosophy.

As they stood by the front door of her car, she said, "Thanks for cheering me up."

He took both her hands in his. "I hope things get better for you at home."

"Thank you. Me too."

"Another hug?"

"That would be nice."

She drove toward her rural dressing room, again appreciating his strength, still feeling the imprint of his body on hers.

***

Ted Aldrich placed the phone call. "Prediction time frame: one."

"Progress, huh?" Berringer replied sourly.

"I should find a confessional and say a few Hail Marys."

Berringer chuckled. "Yeah, right. What's up?"

"I was magnificent today."

"What happened to our fighter?"

"She's fighting, but I'm applying overwhelming force."

***

Michael Ledereaux took her call, although wearily.

"I really need to talk. Matt's gone distant, completely. I'm not proud of this, but I leaned all over Ted Aldrich emotionally."

"What does that mean?"

"Used time with him to feel better; feel happier."

"Did it get physical?"

"No. Well, he kissed me once, for just a second, and held me. I don't think Ted's into physical. He just treats me like a really good friend."

"Do you wish he were into physical?"

"No, Michael. It was perfect."

Michael's confusion about Ted Aldrich deepened. Reading between the lines, the man had likely turned down some kind of opportunity. It made little sense. Regardless Aldrich's motives, Michael wanted him gone.

"What do you know about this man, Jackie?"

"That he's a pilot. That he's kind and attentive. That he makes me laugh."

"But who is he, really? Is he married? Does he have children? Who is he?"

"I really don't care. He's a wonderful man who's playing a positive role in my life right now. I know it won't last forever. I think that somehow, someway, Matt and I will survive all this. But right now, Ted Aldrich is important to me."

Past weary of the complexity, Michael simply said, "It's not good, Jackie."

"Give me a break, Michael. My marriage is a joke right now."

"The answer to your marital problems is not Ted Aldrich."

The following day, Jackie called her sister. "Things are spinning. The parts of my world seem to be flying around me."

"Michael told me you're getting closer to Ted Aldrich."

"Some, I guess."

"Does Matt have any clue?"

"Matt and I are a thousand miles apart."

Blinded by general disdain for the male animal, Mia sighed. "He is such an asshole."

Later that night, alone on the screened porch, Jackie tried to think it through, but it felt completely hopeless. She had been trying to improve a fourteen-year-old marriage. Her husband had returned to high school, fighting ghosts that now haunted him constantly, it would appear. The whole situation felt too heavy for them to handle alone. She decided to talk to him about counseling. She had trouble imagining that Matt would agree, but it made sense to try. And then she told herself some unpleasant truth. It wouldn't hurt if you talked with someone, Jackie Billings. You surely have an issue or two of your own.

Chapter Twelve

Matt Billings wondered if he was living in a new kind of hell. The call had come into his office at about 2:00 this afternoon. "Yes, Mr. Billings," said a male voice, "I'm with Horizon Wireless. We have an odd pattern of calls on twelve series of our lines, and we're asking clients to carefully check their last several long-distance summaries."

Matt said, "I never use my cell phone for long distance."

"In that case, sir," said the voice, taking on a tone of warning that felt personal, and odd, "I'd suggest a *careful* analysis of your wife's calls."

Matt left the office early, premonition filling him, although he tried to tell himself that he needed to ease up. His dad had died of a massive heart attack, and the ton of stress Matt had been carrying felt like a lead weight on his chest.

But he found her phone records and he found the slew of calls to Nebraska. He recognized Mia's number, although the number of calls made no sense. He called the second number. "Panache Art Gallery. May I—?" He hung up, deciding that Mia's workplace made some sense, too. He dialed the third number. A voice message picked up: "You've reached the office of Professor Michael Ledereaux. Leave a message or dial zero for a live human." He dialed zero. "Lincoln Junior College, may I help you."

Matt's mind blanked. He hung up the phone, feeling his heart thundering. He walked into their den and went on-line. Google easily found Lincoln Junior College. A pictorial directory easily found Professor Michael Ledereaux. Matt printed the picture.

Jackie's second ambush hit her at 10:00 that evening, once again on the screened porch. He handed her the marked up phone bill and Michael's picture. "Explain, Jackie. Right now," he demanded through clenched teeth.

She absorbed almost coolly and wondered why. Maybe because she had vowed to never again be caught as verbally flat-footed as she had been during that last horrible moment. Maybe because she was angry with Matt and the truth about Michael—at least most of it—surely made sense. Or maybe because she had nothing else to lose.

"Michael is a good friend of Mia's, and mine now. I met him in Omaha."

"You didn't mention anything about a new friend."

"Surely that doesn't surprise you."

His jaw went rigid. "Everything in my fucking life is surprising me. Since when do we spend hours on the phone with people of the opposite sex?"

"Let me tell you something, Matt. You have beat me up every way but physically. If it wasn't for Mia and Michael and sometimes Sherry, I'd be at Columbus State flipping my lip by now."

He paused, studying her. "So what do you and this Michael talk about?"

"You, mostly, not that you've deserved the attention lately."

"Do you talk about sex?"

"Yes, sometimes."

His face went white. "Is he the reason you became the lady vamp?"

"Only indirectly. He tried to give me some pointers that might help our relationship. That sure hasn't worked very well, has it?"

"So why do you keep calling him, if his advice sucks so bad?"

"God, Matt, don't you see that our marriage has issues that could send us straight down the tubes. There are plenty of things to talk about besides sex."

To her surprise, the comment seemed to stop him cold. He paused for a very long time, turning to look through the screen, scanning into the dimly lit backyard. When he spoke, his voice was thin. "So what are the issues?"

"You've got to be kidding me. We've barely spoken for weeks because I made a mistake in high school. Now you're accusing me of whoring around with a—"

"Well, did you?"

"Did I what?"

"Sleep with him."

"No! There were two other women there nonstop."

"Phone sex?"

"God, Matt. I don't even know what phone sex is."

He stood, glaring at her again. "We have a problem, Jackie. Your credibility is just about zero."

"Are you serious? Because I didn't tell you that in high school I—?"

He walked by her. "A lie is a lie."

"Turn around, Matt. Come back here."

He turned, arms crossed. "Yes?"

"We need to do something about this. We need help. I mean it's almost like the world is trying to destroy us."

"Know what I need?"

"What?"

"I need a break. A break from you until I figure out what the hell you're trying to do to me."

"God, Matt. I'm trying to love you."

"Bullshit." And he walked by her, while she gyrated between frustration with Matt and guilt that his suspicions about Michael had been so close to true.

She struggled through a day at the office, calling neither Mia nor Michael. She invited Jodi and Sean to dinner at the Golden Corral, just for the company. Jodi was Jodi. But Sean's eyes and voice carried hints of unspoken awareness and worry.

Matt fell asleep in his den and came to bed at 2:30. She said, "Matt, can we—?"

He fell into bed, turned his back to her, and said, "No. Whatever it is, the answer is no."

Ted Aldrich called her office the next day, apparently just to chat. He spent twenty minutes with her, calling from a crew lounge in Atlanta. He called again the next day, saying he had sensed the pain and isolation she was feeling. And after twenty minutes of caring conversation, he invited her to another picnic.

Chapter Thirteen

As Jackie drove toward the XYZ Farm, she decided that her mind was nearly out control. She processed major anxiety about a semi-formal attendance warning from her boss. She spent several minutes making mental lists of back-to-school details. She cell-phoned Family Physicians to set up an appointment for Sean's sports physical. She wondered how she could possibly feel so distant from her husband. But she wondered why Matt had begun coming home earlier, being more engaged in the kids' lives and less overtly hostile toward Jackie while the four were together. She wondered whether he would ever speak warmly to her again—or touch her again—when just the two of them were together. And she longed for the oasis of a few hours with Ted Aldrich.

She stopped in the private lane that had become her rural dressing room and wriggled into flippy blue running shorts with white trim, and a matching tank top. She told the little voice that the outfit felt right for picnicking on another sultry summer day. But the voice knew that the outfit was skimpy, and that Jackie hoped that Ted would like it, although there had been no clue of physical interest in her, unless you count the kiss, and she couldn't decide what to do with the kiss.

This time, Ted helped her escape to her oasis without a detour through her problems. He told her a series of stewardess quips after pilots had failed to bring in planes smoothly: "On behalf of Captain Kangaroo and the entire flight crew, I'd like to welcome you to Boston where the local time is nine p.m." … "Please open your luggage compartment carefully, as your belongings have sure as hell shifted during that landing."

He talked about favorite stops in China, Japan, and Southeast Asia. He told her about his latest trip to Africa, and asked, but lightly, whether she would like to join him on a safari some day. She loved watching Ted's eyes while they talked, intelligent, sparkling, but always warm. The face was rugged but also had those great laugh lines. She felt as if she had known him forever.

After raspberry-topped cheesecake, she helped clear away food then asked for a wine refill. She again sat with her back against the giant oak, legs pulled up in front of her. Ted lay on his side, head propped on one hand, eyes twinkling as he studied her—approvingly, she decided, judging from his expression. She tapped her wineglass several times with alternating fingernails, deciding whether to satisfy her curiosity. Finally she said, "Okay, Ted, I need to know. Why did you kiss me last time?"

He smiled, "Do you want the true answer or the bullshit answer?"

"The true one."

He chuckled. "Bullshit first, just for fun." His expression turned teasingly solemn. "Jackie, I wanted to kiss you from the first moment I saw you."

"I think I've heard that one somewhere. So what's true?"

He shifted to sit upright, Indian style, his crossed legs nearly touching her ankles. "I wanted you to know that I find you incredibly attractive in every possible way." He paused, his eyes boring intensely into hers. "And I want you to know that I want you."

Her stomach jumped instantly. She leaned back instinctively, feeling tree bark bite into her back. She was suddenly acutely aware of an outfit too skimpy in a place too isolated with a man too near. "Don't, Ted. I can't—"

He reached toward her and put a finger to her lips. "Shhh. Let me explain—to a woman whose life has somehow robbed her of her confidence." He smiled with new warmth. "I've traveled the world, Jackie. You are a treasure, and I knew it within ten minutes of meeting you. You have a kind and loving heart. You have a combination of spirit, intelligence, and beauty that any man should treasure. So, if ever the stars are right, it would be my great honor to hold you in my arms. Until then, and I mean this sincerely, I'm content being your friend."

She shook her head back and forth sharply, trying to snap herself back into reality. She realized that Captain Aldrich had been too close to mesmerizing. "Honestly, Ted, that sounds like a line, too."

He smiled. "I know. But I defy you to find any part of it that's not true." He rose from the blanket. "Let's walk."

They walked the meadow path, not touching each other as if it were a decision important to each of them. He said, "We are very different, you and I."

"How? I mean what do you mean?"

"All kinds of ways, of course. You know most of them. But we're still very different in how we look at a day like this."

She looked toward him quizzically while they strolled slowly in the bright sunlight. "Explain."

"To you, this is almost as much worry as it is fun, right?"

She smiled. "Well, sort of. It's just that—"

"I'll be dead before you're forty, Jackie. To me, it's a day to cherish, to share with you in any way I can."

She inhaled sharply, realizing that the comment had jarred her physically. "Why will you…? I mean are you sick?"

He turned toward her calmly. "Don't worry. It's nothing that's contagious."

"I didn't mean that. I just… I mean what's—?"

He shook his head. "Let's don't go there. I take my days one at a time. Let me cherish this one."

As they entered the sheltering forest, she tried to grasp that this man would be dead so soon. She hadn't thought about any kind of future with him, but the thought of his death filled her with a dread that made it hard to breath. She reached toward him and grasped his hand. As they walked, she realized that she was gripping, tighter and tighter, wishing that somehow her hand and her will could hold him in this moment. When they reached the location of his impromptu first kiss, she turned toward him. "Here's our spot, Ted."

He embraced her tenderly. She nestled her head against his chest, holding him, fighting tears threatening to erupt from deep within. He lifted her face toward his, his eyes deep in hers. He kissed her, tenderly at first then deeper, more urgent. He stepped back and smiled. "Thank you. I'll cherish this moment and this place."

She smiled up at him. "Again, please." And their embrace and kiss turned fierce. She could feel her will and resistance dissolving, her mind unable to discern whether she was being swept away by the man or the moment or her own loneliness and hunger. She loved the feel of his body pressed tightly against hers. She felt lost in his strength. He turned her, standing behind her, his left hand pressed warmly against her chest, fingers caressing the curve of her neck, his right hand caressing the bare skin of her stomach, his kisses trailing up and down her neck and shoulders. One of her hands fell to her side, almost helplessly. With the other, she reached back to hold onto the muscled hardness of his thigh. When he turned her again, holding her close again, the words poured out of her, as if on their own. "Take me back to the blanket, Ted."

As they walked swiftly back toward the barn, she sensed the dying gasp of fear and concern and resistance. Matt and her children and the events that had hurtled her to this point blurred through her mind, and there was only Ted. They sank to their knees together, their kiss and embrace ferocious. But he eased her onto her back and told her to close her eyes. He kissed her forehead, her nose, her lips, and her chin. And for long minutes that felt like hours, he refused to touch her with anything but his lips. She felt grass tickling her feet as he removed her shoes. She felt warm breezes caressing her body as he slowly undressed her, delivering new kisses, telling her she was beautiful, telling her to be patient, to cherish each moment and each new feeling. She wondered how much time had passed. A lot? A little? She had no idea.

Her breathing turned gradually to ragged gasps, despite her try for patience. Her body began its own sexual dance. She whispered, "I can't wait, Ted." And he began a new kind of torture, almost as if he were a gentle sadist experimenting with methods of arousal, curious about how frequently she could begin again and cry out again. Finally, while his hands and mouth threatened to devour her once more, she whispered, "Please make love to me, Ted. Please." And he became part of her, and she climbed slowly with him, and finally, gloriously, soared with him.

She opened her eyes. "Wow."

He lifted himself on his arms and smiled. "Incredible."

"Did you feel like a rodeo cowboy?"

He laughed his easy laugh. "You are a funny lady. I love that."

He held her gently. She was aware of the heat; their bodies glued together by perspiration; but she didn't want him to be gone. Finally he pulled away and said, "Would you like something to drink?"

"Yes, please; some ice water."

"Do you want to dress first?"

"No, but let me borrow the blanket. I'm going up to the loft for a minute."

He slid off the blanket. She fashioned it into something like a toga, and headed for the wood ladder. As she stood at the bathroom sink, running a cool washcloth over her arms, shoulders, and chest, the stranger in the mirror shook her head, as if trying to decide whether she was excited, contented, or simply bewildered. She returned to the edge of the loft. "Ted, it's cool up here. Why don't you come up for a while?" But, suddenly, the voice within began screaming at her.

For Ted Aldrich, the day had delivered glorious victory, and another of the high points his father had encouraged him to find. Jackie was terrifically appealing, sweet in an almost childlike way, once a man separated her spirit from her screwed-up adult life. She had a marvelous need for tenderness. She had a magnificent need for passion. Jackie Billings might be his best find yet.

He slipped into his slacks, gathered her clothing, entered the barn, and climbed toward her. She stood at the top of the ladder, still wrapped prettily in his blanket, but looking conflicted as all hell. That made sense. Jackie had great difficulty with the concept of relax and enjoy. He smiled warmly, put two fingers to his lips and brought them to her cheek. She tried to smile, but her expression remained tormented. He decided, just for the hell of it, to remove the torment from those eyes, one more time. He smiled inwardly. *If this old body will rise to the occasion, one more time.* He led her through the door, but she stopped well before they reached the bed. He put both arms around her, but she used both hands to hold the blanket closed at her throat, looking up at him, her eyes tortured. She said, "Can I be really honest with you?"

"Sure. Always."

"I've never felt better and worse at the same time in my whole life."

"Jackie, Jackie, I wish there didn't need to be a worse, but I think I understand."

"I really like being with you, Ted. But—"

"Let's just cherish this day, Jackie."

"I'm trying to, but—" He kissed down her neck while invading the blanket with his left hand, knowing any resistance would be brief. "Ted, please, I…oh, God." Her fingers lost their grip on the blanket and twenty minutes later he gave himself credit for a pretty damn good show. Not like the glory days of rock-hard youth, of course. Still, this was excellent.

Afterward, he held her for several minutes, stroking her hair, looking deep into her gentle if still troubled eyes, speaking to her with the thoughtful afterward words that women love and most guys sleep through. She suddenly pulled away and sat up. "I need to start back."

"You've given me the best day of my life." Now she looked at him with more conflict raging, not less. "Are you okay, Jackie?"

"I think so, but I want to go home. Right away."

Ted Aldrich placed his phone call. "The eagle has landed."

"Congratulations, you son of a bitch."

"I'll be using my bonus time."

"I figured that."

Aldrich's tone changed. "I really wish we didn't need to hurt this one."

"Just love her 'til it's over, Theodore."

***

As she drove toward Dublin, Jackie called Mia. She gave no thought to calling Michael. "Guess what, sister, I've just *been* with Ted Aldrich."

"Been as in really been?"

"Yes."

"I'll be damned. I didn't think you could do it."

"I'm not sure I'm glad it happened. I feel really strange."

"But was it good?"

"It was magical, mystical, all that stuff. And I just feel strange."

"God, Jackie, you have got to lighten up. You deserve some fun, and magical sex is fun."

"If I thought it was just for sex, I might feel better."

"What does that mean?" Surprise was evident in Mia's voice.

"I don't even know what it means."

"Are we talking love?"

"No. Not that. Just an attraction. I don't know…"

"Romantic airline pilots are attractive men, Jackie. Don't beat yourself up."

***

Matt Billings reached the decision as he drove toward home, but he had been moving in that direction for several pain-filled days. And he had been prodded just last night when young Sean—growing into a strong, silent version of his father, Matt liked to think—asked, "Are you and Mom okay?

"Sure son," Matt had lied. "Why do you ask?"

And his son looked away for a moment, but met his eyes almost angrily. "Jodi may not notice, Dad. But don't treat me like a seven year old, okay?"

"Mom and I are working through some things right now. But we'll be fine."

"Promise?"

"Yes, son. We'll be fine."

So, finally, painfully, Matt decided that Ty Jameson had been right. To give up the best part of his life because of Jackie's high school romance was just plain stupid. And being surprised that she might need to talk about her life was stupid, too. But man oh man, even thinking about it rips through me like a knife. It's bad enough thinking about her placing phone calls and sharing her feelings with this Michael clown. But the idea that Tom Kerrigan, whoever the hell he is, sweet-talked her, and fondled her breasts, and stripped her and… Holy shit. I've got to shut down my mind; my heart is pounding like a damn jackhammer, again.

So, bottom line, I've got to find a way to chill about all this. Besides, it's not fair at all, in a way. I didn't deliver myself to marriage as a virgin. He smiled into the rearview mirror. Pretty damn close, though. What was her name? Probably Wyoming or Natasha or some damn thing. Showed up at his fraternity love nest, compliments of Ty Jameson, for seventy-five bucks. So I sinned with Natasha and Jackie sinned with Tom Kerrigan and it was a long time ago, so chill out for God's sake.

And while I'm chilling, I need to focus on the good stuff. I love her. And I love the home we share. My life is better than I ever dreamed it would be. Way better than anything I ever saw at home with my father, a guy who spent most of his life being a raging jerk.

He tried to focus on the kids during their dinner, although anxious to retreat with Jackie to their porch where he would try to make peace. Sean ate in near silence, his demeanor something like a watchful judge. Jodi burbled happily about a hiding place she and Brittany Jameson had built in the Jameson back yard. And Jackie participated with an odd combination of kindness toward the kids and emotional distance that Matt knew he had caused. Tonight, though, Matt felt some optimism. He had thought through an approach that would help close the gap.

While Jackie put Jodi to bed, Matt found Sean in his basement nook. He smiled at a son who looked incredibly like Matt had looked at the same age. Strong features, maybe a little too large in the nose department, but strong. Thick brown hair, cut short, with the widows peak on a low forehead that had run through generations of Billings men. Lean and athletic. Probably a tight end some day, just like his dad. Already a helluva soccer player.

"Any chance of you getting lost for an hour or so," Matt asked, grinning a manly grin.

Sean looked up as if startled, probably because they had never shared this kind of manly moment. But he processed and managed a return smile. "Are we going to make up?"

"That's the plan."

"Okay, I'll run over to Brett's and kick his buns at *Crash and Burn*."

Matt found Jackie in her sewing room and took a deep breath to overcome another kind of emotional hurdle. He would try to add some of her kind of excitement to his plan. "Could we talk on the patio?"

She looked up, startled maybe, but in a way that surprised him. "Well, sure. What's up?"

"Did you get rid of that little yellow dress you made?"

She frowned, but oddly. "No. I kind of buried it."

"Will you wear it to our talk? Sean's over at Jamesons'."

She closed her eyes and shook her head. "What's going on, Matt?"

"Will you wear it?" He cleared his throat. "I want you to wear it for me. I'll meet you on the porch."

He waited, listening to the porch's wind chimes, kicking himself in the mental ass for, even now, allowing the thought of Jackie's dress to remind him of Jackie's antics earlier in their life together. *Shit, man, just chill.* She walked onto the porch and he felt Mr. Big stir instantly, however screwed up his jealous mind might be. The yellow of her dress—although it looked more like a shirt—was perfect for her skin and dark hair. She had incredible legs, and it had been too long. "Sit down across from me, okay?"

She walked silently, oddly somber, to the lawn chair across from him. She leaned to clear away a magazine and he exhaled silently. She sat, and he exhaled again, reminding himself to focus on making peace. He met her eyes. "I have two short speeches, seven words altogether."

Her eyes narrowed. "Okay."

"I am truly sorry." He paused; wanting her to know that speech number one had been delivered.

Her eyes narrowed even more. "Okay."

"I love you."

She closed her eyes and put both hands to her forehead. Her breathing turned ragged then became sobs that began gently before gradually overwhelming her, shuddering through her entire body. "Oh God, Matt."

He stared at her, dumbstruck, feeling like a new kind of scum. "Gosh, Jackie, I didn't know…you know, that you were hurting this bad." He hurried into the kitchen, then into the downstairs bathroom to find Kleenex. When he returned, she had apparently steadied herself.

She accepted the tissue box, managing a tear-streaked smile. "Thanks. I kind of lost it. Sorry."

"I've been a total jerk. I know that. And I know that I've got to grow up."

"How did you...? I mean what made you decide...?"

"I just thought about how much I have to lose. And it made me realize how much you mean to me..." He drew in a very deep breath. "Okay, listen to this. I've even decided that if it's important that you call this Michael guy, I won't try to stop you."

"Are you serious? I mean is this really real?"

He practically gagged on the words, but he said, "Yes. It's real."

"Where did you put all the jealousy?"

He managed a pained chuckled and pointed to his stomach. "It's all right here. Every bit of it. But I'm going to deal better and hopefully learn to let it go."

She looked down and ran her hands from the hem onto her thighs. He enjoyed allowing his eyes to follow her hands. Her panties were white with some kind of lace at the front. She spoke without looking up. "This is all kind of unreal, Matt."

His brow furrowed. "Why? What do you mean?"

She sighed, her eyes looking toward the ceiling as if searching for an answer, then back down. "I don't know. Just that we were doing so well then things were so terrible and...and today, all of a sudden..." Her voice trailed off.

"Will you go to bed with me?"

She looked up, not answering as swiftly or as eagerly as he had hoped. "Well...sure."

He grinned a horny man's grin. "Will you walk up the stairs in front of me?"

She nodded, but delivered no return smile.

Afterwards, Jackie lay wide awake beside a deeply slumbering husband who had fallen asleep swiftly. She asked herself the same question in maybe a hundred ways. She failed to answer it, even once. What would today have been like if Matt had talked with her last night? And there were other questions, just as vexing. Would she ever, possibly, be content with Matt as a lover? And worst of all: Did she fail him? Could she have sped up the moment of his apology by focusing at home rather than focusing on Ted Aldrich? And could she find ways to communicate better with Matt—not just about lovemaking, but about love itself and life? *Oh, God, what have I done to us?*

***

During the following three weeks, Ted Aldrich recorded one more triumph followed by two defeats. He dutifully provided profiling information. Daniel Berringer recorded Aldrich's score including penalty points. He updated the three Jackie Billings databases. And he prepared for B-phase, once again fearful that the needy Mrs. Billings would provide no intrigue.

Chapter Fourteen

Jackie took her brown bag lunch to the city park on a Wednesday in late September. The day was crisp and bright with the first color of fall painted on the trees above her. She found an isolated bench, twisted open a diet raspberry iced tea, and sipped slowly while replaying a turbulent month.

Matt had been trying hard to keep the promises of that unexpected meeting on the porch. And Jackie was working hard to build on the positives. His willingness to let her call Michael had astounded her. And she had called Michael three times and tested the water by telling Matt. His eyes told her he hated the idea, but he absorbed it. She had told him she wanted to wear a bikini to the annual end-of-summer pool party at Blakely's. His eyes went grim again, but she bought her first bikini in over a decade, and he tolerated the evening. She drank a little too much rum punch and tried to seduce Matt in one of the Blakely's guest bedrooms. He apparently couldn't deal with that much adventure, but there had been progress, no doubt about it.

But she knew that she didn't really deserve all Matt's efforts. She might not even deserve Matt's love. Ted Aldrich had called her a week after their afternoon together. She had resisted at first, hard, determined to focus on her marriage. But he talked about seeing her at least once more; so he could feel alive again; so they could at least say goodbye in person. She failed to say no, although she arrived at XYZ dressed like a bank's loan officer, determined that they would just talk. But he somehow got inside her head and she let him hold her, and damn it to hell.

And that time, as she prepared to leave the bank, Kaye Lassiter issued a formal reprimand about excessive short-notice time off. That evening, Matt asked her where she had been. He had called, got her voice message, zeroed out, and learned from the receptionist that Jackie had taken the afternoon off. So she invented a meeting in a bank branch, and she knew it was a flimsy lie, and she knew that Michael had been right about her playing with fire, and she vowed to say no to Ted, no matter how hard it might be.

When Ted called, twice more, she held firm. In fact, she might have been proud of herself for her strength, but how can you be proud of yourself when you've been unfaithful to a guy who is dying inside because you had sex during high school?

Then at 10:00 this very morning a young guy in a tan uniform had stopped at her office door. "Jackie Billings?"

"Yes?"

"These are for you."

The guy walked into her office, carrying something wrapped in green tissue. She saw the outline of flowers and felt her heart skip. Surely Ted wouldn't send a gift so blatant to her office. She unwrapped carefully and counted thirteen red roses. She opened the small cream envelope and read the card. *I love you, Jackie. Always! Matt.* She could barely believe it—a stunning moment in the history of their marriage, but a moment tainted because she had let Ted Aldrich into their lives, not just hers.

She shut her eyes, feeling the warmth of the sun touch her face, struggling with where to put Ted Aldrich. She had resisted him, but the struggle had been something like an addict's resistance to the drug of choice. And if she wasn't careful, Ted and those times together crept back into her mind, so she tried to focus on Matt and her home, but—

"Excuse me, ma'am, are you Jacqueline Billings?"

Startled, she jerked involuntarily before opening her eyes and squinting upward into blinding sun behind a man's head. "Yes, I'm Jackie Billings, who are you?"

"It's very important that we talk, Mrs. Billings. Immediately if possible."

"Who are you?" she asked again.

He reached into the breast pocket of his suit jacket, pulled a wallet, and showed her his badge and identification, "Donavon Baxter, ma'am. Federal Bureau of Investigation."

Jackie adjusted quickly. The banking business included multiple opportunities for con artists. Visits from the FBI happened now and then, although usually not in city parks. "How can I help you, Agent Baxter?"

"I have it on good authority that you are familiar with one Theodore Aldrich. Is that correct?"

Her stomach jumped violently. She felt like all air had left her lungs. For one idiotic moment, she thought about telling him she wouldn't speak without a lawyer. She tried to stall. "Uh, may I see your ID again, please?" He retrieved the wallet and stepped toward her without comment, allowing careful examination. It appeared to be authentic in every way. Her throat felt tight. She managed to squeak out, "Yes, I know Mr. Aldrich."

The man paused to scrutinize her. Her breath came in shallow bursts; she feared that her hands were shaking visibly, but she tried to return his gaze. He was rangy, at least six-four, dressed in the traditional dark blue suit. His face was angular with tanned skin stretched taut across pronounced cheekbones. His eyes were wide-set, a piercing gray. His hair was trimmed short, dark brown, but reflecting pale red in the sunlight.

He said, "I assume you'd rather talk here than at your home or office." He was soft-spoken, but the deep voice had an unusual husky quality.

Oh my, that's true. She knew she needed to regain control of her emotions, and her mind. She scrambled for assertive with a try that felt feeble as soon as she said it. "This is very unorthodox isn't it? How can I be sure you're real…really FBI, I mean?"

His tight smile tinged compassion with sarcasm. "I was trying to be considerate, ma'am. Why don't we head on over to the Front Street field office? Perhaps I'll seem more real in one of the interrogation rooms."

"I'm… No… I'm sorry. Here will be fine." *So much for assertive.*

The slight smile returned. "I thought so. I'll get right to the point, Mrs. Billings. We have reason to believe that Theodore Aldrich—Ted to most people—is a major player in the international drug trade. Mostly cocaine. Mostly out of Mexico City. Did he mention flying Mexican routes to you?"

Jackie hesitated. *God, this can't be happening. Ted can't possibly be a criminal. Should I stonewall? No, the stakes are too high. There's jail time for perjury.* She said, "Only once. When I first met him. He mentioned flying to Mexico City."

"Did he give you any clue of the nature of his business there?"

She scrambled backward in time. "No. I just knew he was a pilot, an airline pilot."

"Oh, he is that, ma'am. It lets him move around the world on someone else's dime. I don't know any easy way to tell you this, but while Aldrich travels, he collects lady friends. Fortunately several of them are helping us look into his operation."

Jackie closed then opened her eyes, hoping this wasn't real. She sat silent.

Baxter pulled a folded document from his breast pocket and handed it to her. "This is our sheet on Mr. Aldrich." She held the sheet with trembling hands. Ted's face looked at her, under the FBI logo and the word *BULLETIN*. She tried to read, but her eyes were swimming. Baxter said, "I don't want to overly alarm you, but you'll notice there's suspicion of involvement in several drug-related murders."

She took a sharp breath and exhaled involuntarily. "I can't imagine that."

"I gather our information about your relationship is correct."

Now fear felt like painful shards of glass. Her voice went weak. "I'm…I'm a married woman. I have two kids."

"We're aware of that, ma'am. But that's not what I'm here to discuss."

She knew she was trapped. "Yes, I had a relationship with Mr. Aldrich."

"Had?"

"I haven't heard from him in several weeks. He was visiting more often. I guessed he might have moved on."

"May I sit?" She slid listlessly to the right edge of the bench. He sat beside her, angled toward her, his forearms on his knees. "I need your cooperation, in building our case against Aldrich."

"This is very sudden, Mr.…Agent…what was it?"

"Baxter, ma'am. Donavon Baxter."

"Could we perhaps talk tomorrow, Agent Baxter? I'm a little shaken by all this."

"Columbus is my assignment until this plays out, Mrs. Billings. Tomorrow will be fine. However, I will ask that you contact me immediately if you hear from Aldrich."

"Yes, of course. I will."

"Here's my card. I'll meet you here in twenty-four hours."

"Agent Baxter…does…does anyone need to know about this?"

"I can't answer that question, Mrs. Billings. I'm sorry."

She returned to her office, mind reeling: Why didn't I pay attention to Michael? He was right. There's a reason Ted Aldrich is a mystery man. He told me nothing about his life or his whereabouts or how to reach him. He just blew into town and next thing I knew… Damn it. I've got a soccer game to go to tonight. And tomorrow I'll be talking to the FBI about a drug baron that I… This will wind up in the newspaper, sure as hell. My God, Jodi's Brownie leaders will read about it. My boss. My employees. A thousand other people.

She walked down the hall toward her office, apparently white faced. "Jackie, what's wrong?" asked Connie Sanchez. "You look awful."

"Oh, uh, nothing, Connie, I've just heard some bad news. Family stuff. I'll be fine." Her stomach continued to churn. She could feel her heart pounding. She felt dehydrated, light-headed. She found her water bottle, filled it, closed her door, and tried desperately to calm down.

Minutes felt like hours. Her productivity was zero. She knew she would mangle any piece of detail work she might try. For the first time in weeks, Matt called.

"Hi, Hon," he said. "How's it going?"

"Uh, okay, Matt. What's up?"

"Anything nice happen to you today?"

She tried to get control of her mind. "What are…? Oh, yes. They're beautiful, Matt. Really nice. Thank you."

"Just because I love you, Jackie."

"I, uh, I love you too, honey."

"Is something wrong?"

"No, just, you know, busy." She didn't sound convincing, even to herself.

"I can't make the soccer game tonight. Got to finish a retaining wall before dark."

"Okay, I'll cheer her on."

She hung up the phone without saying goodbye.

An hour later, he called.

"Jackie, this is Ted. I've got to talk to you quickly. You may be tapped."

She couldn't make her mind work at all. She felt close to passing out. "What is—?"

"Has an FBI guy contacted you?"

She had no idea what to say. "What's this about, Ted?"

"A son of a bitch named Baxter is tracking me like I'm some kind of drug lord. It's bullshit—stuff they come up with to make their numbers. Have you heard from him?"

"I…I don't know what to say."

"That's good enough. I'd appreciate it if you didn't mention I called."

"What is…? I mean I don't understand any of this."

"I had to use a day with you as an alibi. Cover XYZ for me if you can. Thanks for the great memories." The line went dead.

She couldn't decide whether to return the thanks or curse him or lean toward her wastebasket and throw up. She hung up the phone.

Her evening became a prolonged nightmare. Jodi's soccer team lost, 9-0. Clem's Pizza screwed up their order. And Matt wanted to have sex. She told him, with complete honesty, "Honey, I've got a horrible headache. I'm really sorry, especially after the great flowers. Maybe tomorrow."

She had the worst night's sleep of her life, and moved zombie-like through the first half of her day. Two co-workers asked whether she was ill. She struggled to noon and walked to the city park, feeling like a woman teetering on the edge of a cliff.

Donavon Baxter waited on the same bench, again wearing a dark blue suit, his briefcase guarding her spot. She scooted the briefcase toward him, sat down, and pulled a small paper sandwich bag from her purse. Today's lunch would be two plums, at most.

He studied her. "Rough night?"

She stared blankly at the paper sack. "I've had better."

"Did you hear from Aldrich?"

She glanced up and back down. "No. I didn't."

He turned toward her, the expression made of granite. "Mrs. Billings, I'll give you one more opportunity to answer that question. My goal is to investigate Ted Aldrich, not to see you behind bars with him. Am I being clear?"

Her stomach roiled. Her voice became a thin whisper. "Yes... he..." She cleared her throat. "He called yesterday at about three-thirty."

"I'll be frank, Mrs. Billings. It is extremely troublesome that you chose not to contact me."

"I know; I mean I was terribly confused. He said you're chasing him unfairly."

He said, "We need to discuss the embedded code," his expression openly suspicious.

"I don't know what that means."

"I'd suggest you not dig the hole any deeper, Mrs. Billings. A comment like 'cover XYZ' is obviously code."

Realization sent new fear deep into her stomach. "Are you...? I mean surely you're not saying I'm some kind of suspect, are you?"

His expression remained hard. "I would like to go from here to our Columbus field office. We'll open a file on you, and let you chat with our decryption expert."

She closed her eyes, trying to breathe deeply. She realized she had twisted the neck of her paper bag into a tight coil, and was still twisting. She turned toward him, sensing an important moment.

"Agent Baxter," she said weakly, "could we start over again? I haven't handled this right; I realize that. But it's nothing like you think."

"What is it like, Mrs. Billings?"

She swallowed hard, clearing her throat. "I was frightened yesterday, really confused. I'm sorry I didn't call you, but it doesn't mean…" Her voice trailed off during a brief internal battle of allegiance. "It doesn't mean I'm trying to help Ted Aldrich."

He scrutinized her with suspicious eyes. "For starters, Mrs. Billings, explain XYZ to me."

She hesitated but only for a second or two. "It's the name of a farm Ted owns."

"Would it be his mysterious flying field?"

"I don't know what that means."

"We've tracked him flying out of Chicago toward Ohio, but he never officially lands. We figured he has a private airport of some kind."

"Yes. Well, I guess so; there's a landing strip there."

"So you've been to this XYZ?"

Her heart rate elevated again, but she sensed a slight change in Baxter's demeanor; less suspicious of her personally, she hoped; more interested in her information. "Yes. That's where I met with Ted."

"Tell me about XYZ."

She told everything she knew: location, Ted's purchase, and layout.

He frowned studiously. "An apartment hidden into a barn?"

"Yes. You'd never know it was there."

"Have you been in the apartment?"

She exhaled slowly. Her face felt warm. "Yes."

He eyed her, his lips pursed into a tight disdainful line. "I assume that's where…"

He paused. She said a soft, "Yes."

His expression changed to something like weary disgust. "I'll want you to take me to this farm. Immediately, if possible."

"I really need to get back to work. Can we go tomorrow, maybe in the afternoon?"

The gray eyes became slits. "That strikes me as very convenient for Ted Aldrich."

She fought a feeling of defeat, a sense that she had slipped backward. "No…I mean it's not about Ted Aldrich. It's just that I've got some problems with being away from the office."

He leaned closer to her, eyes focused intently. "Listen carefully, Mrs. Billings. It would be very unfortunate if I have even a hint that you and Aldrich are in contact, or that evidence at this farm is altered in any way."

"I understand."

"I'll pick you up in front of your bank, tomorrow at three-thirty?"

"Okay, that'll work," she said with confidence she didn't feel. But she could go into the office early and send Kaye Lassiter an e-mail with a time stamp that proved she deserved to leave early.

Jackie tried for a normal family evening: meatloaf dinner, apple cobbler for dessert, a little TV, and parental involvement in homework. But the fear never left her, magnified every time the phone rang. Might Aldrich call? What would she do if he did?

She came to bed in a sheer nightgown, but couldn't get beyond the fear. Matt was patient, even sweet. Finally, he said, "What's wrong, Jackie?"

"I don't know. Things are piling up at work, and… I'm really sorry, Matt."

"I thought a guy's sex life soared when he bought roses."

It was a terrible moment. He was trying, nobly in his way, to comfort her. But she sensed the disappointment, and she knew she had ruined a time that might have been wonderful for their marriage.

She arranged with Sherry Jameson to handle late afternoon kid-duties. Sherry asked whether she felt okay. Jackie fibbed, calling things fine. Sherry appeared unconvinced. Leaving the bank early involved another warning. Apparently early e-mail timestamps didn't always help. Jackie could only say, "I'll watch it, Kaye. I've had a crazy few months. Thanks for being as understanding as you've been."

She approached the unmarked black Ford sedan parked in front of the bank building, looking conspicuously inconspicuous, she feared. As she slid onto the front seat, he nodded formally. "Good afternoon, Mrs. Billings." His jacket hung on a hook behind him; his sleeves were rolled halfway to the elbow. She noticed huge hands and manicured nails.

"Hello, Agent Baxter."

As she directed him toward the XYZ Farm, Baxter began another interrogation. "Tell me what you know about Aldrich's Mexico City connections."

"Nothing. He just told me he flew there."

"How about friends, relatives, or acquaintances."

"He never mentioned anything about other people."

Baxter looked toward her, frowning. "Nothing at all?"

She thought back, hard. "We talked about his parents once."

"His parents are dead, Mrs. Billings. That's not what I'm looking for."

"I'm sorry, nothing else."

"Where did he tell you he lives?"

She swallowed hard. "He didn't tell me."

"What *do* you know, Mrs. Billings?"

She thought of Michael's nearly identical questions. The truthful answer remained the same, although pitifully lacking in details. "Just that he seemed like a very nice person when I needed a nice person in my life."

His jaw clenched. The hands visibly tightened their grip on the steering wheel. He glared, but straight ahead. "May I be perfectly frank with you?"

She leaned away involuntarily, surprised by the tone. "Well, sure."

"In my opinion," he growled, "*nice* is the weakest, piss-ant word in the English language. And you're trying to use *nice* to explain the screwed-up mess that you're involved in." He smacked the wheel with an open palm. "Shit."

She sat still, heart pounding, having no idea what to say, searching Baxter's face in profile as he glared forward. The nose and jaw line gave a strong, determined look, especially now; his mouth turned down in a natural frown.

He took several deep breaths and turned toward her again. "I apologize. Sometimes this job gets to me. Let's talk about any phone calls he made or received while you were together?"

She said, "There weren't any calls," relieved that calm had returned, but dearly wishing she had some relevant information.

"Did he ever reveal a mean streak?"

"No. I can't even imagine a mean streak."

"The murder allegations certainly suggest a mean streak."

"I never had a hint."

"For God's sake, give me something, Mrs. Billings."

She dredged her memory, embarrassed that most of the recollections were so erotic. "He might be dying."

Baxter closed his eyes and muttered, "Oh, Christ." He exhaled loudly and looked toward her. "Your father died when you were nine years old. Correct?"

"Yes."

"Mrs. Billings, you have been taken in by one of the smoothest con men I've ever encountered. The notion that he is dying is, pardon me, bullshit."

She absorbed twin stabs of pain, but analyzed quickly and saw a glimmer of hope. "If he's that good as a con man, you can't be surprised he conned me, can you?"

"You surely wouldn't be the first."

"So why would you think I'm helping him?"

"Think that through, Mrs. Billings. He's a very persuasive man in ways other than sexual."

"Agent Baxter, I am not helping Ted Aldrich in any way. I swear I'm not."

"It will be helpful when I fully believe that."

She directed him to the meadow behind the barn. "He takes off and lands over there," she said, pointing through the windshield. Baxter parked and they walked a circle of about fifty yards on all sides of the barn. He didn't say what he was looking for. He approached the main sliding door, found it locked tightly, and checked the two entrance doors. At the second, he pulled a multi-fingered metal device from his pocket and swiftly attacked the lock. They were inside in seconds.

"Is there electricity?" he asked.

She turned on a light switch. "This place has every convenience." He prowled the lower level, beginning at a long wooden tool bench. Jackie explained that Ted did airplane maintenance with some of the tools, but the hoes, pitchforks, and a hand plow were likely antiques. They passed a large stack of loose straw against the rear wall.

"Does he keep animals?"

"I don't think so. I guess the straw's decorative."

She led him up the wooden ladder into the loft, thinking of the same climb while wrapped in Ted's blanket. Baxter tried to work the lock on the loft-apartment but failed. "I figured this would be more secure. Not a problem; we'll come back later and crack it."

"Do I have to come back again?"

He eyed her disapprovingly. "You are my primary Columbus source. And you are in this, like it or not, very deeply. Is there a problem with that?"

She returned a weak, "No. No problem."

On the return drive, he lightened a bit, asking questions about her family, although even the conversational Donavon Baxter sounded like an interrogator. She managed to learn that he was fifty-two years old, a twenty-five year veteran of the FBI who had made career stops in four field offices. She told him, honestly, that he didn't look to be in his fifties. He managed a real-live friendly grin, and Jackie hoped it was a sign she could interact positively. She knew she needed to rise above fear of this man. They arranged to meet at a northwest branch of Third Ohio at 2:30 Saturday afternoon.

Jackie used near-truth to explain Saturday, telling Matt that the FBI's continuing investigation required her to be at the bank. She wore jeans and an Ohio State sweatshirt. When she slid into Baxter's car, she found a far more casual FBI man wearing light gray denim slacks and a burgundy pullover. But she found nothing casual in his demeanor. After several blocks of stony silence, he asked, "Have you come up with anything else about Aldrich?"

"I really haven't. I've tried."

"I want a swift answer to an important question: Are you in love with Ted Aldrich?"

"No. I'm not."

"I don't need details, but it would help if I understood the relationship."

She gathered thoughts, deciding on honesty. "He came along at a very vulnerable time for me. I married young. My husband and I were having problems. I guess I was restless, more than I really understood. And Ted Aldrich showed up in my life."

"I imagine *showed up* is quite correct. How did you meet him?"

"I was flying to Omaha, and—"

"And you just happened to wind up in the seat next to him?"

"Yes."

"We're not sure how the son of a bitch pulls that off; some kind of cooperation with the counter people, obviously. And then he did the antique plane business, I suppose."

She said, "Yes," but reluctantly, again cursing her gullibility.

"Is it clear to you that you've been conned?"

She hesitated, but only for a moment. "Yes, I see that I've been conned."

He turned toward her, jaw again clenched angrily. "Then let me tell you what I need—I need some real-live, honest-to-God remorse."

"There's remorse, Agent Baxter. But it's all mixed up with a hundred other—"

He sighed audibly. "I'm a simple man, Mrs. Billings. And I believe that a woman in your shoes should be feeling some genuine, gut-wrenching guilt."

She searched almost frantically for the right words. "Agent Baxter, I...I had a large hole in my life then, and he seemed to fill it. And I did like that. It would be a lie to say I didn't. And now I'm still trying to grasp that a man that seemed so wonderful could possibly…" She paused, studying a country church they were passing. "So I'm angry at him. And I'm trying to understand myself. I really do feel guilty—I've done a horrible thing to my husband—but right now I'm mostly confused."

His eyes softened. Not warm, but not accusing any more. "Can I depend on your full cooperation in this investigation?"

She felt a surge of relief, grasping that the danger of being charged as an Aldrich accomplice had finally passed. "Yes. I'll help in any way I can."

Baxter glanced toward her, his expression close to friendly. "This must be a bizarre situation for you to find yourself in."

She definitely liked the new tone. "I really can't believe it. You watch stuff like this on TV, but I never dreamed I'd be here."

Inside the XYZ barn, he used a huge Canon digital camera to snap multiple pictures on both levels. This time he succeeded in picking the lock on the loft-apartment and they entered together. He worked without comment; she tried to avoid feeling like a teenager whose love nest had been discovered by her father.

She held his tape measure while he filled in dimensions on a blue-lined sketchpad. He scraped something off several surfaces and placed the contents in small glass bottles that he stored carefully in compartments in his briefcase. They again walked the outside perimeter; this time he shot photographs from multiple angles. As he packed away the camera, Baxter said, "That'll do it for today, we'll come back one more time and be done with XYZ."

"What else could you possibly check?"

"Good question; the only answer is that I don't know the answer."

"I don't understand."

"The photos go to the lab. Those guys will come back with something we can't see. Sure as hell."

She almost asked whether she needed to come back, but knew better.

On the return trip, they chatted easily, as if Agent Baxter had done his duty for the day and could ease up. He even became *Don* rather than Agent Baxter. Jackie grew steadily more relaxed, daring to hope that somehow this could all end happily.

As they drove, he said quietly, "You know what really pisses me off?"

Although surprised by the informality, she welcomed it. "What's that?"

"That in real life the bad guys get the good girls."

"I gather you're referring to Mr. Aldrich."

"I'm really talking about you: a normal person living a normal life. There's a sweet innocence to it, at least by the standard of crap I see, and some son of a bitch like…" The huge hands tightened on the steering wheel. She wondered if he might break it.

"I sure don't feel very innocent. Can I tell you something personal?"

He looked at her with mock seriousness, "Anything you say can and will…" This time they actually laughed together.

"It's just that, he had me convinced that he didn't care; that anything physical was my idea." She thought back, embarrassed. "That *until the stars were right* he would just be my good friend."

"He's very good, Jackie. A person caught up in the perfect con is actually glad she's being conned."

She noted, happily, the use of her first name. But she required several minutes to deal with the idea that she had been victim of a perfect con. They were just outside the city when he said, "Do you have time to grab a sandwich."

The question amazed her, but she welcomed another indication that they were now something like a team. They had no plans for Saturday evening. She would need to call Matt, but that should work. "Okay, that sounds good."

She spoke to her own voicemail message. "Honey, this is taking longer than I thought. I have to go to another location with Agent Baxter. I should be home in an hour or so." She looked at her watch. "It's ten after six now." She could feel Baxter's eyes. She wondered what he thought of her truthfulness.

They found a place called *The Brauthaus* and entered a restaurant decorated with more dark wood and dead animals than Jackie had ever seen. She and Matt argued now and then about whether hunting is a terrible sport, and about the risk of Sean and friends gaining access to Matt's guns. And, for some reason, she didn't like all those big eyes staring down at her.

Baxter ordered a brand of beer she had never heard of. She said, "That sounds fine for me, too." About halfway into her mug, she said, "You know what your name should be?"

"What?"

"Earnest."

"Earnest?"

"Yes. You are the most earnest man I've ever met."

"I think the FBI attracts earnest people."

"See. That's what I mean. Surely there's some kind of joke you could make."

"It didn't come to mind, sorry."

"Do you know how I've judged the trip back?"

"How?"

"By how many times I could get you to at least crack a smile?"

She saw his expression become nothing short of earnest. "Why would you care how many times I smile?"

"Well, just that you scared me before, and I've wanted to feel more comfortable. Smiling and laughing make me comfortable."

"Don't make me think you're trying to disarm me, Jackie."

"No, really, I'm not. I just like to laugh." She looked at him hopefully.

"Maybe I am a little too earnest. Heard any good jokes?"

She couldn't remember any good jokes, but asked, "Has anyone ever told you that you look like a hawk?"

"A hawk?"

"Yes, your face is all sharp angles, your eyes look like they could see twenty miles. You look like a hawk."

"Is that a compliment or an insult?"

"Neither. Just an observation, Earnest Hawk."

He finally smiled. "I'll admit it; that name would work on an FBI I.D."

They chatted through the braut specialty and a second mug of beer then started the drive toward her car. He seemed relaxed. He actually touched her, a playful backhand to the side of her leg while they drove. She felt good about where she stood with him. But as they pulled to a stop at her parking garage, he said, "I'm sorry, Jackie, but there's something you need to know."

"What's that?"

"My people are saying we'll need your formal testimony."

She felt her heart pounding. "Why? I mean I really don't know anything."

"You've become Aldrich's alibi for several crucial days. We'll need you to testify, primarily about days that you weren't with him."

She winced. "Can it be quiet?"

"I doubt it very much."

"You mean it'll be public, as in the newspaper?"

"I would think so. I'm sorry, Jackie."

Her voice nearly failed. "That could...will...probably ruin everything."

"I'm sorry, but it's—"

"Is there anything...I mean any way I could provide information some other way? Something like that?"

"I don't think so. It looks to be high profile. And my supervisor plays hardball. He'd have my ass on the carpet for even talking to you like this."

"When will it happen?"

"Late next week, I would think. I'll know more by Tuesday."

***

Later Saturday evening, Matt asked, "How did things go with Mr. FBI guy?"

She managed, "Fine. It was pretty routine."

He asked several questions about Baxter the man, and where they had gone. She told several lies, but sensed no suspicion. They popped popcorn and watched *An Officer and a Gentleman*—Matt's favorite movie—for the third time. As she sat curled up on the couch, wearing her fluffy pink robe, munching her popcorn, she declared it all too surreal. She was spending a normal Saturday evening with her husband while an ax hung over their heads. An ax about to fall.

Chapter Fifteen

Jackie lay awake as the digital clock made its way past midnight, heralding the Tuesday that she feared would shatter her family. Beside her, Matt snored peacefully. She reached toward him and stroked his arm, thinking of the irony that he could sleep so serenely, unaware that two hours ago—while he watched Monday night football—she had been standing outside his den, about to walk through the door and blurt the Ted Aldrich story.

She had gone downstairs following a horrible half hour in her bathtub, a time dominated by visualization that she couldn't shut down: Matt reading her story in the newspaper; or Matt being taken aside by one of his employees who had read the newspaper; and Matt sitting stunned in his office, trying to decide what to say to Sean and Jodi. As horrible as the confession would be, she surely owed it to Matt to be the source of the news.

But she had stopped just outside the door; close enough to see the TV flickering in the darkness and hear the play-by-play announcers. At first, raw fear caused her delay. She didn't know where to begin. Did she need to tell the whole twisted story, beginning with the flight toward Omaha? Or could she begin in Columbus—admit to meeting a charming man at lunch? But that would involve more lies, and… So she had tried, over and over, to come up with a sensible set of words, and her mind invariably froze up. Pure, bone-deep exhaustion made things worse. She had barely slept on Saturday or Sunday. In fact, she hadn't had a good night's sleep since the day Baxter ambushed her in the park.

She feared for Matt physically. His reaction during the discussion about phone calls with Michael had been painful, and scary.

She knew his stress went straight to his chest. She knew that her father-in-law had died of a heart attack—no doubt stress related—because Clancy was always stressed about something.

But fear didn't turn her away from the door of his den. Rather, she realized that fear and exhaustion were winning. She had nearly given up, declared the burden too heavy to carry alone. By her confession, she would present herself to Matt, broken and contrite. But Matt wasn't her pastor or counselor. He was a guy with real problems of his own, struggling in his way to make their marriage work, totally unprepared for her devastating news.

So she returned to their bedroom, and she looked deep inside for a reservoir of strength that would get her through twenty-four more hours. She would see Baxter at 2:30 on Tuesday. He might bring dreaded news: details of the timing of her testimony and the public exposure that would follow. The confession to Matt might still be necessary. But maybe, somehow, she could find a way out. And while there was any kind of hope, she should not give up.

She awoke with Matt's alarm clock at 5:30 a.m., guessing that she might have had two hours of decent sleep. Fatigue felt like a living presence inside her head, but she forced herself out of bed and into the kitchen to prepare sausage and a stack of blueberry pancakes, his favorite breakfast.

Matt pulled up to the kitchen counter. "What's the occasion?"

"Just an I love you, and a small thanks for the roses."

"How are my roses doing?"

She said, "They're beautiful, Matt." In fact, they had wilted prematurely, although she had pressed some remembrance petals in a software manual on her shelf.

"You look tired."

"I haven't been sleeping so well for some reason."

"Maybe we should try to get away, just the two of us. It's been too long."

She smiled, though wearily. "That would be really nice."

Matt headed for work at 6:30. Jackie spent extra time with her hair and make-up then walked into her closet and made a selection that she couldn't entirely explain: a short, front-buttoning denim dress hiding in the far corner behind the black gown she had worn to the Gala. She skipped pantyhose, a decision that put her in violation of informal wardrobe guidelines for bank managers. She spent a few seconds studying her reflection in the full-length mirror. She did look tired, despite the makeup. But she knew Ted Aldrich would have liked the outfit. She hoped that Don Baxter might like it, too.

She cleared her work schedule with Kaye Lassiter, absorbing a frown of obvious displeasure as Kaye made some kind of note in her Palm Pilot. Jackie knew she should be more concerned about her boss's reaction. She couldn't afford to get fired. But the challenge she faced today made Kaye's attitude toward time off or bare legs feel minor.

And she waited, with fear rising, for the session that might change everything. At 2:30, determined to be as positive and as proactive as she could possibly be, determined to find any shred of the fighter that might remain inside her, she took the elevator into the bank lobby and strode toward the waiting car.

Daniel Berringer, a.k.a. Don Baxter, watched her exit the glass doors and walk toward his black sedan. He noted the outfit and felt a wave of annoyance that she was unraveling so quickly. Aldrich kept finding corruptible innocents. Why not another pre-corrupted tough gal like the babe from Detroit? That one sensed early on that the game might be a game—making her a damned intriguing broad.

Nonetheless, Don's execution of Jackie's B-Phase had been impeccable: fear, isolation, exhaustion, kindness cycled off and on, hope cycled off and on, crisis. And, of course, submission and payoff. Today, it appeared, would be payday.

In fairness to Ted, the recruiter couldn't possibly know on first meeting the details that Don knew after weeks of profiling an admittedly complex woman. So let's at least grant that Jackie Billings represents a fascinating study. Most Americans simply live their dysfunctional lives, finding ways to deny, hide, or compensate for their weaknesses. And they die normal deaths, untested by high-level rigor and intrigue. So the conclusion of the Jackie Billings project will be interesting. How will she live during her crisis and the remainder of her short life? How will she face death?

She opened the door and hopped in, obviously trying for a cheery smile, but the strain could be easily read in her eyes. "Hello, Earnest."

Don Baxter returned to alias and studied her. Her hem rode at mid-thigh; buttons above the hem barely did their job. He said, "Quite an entrance," his voice intentionally flat and disinterested.

"Oops, that's a problem with this dress." She smiled with an appropriate sense of embarrassment and tugged and adjusted to slightly improve coverage. He decided that Aldrich had correctly assessed her legs as world-class. He also found a bit of grudging admiration. Jackie Billings had no external leverage for today's battle. Despite exhaustion, she recognized, at least intuitively, that her appearance and engaging personality might give her some sort of chance.

Baxter began a new process of withdrawal, threading his way through Columbus traffic without conversation. She tried three questions about the realism of TV crime shows. He answered curtly, returning each time to silence.

"Are we back to being earnest?" she asked, disappointment evident in her voice.

"Yes we are, Mrs. Billings."

"Why? I mean I don't understand." Her voice had turned sweetly plaintive. If he allowed emotion as soft as sympathy, he might feel it for a woman now sensing the abandonment of the only person who might help her.

"I lost objectivity on Saturday evening," he said. "That's not acceptable."

"It was just a beer and a sandwich."

He turned toward her, his expression cold and businesslike. "It became more than that, Mrs. Billings, the minute you talked about consciously manipulating me."

"I was just talking about trying to lighten things up, nothing else."

"I'm sure you understand my conflict."

"I really don't." He could hear the fatigue seeping into her voice.

"I relaxed on Saturday, partly because loneliness is an occupational hazard. Analyzing your comment snapped me back to where I need to be."

She turned away from him, studying the passing roadway, no doubt trying to find a new place to stand. He let fifteen minutes pass—isolation for her, analysis time for him. His respect for her inched upward slightly. An unprincipled woman would have seized on his loneliness comment and made an offer, even if veiled. Ten minutes before arrival at XYZ, he asked, "Why the outfit?" his voice hard, accusing.

She continued to look away from him, her head reclining on the headrest. "What do you mean?"

"Another attempt to influence me?"

After a long pause, she returned a barely audible, "Probably."

He found the admission fascinating; a sign, no doubt, that she was close to emotional collapse. "A more precise answer would be helpful."

Another long pause. She looked toward him, exhaustion clouding her eyes, and back toward her lap. "It's just that, I hadn't given up hope, you know, that… and I thought if you like me, then maybe that would help…. God, I don't know."

Okay, lighten it up. "Jackie, I hope you do know that none of this is about whether I like you as a person." He smiled slightly. "Besides, I'm not a legman."

She glanced at him with those clouded eyes; not even the hint of a smile. He noted that she failed completely to use the opening he had given her. Saturday's Jackie would have surely tried a joke, perhaps something like, *What kind of man are you, Earnest Hawk?*

He barely suppressed a smile as the remaining elements of today's assault clicked into place in his mind. He timed the first step carefully, asking the question with concern filling his voice as he pulled into the opening beside the XYZ barn. "What will happen to you after you testify?"

She looked toward him, fear evident through the exhaustion. This time she held his gaze; valiantly, he decided, all things considered. "Is there any chance at all that…that it can be, you know, secret?"

He shook his head. "I'm afraid not. My people think the media will be all over the airline-pilot-gone-bad angle."

"So Matt will know for sure that I…that I was with a criminal? And my family, and people at work?"

He watched several days of anxiety become stark reality in her mind. "I'm sorry, but it's virtually certain, especially after we interrogate Aldrich."

Her eyes filled with tears. “Matt could never forgive me. I’ll lose my husband. I’ll probably lose my job. My kids will never be able to…” She tried to swallow. Her voice quit working.

“Take my hand, Jackie.”

He watched her wipe tears from her cheek with one hand while extending the other toward him. He took her hand, holding it with a strong, protective grip. “I know this is hard, but life does go on after this kind of thing.”

He heard her sniff. She said, “Matt and I were doing better,” her voice thin, a child’s voice. “I was planning to see a therapist when we could afford it.”

He stroked the back of her hand and resumed his grip. “Why? You don’t seem the type.”

“There are things I don’t understand about myself: doubts, needs, all kinds of things…” Again, her voice trailed off.

“I wish I could help you.”

She sniffed again and managed part of a smile. “I wish you could, too.”

He slid toward her, close enough that their knees touched. His right hand, still holding hers, had made its way to her lap. He met her eyes, trying for something like torment of his own. “I’m a cop trying to do my job, but I’m feeling guilty as all hell. Damn it, Jackie, how did we get here?”

Her eyes closed. She whispered. “I don’t know.” He felt the beginning of soft crying as her hand tightened on his. She said, “God, I’m so tired.” He slid closer, replacing his right hand with his left, putting an arm around her shoulders. He pulled her toward him, ever so gently. He received the expected brief moment of resistance, but she yielded swiftly and was soon cradled nicely against his chest, shoulder, and neck. He knew that isolation, not fatigue, made this piece of physical contact a simple matter. He enfolded her protectively and listened patiently to soft sobbing. *And now, my masterpiece*:

He pulled away from her, reached for his cell phone, and punched the keypad vigorously. He waited expectantly; she watched curiously; and he spoke to the sound of silence. “Phil, Don Baxter. Do you have a minute?” Appropriate pause. “Yes. It’s urgent. I’d like to be able to assure the Billings woman that she won’t be named publicly.” He watched Jackie’s eyes grow wider, searching for hope. “I know, but surely there’s another way.” Baxter waited again, reaching toward Jackie, placing his hand just above her knee, smiling inwardly when her hand made the expected rendezvous. “Damn it, Phil, I understand all that, but we’re talking about publicly demolishing a woman’s life.” Baxter looked into Jackie’s eyes, winced, and shook his head. “Yes. I understand how important Aldrich is.” … “Of course I understand there are risks.”

Baxter enjoyed watching Jackie’s eyes search for hopefulness. He shifted his hand, moving it higher on her thigh. Her eyes never left his, as if she didn’t notice, but he could feel her warmth radiating. “Are you serious? All the way to Washington? Oh, hell, that’s not good.” … “So who’s threatening you?” … “Lindstrom?” … “That son of a bitch. You know it’s all politics; they don’t give a damn about Jackie Billings or Phyllis Hartman.” … “Of course I understand that politics get people fired.”

Baxter closed his eyes momentarily and drew in a deep, bracing breath. “I’m just not going to let it happen.” … “Then if it goes south, I’ll take the hit.” … “Yes, Phil, I know what I’m saying.” … “Yes. Tell them I personally promised her privacy, in return for—” … “Well, yeah. She’s given me some decent stuff.” … “Yes, I’m willing to send you a memo, but for Christ’s sake, Phil, we’ve worked together for fifteen years.” … “Okay. No problem; I’m fine with the memo. I’ll fax it this afternoon.” … “So

I can assure her that…?" Baxter smiled broadly, nodding his head. "Thank you, my friend; thank you very much. I'll catch you later. "

He clicked off the phone. "Everything will be okay, Jackie." And he watched a floodgate burst. Her eyes exchanged disbelief for sparkling joy. Her smile turned ecstatic. She suddenly turned toward him, rising on one knee, practically throwing herself at him, both arms around his neck, her lips trailing kisses from cheek to ear. "Thank you. Oh, thank you; thank you; thank you." Kisses continue and her grip tightened, certainly nothing sexual, but his left hand safely landed on her upper thighs as he met her eyes and said, "I'm glad I could help."

Her embrace became ferocious, delivering pleasant pain to his neck and shoulders. He could hear ragged breathing, maybe sobbing—sighs of relief, not passion, but he returned part of her embrace by spreading his left hand across the exquisite firmness of her ass, pulling her toward him. She continued to cling to him, seemingly oblivious to the invasion of her dress. He leaned back to find her lips with his. She kissed willingly for a moment before resisting—a slight stiffening, a meager try to pull back—all as expected. He held her there. Resistance softened, as expected. He intensified the kiss. He spread the fingers of his left hand, strengthening his grip on her ass, allowing his fourth and fifth fingers to slide lower, to probe carefully the warmth between her thighs. She stiffened, as expected. A shudder rippled through her; her kiss intensified; he felt her hips writhe, just slightly; and he declared this the most passionate body he had ever encountered.

He broke the kiss and leaned back. Her skin was splotched pink and white; her expression had become a quilt of happiness, warmth, gratitude, passion, bewilderment, and maybe a bit of fear. "We'd better go to work," he said, his own breathing coming in labored gasps. He pulled on the door handle.

She touched him on the cheek again and whispered, “Thank you,” before pulling away and taking some note of her wandering hem. She pulled the dress down, but only a little, and slid toward her door.

He met her at the hood of the car and put his arm around her shoulders as they walked toward the barn. As expected, her arm made its way around his waist, squeezing nicely. Just inside the door, he turned her toward him and smiled, but shyly. “Can I tell you something?”

Her eyes signaled warm curiosity. “Sure.”

“You are the most holdable human being in the entire world.”

She smiled with the childlike warmth that Aldrich talked about. “Is holdable even a word?”

He said, “I think so,” as he gathered her in his arms, and carefully built their next embrace. Little resistance this time, as her expression became almost dreamlike. He lifted her off her feet, her arms tight around his neck, and moved as if dancing toward the stack of straw that she had called decorative.

He spoke to her gently, kissed and caressed her knowledgeably, and responded to her “No, Don, we shouldn’t…” with hands and lips brazenly manipulating her body. He sank with her onto the straw when, finally, her knees buckled.

Jackie tried to think through the haze of dying passion. *What am I doing? How did this happen?* She nestled in his arms, but only for a moment, as revulsion washed away any brief contentment—revulsion that coursed through her entire body. She pulled away, jumped to her feet, pulled her dress down, and hurried through the door.

She waited inside the car, shuddering violently. He opened the door and slid onto the seat. "This shouldn't have happened, Jackie. I'm sorry. This shouldn't have happened."

She took several short sobbing gasps. "This is my fault…" Tears welled in her eyes. "I wanted you to like me…to help me… so unbelievably much, that…" Her voice disappeared in sobs that wracked her body.

Several miles later, after she quieted, he said, "We were probably just a few days from avoiding this. I think they're going to pull me."

"Why?"

"Phil talked like I had compromised myself on the Aldrich case."

They drove in painful silence until he dropped her at the parking garage. After she exited, she turned and leaned back into the car with an expression mixing gratitude and deep sorrow. "Thank you for what you did for me."

"I hope the rest of your life goes well, Jackie. You may or may not be hearing from me."

***

Ted Aldrich didn't like the tone of the call.

Baxter said, "The eagle has landed," but his voice sounded flat.

"Congratulations."

"I won't be using the bonus time."

"Why?" asked Aldrich, incredulous.

"It was like taking candy from a goddam baby."

Ted Aldrich needed his friend's involvement—the creative genius behind the games that made life interesting. "How about next year we give you half as many data points?"

"Yeah, we could try that. How about you find a woman with some backbone."

"Okay, Mr. B, I'll work on that. When does C-Phase begin?"

"Next month," replied Baxter. "We can use the cash flow."

Aldrich felt a twinge of regret, since D follows C. But hell, he always felt regret.

Chapter Sixteen

Jackie drove toward her house, her mind an agony of wildly conflicting emotions: enormous relief, gratitude, amazement, confusion, guilt, and rising disgust. She wanted, more than anything, to return to some kind of normalcy: to worry about the evening meal, or Jodi's science fair project, or Sean's concern about signs of budding acne, or paint peeling on the downspouts. She parked her car, slipped through the inside garage door and hurried up the stairs.

She had reached the bathroom before she noticed it. *Oh my God, there's straw all over the back of this thing. In the lining. In the belt loops.* She began to extract tiny pieces of straw, changed her mind, found a plastic bag in her closet, and stuffed the dress and her underwear into the bag. She put on a jogging suit, and started downstairs, heading for the dumpster in their garage.

She ran directly into Matt at the foot of the steps. He had apparently been in his TV nook, or maybe in the garage.

He said, "Oh, hi, I didn't hear you come in."

"Hi, Matt, I just got home."

"What's that?"

She felt her hands begin to tremble. "Just some things I'm taking to Goodwill."

"We can't afford to be giving clothes away."

"I know. It's just old stuff from the back of the closet."

He hesitated, frowning quizzically. Her heart raced. But he said, "Jodi needs help with some homework tonight; will you have time?"

"Sure."

In the garage, she pushed the bag deep into the dumpster, and she checked her car seat, the garage floor, the stairs, and the bathroom for loose pieces of straw.

They finished the math problems, shared Dilly Delights, and Jackie supervised Jodi's nightly brushing of teeth. Jackie had found some blessed normalcy in the evening, but after Jodi snuggled under her covers, she said, "Mommy, will you tell me an Elrod story like you used to. It's been so long."

Jackie couldn't believe it happened on this night. Elrod the Magic Bear had been in mothballs for months, maybe a year. Jackie's father had actually invented the magic character—an easy-going guy who mostly loved people, but once per story helped them out in dramatic fashion. Jackie sat on the edge of her daughter's bed, trying to generate any kind of fresh idea. She limped through a lame story, struggling to weave it between images of herself rolling with Don Baxter and praying that her husband wouldn't discover a straw-covered dress and stained underwear in a plastic bag. Thankfully, Elrod's adventure received a passing grade. Jodi said, "I love you, Mommy," and held up both arms. Jackie held her tightly, while silent tears trickled down both cheeks.

Jackie walked downstairs and out to the screened porch where the only light flickered feebly from an overhead flood in the lot behind theirs. She stared outside, trying desperately to understand. She hadn't been proud of her behavior with Ted Aldrich, but to some extent she understood it. She had no explanation at all for what happened with Don Baxter. Everything happened too fast. There was Ted. Then Ted was gone. No time to process her feelings before being thrust into the middle of an FBI investigation. Don Baxter happened too fast. Desperate fear of losing everything happened too fast.

But what in the world happened this afternoon? Did I give myself to him because I appreciated so incredibly much what he did for me? Without a doubt, I felt something like love for him during that amazing phone call. But I didn't feel *that kind* of love. Is there a chance that the darker side of me—the side that dressed up for him in the first place—gave herself to him just to help reach a goal? Am I that kind of whore? Or am I some kind of round-heeled nympho that winds up having sex every time a skillful guy gets his hands on her? God, maybe that's it. Maybe Matt clamping down on me for all these years is the only reason I'm not like Mia…or my mother.

She shook her head, hating the thought, looking for a place to hide. Is there any chance that Don Baxter took advantage of me? It almost felt like he had a roadmap to my emotions, and my body. But how can I possibly blame him. He helped me in a wonderful way. He didn't force me to throw myself into his arms, or to wear the dress that made me so vulnerable.

She decided, most of all, that she had serious problems—flaws or weaknesses or needs that had to be addressed. She had started the day hoping to protect her relationship with her husband and family. Now she had risked again. She might have succeeded in keeping her secret hidden, but now the secret was magnified, far more explosive. The idea of therapy made sense; but therapy couldn't start immediately. She needed someone to talk to, someone who could help her sort things out. She needed to feel less alone. For a minute or two, she wished it could be Matt. She knew there were couples that shared everything: good, bad and ugly. But that wouldn't work with Matt. No chance. She thought about Sherry Jameson. But Sherry was Ty's wife, Matt's buddy's wife. She thought again about Joy Phillips, her friend from church, but she couldn't imagine confiding in Joy.

After ninety futile minutes, she walked into his den. "I'm going to Omaha, Matt."

He turned, his jaw slack with amazement. "Why in God's name would you do that? We're still trying to survive your last trip."

"I've got to find some help. I'm coming apart."

He took the announcement far better than she expected. She expected anger, especially about the possibility she would reconnect, in person, with Michael; but all she could find in her husband's face was concern mixed with anxiety. "Jackie, I can't imagine that Omaha is the right place to find help. Can't you see someone here? Maybe at church. A counselor. I mean what's going on? I thought we were doing better."

"You may be doing better, Matt. *We* may be doing better. But I'm not."

"Isn't there some way I can help you?"

"I've got to go. It's bad inside my head right now. Please don't try to stop me."

Chapter Seventeen

Matt hated the whole idea of an Omaha trip. He hated the feeling that Jackie had built another barrier between them, hopefully not lying to him, but obviously unwilling to share her feelings. The thought of her seeing the son of a bitch named Michael Ledereaux drove him crazy. But he vowed to keep trying. His mother once told him that love isn't something that happens to us; it's something we learn to do. Damn, Mom, he thought, this is hard work. But he left early from a work project to drive her to the airport. As they pulled onto the access road, he broke an uneasy silence that had lasted for several miles. "How long will you be gone?"

"I don't know. Not long. I'm going to get fired if I'm not careful."

"We sure can't afford that."

"I know. I'll probably call in sick Monday. Then we'll see what happens."

They stopped in the curb lane at the terminal. "Come home soon, Jackie. I love you."

Tears filled her eyes. "I'm sorry to be causing all this trouble."

He slid toward her, putting his arm around her shoulder. "You'll be okay. We'll be okay."

She leaned toward him and kissed his cheek. "Thanks for being so understanding."

He cupped her face in his left hand and met her eyes. And he saw only pain. "I love you, Jackie."

"Thank you, Matt. I really mean that."

He watched as she wrestled her bag out of the back seat, and disappeared into the terminal, trudging along slowly, her head down. *What the hell is going on?*

Matt split the return trip between concern for Jackie and anxiety about his own state of mind. It would be a tough weekend. Sending her back toward Michael was a test too large, too soon. As he rounded the last corner leading to their house, Matt spotted Sean sitting on the front steps.

"Dad, can we talk? I really need to talk."

"Sure, buddy. Let's grab some pop and go to the porch."

When they were settled, Matt waited, watching Sean study his Pepsi can while doodling with his forefinger in beaded moisture. When he spoke, his voice was soft, tinged with pain. "She's not coming back is she?"

Matt processed genuine surprise. "Why do you say that?"

"Cause you guys are just like the Turleys used to be. Hot for a while. Then cold. And Jimmy's mom left and…and now she's married to a guy from Memphis and she's gone." His rugged son had huge tears in his eyes.

"Mom will be back. She's just visiting Aunt Mia for a while so they can talk like women talk. She needs that now."

"What's wrong? What's wrong with you guys?"

"I'm not sure, son. Sometimes parents can get as confused as kids, maybe worse." Matt paused to search for the right words. "People have different needs and don't always understand each other. But here's what I do know. Your mom and I love each other, and we always will."

"Are you sure?"

"Yes, Sean. Nothing will ever make us stop loving each other." Matt said it, but he wished he understood things better.

Sean looked up, straight into his father's eyes. "I hate it when you get angry with her. And it scares Jodi."

Matt felt a stab of pain. "I've been trying to do better, Sean. And I'm truly sorry that...that I've upset you and Jodi."

"I want her to come back, Dad. I really, really want her to come back." Tears began spilling down his cheeks.

"She will, Sean. Don't worry."

They sat silent for several minutes. Sean wiped his eyes with his sleeve and said, "I think I'll see what Brett's doing. As soon as I'm not crying like a damn baby."

"It's okay to cry, buddy." Matt pointed to his own eye where some uncharacteristic moisture had formed.

"Thanks for talking, Dad. See ya later."

Matt Billings had a strange realization. This had been the most intense emotional moment of his entire life. He had shared none like it with his own father. None with Jackie, unless there was anger. He walked to the beer-fridge in the garage, grabbed a cold one, and returned to the porch. He sat alone listening to laughing kids and barking dogs in the yards behind theirs, thinking about his children and about the woman he had always thought was the stronger half of their partnership. He knew he had entered uncharted territory. He didn't understand what was going on in Jackie's head. His mom had always seemed strong; had always handled things, even after his dad had behaved like a total ass, which was a couple times a month, probably more. *What the hell is going on?*

***

Mia picked her up at the airport on Friday night and was shocked by her sister's appearance. Her hair looked tousled. She had deep circles under both eyes, and the eyes had an oddly hollow look. As they navigated I-680 traffic, Mia said, "So you need to disappear for a while, huh?"

Jackie smiled, but weakly. "Yes. I have issues."

"Want to talk now?"

"Know what's been the worst?"

"What?"

"Being so…so alone, while…" Sobs suddenly erupted, choking her voice. She raised both hands to her head, sobbing with each short, gasping breath.

Mia shifted to the right lane and on into the pullover lane. She stopped the car, turned on the hazard lights, and leaned across the console toward her sister, putting both arms around her. "Jesus, Jackie, how bad is it?"

"Bad. It's bad. I'm out of control. I'm risking everything. My reputation, my marriage, maybe even my kids, everything."

Mia found a Kleenex and wiped Jackie's cheeks. "You're safe here, sis. We'll talk things through. Don't worry."

They decided a good night's sleep would be tonight's best medicine, and with a little help from some Mia-provided medication, Jackie slept.

During morning coffee around the kitchen table, Mia asked, "Do you want Michael to come over? I told him to be on standby."

"Maybe a little later."

Ashley Trent finished her coffee. "Shall I leave you two alone?"

Jackie thought for a moment. "No, stay. I need opinions."

Jackie told the whole story. Ashley Trent's expression showed attentive concern. Mia appeared mesmerized. She said, "My God, Baxter showing up in the park must have been a holy shit moment."

Jackie looked up from the coffee cup she had been focusing on. "I've had a lot of holy shit moments."

"Now I see why there are circles under your eyes," said Mia.

They sipped coffee silently. Mia studied the ceiling, as if deep in thought. "There's something strange about all this. Ever watch shows like *Law and Order*?"

"Sometimes."

"Would an FBI guy screw around like that, with his evidence and his witness?" Mia chuckled lightly, apparently enjoying her pun.

Jackie failed to find the humor. "I think I took him by surprise."

"Give her a break, Mia," scolded Ashley.

"No, I'm serious, in a way. Don't you think it's strange that Baxter—?"

"Who can explain what men do?" said the newly assertive Ashley Trent. "I think we should be talking about Jackie." She reached across the table to take Jackie's hand. "I don't see how you've even survived this."

"Thank you," said Jackie, looking into caring eyes.

"For what it's worth, I believe that Baxter took advantage of you. A gentleman—not to mention a professional—would have known how vulnerable you were."

"I don't know. The whole thing just seemed to—"

"I hate to say it," said Mia solemnly, "but this isn't about what Baxter should or shouldn't have done. This is about the curse."

"What is the curse?" asked Jackie.

"Our dear Mother Madeline," said Mia as if delivering a dark secret. "I thought you might have avoided it, but the hard-drinking trollop of my psyche has kept me in major therapy for years."

"I don't think this is Mom's fault, but I am thinking about seeing someone."

"Well then, dear sister, you might as well head on over to Greenville to reconnect. You and your shrink will be talking a little about Dad and a lot about Mom, believe me."

"That sounds heavy."

"It is heavy."

***

Michael Ledereaux had assumed he would wait a full year to see Jackie, so found this bonus visit a pleasant surprise. Of course, his counsel had likely been the real reason she decided to bring her troubles to Omaha. He spent a restless morning waiting for Mia's call to action.

Jackie and Michael sat together in the all-weather sunroom that overlooked Mia's back lawn and pool. Jackie wore jeans and a sweatshirt. Michael was Lands End stylish in chinos and a teal turtleneck. His beard was a bit longer. The nose was still bent in the gentle S. The dark eyes still sparkled. But a lot had happened since last they met.

He mostly listened while she struggled to explain her feelings and actions. He asked solid questions about the impact on her children. He agreed with Mia that a visit with Mom in Greenville would be insightful. He promised to do anything he could to research legal issues. Jackie found herself feeling better. A half-hour into the conversation, Michael suggested a glass of wine. She accepted and felt better still.

He said, "I'm terribly sorry if any of this is my fault."

"I can't blame anyone but myself."

"There's a special tonight at the Ledereaux Massage Salon. Guaranteed stress relief."

"I'll have to think about that."

“A friend helping a friend, sweet Jackie.”

“I’ll think about it.”

At 4:30, Jackie lay in the Wizard of Oz room daybed, struggling to wakefulness after a long nap aided by a second glass of wine. She was also struggling with Michael’s massage offer. Could it be—what would the word be—platonic? If she was even thinking about that kind of time with Michael, where might all this stop?

She heard a light knock on the door. Jackie called, “Come in,” and Ashley Trent entered, pointed the room’s wicker chair toward the bed, and sat down. Jackie pulled herself up and sat upright on the edge of the daybed.

Ashley said, “Can I stick my nose where it probably shouldn’t be?”

“Sure.”

“I think you should take the first available plane, stage coach, or wagon train out of here.”

Jackie asked “Why?” completely surprised.

“I’ve talked with Mia today, and with Michael just a few minutes ago; and I’ve put some things together. Get out of here.”

“I don’t understand.”

“You need serious advice, Jackie. Legal, psychological, who knows? And you’ve come to a frigging funny farm to get it. There isn’t a person in the house, including me, who has the slightest clue how to build a normal life.”

“I don’t have anyone else to talk to.”

“If that’s true, fix it. But get out of here. Mia’s whole life is arranging scenes. Big scenes. Grand scenes. She and I have lesbian arguments in shopping malls just to watch peoples’ mouths drop. Your adventure weekend was classic Mia. Five-cent psychology and dreaming up a meeting between you and your mother is classic Mia. She cares about you more like a movie director than a sister.”

Ashley paused, as if deliberating whether to deliver her second exposé. "Michael can't wait to get his hands on you again. He wants you in the harem. That's all. The guy is a human dildo who can spout poetry."

Jackie had felt some pain during the assessment of Mia, but little surprise. Now she reacted strongly. "That doesn't seem fair at all. Michael has been a good friend to me for months."

"Oh, yes, sorry…a human dildo who knows how to be a good friend because it helps him get laid."

"Is that true? I mean how do you know that?"

"Believe me, I know it."

"Why do you stay?"

"Good question," said Ashley. "Get out, Jackie. Tonight if you can. Tomorrow for sure. Find some real help. And, whatever you do, don't add Michael to your list of issues."

Jackie processed quickly, and decided that Ashley had turned on some kind of light. Her counselors were Mia, Michael and Sherry Jameson who occasionally enjoyed four-hand massages and God knows what else, arranged by her own husband. "Thanks for caring enough to come in here."

"Don't mention it." Ashley laughed. "Please don't mention it."

On Saturday evening, Michael received Jackie's call declining her massage session. He had been certain that an encore massage would lead to fulfillment of his multi-month fantasy. He feared he hadn't handled the turndown effectively. His voice had sounded petulant, even to himself, and Jackie was curt by the time their conversation ended. But damn it, he had invested a great deal of time on her. Where was the gratitude?

On Sunday afternoon, a surprised Matt learned that Jackie had arranged to fly stand-by and would be back in Columbus by 6:30 p.m. He picked her up.

"Matt, I'm going to find a therapist. I need to."

Nothing in Matt's upbringing helped him with this moment. His father had considered therapy the stuff of self-absorbed wimps who ought to, by God, grab their own asses with both hands and get on with life. Matt knew that treatment was expensive and not covered by their medical insurance, but he said, "We'll do whatever it takes, Jackie."

"Thank you."

"Sean needs a hug from his mom tonight. Jodi, too, probably."

She spent time with Jodi, then Sean. She could tell they had talked brother-sister, and had tried to comfort each other. She could tell they were happy to have her back; happy to hear her tell them she loved them. She felt better. Much better. Things would get better.

Chapter Eighteen

Helen Billings hated the phone call. Matt sounded concerned, frightened, vulnerable. She hurt for her son whenever she thought about the vulnerability. He tried so hard to be strong like his father. Always had. But no one could be like Clancy Billings. She smiled. No one *should* be like Clancy Billings. Her husband had ruled his world by sheer force of size, personality, fanatic efficiency, and rage. He had assumed his son would follow in his footsteps. Matt had tried, but it just wasn't in him.

They settled in the living room. Matt sat on the couch, dabbling with the cookies and milk she had placed on the coffee table in front of him. She felt stabs of pain as she studied his face. He had never been able to mask his hurt, another difference between Matt and his father.

He said, "Mom, I may need to borrow some money. No, I *do* need to borrow some money."

"Why, Matt?"

"I thought you would ask how much."

"Men ask how much. Women ask why."

"It's for Jackie. She wants to see a psychologist, or psychiatrist or whatever."

"What's going on?"

"I don't really know. She's just struggling. She's having a really hard time."

Helen worked on frustration with men, at least Billings men. "Haven't you talked to her; really talked to her?"

"I…I…. Well, no. Not really. I'm pretty confused by all this."

"Learn to talk, Matt."

"I will. I mean I'm trying to do better. But do you have some money I can borrow? It may be thousands; I don't know. The business isn't doing well right now, and—"

"I've got some money. Your father believed in insurance, thank goodness. I'd be happy to loan it to you."

With the financial hurdle addressed, Jackie moved aggressively to begin changing her life. She contacted Joy Phillips, a fellow volunteer at numerous church events and a woman Jackie knew to be warm, caring, and well connected. They met for breakfast at a Cracker Barrel, and Jackie delicately described a need for therapy to deal with personal issues and related marital problems.

Joy began by talking about the power of prayer. Jackie confessed to some major doubt about the power of prayer, and suggested that her problems had moved beyond that point, anyway. Clearly concerned, Joy asked where Jackie stood with the Lord. Jackie admitted that she and the Lord had been somewhat out of touch since the long-ago night that a little girl prayed ferociously in the back of a medical van. Joy was sympathetic, non-judgmental, and even admitted to confusion about the mystery of unanswered prayer. She suggested various church programs run by the Minister of Counseling. Jackie held firm, insisting that she had issues she would rather discuss with professionals outside the church family. And, finally, Joy promised to refer Jackie to a local clinic she knew to be doing excellent work.

Jackie called her mother that Thursday afternoon.

"Mom, it's Jackie."

"Whuzzup, missy?"

"Have you been drinking?"

"Of course, it's almost three; haven't you?"

"I'd like to visit you Saturday morning, okay?"

"Saturday morning, why?"

"I'll be off work and you'll be…you'll be able to concentrate."

Marilyn snorted. "That wasn't very nice. But, sure, come and see me."

Jackie started the ninety-minute drive at 7:00 a.m., taking I-70 to Ohio 49, which led across farmland and into Greenville's familiar tree-lined streets. The trees were near high-color, flaming brightly in reds, oranges, and yellows. In a way, most of the homes in Greenville looked like their house, large porches, rooflines running at all angles, and mature trees and shrubs everywhere. But they were all different.

She decided on a six-block side trip and drove through the Greenville City Park, her favorite place as a kid, a place rich with memories of her dad. She remembered picnics, fishing with him in the little creek, flying kites with him, and zooming down the twisting circular slide where he would always catch her and laugh and squeeze her really tight. Sometimes, especially while they fished, her dad talked to her about his life; about some of the things that made him happy and sad. He even told her stories about the Korean War, about how it felt to be a soldier. She treasured those special times, partly because she was pretty sure he never talked to anyone else like that, especially about the war. But she kept those talks a secret.

She thought about today's meeting with her mother. She would dump the whole load, confess everything, and learn as much as possible about her roots. She smiled at a random thought. *It's a testimony to our pitiful relationship that confessing the whole thing isn't frightening at all.*

Jackie entered through the front door and yelled, "Hello…"

“In the kitchen,” rumbled Madeline Morris. Jackie walked into a kitchen that had not changed in her memory except for a new microwave by the sink. The same old Frigidaire was still running. The GE stove had never been replaced. The gray Formica table was the same table where her dad held court after dinner, sessions about life, history, or current events that Jackie loved and Mia hated.

“Hi, Mom.” Jackie knew there would be no hugs or kisses, so remained standing across the table, taking stock of her mother’s appearance. She had thickened a bit over the years, and some wear and tear showed, especially around the eyes. But she looked absurdly good for a fifty-seven year old hard-drinking unrepentant chain-smoker. Her latest hair color was blonde, full, pulled back into a ponytail. The whole look should really be reserved for those under thirty, but it was typical Madeline.

Her mother studied her with blue eyes surprisingly clear. “To what do I owe the honor of this audience?” The voice was raspy, guttural, and had sounded that way for as long as Jackie could remember.

“I need some help understanding what’s going on in my life.”

Madeline didn’t seem surprised, likely indicating that Mia had prepped her, but she asked the expected question. “When’s the last time you came to me for anything?”

“A long time ago.”

“Well grab a coffee and pull up a chair. I can hardly wait to hear this.”

Jackie told the whole story as unvarnished truth: her encounters with men, her problems with Matt, her growing fear that she was both exhibitionist and nymphomaniac, although she wasn’t sure what it meant to be either. Madeline sipped and puffed through the long discourse, betraying not the slightest surprise.

"That's quite a story, missy; more like the adventures of Mia than Jackie."

"I know."

"And, one more time, why are you here?"

"I don't understand what's happening to me. I've decided to get help, to do whatever it takes to get my life under control."

Madeline stood, poured another round of coffee, and opened a new pack of cigarettes. She returned to her seat and lit up. "I'm not smart enough to understand what's in your head, but I can sure see what's happening to you."

"What?"

"*Life* is happening to you. What were the men's names again?"

"Aldrich and Baxter and Michael Ledereaux."

"Okay, then, Aldrich and Baxter and Michael Ledereaux happened to you. All you did was put yourself somewhere where it could happen."

"But it was me…I—"

Madeline put fingers to both temples, as if her head had suddenly begun aching. "Jackie, Jackie, I should have taught you more. This Michael is a scumbag, but your pilot and the FBI agent are appealing, worldly guys. Just think back. They are suddenly the answer to a desperate need; they create an opportunity; next thing you know, you're on your back. Right?"

Jackie frowned, dredging her memory, realizing that her mother's simple explanation had a ring of truth. But surely it didn't explain everything.

Madeline rolled on. "Are you an exhibitionist? Sure as hell sounds like it. But let's be honest; what woman isn't, if she's got something worth showing? It doesn't make us wanton women. Know what I mean?"

This time Jackie smiled. "I guess so, Mom."

"Are you a nymphomaniac? I don't see it." Madeline paused to smile slyly. "Although healthy appetites sure as hell run in the family. No, I think you finally ran into a couple guys who knew how to turn your knobs. And any woman who's honest—which damn few are, in my opinion—will tell you she enjoys a good knob turning."

Jackie smiled again, although she now questioned the educational value of this trip. Still, she might be closer to understanding Mia's so-called curse.

Madeline closed one eye and exhaled a stream of smoke. "Here's the real enchilada, if you ask me. You married too young, chasing after security. When it was time to explore, you chased after older men. Hell, Jackie, listen to your own Baxter story. You were a little girl trying her best to win her father's approval."

Jackie found no smile this time. Her throat tightened. She looked up to study her mother's face, wondering if the cruelty had been intentional. Madeline just sipped her coffee, her face thoughtful as if preparing to unload her next barrage.

"For Christ's sake," she rumbled, "I can't decide whether you remind me of a wandering butterfly or a bitch in heat. Either way, make a decision about your marriage. I can't believe Matt's been able to survive you; and I'm not talking about the infidelity."

Jackie now remembered why discussions with her mother rarely ended well. This was the moment when she stomped upstairs and slammed her door. Today she would hang in there. "He was smothering me, Mom."

"Give the guy a break, for crying out loud. You married him in the first place because he was protective. Now you're busting his balls, not to mention prowling, because he is. I don't even like the guy—probably because he reminds me of his asshole father—but I'm on his side in this mess."

"I am working on my marriage, Mom."

They took an unspoken time-out while Jackie warmed bagels in the toaster. She returned to her chair, prepared to probe. "Here's something that may be harder for you."

Madeline looked surprised, as if she couldn't imagine that problems and issues remained unresolved. "That sounds like trouble. What's up?"

"Am I Daddy's daughter?"

Madeline nodded casually while adding cream cheese to her bagel. "I was thinking about that yesterday. You are most certainly your father's daughter. It was always Mia and I, and you and—"

Jackie hadn't prepped for this line of discussion, but she took the detour. "Did he really love me? I mean a lot?"

Madeline nodded. "Yes, Jackie. A lot."

"What about you, and Mia?"

"Us, too." Madeline suddenly looked troubled. "In his way."

"Did you love me?"

"Well, I…" The woman who talked constantly paused, thoughtful, as if unable to find words. "I didn't understand you, Jackie. And you were so hostile."

Jackie nearly asked whether her mother realized that Jackie had gone seven full years without a single hug. But that water was too deep. "Am I Daddy's biological daughter?"

Madeline looked at her with wary eyes. "Yes, you are."

"Is Mia?"

Madeline studied her coffee cup, looked up at Jackie as if considering *a mind your own business* comment, but said, "I don't know for sure. Probably not."

"Did Daddy know that?"

"Yes, he knew that."

"How did he find out?"

"Guy talk at a bar started the rumor. Henry asked me if it was true. I admitted I was seeing a man."

Jackie asked, "Mitch Upton?" dredging up the ancient rumor.

"Yes."

"And Daddy stayed with you anyway?"

"It was terribly hard for him. Partly because I didn't really change. He always feared I was bed-hopping."

"Were you?"

Jackie watched intense sadness flood her mother's face. "Do we really need to discuss this?"

"I want to know, Mom. I need to know."

"He was a wonderful man in many ways. Remember all the medals we kept in the china cabinet?"

"Yes, his war medals."

"I described him once as a good soldier. Courageous, dedicated, loyal. But he was fourteen years older than me, and serious. So serious. He hated my plays and my parties. And he grew to hate my friends."

"Still, he didn't leave you."

Her mother looked at her through eyes filling with tears. "God, Jackie, he did leave me. Don't you see? A healthy man in the prime of his life. He left me. And I regret it every day of my life." Madeline Morris now spoke through broken sobs. "And I regret that I was a horrible mother, and oh, God, I'm so sorry..."

Jackie studied her, feeling emotionally blindsided. She couldn't decide whether to be comforting, or to let her mother wallow in richly deserved guilt. Then she felt a wave of fury at the possibility this woman really had killed her father; then a wave of sadness that the wreck in front of her was the only parent she had to love, or turn to for support. Jackie walked around the table, leaned forward, and wrapped her arms awkwardly around her mother's shoulders. "My problems aren't your fault, Mom."

Madeline kept sobbing, possibly a bit melodramatically, Jackie decided. "I've not been a mother to you. I didn't know how to be a mother to you."

"You got me to adulthood. I'm on my own now."

Madeline called Mia. "Well she's come and gone."

"And?"

"And it was the most grueling damn session I've ever been in. I couldn't decide whether I was a mother or a priest or a marriage counselor."

"And?"

"I really did want to help, so I was all prepared. I talked with Kenny Gerard yesterday, and—"

Mia laughed. "Your G.P.?"

"Kenny's a very intelligent man, well read," Madeline replied in a wounded tone. "I even took notes. Anyway, I think I came pretty damn close to being a marriage counselor. I think I might have done some good."

During her drive home, Jackie looked for the silver lining, although from the distance of even a few minutes and a few miles, it was obvious that her mother was even more of a mess than expected. Still, Madeline understood a thing or two about life, and Jackie better understood the curse. She vowed not to be controlled by it.

And her mother had spoken some truth about Matt. Jackie had been horribly unfair to her husband. The days ahead were uncertain, but not hopeless. She might need some breaks. Baxter and Aldrich needed to stay gone. Matt needed to stay understanding. She needed to grow. Seeing a therapist would help; she was sure of it. There was hope.

Chapter Nineteen

Jackie's first visited the Tollison Clinic at 11:00 a.m. on Monday morning in the last week of October. Joy Phillips had spoken personally with Dr. Frank Tollison, assuring him that Jackie had real needs and asking for an accelerated appointment schedule.

Jackie entered through oak double doors and soon found herself in the office of Dr. Tollison, a silver-haired man of about fifty, warm with a ready smile. The facility was as warm as the man: earth tones, lush plants, nature paintings, and gentle music. She sat on a soft leather couch. He sat on a chair opposite her, taking detailed notes on a legal pad as she summarized her life story. Toward the end of the session, Tollison said, "I'm going to recommend something, Jackie. You will be better served by a woman therapist."

"I don't understand."

"You'll need to trust me on this. Our Doctor Laura Geiger will be a wonderful choice for you. Is that agreeable?"

Jackie began meeting with Dr. Geiger twice weekly. Laura Geiger was a married woman, just two years older than Jackie. She was petite with short black hair and dark brown eyes that danced when she was making important points. She was something of an eccentric, often removing her shoes and using them as props during their sessions; sometimes depicting conflict by pointing them toward each other, even kicking each other. Sometimes the shoes walked beside each other; sometimes one walked in front of the other; sometimes one stepped on the other's toes. They were very active shoes.

During Jackie's second full week, Matt met privately with Dr. Tollison, and set up his own schedule. For Jackie, simply entering the process helped greatly. "Problems are less fearsome if we identify, understand, and address," said Dr. Geiger. They talked about the role of Jackie's long dark period in shaping her tendency toward exhibitionism. Geiger said, "It's not about a cheerleader and a football player. When young Tommy Kerrigan came along you still felt ugly, at least in your own eyes. And he showed you what it means to be pretty and sexy and loved, at least in his eyes."

Jackie learned without surprise that she possessed what Dr. Geiger called a highly charged body. "Women do vary in need and in responsiveness. Why? There's constant debate, but the reasons are likely a combination of physical and psychological. Whatever the reason, you received your share and then some. And like most things in life, that can be either good or bad."

They discussed mother Madeline, but not deeply. Geiger said, "I have a feeling that we'll be spending a good long time on that subject. Let's work on the things that we can address more quickly."

They delved into the multiple impacts of her father's early death, and connections that seemed almost trite between the loss of her father and her attraction to the men who had entered her life. "They played you like a master plays a violin, Jackie. The dying Ted Aldrich reached deep into your psyche. Donavon Baxter couldn't have played it better if he were a trained psychiatrist."

Jackie began to see that Matt was struggling to climb a very high mountain. Geiger said, "You ran to Matt to escape dysfunction, but soon you were comparing him, subconsciously, to a myth: a father you idolized, frozen in your mind as a heroic figure, a warm and loving heroic figure."

They talked about Jackie's problems with self-respect, with loving herself. It was a concept so foreign to her that she had trouble even grasping it. She knew there was work to be done on that subject.

By their fifth session, Dr. Geiger had a clearer picture of Matt's jealousy issues, and she suggested a joint session. She was greatly encouraged to learn that Matt, like Jackie, had committed to finding answers and to improving their marriage. Too often, the fiercely possessive are not open to change.

She learned that Matt never quite made it into the in-crowd, in either high school or college. He lost his high school sweetheart to a guy named Dean Volmer who drove a black Camaro and was viewed as a high school stud. He suffered a similar loss—a Columbus townie named Kim Delp—during his sophomore year in college. By the time he met Jackie, he anticipated the losses. Almost to his own surprise, he didn't lose Jackie, but thanks to his father, Matt soon found his insecurities fanned into uncontrollable jealousy.

Helen Billings filled in that part of the story. Shortly before Jackie and Matt became engaged, the families met at a restaurant near Dayton, Ohio. The early part of the evening had been cordial, but Madeline Morris downed several cocktails and, according to Clancy Billings, showed herself to be a complete slut. Her language became raw. In the parking lot after the dinner, she embraced Clancy in a way that he viewed as wanton. He called a detective friend the following morning and soon knew that Madeline was well traveled and poorly regarded in her own hometown. Clancy tried, without success, to sidetrack his son's interest in Jackie. He barely tolerated the wedding, again disgusted with Madeline Morris's behavior. And at a trade convention in Chicago, when Jackie appeared to flirt with the men who were admiring her barely covered backside, Clancy declared her a wanton woman and began planting the seeds that would influence the next fourteen years of his son's life. Matt's insecurity became jealousy that steadily fed on itself, becoming a factor in his psyche that Jackie could not begin to understand.

Laura Geiger struggled with the irony. Clancy Billings was an opinionated ass, but his fears about Jackie, hence Matt's fears, had virtually come true. The irony might make a wonderful doctoral thesis, but it was attacking a real family, before her very eyes.

At Laura Geiger's suggestion, Jackie visited a clinic to be tested for STDs. Geiger dearly hoped that the truth Matt would someday face wouldn't include potentially deadly disease. All tests came back negative, hopefully part of a developing pattern of improvement.

Jackie and Matt also did their homework: striving to communicate feelings at a deeper level, learning to process their disagreements in a few hours rather than a few days. Jodi and Sean were noticeably happier. Kaye Lassiter's most recent job evaluation had been positive, although she mentioned the absences. Jackie heard nothing at all from Don Baxter. The lack of any contact puzzled her, but she decided to be grateful for every day that passed.

Jackie decided that tonight would be the night. Dr. Geiger had suggested that indirect communication about sexual needs is often less threatening than giving a man a set of new requests. So Geiger gave her an idea that Jackie struggled to even imagine, but she said she'd give it a try. She geared up mentally during a long, hot bath, slipped on a sheer yellow baby-doll, and slid into bed beside Matt. She processed quick annoyance that perfume and baby-doll had failed to cause him to even glance her way. He was reading *Field & Stream,* for heaven sake. But she remembered he had had a hard day, and she forgave him.

"Matt, I need you to do something for me."

"Sure, what?" he replied, still reading.

"Come over here and pull my nightie over my head. I need to test something, purely in the interest of science."

"You're not going weird on me are you?" She understood the question. Matt still called unnecessary variations *Cosmo* moments.

"No, this is a serious experiment."

"Okay."

She put her arms over her head and he tugged her top off.

"Yes. Very good. Now listen carefully. My left nipple is the finger nipple. My right nipple is the mouth nipple. We will be conducting a comparative stimulation test. Do you understand the objective, Dr. Billings?"

She read him as somewhere between suspicious and incredulous, but he went along with the routine. "I believe so, Dr. Billings. What is the duration of the test?"

"The experiment lasts ten minutes. However, at five minutes, you are to pause and allow me to report my findings. I may direct you to slightly revise your manipulation technique. Is that clear, Dr. Billings?"

"I understand, Dr. Billings."

He started caressing and sucking. She guessed he was trying to figure out how to kill five minutes on such a menial task, but he stayed on the job. "Five minutes are up," he said, "what are your findings?"

"Mouth stimulation is at seven point six," she reported between short breaths, "digital is at five point three. Now bring my body lotion for the digital breast, and prepare a clockwise tongue swirl for the mouth breast."

He got up to search for body lotion. She was pleased to note that his flag was flying at well past half-mast. "I will apply the lotion," she said. "Your job is to massage it thoroughly. And remember that we twirl the tit for this session, clockwise only."

He laughed. "You are nuts."

"Perhaps, Dr. Billings. Perhaps. But science must prevail."

Five minutes later, Jackie moaned, "I'm losing focus, Dr. Billings. Seemingly I need attention to other body parts."

Her associate needed no further instruction.

Dr. Billings and Dr. Billings experimented the next night, introducing an initially reluctant Matt to oral possibilities. They committed to more nights of honest communication, and finally they shared a wonderful climb up mutual-mountain. Jackie felt closer to Matt than ever in their lives, and realized happily that the reasons ran far deeper than sex. Their time together was better. Their time with family was better.

But the deceit loomed as a giant negative. Jackie talked with Dr. Geiger about ways to gradually share the truth with Matt, for example beginning by confessing the massage session with Michael. "Not yet, Jackie," said Laura Geiger, holding up her right shoe as if it were a stop sign. "I've discussed that with Dr. Tollison. Matt's just not ready yet."

***

On more nights than he would ever confess to his macho-buddies, Sean Billings spent time with his little sister. He liked her. She made him smile. And he knew there were many nights when Jodi needed some company. Usually he just sat on her bed for a while before she fell asleep. During the bad times, she sometimes cried while they talked. Of course, he never did. Tonight she said, "It's happy in our house again."

Sean said, "I know."

"I'm glad."

"Me too."

Chapter Twenty

Because the Tollison Clinic was within walking distance of her office, Jackie scheduled her sessions over the lunch hour whenever possible. She had stopped for Wendy's-to-go after her Monday appointment and returned to her office at 12:55. She walked through her door and picked up the ringing phone. "Jackie Billings, may I help you."

"Ah, yes, Mrs. Billings," said a clipped, high-pitched male voice.

"Yes, may I help you?"

"I'll pick you up. Broad Street side. Exactly 1:15. Dark green Town Car. Be there."

"Who is this?

"Max Collier."

"What do you want, I mean why are—?"

"I'm an associate of Donavon Baxter's. There is unfinished business."

She exhaled as her stomach churned. "Are you with the FBI?"

"No. However, Baxter has made me aware of *everything*. Do you understand?"

"No, I don't understand at all. What's this about?"

"You do not want me to share my knowledge." The line went dead.

Jackie spent five anxious minutes considering Collier's meaning and her options. The man knew about Ted Aldrich, almost for sure. Baxter wouldn't have revealed his own time with her, or would he? But why wonder? She fished Baxter's card out of its desk drawer hiding place, dialed, and listened to a woman's recorded voice: “This is the mobile line of Agent-at-Large Donavon Baxter, Federal Bureau of Investigation. Leave your message at the tone.” Jackie checked her watch, decided she didn’t have time to wait, decided that leaving a message wouldn’t help, and hung up the phone. She saw no option but to find out what Max Collier was all about.

She walked past the department’s twin rows of cubicles, telling her people she would return in a few minutes. She rode the elevator to the lobby, exited through the Broad Street doors, and easily spotted the car, parked half a block to her right. She walked quickly toward it and knocked on the window, hoping the driver would speak with her while she stood on the sidewalk. He made no move except to gesture toward the seat with his forefinger. She reluctantly opened the door and slid into the front seat.

“Mrs. Billings. At last.”

She quickly studied him. A bent-rimmed safari hat pulled low. Dark eyes. Prominent nose. Faint pock marks among the stubble of a salt and pepper beard. "Who are you? What’s this about?"

“To be revealed.” His deep-set eyes slowly scanned her, hair to shoes, while his head nodded slightly. He reached for the gearshift lever.

“Wait. Please. Tell me what this is about.”

“Patience, Mrs. Billings” He put the car in gear and pulled away from the curb.

She reached for the door handle. "I want out of this car, right now.”

His head snapped toward her, the eyes suddenly painted black by some kind of inner fury. “Shut the fuck up! Just shut the fuck up!” He looked forward, pounding the steering wheel three times with his right fist. “Shit. Shit. Shit.” Then he turned back toward her, eyes blazing. “You angered me. You must not anger me.”

She felt herself shrink backward from a blast of raw rage unlike anything she had ever seen. “Won’t you just tell me what’s going on?” Her voice had gone thin, weak.

He studied traffic and appeared to be talking to the windshield. The voice mellowed but sounded singsong. “Three things anger me: failure to pay attention, failure to answer questions, and failure to follow instructions. I wonder if Mrs. Billings understands?” He glanced toward her inquisitively.

She considered jumping from the moving car or trying to escape at the next light. But she would need to flip the lock lever and pull the handle. She guessed it would take too long, be too obvious. Apparently she had waited too long to reply, the eyes began to blacken with rage. “Yes, I understand,” she said softly.

“Silence then, while I seek isolation.”

He drove west then south. Finally he pulled onto an industrial side street in an area that looked like a locale in a depression-era movie. She saw old brick buildings, long runs of rusting chain link fence, but no cars or people. He pulled into a barren parking lot, switched off the engine, moved his power seat back, and turned toward her. She leaned away, feeling the armrest hard against her hip, searching her mind frantically for escape options, but finding nothing.

He mixed frown and smile, this time allowing his lips to part. "Would you agree that I was not blessed with good looks?”

She could see stubbed teeth, widely spaced in front. He had the kind of face with pieces that just didn’t fit: the nose too large, the eyes too small and so deep set they sometimes disappeared into shadows under black eyebrows; the stubbled chin was slightly receded. She decided to say nothing.

“Hence I appreciate Agent Baxter’s help in making your acquaintance.”

She realized she must to get into this game, mentally and emotionally, although she feared that Max Collier was seriously unbalanced. “But Agent Baxter was here to investigate, and—”

“And he has behaved badly. So badly. Revealing Aldrich. His own dalliance.”

She felt fear rising from the pit of her stomach: fear of this man and the reason for his intrusion; fear that everything she had worked for was about to be crushed. But she tried to stay in the game. "Does Agent Baxter know you're here?"

He frowned. "Oh, no. Not now. Not ever."

"I need to get back to work."

"In due time. We will now negotiate for my silence." He shifted again into singsong. "Potential recipients of fascinating news: Matthew Billings, Sean Billings, Jodi Billings, Kaye Lassiter; Vaughn Whitmore, reporter, *Columbus Dispatch;* Kitty Levine, reporter, *Channel Six News*…. Listening?"

She exhaled long and slow, and nodded.

"Demand number one: Be at XYZ Farms, at noon on Wednesday with one hundred and fifty thousand dollars in unmarked bills."

A new kind of fear surged through her. "No…I mean there's no way—"

He raised a hand. "I'm not interested in obstacles. Listening?"

She nodded her head, her mind reeling.

"Number Two. You will deliver the funds to XYZ while wearing a suitable coat, no more, no less. You will participate in a favorite little game wherein you resist me, futilely, of course. We will utilize Agent Baxter's favorite spot."

This nightmare has to stop. She met his eyes while snaking her hand toward the door, searching for the lock lever. "No, I won't do any of that." She tried to flip the lever.

His hand shot toward her, grabbing her left hand in a vice-like grip, twisting her wrist backward. Pain shot up her arm and into her body. "God, stop, you're hurting me."

The eyes were black. With his left hand, he reached toward a cell phone mounted on the dash. "I believe the number is 6 - 9 - 1 - 1 - 0 - 4…" He dialed as he spoke; Matt's mobile number. Collier's finger paused above the keypad. "And a three I believe."

"No, don't do that." Pain pierced through her wrist. She felt sick to her stomach.

He released her arm and sat back slightly, but his hand remained at the cell phone pad. "Listening?"

Fear raged through her. Her mind had hit overload; nothing would register. She looked at Collier with a hopeless expression and nodded.

"Number three: Your brassiere. Right here. Right now. I do so enjoy brassieres."

She tried for resistance, for anger, for anything but the feeling of complete, cruel manipulation. She watched his finger descend on the cell phone and hit *3*. He paused just above the *SEND* key. "No, stop."

Her eyes filled with tears, a mixture of anger, fear and humiliation. She sensed that yielding to this horrible man would be a dangerous decision, but she couldn't imagine destroying her marriage over a bra. He leaned back, watching intently as she pulled her arms out of her sweater sleeves, reached back to unclasp the bra, slid the straps off her shoulders, and handed it to him.

He wiped the garment across his face, inhaled deeply, and tossed it into the rear seat. "You may put your sweater on." She reached upward to slide her arms back into the sweater. He stopped her, again clamping her left wrist with his right hand.

"There is one small matter, to assure your purity until we meet." He used his free hand to yank the bottom of her sweater, pulling it nearly to her shoulders. She struggled against the assault but her arms were tangled in the sleeves. His face darted forward; she felt his teeth on the soft tissue around her left nipple. And he bit down, hard.

She clenched her teeth, trying not to cry out as pain seared through her, but she couldn't stop a long gasp from deep in her throat. "Oh…Oh, God…"

He slid behind the wheel, turned the ignition key, and drove across the parking lot toward the cross street. She put her arms into the sweater and leaned back, eyes closed. Her head felt light. She felt the warmth of blood on her breast, seeping into her sweater. Pain burned through her. They drove in silence.

He pulled to a stop directly in front of the bank building. She sank deeper into the seat, terrified that an associate would somehow know of this moment. His voice went soft, but seemed almost to hiss. “Do not, ever, make me angry.”

She looked at him with an expression gone blank. Her mind was numb; her breathing shallow. She felt nausea rising in waves. As she closed the car door, she could hear him talking to himself.

Jackie crossed her arms over her chest while struggling toward her parking garage. *Damn, I wish I’d brought my jacket, and my purse. But I was in a hurry.* She wanted desperately to be at home. But she felt faint; her legs weren’t working right. She was only a few feet away from the parking garage entrance, worrying about driving without her license, when her world went black.

She next saw the concerned face of a young paramedic, from inside an emergency vehicle. She heard a siren blaring, apparently on her behalf, as the van rocketed along, swerving through traffic. “How are you feeling, ma’am?”

“What’s happening? Where am I?”

“You’re heading for ER at Ohio State Medical. We found you on the sidewalk. Your blood pressure was way down. You’re stable now.”

“I’ll be fine. I don’t want to go to ER.” She tried to sit up, but felt the stab of an IV needle in her right arm. Her eyes wouldn’t focus.

“Take it easy, ma’am. You’ve had a serious shock to your system. What is your name?”

Through her mental haze came an urge to say Smith. Mrs. John Smith. But she said, “Jackie…Jacqueline…Billings.”

"*Mrs.* Billings, I assume?" She nodded. He said, "It's obvious that you've been attacked, Mrs. Billings. The police will meet us at the hospital."

She leaned her head back and closed her eyes, speaking just above a whisper. "I don't want to talk to the police. I just want to go home."

"It's routine. And you need to be checked out. A healthy woman shouldn't wind up on a sidewalk in the shape you were in."

Aides transported her into the hospital on a gurney and helped her onto a permanent bed in a green cloth cubicle. Within five minutes, an administrator had taken preliminary information, accepting Jackie's assurance that she had medical coverage but had left her purse at the office. Five minutes later, a uniformed officer approached her bedside. The officer appeared to be about Jackie's age, attractive in a trim, efficient way, with darkish blonde hair falling just below her cap. "I'm Lieutenant Carolyn Trask of the Columbus Police Department," she began, dark blue eyes searching Jackie's face. "Do you feel up to talking?"

"Yes, I'm feeling a little better."

"Were you attacked?"

Jackie tried to think. Maybe a simple fib and all this goes away. "No, no, nothing like that."

"The paramedic said you suffered a bite, a human bite."

Jackie sensed the importance of the moment. She tried to analyze carefully but it was too complicated, and she felt like she was thinking through a fog. "I was with a man. He got carried away. It was an accident."

"I'm told the wound seemed vicious, not playful."

Now Jackie couldn't make her mind work at all. *Should I tell the truth? What is the truth? I can't imagine explaining Baxter and Aldrich and...* "He got excited. It's a game we play."

Officer Trask jotted notes. "You were not attacked against your will?"

"No. I wasn't."

"You were not abused in any inappropriate way?"

"No."

"I assume this man was not your husband."

"Yes. I mean no. He was not my husband."

"And that you won't be pressing charges?"

"No. No charges."

"I will need some additional information for my report."

"Does there need to be a report?"

"Yes, Mrs. Billings. Sometimes accidents keep happening. We need a report."

"Okay…"

After completing her form, Officer Trask said, "Here's my card. Call if you need anything. And take care of yourself."

The doctor cleaned and dressed the wound, administered a tetanus shot, and ran heart and circulation tests. At nearly 4:30 p.m., Jackie made the phone call that she knew should have been made earlier.

"Matt Billings here."

"Matt, it's me. I've had a…an accident. I'm in ER at OSU Medical."

She heard him gasp once for breath. "God, Jackie, what happened?"

"I'm okay now. I fainted on the sidewalk in front of the bank. I got cut a little. On my boob of all things. Can you get away?"

"I'll be right there."

She called her boss. "Kaye, this is Jackie. I'm terribly sorry. I'm in ER at OSU Medical. I fainted on the sidewalk."

"We were worried about you. One of the people in biz loans thought he saw you being put on a stretcher. What happened?"

"I don't know. I just passed out. I'll be in tomorrow."

Lassiter said, “Don’t push it, Jackie. Take time off if you need to,” but impatience was evident.

“No, really, I’ll be fine.”

Matt hurried through the ER tent, his expression a blend of concern and love unlike anything she had ever seen. He gently helped her from the wheelchair into their van. He tended her every need through the rest of the day. And just before falling asleep, Matt said, “I love you, Jackie. God, I’m glad you’re all right.”

But she wasn’t all right. A day ago, her life had been moving gradually toward truth. She longed for truth. Now she had sunk deeper into deception, including secretly burying her sweater in the trash after realizing it lacked the rip or tear necessary to make her latest lie work.

She stared into the darkness, studying her options. As much as Matt thinks he loves me, he couldn’t possibly absorb what is happening. So whatever I do, I must do alone. Or could I call Dr. Geiger? At least to talk about options. Maybe. I’ll think about that. But Dr. Geiger can’t make Max Collier go away.

Can I get the money? Maybe. There are two possible ways. I could use inside clearance to get close to that kind of cash. Or I could quickly process and approve loans, and divert the proceeds somehow. Do I have time? Probably not. Will Collier give me more time? I don’t know. Would my theft be discovered? Would I end up in prison? I don’t know. Bank security is good. The only thing going for me would be complete surprise. I’m a model employee. Or am I?

Why am I even thinking like this? I’m not a criminal. I’ve never dreamed of stealing from the bank. But this is a cruel man. I believe his threats.

Could I handle the sex session with Collier? God, I can’t believe I’m even thinking this way. But it’s my own fault that I’m in this mess. Could I shut my eyes and endure an hour or two or whatever it would take?

Could I just go to the police? Tell them what's happening. Maybe they could arrest him based on the bite and the threats. Will they believe me now? Why didn't I just tell Officer Trask the truth? That's not a hard question to answer. I couldn't imagine telling the truth, especially with my mind all mush.

But there might be a way. If I say I'm being stalked and the guy has threatened me if I don't show up at a certain place. If I could make that believable, maybe they would arrest him at the barn. That might work. But the barn's way out in the country. That wouldn't be Columbus Police stuff. Who would I even talk to? Then all the old questions are back again. Would I have to testify? Would Collier testify? Would Baxter? Would all that lead back to Aldrich? And to the newspaper? Channel Six News?

The key to this may be Donavon Baxter. I can't imagine that the earnest Agent Baxter would be directly connected with someone like Collier, but there's obviously a connection of some kind. I could contact Baxter; find out what's going on; see if he can help. He helped me once; he surely still likes me, even if things got out of control at the end. But what about Collier's warning not to contact Baxter? That feels like an acceptable risk. Baxter's a strong guy; Collier is more like slime. Baxter could handle Collier.

One thing is certain. I will not be passive. I will not let life just happen to me. I'll make a decision and I'll try my best to fight my way through this.

Chapter Twenty-One

Jackie gave no thought to staying at home on Tuesday; she had been absent too much, and she guessed she would be absent a time or two while dealing with Max Collier. She worked through a surprisingly productive morning and decided to make her decision during a lunch hour in the park. The day was cool but not bitterly cold, typical late November weather. She had slipped into her coat when the phone rang. "Jackie Billings. May I help you?"

"How's the tit, babes?"

She didn't answer.

"You were wise not to involve the police. Good girl."

Now past weary of being pushed by Max Collier, she said, "Maybe I did involve the police."

He chuckled. "I monitor these things. Don't try to bullshit ol' Maxie."

She puzzled over the new swagger in his voice, and a new crudeness. Yesterday, she thought there might be two Max Colliers. Now she wondered if there were three. "What do you want?"

"I'm certain you need more information. We'll meet tonight at eight-thirty."

"No. I won't…I can't. I've got a meeting at—"

"Be at this phone for instructions at eight-fifteen." After an uneasy pause, the voice turned dark. "Don't even think about crossing me, lady."

She lunched in the park, but with a revised agenda. Should she defy Collier? If not, could she possibly arrange to be at her office at 8:15? She needed to be at a PTO fund raising meeting at 7:00. She would have to show up, ask to be put first on the agenda, and rush back downtown. What would she tell Matt?

She sensed a physical problem as well. Yesterday had been a draining day, and her energy burst from this morning had faded. She called it a terrible sign that she was considering complying at all. When would Collier's control ever stop? She knew when it would stop. Would it even stop then?

She thought again about the police, but all the questions and answers remained the same. She could think of no scenario that didn't end with explosive public exposure. She decided to call Baxter, despite Collier's warning.

She returned to her office and listened again to the recorded message. "Don, it's Jackie Billings. Please call me right away. It's urgent..." As the afternoon dragged along, she tried to concentrate on her work, but spent more time staring at her telephone than working on loan files. He called at 3:40. "Jackie Billings, may I help you."

"Baxter here. Do we have something new on Aldrich?"

"Just a minute." She rushed to her office door and closed it. "That's not why I'm calling. There's a guy in town named Max Collier. He's...what do you call it? Blackmailing me."

"I'm not following."

"A guy just showed up. He knew all about me and Ted Aldrich; and about you."

Baxter paused, but briefly. "I've never heard of Max Collier."

Jackie's mind spun backward to Collier's claims. "He called you an associate. He said something about you helping him meet me. Now he's demanding money and...and that I meet him at XYZ."

Baxter paused again. "This isn't some kind of trick is it? I can imagine you're angry about that afternoon, but—"

She felt totally blindsided, but this time anger led a host of emotions. "This is not a trick. You gave information to a horrible man who humiliated me yesterday. Now I'm supposed to play some sick game and give him a hundred and..." She stopped and glanced around her office as if security officers might be listening. "What is going on?" she snapped.

Baxter's voice remained steady, maddeningly calm. "I have no idea what's going on, but you're on your own. If you're making this up, I'll ask you to quit playing games. If I accidentally spilled some information, I must deny it, obviously. I'm sorry things are ending like this, Jackie. Goodbye."

She slammed down the phone, still furious. But anger dissipated quickly, replaced by confusion and frustration. Once again, she thought about talking with Matt. She desperately needed a partner. No. There was no chance he could handle it. She found Lieutenant Trask's card and stared at it, trying to visualize the conversation. *I lied yesterday. The guy that bit me is a bad guy who's blackmailing me because he knows I had sex with...* She couldn't imagine it.

She asked herself whether Collier might be dangerous. Another bite? A rape? Worse? Hopefully not. I'm his avenue to $150,000. Apparently he wants his sex at XYZ, playing his damned fantasy game. And he's right; I need more information. Then maybe, possibly, I can find a way to talk myself out of all this.

Jackie sped frantically through her early evening, feeling like a video in fast-forward. Rushing home. Preparing a quick meal for the kids. Securing Sean's services as babysitter. Dashing to the PTO meeting. Calling Matt to tell him there was a surprise birthday party downtown for one of the bank employees. Apologizing for forgetting to mention it. Cooking too fast, talking too fast, and definitely driving too fast, especially after an accident delay cost her nearly ten minutes. Hank Pauley, part of the night security crew, wanted to chat in the lobby. She felt guilty about brushing him off, knowing that Hank's daughter had miscarried and the family was devastated. But Jackie reached her office, exhausted, seconds before the phone rang.

"You used good judgment again, Mrs. B. And I see you have high-level security clearance. That's very good."

She had worked on a plan of sorts. "I'll only meet you in a public place."

The voice went dark. "Do not ever tell me what you will and won't do, lady."

She waited, hoping she hadn't tweaked the rage.

He said, "But for tonight, you are correct. Public is correct. Drive to the corner of Platte and Thornbush. Park near the Thornbush bus stop. I'll drive by. Follow me. Are you driving your Taurus or the Pathfinder?"

His detailed knowledge sent a tremor through her stomach. "The Taurus. I…I don't know where Platte and Thornbush is."

He gave her directions. "See you in a few, Jackie."

Fifteen minutes later, she slowed to a stop on a desolate street in a desolate section of the city. She waited, watching sparse traffic. In her rearview mirror, she saw the flash of headlights, alternating bright and dim. The Town Car drove by and she followed. Collier led her into a parking lot beside an ancient brick two-story building that ran for half a block to her left. The lot was a canyon created by old brick walls, going dark in the fading evening light. She saw only two cars. He parked about two-thirds of the way into the lot, exited, and signaled her to park beside him. He wore blue jeans, black cowboy boots, and a long-sleeved black shirt with western-looking silver trim. As he swaggered toward her, his expression smug under the tan safari hat, Jackie decided that all the logic that had caused her to be here now felt like insanity.

They walked to the sidewalk and turned into the second storefront, where a dingy window sign read, *Jim's Neighborhood Tavern*. Collier said, "Good place to talk. I don't know if there's a Jim, and if there is, he don't care much about sellin' booze." As Collier led her toward a back corner booth, she saw a tall red-haired woman behind the bar, pouring a drink for a sleepy-eyed guy sitting behind alternating beer bottles and shot glasses. They were the entire crowd. A twangy country song played on an ancient jukebox that appeared to have lost a bar fight; the curved glass of its crown was cracked in all directions.

She hung her coat on a wood peg and slid into the booth, feeling cracked leather bite at her slacks. Collier remained standing. "What'll it be, lady?"

She looked up at him, nervous, angry, curious. This man could be Max Collier's lowbrow twin. "Nothing."

His eyes, barely visible under the safari hat, darkened. "Wrong as all hell."

"Diet Coke, then."

"Wrong again. We're here to have a by-god drink, lady. What will you have?"

She studied another nasty expression, deciding that the man could turn on anger like a faucet. "Rum and Diet Coke."

"That's more like it." He walked to the bar, ordered up the drinks, and returned, carrying her rum and Coke and a tall glass that appeared to be straight dark booze of some kind.

He raised his glass in a silent toast, waiting until she raised hers. Now he smiled his gap-toothed smile. *God, this is awful.* She sipped tentatively, worried about the interaction of alcohol and yesterday's ordeal and medication. He drank deeply, his eyes alternating between staring at her face and repeatedly, blatantly, scanning her neck and chest. She couldn't imagine that a sweater with a shallow V gave him much to stare at. He spoke straight at her chest. "What did you think of yesterday's Max?"

"I don't know what you mean."

"That was man-of-few-words Max. What did you think?"

His expression had turned pleasant. Maybe she could begin some dialog. Things had gone better with Baxter once she rose above the intimidation. "Can I be honest?"

He grinned, keeping his lips compressed, eyes still cast down. "Only if I like what you say."

"It's hard to like someone who hurts you. And you hurt me."

His grin became a leer. "I really need to break that tit biting habit." He raised his glass and, finally, his eyes. "Here's to the speedy recovery of Jackie's tit."

She eyed him, hoping he couldn't read her disgust. An emotional door had slammed in her mind. She didn't want to banter with this man. She wanted to get out of this horrible place as quickly as possible. "So give me the information."

She saw the eyes going black. "I don't care for your tone, lady."

She sighed. "I'm tired. I don't feel well. Please tell me whatever you're going to tell me, and let me go home."

"Drink."

She raised her glass and gulped once, hoping for some kind of lift of her spirits and her energy.

"Let's start with an idea you need to get, Jackie. You work with me, I'm nice. I'll even be nice, in a way, while we play our game. You screw me up, I'm the meanest so'bitch that ever lived. Clear?"

She nodded, trying to focus on a voice now echoing from some distant point.

"I'm a fair guy, a reasonable guy. Money by tomorrow is impossible, right? Deadline is now Friday, same gig, XYZ at noon."

"There's no way. Not by Friday. Probably not ever."

He smiled. The gapped teeth she knew too well were back, but the rage had departed. "Here's the deal, then. Cool by me on a delay. I've got all kinds of time. We meet at noon, Wednesdays and Fridays, at a nice little motel I've found—until the Friday you decide to meet me at XYZ." The smile broadened. "See. Reasonable, clear-cut answers, compliments of ol' Maxie."

"I…I don't know if—"

"Shut up a minute. I want to listen to this song."

She sat back, sipping silently, now hoping the drink might help her remain calm in an awful place, with an awful man drumming his fingers on the table, singing off-key, staring at her chest. The image of Collier—now signaling for silence through another song—began shimmering in front of her. She felt hot, although the place was drafty. She should have been growing restless, she thought, but she was oddly mellow, her mind a little hazy. Getting hazier.

The song ended. He leaned toward her, eyes black, intense. "Listen carefully, lady. I've been doing this for a long time. You're thinkin' bullshit like going to the police. You're thinkin' bullshit like telling me to stick it. No sex for Maxie. No money for Maxie. Don't think that kind of bullshit. I'll do more 'n tell your fucking story, lady. I know where you live. I know about Jodi. You'll just never know when I might drop by. I love seven-year-olds named Jodi. I'd love hearing her say 'oh, please, no'. Did you hear me, lady?"

She heard him. She tried for anger, for resistance, but something was terribly wrong with her brain. "So, Jackie. You be nice. 'ol Max is nice. You screw me up…" She blanked for a moment, but struggled back. She felt him take her arm, carrying her purse and coat, leading her outside toward her car. He had her electronic key. He unlocked the doors. He pushed her into the backseat.

She awoke slowly, as if floating upward out of a deep black sea. She was cold, shivering, although her coat had been thrown over her. She shook her head, hard, trying to clear her brain. *Oh, my God, I'm in my car. On my backseat. It's dark. Almost pitch black.* She reached up to turn on the dome light, trying to decide whether to be more afraid of what her wristwatch would tell her, or what her body would tell her. *Oh, God. 2:35.* Her breasts were bare; her sweater bunched at her shoulders. She reached beneath her coat, gritting her teeth when she touched the bite marks, exposed, still raw.

With fear spreading through her, she slid her hand down her stomach. Fingers hit her belt buckle and slacks. No sign he had undressed her, or worse. Her sense of gratitude ended swiftly. *God, this is horrible. It had to be a drug. What a miserable wretched bastard. What do I say to Matt?*

She sat up, looked for her bra, but couldn't find it. She pulled down the sweater, struggled into her coat, and fumbled on the floor for her purse. She found her cell phone, and checked the screen. Five messages. *Oh, damn. No need to wonder who called.*

She started driving, made her way toward downtown, and pulled into the empty parking lot of an Italian restaurant. Fear and anger had definitely blown the fog out of her brain. She called home. He answered instantly. "Jackie. Where the hell are you?" He sounded frantic.

"Matt, I'm so sorry. This is unreal. I'm in the back of the parking lot at Antonio's. I felt kind of sick after a glass of wine. I got in the car, leaned my head back, and I just woke up. I don't know what happened."

There was a long pause, a frightening pause. "But…who were you with?"

The trap was clear. "Some people in the audit department. I don't think you know any of them?" She hated being so glib. She hated Max Collier for making it necessary.

"Jesus. I've been calling everyone I could think of."

"I'm heading home now."

"Are you sure you're okay to drive."

She tried for a laugh. "I'm fine. I've had a nice long nap."

At home, Matt's attitude of loving compassion had suffered a clear setback. He told her about emotions starting with worry, shifting to anger, and ending with terror that she was injured or dead. He had been minutes away from calling the police. She tried to read him for suspicion or jealousy and saw clear signs of both. She didn't blame him. Her story was lame. She had to sneak off to re-dress her breast. She told twenty lies to cover the first set of lies. She got a miserable night's sleep. She felt fury rising.

At work she covered more lies. Matt had called Kaye Lassiter and three of her employees. "He was confused," she said. "I was with some old sorority sisters. I'm really sorry for all the concern." That was lame, too, and Kaye's raised eyebrows signaled major displeasure that Jackie had partied late on a work night.

At 11:15, Max Collier called her. "Surprised to be a virgin this morning?"

She sat silent, rage seething.

"I enjoy some things as much as sex, lady. Know what I mean? Sorry about the bra, though."

She sat silent.

"Who do you like better? Man-of-few-words Max, or cowboy Max?"

She sat silent.

"Don't piss me off, lady. I'd like to hear your voice now."

"Hello, Max."

"Do you remember everything we discussed last night?"

"Yes. Yes I do."

"I'm looking forward to seeing you at the motel today. Let me give you direc—"

"You'll see me at XYZ, at noon on Friday."

"Well, well, a pleasant surprise from my favorite set of tits. I trust you remember the rules."

"Yes, Max. I remember the rules. I remember everything."

"Good girl. See you then."

Chapter Twenty-Two

Jackie had made all necessary preparations, fairly simple compared to the decision itself. But she reached the decision based purely on a wife and mother's lack of alternatives. On Thursday night she tucked Jodi into bed and told her a feature length Elrod the Bear story. She then held her daughter, apparently a bit too tightly. "Golly, Mommy, you're gonna break me in two."

She spent a full half-hour in Sean's room, a conversation that started uneasily but warmed as she talked about computer games and asked whether there was a chance Tara Essinger would go on the hiking trip with him.

And, somehow, Matt forgave her enough to hold her and make tender love to her, despite a left breast that needed special consideration. Awareness of his love had become a wonderful but bittersweet part of her life. She appreciated him more than he could possibly know. But she regretted the shallow years. And she feared the abrupt end of the joy they were learning to share, because she couldn't see even twenty-four hours into the future.

After the kids headed for school on Friday, she held Matt in her arms, head against his chest. "I want you to know that I love you completely, no matter what happens. I wish I could just freeze this moment."

He touched her face and could feel the tears. "I love you too, but what's wrong?"

"It's just an emotional moment. I want you to know I love you and I'm sorry for making our lives so difficult."

"Everything's okay, Jackie. We'll be fine if we keep communicating."

***

Mark Coffey, a.k.a. Max Collier, rechecked his props inside the barn and swaggered across the clearing. Blustery clouds churned low hanging clouds above him. He entered the old farmhouse and anxiously checked the kitchen wall clock: 11:45.

He sat briefly at the kitchen table, glancing through the sports page. He walked into the living room—XYZ's high-tech command center—where he again checked the police monitor. They all think about involving the police, although this one is less likely than the others. She would rather die than let hubby know what she's been up to. He grinned. Okay, babes. No problem, compliments of your friend B.

Man, this is a kick-ass day for me. Absolutely kick ass. Too bad it can't be more often. Nah. I'm doing enough. This damn thing is risky and I damn sure can't go to jail. Prison camp fucked me up bad. No doubt about that. And I came too close to jail—what was it, five, six years ago when the bitch went to the cops? She sure as hell changed the game.

And now we have Jackie—soft in a way, tough in a way, and tough will make spreading those thighs a hundred times more fun. Wimps wimp. Whores pretend. Jackie is just right. Who knows? The broad might even like me. Ted and Dan both called her a real live genuine hottie.

All right! There's the signal. She's inside the perimeter. This monitor is cool as an Eskimo's balls. I like security. No surprises while I'm busy banging away. She's around the farmhouse, down to the barn. Out of the car.

These are kick-ass binoculars. What a looker. So good. So bad. So much going on inside that head and body. Kick ass.

Good girl, wearin' your trench coat just like you paid attention. Man, the thought of that babe, naked, cowering in front of me, is kick ass. Why do I like to humiliate them so much? Something my worthless piece of crap mama did to me? Or is the game screwing me up? Or the porn? Or the pills? Who am I, anyway? Hell, I used to play in Ted and Dan's league. Now I try just try to fake 'em. Oh, well. Time for fun now.

Good girl. Two briefcases, dead on for a hundred and fifty Gs. Now she thinks she can endure me for an afternoon and live happily ever after. Oh, Jackie.

Man, unreal, it's stiff-dick time already. Kick ass. She's inside. On the closed circuit. Money's on the tool bench. Very good. This is one hell of a system. Nothing like adding to your video collection, I always say. I'll make this one last all day. Play rape for a while. Straps and chains for a while. Improvise after that. Here's to Jackie Billings liking it. At least the first part. What a kick ass thought.

I'm going to do the same thing I did last time. Walk into the barn and drop my drawers right away. I love the look in their eyes. I'll bet they think, Man, I wouldn'ta thought that scrawny shit would be hung like a horse.

Okay. Here we go. A short stroll down to the barn, and the fun begins.

Okay, by the haystack, just like she's supposed to be.

"Time to take off the coat, Jackie."

I'll be damned. Look at the eyes. Not as afraid as I thought she'd be. That's okay. It's more fun when they aren't afraid at first.

"It's too cold, Max. But see, everything's fine."

Okay! Nice flip. Nice thighs, even for a big time tit man.

"Take the coat off, Jackie."

"Hey, Maxie, I thought we might just talk for a while. Okay?"

Whoa, bitch. Don't go getting flirty with me. You may decide you like me later, but don't be flirtin' around now. That's bullshit. Let's see what she thinks of this. Here bitch, here's today's star pecker.

"You're looking good, Maxie."

Son of a bitch. This is big time bullshit.

"I explained the game, Jackie. This kind of flirty bullshit isn't part of it."

"I want to play a different game."

"Don't screw with me, lady. Play my game or…"

Okay. She's backing up. Lying back on the hay. Lookin' good, but still in the coat. And the eyes. What the hell?

"C'mon, Maxey. Play my game. Why don't you come over and see if you can do some good."

Okay, Jackie. Time for all the bullshit to stop.

"I'll do some good all right, right after I loosen a couple of your fucking teeth. Get ready, you smart ass bitch."

What's that? Shit. A gun. A fuckin' .38. Clever try, babes, but I'm not buyin' that bullshit. We've studied you like a bug under glass. Here I come, bitch. How 'bout I take your gun and pistol whip your ass—maybe ram it inside you.

The eyes. God. Steely. A soldier's eyes.

Jesus, Jesus, Jesus, she shot me. My stomach. Oh, god, what the hell?

"Stop, no… Aaah, fuck…"

God, my chest, no... "Aaah." … *Shot me again...oh, fuck... her eyes... steel... falling... falling ... blood everywhere... not supposed to be my blood... I'm going to die.*

Jackie rose from the straw and brushed off her coat. She put on her slacks, found a shovel, walked to the nearest tree stand, and dug a hole as deep as her strength and the cold Ohio soil would allow.

She dragged the twisted body of Max Collier to the edge, pushed him in, returned the dirt, pounded it down, and covered the site with brush and branches. She returned the shovel, cleaned up blood, and used a broom and a rake to smooth away marks in the dirt and gravel. She put a gun and two briefcases full of newspapers into her trunk. And she drove toward Columbus in a green Town Car. She had no idea where that part of her plan came from, but she followed it as if scripted, vaguely aware that her focused fury had become cold but focused determination to be done with this business and return to her home.

Jackie drove in broad daylight into the inner city and easily found two men happy to believe that her "miserable two-timing husband doesn't deserve a Lincoln Town Car." She would happily trade it for a ride into the country. She suggested they use it for parts. They told her they knew what to do with Lincoln Town Cars. She returned to the XYZ Farm's out gate, thanked her unlikely new friends, headed for her own car, and drove home. She left Matt's pistol in her trunk, wrapped in rags and newspapers.

She entered the kitchen and decided to microwave a cup of water for tea. And in the 2:30 that she waited—studying with a new kind of interest the warm decorations and refrigerator-mounted photos of the place her family often gathered—Jackie's mind refused to grasp that she could have killed a man or coolly entered the inner city. But she grasped one thing, with every fiber of her heart, mind, and soul. The miserable bastard loved seven-year olds named Jodi. He would love to hear Jodi say, *oh, please, no*. Her Jodi was safe.

Only when she reached her bathtub did the enormity hit her. She cried for over an hour, a deep, sobbing, cleansing cry. She tried to talk to God about it, even though she didn't know or understand Him very well. She tried to find compartments for her guilt and fear. She tried, but failed completely, to analyze the link between

Collier and Agent Baxter. And she tried to visualize the avenues her life might take.

When Matt came home, he noticed that she was quieter than normal; her eyes looked almost haunted. But they shared a near-normal evening including pizza and a video with the kids. She wanted to make tender love again. His aggressive lady suddenly loved making tender love. But he was okay with it. He realized that he was a long way from understanding her. He hadn't finished struggling with Tuesday night. Not a guy in a hundred would buy a story about falling asleep in a restaurant parking lot. Thinking about the possibility of another man ripped him apart. *But I love her. I just plain love her. And since Sean hit me with the idea that I frighten my own family, I've been even more determined to do better. So please, Jackie, let the Tuesday story be true. Please love me back. Always.*

Chapter Twenty-Three

Jackie's Saturday began at 12:01 a.m. She had found temporary solace in the normalcy of their Friday evening. But sleep had eluded her completely. Beside her, snoring peacefully, lay her husband, oblivious that she had snuggled up against him, as close as she could find a way to be. She tickled his cheek with her hair and gently stroked his chest, smiling when he twitched or snorted. She tried consciously to enjoy those few playful moments, because she had made the hardest decision of her life, a decision she prayed Matt would survive.

She couldn't possibly handle this alone. She faced terrifying decisions and she couldn't even think clearly. She couldn't talk to friends or relatives. She remembered reading that they would become accessories or something like that. She guessed that an attorney would be important soon, but she had no idea where to turn. Their attorney was a guy named Paul Dorsett who did Matt's corporate work. She couldn't imagine talking to Paul, a longtime friend of the Billings family and their neighbor.

Only Matt gave her a chance for real support, but it could only work on an honest basis. No more lies. No deceit. No secret attorney meetings or hidden invoices. No fear that someone would reveal something horrible and destroy their marriage. She worried that her mind was hazy, maybe even in shock; that telling Matt everything might be a terrible idea. Dr. Geiger had said to go slow. Jackie also worried about his physical reaction, about his heart. But she couldn't wait.

***

At 7:00 a.m. on Saturday morning, Daniel Berringer called Ted Aldrich. Per their guidelines, Berringer would continue to use his alias until project's end. As always, Ted Aldrich played boldly, using his given name.

"We have a problem in Columbus."

"What was the timetable?" asked Aldrich.

"C-Phase wrap up was noon yesterday; D-Phase at midnight. No signal."

They didn't need to discuss the reason for concern. If Collier had been arrested, he would have used his allowed phone call to contact their crisis line. Baxter would have launched L-Plan, their legal contingency.

"Scenarios?"

Baxter paused, assessing. "Took the goodies and ran. Probability close to zero."

"Agreed. Flaky but loyal."

"Dead. Ambushed by the law. Fifteen percent."

"Tops. He's careful. I can't see her going to the law."

"Being held by the law as bait. Five percent."

"Agreed, same analysis. But let's be careful of that one, old buddy."

"Unrelated accident. Ten percent."

Aldrich's chuckle lacked mirth. "You're seriously short on probability points."

"That would be correct. I'll launch R-Plan and get back to you."

Daniel Andrew Berringer put his huge hands behind his head and rocked back in his swivel chair. He gazed out wide-paneled walkout doors. In the valley below him, two deer foraged at the edge of an increasingly barren west Pennsylvania forest. Of course, the reconnaissance job would be his, and Daniel felt some of the old fire return to his belly. He relished every minute of slipping into a city, doing his job, and escaping in the nick of time, hopefully before the gunfire began. But a little gunfire would be okay.

Daniel stood, gave two deer a farewell salute, and ambled up the stairs into the kitchen. "There's an emergency in Ohio. I've got to head over there right away." His wife looked up from her computer and nodded. They never asked questions.

***

Matt Billings began his Saturday morning by whipping up buckwheat pancakes for the family, contributing his only culinary skill other than peanut-butter sandwiches and burgers on the grill. He coached Sean's team to victory in a good soccer game. They lunched at McDonald's. Sean left to spend the day with Matt's mother. Jackie had arranged playtime for Jodi at Jamesons', so Matt wondered whether his wife might be planning an afternoon adventure. He had begun, if slowly, to enjoy her unpredictable erotic side. *Dr. Tollison is right. Therapy can be fun.*

She asked him to join her for hot chocolate in the living room, their home's adult retreat. "Build a fire, Matt." They shared a brief smile as he pointed the remote toward their gas logs and flicked. They settled into twin recliners flanking the fireplace, sipping the hot chocolate. She was wearing a lavender sweat suit; he was speculating about what she was wearing under it. But something changed in her. She began visibly struggling for breath. The cup trembled in her hands. He knew that this meeting would not be about playtime.

"Matt, I would almost rather die than have this talk." She continued to stare into the flames, her voice soft, pained. "I've got things to tell you that…that no man should ever have to hear from a woman."

Man, that's a scary opening. We were just eating Big Macs together.

"I'm going to start with the worst. I'm afraid if I start at the beginning, we may not make it to the end."

He felt palpable fear grip his chest, "What the hell are you—?"

"Matt, I…I killed a man yesterday."

His mind reeled. At first he couldn't believe it. He almost laughed. But her eyes told him that something had happened. "What? In a car? Hit and run? What…?"

She shook her head. "No. With your gun. With the pistol from the cabinet downstairs."

Now his mind felt like tires spinning on ice. At first he couldn't imagine it at all, but he remembered that she and Sherry had taken a firearms class after a rapist struck in a nearby neighborhood a few years ago. Matt had fully supported her knowing how to defend herself. Finally a possibility came to him. "Was he attacking you?"

"In a way. But now I have to start at the beginning." She stared into the fire for a long moment then turned to look into his eyes. "Do you remember what I said yesterday, about loving you no matter what happens?"

"Yes," he replied, his voice husky, his heart thudding.

"I know I don't deserve it. But I wish that somehow you could feel the same way when I'm finished."

He felt his eyes glazing. His throat went tight. *Your wife tells you she used your gun to kill a man then braces you for the bad news. What the hell?*

She started in a flat monotone, never looking up from the fire. She told of meeting a man named Ted Aldrich on the plane. He teased her with the idea of being more adventuresome. Mia helped her arrange a Michael massage. It turned incredibly erotic and ignited a kind of fire inside her that she didn't even know was smoldering.

Matt tried forlornly to block the vision of his nearly naked wife being aroused by a stranger. He tried to block memories of all the deceit. He felt his heart pounding too hard; his breathing had gone shallow. "Stop for a minute. I need to get some water." He went to the kitchen, drank, refilled the glass, and walked twice around the oval made by their kitchen, dining room, family room and entryway. He returned to his chair, holding the water glass in hands now trembling.

She told him about Aldrich. About their times together and how he taught her about sexuality. This time Matt dragged himself up the stairs to their bedroom. He lay on his back, staring at a ceiling that shimmered in front of his eyes. His mind felt numb, as if a blow had knocked him nearly unconscious, but not numb enough. There were too many images. He could feel his heart racing. He closed his eyes, took a long series of deep breaths, and returned to the chair.

She told him about Baxter's investigation and her fear of exposure and about another seduction, though brief—the moment that convinced her that she must face serious problems of her own. She told him about Collier and the demand for both sex and money. She told him that Collier was trying to destroy everything; that Collier had even threatened Jodi. "So I killed him. I shot him three times, and I buried him, and I tried to make the evidence go away." She turned to look at Matt, her eyes liquid, pleading. "I'm so sorry for all the lies. It just started and it got out of control and God, Matt, I don't ever want to lie to you again. I don't know what to do. You're the only person I can talk to."

Through the last ten minutes, Matt had not moved except for the slow circular motion of his jaw muscle. His eyes now stared blankly at the dancing flames. He sat silent for five more minutes, waiting for his heart rate to slow. The wood clock on the fireplace inched slowly toward three o'clock. He turned toward her, tortured eyes filling with tears. "Jackie, I think you've killed two men."

He pulled himself up slowly and looked down at her. She met his eyes for a few seconds, but looked away. He climbed the stairway, found a leather bag, and threw clothing and his shaving kit into it. He carried the bag downstairs and opened the front door.

She had walked into the foyer as he descended the stairs, her face anxious, her eyes fearful. He said, "I've got to go somewhere, Jackie. I don't know where. I don't know when I'll be back. Or if."

And he closed the door, softly, behind him.

***

Don Baxter drove west, stopping once to change personas. He transformed the angular face into a face with beard and mustache. The hawk-like gray eyes became blue. R-Plan assumed the worst: that the posse might be waiting for him at the edge of town and another posse might be formed up at XYZ.

At 3:25 p.m., he passed the Dublin city limits sign. Ten minutes later, he pulled the dark blue sedan to a stop in front of 4146 Duncan Place in the White Oak Estates subdivision. He waited patiently, watching, needing to know the answer to a crucial question, perhaps several.

At 4:15, a pony-tailed little girl skipped up the sidewalk. "Are you Jodi?" he asked through the open window.

"Yes, but I'm not allowed to talk to you, mister."

"It's okay, Jodi." He showed his badge. "I'm one of the good guys. Is your mommy home?"

"Yes, she's inside"

"Is your daddy home?"

"No, he went somewhere."

"Tell your mommy that Agent Baxter would like to speak with her."

"Okay, mister." She dashed up the sidewalk.

Jackie looked out the front window at the man leaning against the front bumper of a plain blue sedan: definitely Baxter, but different. She searched her mind for options and found none. She wondered whether she could find the strength to deal with him, but knew she had to try. She thought back to the emotion-filled afternoon they spent at XYZ and marveled that its significance felt dwarfed by new events. Hopefully, though, Baxter still had positive feelings for her. She put on her coat, told Jodi to stay inside, and walked through the front door.

"Hello, Jackie."

She tried for casual as she strolled out the sidewalk. "Why the disguise?"

"I'm undercover in Cincinnati." He looked left and right, as if checking for possible listeners. "We may have a problem."

"What kind of problem?"

"The man named Collier who visited you."

Her stomach jumped; her mind raced, but her thinking seemed clear. She wondered whether some kind of survival instinct had gone to work. "I thought you didn't know anything about him."

"I was less than forthcoming about Collier. He's a problem."

She tried to analyze on the fly. She would admit what he could easily verify, but nothing more. She knew that she should have sought an attorney's advice, but it was too late to worry about that now. "Why do *we* have a problem?"

"Collier is an FBI informant who turns out to be a punk shakedown artist. I was careless with some information. The ballsy bastard set up a way to end my career if I didn't back off."

"He made it sound like you were helping him."

"That's surely not the case, but I'm not surprised the little bastard would say it."

"He's not a nice man."

"So the S.O.B. extorts you, too. Damn it. I am truly sorry, Jackie."

She tried for a sarcastic smile. "Sex and money, that's all."

"Did he get any?"

She sensed no try at humor "No. He made a mistake."

"Which was?"

"He bit me so hard that I went to the hospital."

Baxter shook his head. "Unbelievable. Was there a police report?"

"I thought you would already have it."

"I'm not in that loop. What did you tell them?"

She processed rapidly. Admitting to the FBI that she had lied to the Columbus Police would be risky, but Baxter appeared genuinely uneasy, apparently fearful of being personally implicated with Collier's misdeeds, whatever they were. "I told them a boy-friend bit me. The truth was too, uh, too complicated."

He reflected for a moment then smiled broadly. "That is very good, Jackie. You saved both of us some trouble." He paused again, brow furrowed. "What did you tell your husband?"

"I told him the truth, all of it. Even about you."

Now she saw surprise in Baxter's face, possibly concern. "I'm amazed. So what became of Max Collier?"

She didn't hesitate. "I have no idea."

"What's your best guess?"

She had anticipated this question. "He probably saw me faint; probably knew I was going to the hospital and there would be a police report. Maybe he just ran away."

"So he didn't contact you later, to try to cash in?"

She sensed deep water but could find only one answer that didn't lead down the road toward discussing her final meeting with Collier. "No. I didn't hear from him."

He frowned before his mouth lifted in a tight smile. She felt a tremor ripple through her stomach. "I'll be in touch, Jackie."

Back in her kitchen, Jackie tried to analyze the Baxter exchange. At first he had been friendly, but at the end he had gone into a mode she hadn't seen before. Had he seen through her lie? If so, why hadn't he challenged her on it? What was he doing now? The tremor in her stomach became terror rising. She considered trying to reach Matt but decided he had endured enough for one day. She called Sherry Jameson. "Can Jodi and I come to your place for a slumber party tonight?"

"Sure. What's up?"

"It's too long a story, Sherry. I just need some company."

They spent a quiet evening, happily absent deep discussion. They put Jodi to bed early, sipped a little wine, and watched *Elmer Gantry* on AMC. Ty became an oddly gracious host, attentive to Jackie's opinions and need for wine refills—friendly to an extent that sometimes felt awkward as a threesome. But Ty was gulping manhattans from a very tall glass, so Jackie declared his attention understandable, and barely on the radar screen of her life's challenges.

Chapter Twenty-Four

During Don Baxter's drive toward XYZ Farm, he carefully analyzed his session with Jackie. She had been remarkably cool—too cool to make sense—almost as if coached. For a few minutes there on her sidewalk, he had actually feared a worst-case scenario: that Collier had been nabbed and had implicated Baxter-Aldrich. And that Baxter was talking to a wired police accomplice while a hidden squad listened intently.

But if that had been the case, he would now be wearing handcuffs. Therefore, he had to conclude that Jackie Billings had been operating on her own. She told a piece of fascinating truth when she admitted lying to a law enforcement agency. At the moment of that confessional, Baxter assumed he was dealing with a completely forthright woman. Then she told a bald-faced lie. Collier had called him late on Wednesday morning to report pleasant surprise that Jackie would be visiting XYZ on Friday. Baxter had gone on alert, ready for the signal that would launch D-Phase on Friday evening. Collier had most certainly contacted Jackie after the police report.

Collier is dead, he thought, at a ninety-five percent certainty. If alive, he would have called, unless law enforcement was holding him as bait, and we just eliminated that scenario on Jackie's sidewalk. An unrelated accident would explain his death but would have been covered in the media that Baxter monitored carefully. A police execution would have received media coverage. So who killed him? Son of a bitch; I can't believe where this analysis is leading. A wry grin formed as he shook his head. No. Can't be. There's no way in hell that Jackie Billings actively participated in a scenario that handled Collier. I've studied her too closely, defeated her too easily. Hell, candy from a baby. There has to be another explanation, and I need to find it quickly.

He drove to the farm but did not enter. He drove all roads surrounding the farm, but saw no signs of activity. He called Aldrich. "Jackie Billings is safely at home. I'm at XYZ now."

"Any clues?"

"Nothing yet. I'll wait on the perimeter until morning."

"Why the delay?"

"It's almost dark, and there's a chance this place is a trap."

"What are you thinking?" asked Aldrich, detecting unusual uncertainty in his long-time associate.

"This thing is very strange. Very complex. I'll fill you in later."

"I wonder if our video feed will show anything."

Baxter chuckled. "Maybe. In at least one of my scenarios, we might have some damned interesting footage."

***

Jodi snoozed peacefully in one of two single beds in the Jameson guest room. Jackie lay wide-awake in the other, her mind racing uncontrollably: I don't think I handled the Baxter meeting well, especially the last part. Why did I even try? How long will it take the FBI to figure out what happened? What will it feel like when they show up at the house to take me away? Will they handcuff me? What if Jodi and Sean are there?

I can't get Max Collier's face out of my mind. I hated the awful, obnoxious leering. When the leer turned to terror, I thought he deserved it. But then the face twisted into a kind of pain I've never seen. And I can't forget the sound when his body thudded into the bottom of the hole I dug.

I can't get Matt's face out of my mind. Twisted in pain that I caused. And the sound of the door closing. Did I make a terrible mistake? Was I focused on me, and not thinking enough about Matt? Did I do the very thing that would drive him away, at the time I need him most? Could I have explained things better? Maybe a little less honest, but still honest enough? Will he divorce me? Will I ever get to sleep?

***

At sunrise, Don Baxter opened the gate and drove to the XYZ barn where he found the door unlocked. Once inside, his practiced eye left him ninety percent certain that he need not fear police surveillance. He walked to the farmhouse and filled in the other ten percent. As anticipated, Collier planned to add to his video collection. Although slightly grainy, the images told the whole story, sight and sound, shot from above and behind Collier.

I sure as hell underestimated that lady, thought Baxter, as he rewound and played for the third time. She took him apart, not only physically but also psychologically. His face twisted into a sardonic smile. In a way, the shithead got exactly what he deserved. I wonder if she shot at the dong he was so proud of.

He chortled at her weak efforts to cover the crime scene—definitely a first-timer, although she apparently knew enough to ditch the car. His admiration for Jackie Billings soared. He ejected the video, placed it carefully in his briefcase, and called Aldrich.

"Prepare for a shocker, Theodore. Your long-legged, cuddly brunette blew the balls off Mark Coffey."

"What the hell are you saying?"

"Hit him three times, dead center, with what looked like a .38 and dragged his ass offstage, pecker still fully erect."

"I'll be damned; dead for sure?"

"In living color; as good a job as I've ever seen; surprise and result."

Aldrich chuckled. "You apparently missed something on her profile."

"Apparently."

"Do we have a plan?"

"No," replied Baxter, "no contingency for this."

"I'd say you need to take her out."

"There's no hurry. Obviously, she's not talking. There's no way the law knows he's out here. I'll meditate a bit."

"Take her out."

"I thought you loved her."

"Not that much."

Baxter understood Aldrich's assumption that Jackie Billings would be eliminated. He thought back to their Pittsburgh project. What was her name? Alice, Alicia, something like that, Radcliff. Got so pissed at Coffey—Max Cavendish at the time—that she headed straight to the police. At least C read it and delivered a swift warning. Her death was a B masterpiece. Less than twenty-four hours to assess and strike. A lady who enjoyed quaffing a few. Husband gone in a jealous rage. Alone in a fifth-floor condo. Surprised her after work. Ten or twelve, what were they? Gin and tonic, I think; her favorite drink, at gunpoint. Passed out. Over the balcony. Beautiful. The law was all over that one, but couldn't prove murder and must not have had time for sketches of Coffey's sorry mug.

So what to do with Jackie? Ted's right. Letting her live is dangerous. But C bit Jackie's tit. There's a chance C bit Pittsburgh's tit. Damn it, I should've checked before I tossed her off the balcony. Two dead women with bit tits, and we have the FBI in the game, sure as hell. Do I want that much intrigue?

***

The phone rang at 4:30 on Sunday afternoon. Sherry rose to pick up the rec room extension. Jackie looked up from the *Flubber* movie they were watching, hopeful.

"Hi, Matt. Yes, Jodi and Jackie are here. Sean and Brett are over at Fitzwater's. Where are you?" Sherry listened and nodded.

"Okay. I'll tell her."

Sherry hung up the phone. "Matt's at home. He wants you to go over. He asked that Jodi stay here for a few minutes."

Jackie put on her jacket and walked toward their house, eerily aware that she might not be welcome in her own home. She opened the front door and started down the hall toward the kitchen. She could hear the gentle hiss of the fireplace, and she found him sitting in the same recliner, watching the flames. He didn't turn toward her. She moved to her chair and sat silently, waiting, not knowing what to say.

He turned toward her. The rugged face looked haggard; his eyes were deeply rimmed; his expression etched with pain. "Jackie, I don't know if I can do this for the long pull. I just don't know. But I won't leave you now."

Her eyes filled with tears. She started to speak, but her throat seemed to close. She cried softly at first but couldn't hold back the flood.

Matt rose to find Kleenex then watched as she sat huddled in the chair, sobbing, dabbing her eyes and nose. He felt waves of compassion doing battle with still-seething pain and fury. He guessed that his father would have called him pitifully weak, but he held out his hand, lifted her gently from the chair, and wrapped her in his arms.

She stood on tiptoes, arms around his neck, kissing his cheeks and lips. "Matt, I love you more than I could ever say." She managed to smile through her tears. "Sorry." And she raised a soaked Kleenex to his very moist cheek.

He met her eyes but could not muster a smile. "I'm doing my best, Jackie."

"Will we survive this?"

"Let's just survive today."

Jodi skipped down the hall and around the corner. "Hi, Daddy. Wow, what's the matter, Mommy? Your face is all wet. Both your faces are all wet." Matt picked her up and they surrounded their little girl in a silent love circle.

They struggled through an evening having normalcy as its own goal: the family's favorite meatloaf dinner, a video, computer games with Sean, an Elrod story for Jodi. But at 11:00, Matt and Jackie lay in bed, side-by-side, staring upward into the darkness.

Matt said, "I feel mostly numb, like this isn't real; that it will somehow go away."

"It isn't going away. Baxter from the FBI was here today, looking for Collier."

"Why didn't you tell me before?"

"I thought you had enough to deal with."

After several silent minutes, he said, "We aren't smart enough to decide how to handle this; whether to go to the police, or hope it's never discovered, or…"

"I know. I've been thinking about all that, non-stop."

He tried for quiet assurance. "We'll come up with a plan."

Chapter Twenty-Five

After the kids left for school, Matt said, “I’m going to get us an appointment with Paul Dorsett, today if possible.”

“This isn’t his kind of case is it? And he knows a lot of our friends.”

“We’ll tell him we’re asking for a family friend from Dayton. It’ll work.”

She couldn’t imagine that it would work. “I don’t like it, Matt.”

“Damn it, Jackie,” he snapped, “I don’t like it either, but we’ve got to know where we stand. You haven’t given us many good choices.”

She couldn’t blame him for the anger, and she had no better alternatives. “Okay, let’s try Paul.”

Jackie struggled through a reasonably productive morning at the office. The guilt she expected hadn’t hit her. *I love little girls named Jodi...hearing her say oh, please, no.* She had less success quelling the fear. At 11:00, he called.

“This is Baxter. I’ll be at your house tonight at nine sharp. Be there.”

“Why are you coming?”

“To discuss Max Collier,” he said tersely, a sharp edge in his voice.

She closed her eyes and exhaled silently. “What about Max Collier?”

“His strange disappearance.”

She tried to keep her voice steady. “All right. Nine will be fine.”

Jackie got up and paced her small office, fighting waves of anxiety that threatened to overwhelm her. Why did she even dream she could deceive a veteran investigator? Now she agreed completely with Matt's decision to contact Paul Dorsett. They needed information, quickly. She spent a long, restless morning, no longer able to focus on anything.

***

Baxter called Aldrich. "Jackie Billings may be bulletproof."

"Meaning?"

"The Columbus police may have enough information to link her to Pittsburgh."

Aldrich paused to contemplate. He hadn't liked the D-phase decision, but now that die was cast. "I think it's safer to take her out, no matter what."

"It's complicated. The woman in Pittsburgh talked to police about extortion and being with two men. Our M.O. is in that file. If Billings dies, the link may be simple."

"How could they possibly link her?"

Baxter hesitated before delivering truth he had never mentioned. "Regrettably we have the possibility of Coffey's trademark."

"What the hell is Coffey's trademark?"

"A major chomp into a target's left tit."

"That asshole bit Jackie Billings?"

"Affirmative."

"Are you saying there was a bite in Pittsburgh?"

"Unclear."

"Wouldn't the press have covered it?"

"They didn't. It might not have happened. They might have respected her privacy. Or the police might have suppressed for investigative reasons."

"Odds assessment?"

"Fifty-fifty."

"Well shit," growled Aldrich. "So you knew about this damn trademark?"

"I thought it added intrigue."

"Let me suggest a place for you to stick your goddam intrigue."

Baxter laughed. "Fear not, Mr. A. All is under control."

***

Paul Dorsett sat at his cluttered desk in an office piled high with blueprints, proposals, and contracts, hands folded in front of him, striving to appear remotely calm. Dorsett was a slight man, not tough, even in his own mind. He had been practicing law for twenty-two years and had been fortunate enough to find a slice of the legal business that let him eke out a decent living. But he struggled, even in his specialty, and stress more than heredity had robbed him of his hair. Painfully, his self-confidence had receded with his hairline.

Of course, he had happily agreed to meet with Jackie and Matt. He went back fifteen years with Billings Construction, although he had barely survived old Clancy. But he had expected to be talking zoning and construction, for God's sake. And now they were talking criminal law, hiding behind transparent baloney about a cousin in Dayton. They were either talking about themselves—a notion he couldn't grasp at all—or someone they cared about deeply. His best guess was Ty and Sherry Jameson, although even that possibility was hard to fathom.

And then Matt delivered the crown jewel—that the cousin shot an extortionist three times and buried the evidence. Dorsett gulped, embarrassed that his astonishment had become audible. "Are you shitting me? Pardon my French. Shot him?"

Matt nodded. "Yes."

Dorsett knew his voice had sounded high-pitched. He could feel perspiration forming on his brow and under his armpits. He wiped his glasses for several seconds, trying to silently clear his throat. "And why didn't she just go to the police in the first place?"

Matt answered. "He was a vicious man; she was frightened; she was certain he would harm her daughter."

"Was there any documented threat to the daughter, other than the verbal representations of the mother?"

"I don't think so."

Dorsett began to think it odd that Jackie was here, yet so uninvolved. He asked, "Where did the shooting take place?"

"In a barn in the country."

"Did he force her to go with him to the barn?"

"No. Well, yes, in a way. She went because of his demands."

"Was she physically forced to go to this barn?"

"No."

"Did she take the extortion money with her?"

"No."

"Was he armed?

"No."

"Did he attack her?"

"She thought he was going to."

"Was he attacking her when he was shot?

"No."

"So we're saying she pulled a gun she had brought with her, shot an unarmed man three times, and buried the evidence?"

"Yes."

Dorsett looked at Matt, at Jackie, and back at Matt. He inhaled, exhaled slowly, and ran an unsteady hand across his brow. "If you're here to ask my opinion about the charge, I'd say murder one."

Color drained instantly from Matt's face. "Even if he threatened her child?"

"I'd say a sympathetic jury might give her murder two. Maybe. Maybe not. On murder one, she probably avoids the death penalty, just life in prison. On murder two, maybe twenty, thirty years."

"Any chance of temporary insanity?"

"It sounds calculated. Cold blooded. I'd say you'd... she'd... never get insanity."

At that moment, Paul Dorsett knew they were talking about themselves. They shared an expression unlike anything he had ever seen. "Excuse me for a minute, guys, I've got to look something up." He closed the office door behind him, rushed to the disheveled cubbyhole he called his library, and frantically flipped pages: *attorney-client privilege, duty of an officer of the court, client confidentiality.* Twenty minutes later, he felt slightly more qualified to advise them, but he knew he was a fish out of water.

"Matt, Jackie, I'm going to choose my words carefully. If your cousin goes to an attorney, and probably she should, he must encourage her to confess the crime. However, he can't force her to confess, and he has no duty to inform authorities of the crime. He might tell her to leave; in other words, that he does not want to take the case. Or he might discuss the defense options. Does that make sense?"

Matt said, "Yes, I think so." Jackie remained silent, her mouth a tight, grim line.

Paul Dorsett wiped his brow with his fingers, adjusted his glasses, and cleared his throat. "Is there any chance the woman's husband has been involved in a cover-up?"

Matt said, "I'm not sure," his voice thin, strained. "I think he might have cleaned the gun, or maybe got rid of it."

Dorsett blew breath through pursed lips. "If so, he is likely an accessory after the fact. He might be facing three to five years. The children might become wards of the state." The lawyer watched as Jackie blinked her eyes.

"Thank you, Paul," said Matt, as he helped his wife to her feet, put his arm around her, and guided her through the door.

Paul Dorsett closed his office immediately and walked across the street to the bar at the Klondike Restaurant. He would miss dinner again. He would miss little Angela's piano recital. Kate would be furious. He would be lucky to get his car and himself home in one piece. But he didn't care.

***

As 9:00 p.m. inched toward them, Jackie and Matt waited in the family room. They had asked Jodi and Sean to remain in their rooms, an unusual instruction that painted new concern onto the faces of two kids who had already weathered enough concern. Jackie hated that more than anything. They had tried twice to discuss the news delivered by Paul Dorsett, but the enormity stopped them cold. On the third try, they decided that confessing made no sense. There was at least a chance of avoiding discovery. Confession brought consequences too awful to contemplate.

At precisely 9:00, the doorbell chimed. "I guess that's him," said Matt. He started to rise, but slumped backward. "I don't think I can open the door for him."

Jackie understood and went to the front door. Don Baxter, wearing a dark suit under an unbuttoned topcoat, entered without comment. She led him into the family room. "Matt, this is Agent Baxter. Don, this is my husband."

The two men nodded slightly "This won't take long, but I'll need a video player," said Baxter, gesturing toward their entertainment center. "Is it working?"

"It's working," said Matt.

Baxter handed Matt a cassette. "Your copy. Play it."

As Matt activated the system, Baxter folded into his chair. Matt sat beside Jackie on the couch. From the first frame, Jackie sensed disaster. She feared for herself, but mostly for her children. "No, no, wait! Matt, pause it. Turn down the volume. Let me close some doors."

Baxter allowed the preparations and ordered Matt to resume. The action played like a scene from a B movie. She waited for Collier. She flipped her coat hem before lying on the straw to taunt him into coming closer. She could imagine what it would look like to a jury. Her face didn't say fright or even confusion, just focused determination. The first loud pop. Collier staggering backward. Two more pops. Collier sprawling, twitching, then still. Jackie slipping calmly into her slacks, her eyes hard, mouth set in a grim line…finding a shovel…fast-forward…dragging Collier's body away…fast forward…trying to sweep away all evidence.

Jackie closed her eyes, her breathing audible. Matt sat dead still; his eyes two blank slates. Baxter said, "Anything to say?"

"Don't say anything at all," said Matt. He shook his head as if trying to engage his brain, and turned toward Baxter. "What happens next?"

"Probably not what you're expecting." Baxter looked at them with an odd smile. "I told Jackie on Saturday that *we* have a problem. That is true. This entire episode cannot come to light, including my indiscretion with Jackie. My offer is straightforward. I will go to XYZ and cleanse your crime scene. It would not survive two minutes of professional scrutiny. I will not reveal the murder. You will not reveal my unfortunate professional lapses. You will quietly live your lives. To monitor your compliance, I will call Jackie's office daily at eleven a.m. for the next sixty days. Weekly after that for six months. Do you understand my offer?"

They sat for a long moment, trying to grasp that the assassin's gun had misfired at pointblank range. Finally, Jackie said, "That's it?"

"Yes. Do we have an agreement?"

Jackie and Matt looked at each other with expressions mixing relief with disbelief. They nodded.

Baxter's gaze moved slowly from Matt to Jackie before locking ferociously on Matt. "Don't ever cross me, guys. I like Jackie. I've busted my ass for her. You got a break, too, friend. Don't ever cross me." He rose, looked once more into their faces, and left the room. The front door slammed loudly behind him.

"Where will it end, Matt? It just gets deeper and deeper."

"If we're lucky, it will end now. Then we can see if we have a marriage left."

"This doesn't make any sense."

"I don't care if it makes sense. We just need it to end."

"Did we have any choice?" she asked. "The deal, I mean."

"I don't think so."

"Neither do I."

***

For Matt and Jackie Billings, a new kind of life began. The sound of a siren delivered terror. They read the daily newspaper with fear. They listened to the nightly news with fear. They tried to love their children with new awareness of the precious gift of time—but the possibility of loss hung like an ominous, ever-present cloud.

But a blessedly uneventful week passed. Baxter called daily as promised. Jackie assured him that all was quiet and normal. But in their private conversations, Jackie and Matt wondered whether life could ever again be truly normal.

Chapter Twenty-Six

Link Pettigrew alternately pounded the keys of his keyboard, mouse-clicked his way among multiple databases, and jotted notes into the spiral-bound tablet that he clung to, despite the great march of technology. Link worked in an FBI department that looked for unusual crime patterns, and he may have found a prizewinner. He scanned his notes while waiting for the daily walk-through of his departmental supervisor.

Pettigrew was a twenty-two-year FBI veteran. In his early years, he had served in four field offices, facing his share of con men, con women, mobsters, thugs, and gunfire. For the last five years, he had been assigned to the FBI's sprawling, catacomb-like headquarters facility in Washington. His latest assignment blended his fascination with computers and a seasoned veteran's talent for intuitive analysis.

Pettigrew's opportunity evolved from a piece of blatant empire building by Darren McSoley, an attorney turned FBI agent turned computer guru. Aware that the twenty-first century FBI had been stung by criticism of its antiquated computer system, McSoley conceived and sold a new department now known as CAP: Computer Analysis of Patterns. In layman's terms, McSoley's department, which he smugly called *Mac's Team*, used ingenuity and technology to cross-index unusual occurrences that might suggest criminal activity.

Mac's Team scored early in the field of white-collar crime because their methods were ideally suited to uncovering patterns such as stock manipulation and price fixing. But McSoley was eager to build a reputation in terrorism and street crime as well.

Always politically astute, McSoley had focused four of his twelve investigators on terrorism. Three studied white-collar crime. Two dealt with violent crime. One concentrated on drug-related activity. The other two, Link Pettigrew happily included, were free to roam wherever their imaginations, or McSoley's ambition, took them.

Link Pettigrew, under orders from Mac, was now exploring serial murder. He knew that McSoley's goal was political: to discover, solve and publicize a high-profile case. But Pettigrew enjoyed the challenge. He also knew that McSoley would allow him to actively investigate. Working the computer was challenging, and safe. His wife liked that, mostly because she never overcame fear of receiving that solemn visit: *Your husband died heroically, Mrs. Pettigrew, in the service of the Bureau and of justice.* But Link needed to get into the field now and then. Darren McSoley could be a major pain in his backside, but Link Pettigrew had found the perfect assignment.

McSoley entered the oversized cubicle that served as Link Pettigrew's office. They were an odd couple. McSoley was blonde and blue eyed, with a perpetually youthful face. Some joked that he could be poster boy for the next FBI recruiting campaign. Link Pettigrew was black, lean, and muscular, the result of an hour daily in the onsite gymnasium. His hair was close-cropped and flecked with gray that he called premature. His eyes were deep-set, probing, usually friendly, always alert. He had no interest in being promoted to management, no tolerance for politics, and a history of edgy relationships with his superiors.

"Come up with anything?" asked McSoley.

"Maybe," said Pettigrew. "In five of the last six years, a woman in the Midwest has embezzled a hundred grand, more or less, then vanished."

McSoley grinned. "A busy lady, huh?"

Pettigrew ignored the tired old joke. "If we have a pattern, it has completely eluded local law enforcement. The women worked in a metro financial institution and lived in an incorporated suburb. They were listed as missing from one police jurisdiction and the embezzlement occurred in another. We've got four states involved: Ohio and surrounding. Never back-to-back occurrences in the same state. No known threats. No evidence of violence. They just drove out of their own lives."

McSoley's grinned smugly. "That is surely Mac Team stuff." He paused to analyze. "But might we have *took the money and ran*?"

"I don't think so. These are women in upscale suburbs, always attractive, always mothers of small children. The bucks they embezzled don't feel high enough."

"I'll be damned. Murder?" McSoley's face took on a lustful expression that Link Pettigrew truly despised.

"That's what I'm working on, but I can't make it make sense. We would have extortion forcing an embezzlement followed by the extortionist committing murder."

McSoley nodded. "You're right. If she embezzles, she isn't going to talk. No need to kill her."

"It's more far-fetched than that," said Pettigrew. "We would have an angry loner serial killer who pauses for a quick bit of extortion. How's that for a profile?"

"I haven't heard of that one."

"I'll shower on it."

Link Pettigrew had earned a bit of fame in his shower. He planted seeds in his mind, watered them in his morning shower, and astounded all who knew him with the stuff that grew. Now and then, he even astounded himself. His latest shower brought a revelation and an idea.

If his pattern involved serial murder, the odds were high that the perpetrator was intimately familiar with law enforcement. The scattered pattern of occurrences was likely not coincidence.

If he had a pattern, its discontinuity occurred five years ago. A woman went missing in the previous four years, and in the sixth. Could he find an event in the fifth year that *would have been* in his pattern if not sidetracked? It was a long shot, a scenario that would involve a woman who fit his victim profile facing an extortion demand, going to the police, succeeding in thwarting the extortion demand, but failing to help secure an arrest. Even if all that happened, could he find the file—and find the woman for interrogation—five years later? A very long shot.

Pettigrew dug for four days using high-tech computer analysis and low-tech grunt. He contacted every FBI field office in the five-state region and checked with every major police department. His search yielded a possibility in Pennsylvania: a woman who lived in the suburbs and worked in Pittsburgh. The pieces fit, but this woman could not help his investigation. Her name was Alicia Radcliff, age thirty-three at the time. Outraged by an extortionist's demand, she took her story to the Pittsburgh Police Department but died twenty-four hours later. Her death had been investigated as murder, coincidental accident, or suicide, with most attention focused on the possibility of murder. But Pettigrew ran across the case while computer searching *extortion*. The Radcliff file included the entry, *Extortion demands included both sex and a cash payment of $125,000.*

The extortionist, a man named Max Cavendish, used knowledge of two recent sexual encounters as leverage for his demand. Threat of exposure was apparently relevant leverage. When he learned of her infidelity, the woman's husband, Thom Radcliff, reacted with such fury that he became the prime suspect in the murder investigation. At time of death, her blood alcohol content was .28. Although she plummeted from a fifth-floor balcony, Pettigrew thought suicide unlikely. A woman strong enough to come forward with information so damning would not likely kill herself after doing it.

Pettigrew admired Alicia Radcliff's willingness to discuss an ordeal that included the additional indignity of a breast bite inflicted during her initial meeting with Cavendish. An arrest appeared likely if she had lived.

Link Pettigrew's gut told him that he might have a breakthrough, although the investigation remained spectacularly speculative. He had no hard evidence that his five missing-person cases involved either extortion or murder. He could only speculate that Alicia Radcliff in Pittsburgh would have been murdered if she had submitted to the extortion demand. But she fit the profile in every other way, and her file gave Link something to work with.

He grasped that action should be immediate. The missing women vanished in November or December, so a repeat might be imminent, creating the possibility of preventing the next occurrence while advancing the investigation. Link scoured the Midwest for recent embezzlements. He came up with nothing that fit the pattern, indicating either that the embezzlement had not yet taken place, or that the targeted financial institution had not yet discovered that funds were missing.

To that point, by Link Pettigrew's self-imposed high standards, he had been doing normal investigative work that should have been initiated long ago. But his Wednesday morning shower generated an idea that could reasonably be called inspired, and the inspiration involved breasts. He smiled during that shower, guessing that his wife wouldn't be surprised. Myra occasionally ribbed him, usually good-naturedly, about excess interest in the female form.

Although aware it was another long shot, Link asked for database analysis of recent assaults involving human bites in the Midwest. A day later, he reviewed a list indicating that Midwesterners have a surprising proclivity toward biting each other: twenty-nine reports in the target area. He immediately eliminated twelve cases that involved woman-on-woman biting. He selected by age. He selected by marital status, by neighborhood, and child-count. He selected by employer category and by location of the bite.

When the analysis wrapped, he had a list of two: Marla Jean Kalbach of Bloomfield Hills, Michigan, and Jacqueline Sue Billings of Dublin, Ohio. By noon, he had reached both investigative officers. Marla Kalbach's attacker had been identified: a recent parolee, a repeat sex offender who had been in prison for much of the previous five years. Link found no activity related to the Billings case, nor was Jacqueline Billings listed as dead or missing.

Link asked Lieutenant Carolyn Trask of the Columbus Police Department to contact Billings, to verify her safety, and to warn her to avoid any kind of contact with a potential extortionist. He also asked Trask to inform Billings that the FBI would likely be in touch with her.

Link dropped by Mac McSoley's office. After hearing the analysis and Pettigrew's request to fly to Columbus, McSoley said, "I'll be damned, that's quite a piece of work."

"It's still speculative as all hell, but I'd like to follow it up. If I'm right, this woman may have only days to live, if she isn't dead already."

After a long pause, McSoley nodded gravely. "My gut's pretty good on this kind of thing. We're onto something. In fact, I may fly with you to Ohio. I like to keep my hand in field work."

Link Pettigrew shook his head in silent disgust. McSoley's look of lust had returned, and Link could feel FBI-issue bullshit rising past shoe-top level, but he went to work.

Chapter Twenty-Seven

On Wednesday morning, Jackie cancelled her third consecutive therapy session. She knew that time with Dr. Geiger was useless without honesty, and she hadn't decided whether, or how, to be honest.

Her life felt something like suspended animation. She worked, drove carpools, and sold PTO raffle tickets, but days dragged interminably and an air of unreality would not go away. Nor would the horror of memory and the fear of discovery. Not surprising, Matt had been physically and emotionally distant since Baxter's visit.

Just after 1:30 on Wednesday, Jackie received the call.

"Mrs. Billings, this is Lieutenant Trask of the Columbus Police Department."

"Yes?" Her stomach churned. Her throat felt dry.

"I've been contacted by the FBI in Washington. They asked me to contact you."

"The FBI? Why…what…?"

There's some concern about your safety."

"My…? What do you mean?" Jackie now felt as much confusion as fear.

"There's concern you might be the victim of an extortion plot?"

"I don't understand."

"No one is presently asking you to embezzle from your bank?"

She focused on keeping her voice even. "No. No one."

"I'm going to ask you to meet me tomorrow at the FBI office downtown: 500 South Front Street, tenth floor. Ask for Agent Carmody. Special Agent Pettigrew from Washington will be here."

Jackie had jotted the address and names, temporarily delaying awareness of the strangeness of the call. Finally, confusion swept through her. "But I'm already…should I bring…?"

"What, Mrs. Billings?"

Lieutenant Trask's voice had transformed from concerned to curious. Through her confusion, Jackie sensed that she could handle this moment very badly, and she had come close. She took a breath. "Nothing. I'll, I, uh, I think I can make it okay."

"Do you still have my card?"

"Yes. I have it here."

"How about ten o'clock?"

"Uh, not good," she said, aware that Baxter's 11:00 a.m. call could shed light. "I need to come in the afternoon."

"Say one o'clock?"

"That will be fine."

Jackie and Matt sat in their fireside recliners. He said, "How the hell can two parts of the FBI be involved?"

"I have no idea. I almost jabbered to Officer Trask, trying to figure that out."

"It sounds like they suspect nothing, right?"

"I guess not. She said they want to protect me."

Matt shook his head, leaned back in his recliner, and closed his eyes. "I don't even know what to say."

She said, "Hopefully Baxter can straighten all this out, or at least tell me how to handle it."

***

At 11:00 a.m. Thursday, Baxter placed his daily call.

Jackie had spent the previous ninety minutes trying to work, but feeling increasingly paralyzed. Her stomach actually ached. She said, "The FBI—people from Washington—want to talk to me, this afternoon."

"Who called? What did they say?" Baxter asked. She read surprise.

"A Columbus police officer. The one who took my report at the hospital. She said the FBI's looking into embezzlement, and they're concerned about my safety. What's going on, Don?"

"Jurisdictional crossover. It happens all the time."

"Can you make them go away?"

"They're working a different angle. I can't stop it."

"I don't know what to do; what to say."

"Let me call you back in a few minutes. I've got to think this through."

For lesser mortals, Don Baxter's think time would have been frightening. Apparently database analysis beyond anything Baxter anticipated had allowed the FBI to link Jackie to the target in Pittsburgh. Of course, Don Baxter must now build a wall between Pittsburgh and Billings. He called Jackie to explore a possibility.

"You're in a very tight spot here, Jackie."

"I know that."

"Did the Columbus Police press you for details about the breast bite?"

"We talked about it."

"I'm talking about in depth. Things like photographs."

"No. No photographs."

"Tell me again how you explained the bite."

"A male friend, not my husband, got carried away and bit me."

"Stick to that story, refuse to identify the boyfriend, and you'll be fine."

"Shouldn't I take a lawyer with me?"

"I don't think so," said Baxter, chuckling. "Showing up with a lawyer, to protect you against their efforts to protect you, wouldn't look good."

"Okay. I'll do my best."

"Don't screw this up, Jackie. Jail time awaits."

"I know."

***

Baxter called Aldrich. "Well, Theodore, say a little prayer for Jackie Billings."

Aldrich snorted. "Right. I'll catch it in my daily devotional. What's up?"

"She meets with the FBI today. They're trying to protect her from Max Collier."

"Christ, how did that happen?"

"They linked her to Pittsburgh."

"Is this enough intrigue for you?"

"Plenty. I knew they might link a dead Jackie to Pittsburgh. But a live Jackie is nothing but the victim of a boyfriend's bite. Someone did a hell of a piece of analysis."

"Do you still think it was smart not to take her out?"

"No. I should have killed her."

"Now what?"

"Depends on how she weathers the FBI. It could go either way. There was no way I could brace her for what she'll learn about Pittsburgh."

"Well keep me posted, you son of a bitch."

Baxter chuckled. "Admit it, Mr. A. You're enjoying this."

"Try to remember, Mr. B., that I enjoy the screwing. And jerking off in a prison cell is not an acceptable contingency."

"No prison cells, my friend. Guaranteed."

***

Jackie had never been inside a law enforcement facility larger than the Dublin police headquarters, and that was a two-year-ago mom role when Sean and friends decided it would be fun to explode cherry bombs in a mailbox.

She entered the South Front Street building that houses the FBI's Columbus field office. After she cleared the most intense security checkpoint she had ever faced, a uniformed officer directed her to the tenth floor where she entered a glass enclosed holding area. The familiar Federal Bureau of Investigation logo loomed over her as she logged her arrival on an Arrival/Departure sheet and told the reception officer that she was to meet Agent Carmody. "He'll come for you in a few minutes, ma'am."

A stocky young man opened glass doors in front of her. "Mrs. Billings, please come this way."

They pushed open a door marked Conference Room B where two men waited along with Lieutenant Trask of CPD. Carmody said, "Mrs. Billings, this is Special Agent Pettigrew and his supervisor Darren McSoley. They're out of Washington." They stepped toward her and extended right hands. She shook Pettigrew's hand then McSoley's. Carmody said, "I believe you know Lieutenant Carolyn Trask. I'm stationed here also, and will be FBI liaison in the event of local follow-up."

Carmody motioned her toward the chair at the head of the table. Pettigrew and McSoley sat to her left; Trask and Carmody to her right. The three men pushed business cards toward her. She collected the cards, slowly unzipping her purse and inserting them, while trying to fight rising nervousness.

"We're happy to meet you, Mrs. Billings," Link Pettigrew began, pausing to smile warmly. "Actually, for more reasons than one. We feared you might be dead."

"I…I don't understand."

"May I call you Jackie?"

She nodded, aware that eyes around the table were watching her every reaction.

Pettigrew said, "We don't mean to frighten you, Jackie, but we're pursuing a possible serial murder case. If we're correct, victims are targeted based on employment at institutions handling large sums of money. They are coerced into embezzling funds in the range of a hundred thousand dollars. They then disappear."

Jackie's mind reeled but she managed to suppress an instinct to gasp. "Well, I'm here. I'm…I'm okay."

"We see that," said Pettigrew, his tone friendly, almost soothing. "We're hopeful, though, we can help you avoid danger and advance this investigation."

Darren McSoley suddenly leaned forward, his eyes intense. "Mrs. Billings, let's get straight to the point. I've been carefully studying Agent Pettigrew's files. Several elements fit a pattern, but I'm particularly interested in your breast."

Pettigrew looked at McSoley in open amazement, visibly trying to stifle a laugh. Agent Carmody bit his own lip. Carolyn Trask shook her head. Jackie could feel the warmth of her blush, but appreciated a moment of comic relief that seemed to give her an energy boost. "I'm not sure what to say to that."

McSoley's cool professionalism had slipped; his face turned deep crimson. "I'm sorry. I mean that the bite you suffered ties closely to a case in Pittsburgh five years ago. That woman died mysteriously. We're very interested in who bit you, Mrs. Billings."

Jackie's burst of energy evaporated. She scrambled to process the information while trying to appear calm. Was it a coincidence? Could Max Collier have killed the woman? Where is Don Baxter in all this? There were probably a hundred other questions but this was not the time to ask them. She cleared her throat, grasping that a bit of nervousness would be accepted. “I just don’t see how this applies to me. A male friend bit me. Not my husband. This is all very embarrassing.”

McSoley pressed on. “Mrs. Billings, we want to talk to that male friend.”

Pettigrew glared disapprovingly at his boss.

Jackie said, “I don’t think I have to tell you who he is, do I?” but weakly.

McSoley leaned toward her, his voice stern. “Why wouldn’t you, Mrs. Billings? What are you trying to hide?”

Carolyn Trask said, “Agent McSoley, with all due respect, I think it’s clear why she might prefer that this incident remain private. She declined to press charges. I believe that is her right.”

“Jackie, we’re concerned about your safety,” said Link Pettigrew, obviously trying to regain control of his meeting, “and we want to pursue any possibility that might uncover the murderer of five women, maybe more. These are women just like you in every respect.”

Jackie met his eyes. “I appreciate your concern, Agent Pettigrew.”

Pettigrew’s expression grew more intense. “So you have not been asked to embezzle money from your employer?”

She concentrated on meeting his gaze, speaking calmly. “No, I haven’t.”

“No threats?”

“No, no threats.”

Pettigrew paused, stroking his chin, his eyes locked on her eyes. “We have ways to help you, and to protect you.”

She considered briefly, but truth felt too complicated, and too risky. “Thank you, but I don’t need any help.”

Pettigrew focused intently on her eyes for a moment that felt long. "We appreciate your coming in, Jackie. We might want to speak with you at a later time."

"Yes, of course."

"Please call me if you think of anything, or are contacted."

"I will."

Carolyn Trask said, "I'll show you out, Jackie."

In the outer lobby, Lieutenant Trask said, "If you want to talk about all this with another woman, call me." Jackie nodded, but did not reply, feeling too much relief to even consider another discussion.

The three men sat silent. Link Pettigrew frowned quizzically while smacking an open palm against a clenched fist. "That was very strange."

"Because she was so jittery?" asked McSoley.

"No. Jittery makes sense in any scenario. I think she wanted to talk."

"She may be involved with a seriously sadistic guy," said Carmody. "The whole thing is probably twisted. You can see why she wouldn't talk."

Pettigrew's frown deepened. "Possible, but she sure doesn't seem like the type."

"They never seem like the type," said McSoley smugly, as if he had recited mantra directly from the J. Edgar Hoover handbook.

Pettigrew ignored him. "I *really* don't think she's the type. She wanted to talk."

"Might the extortion be underway," Carmody speculated, "including a demand for silence?"

"Possibly," said Pettigrew. "That would make some sense." He paused, his face a studious grimace. "Or does it?"

McSoley said, "Damn it, Link. If you were suspicious, why didn't you press her? I sure tried."

Link Pettigrew had reached his McSoley limit for one day. "Good God, Mac, what's our probable? She comes in here without an attorney believing we're trying to protect her, and you want to beat her up. The judge would love that one. Your Honor, we believe she's a suspicious character. Why? Because she didn't show up at our interrogation dead."

Carolyn Trask returned as the meeting was breaking up. Pettigrew said, "Lieutenant Trask, I suggest we open dialog with Jackie's bank. Would you coordinate?"

Trask nodded.

"Don't use her name; call it speculative; but warn of a possible embezzlement in the range of a hundred thousand. Reveal the department if you need to, but not her identity."

McSoley said, "That's more like it, Link."

Jackie drove home with something approaching terror in the pit of her stomach. She felt surrounded; not at all sure she handled the questions well. And a frightening new picture of Don Baxter had begun to form. She hadn't thought about suicide since she was seven years old, and that moment had been based on childlike fury over some disappointment her parents had inflicted. Now she better understood how it happens. If life feels like a downward spiral, swirling, dark, from which you can see no escape…

But at home, she ordered a pizza, fed her family, helped Sean with algebra and helped Jodi try a cool new hairstyle. Later, while she tried to relax in a hot bath, a vision nearly broke her heart. She could see Jodi's wedding day. But Jackie had no role in the planning, no walk down the aisle, no tear-filled joy as Jodi and her groom exchanged their vows, no special dance. And from deep inside, she felt resolve rising.

They waited to discuss her afternoon. As Matt slid into his side of the bed, Jackie said, “The FBI suspects that Collier was a serial murderer.”

Matt turned toward, confusion and fear swirling. “A murderer?”

“That’s what they said.”

His head jerked visibly. “God, this whole thing is scaring me to death.”

“I know. And it just gets deeper.”

“Maybe it’s good, right? I mean a jury might be more sympathetic if…”

“Maybe, but there’s something else. Do you believe in women’s intuition?”

He snorted. “Every guy ever caught lying by his mother believes.”

“Don Baxter is a fake, a con man. I suspected it before. Now I’m sure.”

“How do you know?”

“Intuition; the way he’s worried; the odd way he’s trying to help me; things he said; things Collier said. The two of them are connected somehow.”

“That would make him dangerous wouldn’t it? A lot more dangerous than an FBI guy with a secret to keep.”

“I’m afraid so.”

“And if the serial murder theory is right—”

“It’s hard to imagine Baxter being involved in that, but he’s nervous about something, and I have a plan.”

Matt sighed deeply. “I don’t know how much more I can take.”

Matt Billings lay awake far into the night, this time listening to the occasional gentle snore of his wife. He tried to analyze his role in all this. He wanted to be strong, a protector. That's why he came home. He had little idea whether he could rise above the hurt she had inflicted, but he wanted to be strong for his family, to keep them safe, at least until the crisis ended.

But he didn't feel strong. He felt more like an animal caught in a trap; an animal trying to decide whether it's worse to be taken by the humans, or killed by a larger predator. Matt could see no happy outcome. Even a sympathetic jury would call it murder two. He would be a single father, if not an inmate himself. Unless Don Baxter found them, caught in the trap, before the law did.

Chapter Twenty-Eight

Don Baxter called on Friday morning at 11:00 sharp, eager to hear her story, eager to plan his next set of moves, aware that this would be a life or death phone call for Mrs. Billings. He asked, “How did it go?”

“I think okay.”

“How were you emotionally?

“I was afraid at first, but I got better.”

“Who was in charge?”

“A guy named Pettigrew from Washington.”

“Sharp?”

“I guess so. He was nice to me. His boss was an ass.”

“A supervisor came from Washington?”

“Yes. A guy named McSoley.”

“What did they ask you?”

“Whether the man who bit me was an extortionist who might fit a pattern they’re working on.”

He noted that her voice sounded stronger, edgier. “And?”

“I said exactly what you told me to say.”

“Did they believe you?”

“I think so. I did my best.”

“Did they suspect more than one man was involved?”

“They didn’t say anything about that. But here’s a question for you. Would Collier have killed me if I hadn’t killed him?”

The change in her demeanor fascinated him. Even stronger. More aggressive. He laughed casually. “That wimpy slimeball? Of course not. Why do you ask?”

"They said a woman just like me has disappeared, for several years in a row."

Baxter laughed. "So they ride into town to save a damsel in distress. You'd think, as screwed up as their world is, they'd have better things to do."

"What's going on, Don?" she demanded.

"Damn good question. I'll see what I can find out, but I know one thing: they're flailing, desperately. I'm not proud of being connected with Collier, but hell, Jackie; I went fishing with the guy once. The wimp wouldn't even clean the fish. Serial murder is an absolute joke."

Don Baxter looked out into his Pennsylvania forest, now white with snow. He grinned broadly and raised a clenched fist. We have a worthy opponent in Washington; in fact, we may have a genius for an opponent in Washington. The case has already attracted supervisory interest. Jackie Billings has become a fascinating player. It will be close. It could go either way. Excellent!

He replayed their conversation in his mind, and he recognized a small but uncharacteristic error that suggested a bit of rust in the high-level intrigue department. Asking whether the FBI suspected the involvement of more than one man tipped a scenario she couldn't have imagined on her own. He wondered whether she picked up on it. Quite possibly. She just keeps getting stronger. But it didn't really matter. Jackie knew too much. She was operating too near high-level law enforcement personnel. Her husband knew too much, as well. Elimination involved risk, but letting them live would eventually lead the FBI's miracle sleuth to the door.

Baxter leaned backward, hands locked behind his head, grinning toward the ceiling. This whole damn thing is fascinating. Jackie has no clue that she killed one of the cruelest sons of bitches who ever used whips and chains. But he wouldn't have killed her.

Mark Coffey, a.k.a. Collier the fuck-up, had no stomach for killing, although death number one was pretty close. What was her name? Kathy, Katie, something like Culbertson. That poor bitch literally died of fright. Had to be an aneurysm, right in the middle of his playtime. So Jackie Billings kills a guy who probably deserved to be horsewhipped before being shot, and she's terrified of going to prison. Of course, she should be terrified. If this thing ever hit the courts, a good prosecutor probably sends her down. A good defense lawyer maybe gets her off. But all of that will be academic in a few hours.

Baxter called Aldrich. "I'm going back to Columbus. She's too hot."

"How so?"

"The FBI is close to a direct link to Pittsburgh, and she's too close to the FBI."

"So she dies?"

"Yes. Now the lesser risk. Our opponent is good, and Jackie is gaining on good herself. You need to be ready for the possibility of flight, and I don't mean your damn 747s."

"I don't want that to happen."

"I know, but be ready."

***

Baxter called from the cell phone as he drove west. "Jackie, I want to meet you and your husband tonight."

"Why?"

"This is not a request. This is an instruction. I want to be sure we're all on the same page."

"Where?"

"At XYZ."

"Why there?"

"No chance of eyes or ears."

She fired back, "Why do you care, Mr. FBI man?" her voice defiant, almost mocking.

He didn't tolerate defiant, mocking housewives. "Meet me at XYZ, Jackie."

"Not a chance."

"You're in no position to be setting rules."

"We're not meeting you at XYZ."

"I'll call you from somewhere east of town. Carry your cell."

Jackie tried but failed to understand her own behavior. She felt strong. She felt confident that her plan would work, now that she fully grasped that Baxter feared exposure as much as she did. She called Matt. "I want you to take Sean and Jodi to a movie tonight."

"Why?"

"I'm meeting Don Baxter, and I want you guys to be somewhere else."

"I won't do that, Jackie. You said he's dangerous."

"Don't worry. I also said I have a plan."

After several difficult minutes, Matt agreed to let her go alone.

Don Baxter brought his sedan to a stop in dark shadows on the east end of the eastbound I-70 rest stop. He felt as if he had negotiated the location of a meeting between diplomats of warring countries. He first insisted on meeting on an isolated country road. Jackie said they would meet in a restaurant. He said they would meet at an interstate rest stop, in his car. She said they would meet at a rest stop, outside either car. Baxter decided he could make that work.

Baxter played out scenarios while he waited. If possible he would use his assault rifle—now hidden beneath a creatively customized rear seat—to execute a quick hit through his window.

Because of his isolated location, he could be safely holed up in Pennsylvania before discovery and any kind of law enforcement reaction. If he spotted potential witnesses to riddling their car, he would approach the Billings and begin a conversation. He would either invite himself into their back seat or, if they resisted, let Matt see the metal of his Beretta. A threat to Jackie would turn Matt to jelly. Surely no man on the planet is more of a sucker for love than Matt Billings. How else to explain no divorce papers? Once inside their car, he would force them to drive to an isolated location where the job could be finished.

Jackie drove east on I-70, while working on maintaining her confidence. Her trip odometer now reported 26.5 miles east of Columbus, not quite two miles to go. Her dash clock said 10:15. Increasingly heavy snow swirled in her headlights. The clouds above her hung so low she could see them in the night sky. She spotted the rest area's one-mile sign, and she tried several sets of deep breaths to steady herself.

She carefully negotiated an entrance ramp now slick with snow and pulled into a west-end parking area lined with eighteen-wheelers. She inched along, looking for light in the trucks having sleepers. She stopped across from a dark-blue Mack and stepped into the blustery night. Nervous pangs in her stomach reminded her that this part of her plan might not work at all.

Jackie climbed onto the passenger-side running board and knocked on the Mack's window, softly then louder. No response, although she could see the flicker of a TV behind a blue curtain. She walked to the next lighted truck and tried again. This time a hand emerged from behind the curtain and shooed her away. She returned to her car, drove toward the next cabin light, and stopped in front of a wine-colored Kenworth.

A bear of a man wearing a dark plaid shirt over stark-white long johns emerged from the sleeper and flipped on the cab light. His eyes were bright blue above a full red beard. He lowered the window. “Sorry, ma’am. I’m a happily married man. Ya’ll can just move on down the line, unless you’d like to set a minute and talk about the Lord.”

She smiled, relieved at the indication of kindness, aware that she hadn’t thought of everything. “I’m not here to, I mean for... My name is Jackie Billings. I need some help.”

“How so, ma’am?”

“I’ll be talking with a man in a few minutes. I’m afraid he might try to hurt me. Will you shine your lights on my car and maybe keep an eye on me?”

He studied her, but only briefly. “I’ll do more’n that, ma’am. He so much as lays a hand on you and I’ll bust his head.”

Jackie smiled again. “In the name of the Lord?”

“My Lord don’t cotton to no one hurtin’ a woman.”

“What’s your name?”

“John Sullivan, ma’am. But folks call me Red.”

“Just watch me, Red. I’ll be all right. And thank you.”

She walked back to her car and leaned against the front fender, now brightly illuminated by Red Sullivan’s headlights.

Don Baxter checked his watch. She should be here. He looked around the rest stop. At the far end, probably half a mile from his position, he could see truck lights illuminating a parked car. What the hell? Was that Jackie? He pulled his field glasses, ID’d Jackie, and rubbed his temple and forehead with the thumb and fingers of his left hand. He called her cell phone and watched her answer. “Wrong end of the rest area, Jackie.”

“It’s my end, Don.”

“Drive down here.”

"I'm not moving from here."

"Where's your husband?"

"He couldn't make it."

This lady is becoming difficult, that's for damn sure. "Does he know you're here?"

"Do you think I'm dumb?"

"No, Jackie. I don't think you're dumb."

"You really do want to hear what I have to say." She clicked off.

He hit *End* and considered options. To meet her, he would need to back his car to her position. He considered exiting east, doubling back, and blasting her with a drive-by. But Matt likely knew she was here. Worse, she had apparently formed an ad hoc posse of truck drivers. Either her new friend, or the drivers he would reach by CB radio, would be all over him on I-70 East. Okay, I need to know what she's talking about. I'll back up and try to charm her. She's still not sure I'm not FBI, although she sure as hell doesn't trust me much. If that works, I'll talk her into an isolated meeting. If not, I'll tail her, finish it from the car, and find Matt later. He shifted into reverse and backed toward her, pulling to a stop just in front of her car.

Baxter found tinted glasses in his glove compartment, pulled his hat low and his collar up, and exited the car. He studied her carefully as he strolled toward her. She wore a long blue winter coat, holding it closed at the neck with both hands. Dark waves fell below a white wool cap. The mist of her breath swirled in the winter wind. God, she's a hundred times more attractive now than when she moaned under me at XYZ. He thought of Collier's last moments and smiled wryly. Maybe I should be the one who's glad we're meeting in the glare of lights. But she looks tired. She's lost some weight. Stress will do that. He glanced above the lights that had turned his night into day and saw a bearded face peering from the driver's side of the truck cab. He approached to within three feet of Jackie. "Who's your friend?"

"That's Red."

"What the hell's going on Jackie? I thought we had an agreement."

"So did I, until I realized you would like to kill me."

What the hell? Is this a trap? Is she wired? Surely not. "That's crazy. I would never hurt you. Can't we go somewhere where it's warm."

"I'm not going anywhere. I can get warm in Red's truck if I need to."

"What's this all about?"

"I bought myself some insurance. I got pictures of Collier off the video. I told my whole story, every bit of it, with all kinds of details in writing. It's in a safe place, and several people know where to find it if anything happens to me or my family."

I'll be damned; a Dublin housewife is kicking my ass at my own game. But, of course, I hold the trump card. "I don't understand any of this, Jackie. We have a mutual silence agreement. That's all there is to it. What's this about?"

"I think you would rather have me dead."

"Why would you think that?"

"Because you and Collier were in Pittsburgh. And the FBI—the real FBI—is closing in."

Christ, it's cold out here. How can she not be frozen? How has she figured all this out? "Jackie, have a coffee with me somewhere. I'll tell you the whole story. I'm not FBI. But I'm not what you think."

"Talk to me here, Don; or whatever your name is."

Okay. Let's play the trump and get out of this wind. "Ted Aldrich and I had a sexual conquest contest all through college. Collier kept score. We got together at a reunion when we all turned forty. We cobbled up a new game, even gave Collier a way to play and to help us finance the fun. We called ourselves the ABC Gang, until you rubbed out our C." *That was a good shot, close to true, except for the college part. The cool Mrs. Billings is looking a bit troubled.*

"Why should I believe that?"

"Think about it. It's obviously true. You missed, they all missed, that I knew things that Ted had to tell me. Ted's job was to pick the right mark. To score a point, he had to get them to ask for it—their screwing, I mean. My job was tougher, because so many of them fell deeply in love with Ted's ass. But he had to level the playing field by telling me everything he learned. Then Collier got his jollies and picked up a few bucks to finance the program." *This is fun, now. She's crumbling before my eyes.*

"What about Pittsburgh?"

"Collier pissed a woman off. I was in Pittsburgh trying to smooth things over, and I was too damn close when she died; no doubt about that. But hell, Jackie, she was drunk out of her mind. She probably thought she could fly off that balcony. It was an accident. No murder was proven, because there was no murder."

"What about the five other women Collier killed?"

"That is pure unadulterated bullshit."

"Agent Pettigrew doesn't think so."

"Agent Pettigrew is full of crap, dreaming of a big-time score. I can take you to see our other women if you'd like to meet them." *Hmm. That'll take a little work, but it can be arranged.*

"I don't believe anything you say."

Okay, let's end this. "Jackie, I like you. I admire your moxie. But don't you see that you made a horrible mistake—a mistake that robbed me of a friend and made you a cold-blooded murderer?"

Her eyes narrowed. He could easily see fear rising. "What do you mean?"

"You were supposed to negotiate with Collier. They all did. Hell, he let a couple of them off with a hand job and a few hundred bucks they could borrow from aunts and uncles. Out of the whole bunch of them, only two hit up their employer directly, and those two had inside connections that made it foolproof. What the hell were you thinking?"

He waited through a long reflective pause, watching her bravado die before his eyes. "God, Don; is that true? I mean he—"

"Of course it's true. Didn't it ever occur to you to just say, 'I can't do that, Max. What can we work out?'"

"He…he was controlling me. He threatened Jodi. He—"

"Max Collier was a sad little man living a sad little life; a frustrated actor who hadn't had a gig in years. He was angry. Maybe a little mean, but the guy wouldn't kill a fly, much less a woman." *Mission accomplished. Look at the tears. Damn, I'm good.* "Go home, Jackie. Before I change my mind about turning you in. The ABC gang was cruel—if you call playing with women's heads and bodies cruel—but you killed our innocent."

Her eyes had turned to liquid, glistening in the bright glare of the Kenworth's headlights. She walked past Baxter, toward the truck. The driver stretched to open the door, and Jackie climbed up and in. Baxter decided he had accomplished enough, and he could drive home without worrying about a pursuing posse. He would need to monitor her. He might need to kill her. But for now, she was shut up, tight.

She huddled on the huge leather seat, shivering, tears beginning to escape from beneath closed eyelids.

"Coffee, ma'am?"

She looked toward him. "Maybe in a minute."

He returned a green Philadelphia Eagles cup to its holder. "Want to talk? Ol' Red's a good listener."

She shook her head while fishing in her pocket for something to help stop the sniffling. “Do you have any Kleenex?”

He pulled a man-sized box from a console compartment. “The world’s a heavy thing for one little gal to carry all by herself.”

She tried, but couldn’t speak. Her agony erupted from deep within, and she began sobbing in deep, uncontrollable bursts. Red Sullivan reached toward her, putting a huge hand on her shoulder then gently stroking her arm. She reached across her body to hold onto rough and gnarled fingers. When the sobbing subsided, she looked into his eyes, speaking in short bursts. “ “I’m going to lose my husband. I’m going to lose my kids. I’m…I’m…” A new wave of sobs overwhelmed her.

“May I pray for you, ma’am?”

She sniffed. “No, thank you. I’d just as soon God didn’t hear about all this.”

“I don’t reckon that’s how He looks at it, ma’am.”

Jackie found the door handle and stepped onto the running board. “You’re a wonderful man, Red Sullivan. Thank you.”

***

Baxter called Aldrich. “She’s clever. Planted evidence; enough evidence to make our lives miserable. She called it life insurance.”

“Now what?”

“I’ve got to keep her shut up. I laid one on her tonight.”

“Will that be enough?”

“I’ll pound on her a little more, but we’ll be fine. Tonight was one of my finer hours, if I do say so myself.”

***

Jackie drove home trying to grapple with the inclusion of Ted Aldrich in the scheme Baxter had described. The possibility of a connection had flickered through her mind when she wondered why Collier used the XYZ Farm. But she couldn't make herself believe that Ted could be connected with Collier in any way. Ted Aldrich had a kind, gentle spirit. She had never believed Baxter's assertion that Ted might be involved in drug related murders. She couldn't imagine now that he could be part of Link Pettigrew's suspected murder ring.

But the sexual conquest part rang disgustingly true. The idea that she was so thoroughly duped made her sick. A hundred Ted Aldrich lines tumbled through her mind. She thought of her first meeting with Baxter. If she had called the con man's bluff about going to the FBI field office, she might have avoided all this. She recalled Baxter's performance on the telephone, and she clenched her teeth and smacked the steering wheel, over and over.

When she told Matt about the ABC gang, he reacted as if she had stabbed him with a knife. "I don't even know what to say—knowing that you got yourself into such a sick…" He exhaled, long and slow. "I just don't think I can handle it anymore."

Chapter Twenty-Nine

Don Baxter anticipated correctly that Jackie would continue to accept his calls. She had reached a remarkable level of street savvy. She would want to keep communication lines open to keep tabs on him.

He began his next regular call with a revelation. "There's an excellent chance that Pettigrew will suspect you killed Collier."

"How could he possibly know?"

"He won't know. He'll get there by scenario analysis."

"I think I'll deny that."

"That is correct. Absolutely never forget that he has nothing but a string of circumstantial evidence. No extortion. No money missing from your bank. No bodies. Nothing. So you're right. Deny. Deny. Deny."

"Isn't Collier missing from somewhere?"

"Not to worry. Collier, an alias by the way, has been missing since 1982. Total loner, except for our little game. Secondly, hit Pettigrew with a simple question: 'Do you think I would dream of facing the FBI without an attorney, if I had killed a man?'."

Shortly after lunch, Jackie answered her phone. A woman's voice said, "I can only speak for a moment. Don Baxter demanded that I call you—although his name was Don Breckenfield when I knew him. My name is Marianne Lake, last year's ABC target."

"You wouldn't, by chance, be a friend of his playing with my head?"

"I wish I were. I owe my uncle twelve thousand dollars that I can't repay. My husband is gone. And I feel like America's biggest fool."

"Tell me about it."

"I'm a writer whose husband never read a word I wrote. Ted Aldrich made me feel like the next Mary Higgins Clark. Breckenfield had me feeling like a character in my own thriller. And I endured that sorry little prick Carmody, who left with twelve thousand dollars and the last shred of my self respect."

"What color are Aldrich's eyes?"

"Glorious sky blue, that miserable prick."

"What kind of insignia on his flying suit?"

"He always wore a dark leather bomber jacket. There was no insignia."

"Where did you meet Baxter…Breckenfield?"

"He just showed up. He banged me in the loft of their damned playhouse."

"So you're really real?"

"I'm afraid so, and I'm sorry for what you're going through."

"May I call you later?"

"Only if Breckenfield makes me remember any of this again. That miserable son of a bitch. Good bye."

Jackie checked caller ID but found the call untraceable.

***

The possibility hit Link Pettigrew during a Wednesday morning shower—a startling theory, even for a veteran rarely surprised by anything: Jackie Billings killed the extortionist, directly or indirectly.

Link smiled, realizing his shot at McSoley had been relevant. Indeed, Jackie did not show up dead in Conference Room B. She dodged FBI protection against a man likely to be planning her murder. What else would explain it? She knew the man was dead. She feared prosecution. She hoped to avoid discovery rather than turn herself in and risk a murder charge.

He recognized the potential flaw in his analysis. No one else in the interrogation room picked up the vibration that she had wanted to talk but decided against it. If Link had misread that element, her story likely held up—a woman caught up in a sordid sexual relationship, anxious to minimize revelations. He recalled that Columbus Police Officer Carolyn Trask had left the room while the men discussed Jackie's reaction to the interrogation. By mid-morning, he reached Trask in her squad car. Electing not to reveal his new theory, he asked, "Did you have any sense that Jackie Billings had a lot on her mind that day, things she would have liked to discuss?"

"No doubt about it. I even suggested that she call me when she was ready to talk."

Link processed the possibility that Jackie's husband was involved—possible but unlikely in a case of infidelity-based extortion. Also essentially irrelevant. Even if Matt Billings had been the trigger, Jackie would be primary interrogation target. Link considered the possibility she had arranged a professional hit but discarded it immediately. He was already stretching credulity. A Jackie Billings involved with the seamy side just didn't work.

Link Pettigrew told McSoley that he would be visiting Ohio again, Just a routine fact-find, he said.

***

Jackie waited in a corner booth at the Pancake Boutique, as ready as she knew how to be for Link Pettigrew's visit. The passing of several days had made room for clearer thinking. The scene at XYZ could, sometimes at least, be shoved into that corner of the mind reserved for bad dreams. A part of her that felt almost detached had been listening to Baxter, analyzing risk and danger, and preparing for Link Pettigrew. Her heart was at home. There were Christmas presents to buy, a house to decorate, a family to hold together. So she made cookies, told stories to Jodi, and counseled Sean, when he would let her, on the mysteries of teenage girls. And she tried, mostly forlornly, to find ways to connect with her husband.

As Pettigrew approached the booth, she quickly assessed the man. This one appeared to be a sincerely earnest FBI guy. But she knew what she had to do.

Before serious discussion, they established that he was Link, not Agent Pettigrew. And he dived in. "Jackie, this is delicate for both of us. Perhaps you should consult a lawyer before we talk."

She could feel the scrutiny of his eyes. "I don't need a lawyer."

"If my theory is correct, I want to help you."

She waited, stirring her coffee, concentrating on the swirling spoon.

"I believe you were extorted by the same man who bit you. That you met with this man and that, perhaps in an accident, the man died."

Now she looked up, trying for a tone of incredulity. "Are you saying you think I killed someone?" She didn't like the way her voice sounded, but my God, an FBI guy had already figured it out. At least Baxter had forewarned her.

His intense scrutiny continued. "It is my theory."

"That doesn't even make sense. I'm here because I'm willing to help you. I can't imagine you think I killed a guy, and dropped by to chat without an attorney."

He returned his cup to its saucer and met her eyes squarely. "I've thought of that."

"So how can you possibly think I killed someone?"

"Analysis. A good gut. I've been around a long time."

She sensed success just ahead. "You're wrong. Just plain wrong. I'll contact you if anything happens. But nothing has happened yet."

"You weren't as well prepared during your visit to the office."

She frowned, puzzled by the new direction. "For what?"

"For questions. I had a strong feeling that you wanted to talk."

"I was scared to death. That's an intimidating place, and this is all very bizarre."

His eyes narrowed, focusing even more sharply. "Have you been involved with a man, outside marriage?"

She felt ambushed. Attacked from a new direction. Her neck and face felt warm. She wondered how much blush was showing. "That seems a bit personal?"

"Please answer my question, Mrs. Billings."

"I'm…I'm not going to talk about my sex life. It's really none of your business."

"A simple yes or no would have been better."

"Better for what?"

"For my understanding of where you are."

"My sex life is not relevant. May I go now?"

He stood. "Thanks for meeting with me."

A new revelation hit Link Pettigrew as he sat in a Columbus airport coffee shop, waiting for a delayed flight to Washington. *She was coached, brilliantly coached, from the first interrogation—almost certainly by a veteran of law enforcement.* He called his wife then Mac McSoley to tell them his itinerary had changed, and he booked a commuter flight to Pittsburgh. While in the air, he contacted the FBI field office and started the process. "I want to reopen the Alicia Radcliff murder case, strong probability of a multi-state serial. I'll want to talk with her husband and any friends who might know about her sexual encounters. I'll want autopsy photographs." Agent Kathleen Larsen made necessary contacts with the Pittsburgh Police Department and the coroner's office.

***

Although Link Pettigrew stressed that he was exploring new angles, Thom Radcliff would not talk without his attorney. After his wife's death, Radcliff had faced intense, multi-day interrogation as the only suspect with apparent motive. The police had rejected the idea that the extortionist might have killed her. Cavendish had committed no violent offense worse than biting her. Seedy small-time extortionists don't pull off professional assassinations, or need to. Besides, all fingers pointed toward Thom Radcliff. He was a powerful man physically, an ex-football star turned insurance salesman. He had handled her confession of infidelity so badly that witnesses to his fury were available in his office and in their neighborhood. Relatives and neighbors reported a pattern of past abuse, both emotional and physical. When his alibi checked out, he faced more interrogation about the possibility he had arranged a hit. The grand jury failed to indict, but it was close.

They met in the opulent office of Radcliff's attorney, a silver-haired man named Ned Foley. The protocol was straightforward. Link would ask. With Foley's head nod, Radcliff would answer.

Link said, "I'm pursuing the possibility that the extortionist had an accomplice. What do you know about the men she was with?"

Foley nodded, but Radcliff hesitated, visibly angry. Link marveled at the power of jealousy. Radcliff's wife died over five years ago; he had remarried, apparently happily. "Almost nothing," he growled. "I was so pissed that I wasn't talking to her at all."

"Any idea how she met them?"

Foley nodded. "She attended a sorority convention in St. Louis. I think she met the first guy during that trip."

"Where? How?"

Foley nodded. "No idea," said Radcliff testily.

"And the second man?"

"No idea. Listen, friend, do you have any idea how it feels to know—?"

Foley interrupted. "Just answer the questions, Thom."

Link said, "According to the report, the extortionist knew about both of them. How could that be?"

This time, Radcliff returned a swift answer without counsel. "Look, I have no idea how the hell he could know. She might have confided in a friend who wasn't a friend. I have no idea."

"Why do you think she was killed?"

Radcliff looked toward his attorney. Foley said, "He has testified that he has no idea why she was murdered, or whether she was murdered."

Link said, "According to the transcript, her closest friend is Terri Mellinger. Is she still in the area?"

Foley nodded. Radcliff said, "Yes. She still lives in our old neighborhood."

"And her sister? Still in the area?"

"Yes."

"Thank you, gentlemen," said Link Pettigrew.

Terri Mellinger agreed to meet with Link, but had little to share. "It was a strange time in our friendship. I knew she had a lot going on. She was up, down, happy, sad; but she never talked to me. I even asked why, but she wouldn't talk. I think she was so afraid of Thom that she didn't tell anyone anything."

"So why was she willing to go to the police?"

"She was like that. You could only push her so far and she lashed back. She quit a job once because of sexual harassment, but only after she brought the guy down. Hearings. The whole deal. Thom hated every part of it, but she did it anyway."

Alicia Radcliff's sister met with Link at her home. She said, "She came by once, scared to death. She was involved with an airline pilot; afraid that Thom might find out; then the FBI showed up investigating her lover's possible drug dealings. She was terrified that she might need to testify."

Link Pettigrew's life had required him to install personal shock absorbers. He had encountered the petty, the disgusting, the disappointing, and the appalling. He processed a mixture of those emotions while contemplating an FBI agent using case knowledge as an extortion-murder lever. "Why did none of this come out during the investigation?"

"It just never did. Everything pointed to Thom. I still think he killed her. I wish to heaven she could have divorced him, but she just couldn't go against her vows."

"Was an FBI agent the second sexual partner that Cavendish knew about?"

Until that moment, she had been open, a helpful young woman. Her wide-set eyes narrowed. "Is all this really relevant now?"

Link hesitated, not wanting to conduct an internal affairs investigation in front of this woman. He decided to wade just a bit deeper. "It would help my investigation. I think there's a chance other women are in danger."

She paused again. "Yes, she slept with the FBI guy."

"Was he from Pittsburgh?"

"I don't know. She didn't say."

"Did she tell you anything about Cavendish? How he got his information?"

"No. I didn't know anything about Cavendish."

Link returned to the field office and transcribed his notes, now speculating that Mac McSoley would indeed have his high-profile case, a conspiracy of a very different kind.

At the field office, he asked Agent Larsen for help tracking any FBI investigations conducted just prior to the Radcliff death that pertained to an airline pilot involved in the drug business. She turned up nothing, suggesting three possibilities: Documentation might have been sketchy. The agent might have been from another office, conducting a multi-city investigation. Link would explore that possibility from Washington. Or the agent might have buried the investigation after passing along its sordid details to his extortion buddy.

During the ride to the airport, Link Pettigrew analyzed scenarios, trying to determine the next investigative step. He reached only one firm decision. He must meet with Jackie Billings, swiftly. Today was December 21. He gave thought to allowing the holidays to come and go, but the risk felt too great. His adversary was taking shape in Link's mind—a worthy, if disgusting, opponent.

He struggled with another troubling aspect of his theory. Serial killers are typically male loners. The idea of a co-conspirator fit neither Link's experience nor intuition. But it had been a strange case from the start.

Link flew toward Columbus. The expanding set of files in his briefcase included an autopsy photograph.

Chapter Thirty

Jackie had hoped that somehow it would all go away, at least for Christmas. She took Pettigrew's call with a kind of reluctant resignation. "Yes, I'll meet with you. But after work, and only for a few minutes."

Baxter had prepared her. He explained that Pettigrew might float an immunity offer that could be withdrawn after more of her grim truth came to light. He explained that Pettigrew would be vulnerable if he failed to notify of his real intention and to advise her of her rights. She might even be able to go on the offensive if Pettigrew mishandled Miranda.

A second "survivor," as Baxter now mockingly called them, had contacted her to confess involvement with the ABC gang. Her name was Meg Oakley, a thirty-two year old from Charleston, West Virginia. She knew things that only an ABC victim would likely know, and she mentioned hating Collier—Claypool, to her—for scarring her left breast. Jackie again tried but failed to I.D. the number. She feared that Baxter continued to con her, but he had easily deflected her questions. "Jackie, Jackie, try to understand that you and I are in the same place. I'm a married businessman who played a game I shouldn't have played. It exploded in my face, almost like God himself said 'enough.' You're a wife and mother who got sucked in, and made a terrible mistake. Let's quit distrusting each other and try to get out of this in one piece."

They sat in the same booth at the same restaurant. Link battled mixed emotions as he noted the strain etched on Jackie's face: eyes weary, face gaunt. He believed that this woman was the emotional hostage of a very intelligent, very cruel man. She was likely terrified of a prison term. But somehow she continued to hold up. He thought of POWs battling the tremendous advantage held by their captors, and he couldn't avoid admiring Jackie Billings' determination and resilience.

He said, "I've been in Pittsburgh. I now believe that Alicia Radcliff was killed to hide a conspiracy. Killed by a vicious criminal."

She studied him silently, eyes steady if troubled.

Link said, "Please forgive me, but you need to see this." He slid the photograph toward her. Although not deep, the tooth marks were clearly visible, wide spaced.

She looked down, pushed the photograph back toward him, and looked up to meet his gaze. An amazing try, he decided, but a veteran could easily read her eyes.

He said, "Are they the same marks?"

Her eyes steadied. "Of course not. How could they be?"

"Jackie, I've been in this business for a long time, but I've never been in anything like this. Right now, the only thing I know for sure is that I want you safe."

"I'm safe, Link. But thank you."

"If you're safe at all, it's only temporary. He's vicious. You can't trust him."

All unease had left her eyes, almost as if blown away by a wind gust. She said, "I don't even know what you're saying."

He nearly smiled at the recurrence of their pattern. If an interrogator wants to learn anything from the resilient Mrs. Billings, he'd better ask it quickly. "Help me investigate this. Help me bring him down."

"Be honest, Link. You're trying to weave together a hodgepodge of circumstantial stuff, right?"

He locked onto her eyes, trying for some kind of rapport, some kind of breakthrough. “Sure, any veteran cop operates on theories and speculation. But please listen to me. I believe you’re tangled up with the wrong person. And you don’t deserve to live, or to die, with such filth.”

“I thought you suspected me of murder or something.”

“If so, only in self-defense. There’s an excellent chance for immunity.”

“If anyone would buy your string of circumstantial, right?”

He again despised the savvy of her coach. “True.”

“Be honest with me, Link. You know what you’re asking me to do. Are you sure of any of this? Even a murder in Pittsburgh?”

He exhaled slowly, shaking his head. “No, Jackie. I’m not sure of it. My game is all about probabilities.”

“If I thought I was in danger, wouldn’t I jump into the lap of the FBI?”

“Not if you feared a greater danger.”

“Now you’re confusing me.” She stood and reached for her coat. “I need to run. Merry Christmas.”

He watched her slip into her coat. “Call me when I can help you.”

“I will.”

Chapter Thirty-One

Sean Billings couldn't make Christmas Eve feel right, at all. The family had gathered around the fireplace, drinking hot chocolate, listening to Dad read the Bible story of the first Christmas. It was one of their traditions, just like the trip to the Cut-Your-Own-Tree Farm, the annual argument about long-needled or short, and the fatherly scolding about throwing icicles on the tree rather than placing them carefully, one-by-one. They had attended Christmas Eve services earlier in the evening; they had driven all over Dublin, looking at Christmas lights; they had sung carols. And Sean felt the kind of fear that he hated: the kind that gnaws at your stomach, that almost makes you feel sick.

He knew Christmas was going to be lean this year. He had spotted the arriving Wal-Mart sacks. He had overheard discussions that told him that Dad's construction business wasn't doing well. That was okay, though. Wal-Mart was okay. But things weren't okay between his mom and dad. Sometimes he just wanted to scream, *Quit pretending! I know both of you had screwed up childhoods and you're trying to make our Christmas happy. But quit pretending and tell me what's wrong.* But he couldn't bring himself to talk about it. The fear was too great. So now he was pretending, too.

His dad finished the reading and picked up the package he had put beside his recliner. His mom picked up the gift beside her chair, too. Sean rose from the hearth ledge, walked to his mother, took the package, and carried it to his dad. Jodi rose and took Mom's gift to Dad. Then the kids returned to their seats and watched. It was tradition.

Dad opened his gift first. It was a leather wallet, nice, but definitely not expensive. He looked toward Mom, tried for a smile, and said, "Thank you."

She tried to smile back. "You're welcome. Merry Christmas."

She opened her package, a cream-colored sweater with rows of dark blue triangles. Lots of years, her gift was jewelry, sometimes with diamonds. She looked at Dad and said, "Thank you." But it was easy to see that her eyes were wet with tears, and not because she was happy. The gnawing feeling in Sean Billings' stomach started trying to eat him from the inside out.

Everyone hugged and said Merry Christmas. Sean hugged his mother harder than usual. He was uncomfortable hugging her most of the time, but Christmas was a good excuse, and he really wanted to hug her. His hug with his dad was awkward. Maybe next year they would just shake hands. If there was a next year.

His mom and dad took Jodi upstairs. They would tuck her in, maybe tell her a story. Sean was allowed to stay up a little later, of course. He decided to spend the time in his basement nook. He tried a couple video games, but got his butt kicked both times. He flipped on the TV but nothing was on but Christmas stuff. How many times can they run *It's a Wonderful Life*? He surfed the net for a while. Checked some movie reviews. Wondered which shows his parents might let him watch with Tara Essinger. Not a date; just the gang. Still, he kind of liked Tara Essinger. But he couldn't even get his heart into thinking about Tara.

He walked back upstairs. His parents were beside the fireplace again, not talking; just looking into it. He said, "Good night, Mom; night, Dad."

His mom turned toward him. "Good night, Sean. Sleep tight." But she barely smiled. Her face looked almost pinched. His dad didn't even turn, but Sean thought he heard a mumbled *good night*.

He walked by Jodi's door. It was open, of course. Jodi didn't like being alone behind her door. He noticed that the entire wall against her bed was lined with stuffed animals. He knew what it meant. "Are you asleep?" he whispered.

Her head stayed down; her reply was a whisper, but distinct. "Yes, are you?" It was a joke they often shared, and he liked it that she was trying to make them laugh.

He walked into her room and sat on the edge of her bed. She turned to lie on her back, her hands behind her head, looking up at him. He really liked Jodi. She was funny, and as cute as could be. There was barely room to sit because of the mob of stuffed animals on the other side of her. He said, "You okay?"

"I guess so, but I don't think this is our merriest Christmas."

"I see you've got a few friends with you tonight."

"Yep."

"Why?"

"Cause."

"Cause why?"

"Cause cause."

"Things will get better, baby sister."

She tried for her smile. "Don't call me baby."

He smiled back. "Sorry. Get to sleep so Santa will come."

"There isn't a Santa. You know that."

"Sure there is." He leaned toward her and gave her a kiss on the forehead. "Good night, sweet Jodi."

"Thanks for coming to my room."

Twenty minutes later, she got out of bed and knelt beside it, eyes closed, hands folded. "Dear God, this is Jodi Billings, and I live at 4146 Duncan Place in Dublin, Ohio. I guess you already knew that, right? I haven't been praying as much as I should, so I'm sorry about that. But I bet you hear 'Now I lay me down to sleep' 'til you're 'bout sick of it, right? Anyway, my Sunday school teacher says I can talk right to you, and you'll listen. I don't see how that can work exactly. But I hope it does, 'cause I need to talk.

"Things are really bad at my house and I don't know why. Christmas is our most favoritest time, and this year it's been really bad. My mommy looks really worried and sad all the time. You can see it in her eyes. She has the prettiest green eyes. When she looks at me, like when she's telling me an Elrod story or something, her eyes make me happy. But now they're always worried and sad.

"My daddy looks different too. It's almost like he's there, but really he's not. Like a couple times this week, Sean—that's my brother—or me would ask him something or say something to him, and he didn't even hear us.

"Here's what I'm afraid of, God. I'm afraid my mommy is really sick. I think she's losing weight. She's still pretty and everything, but I think she's losing weight. Last year my friend Casey Fishman's mom lost lots of weight, and then she died. I guess she's there with you, but Casey really misses her still, and if my mom died, I just don't know what I'd do. And I'm afraid she's worried and dad's worried because she's sick, and they just haven't told me and Sean yet.

"So, please, God, don't let her be sick and don't make her come to heaven yet, because I really, really want her here.

"Okay, thanks for listening to me. Say happy birthday to Jesus for me.

"Amen."

***

On New Years Eve, Jackie and Matt emerged temporarily from their self-imposed gloomy exile, accepting an invitation to an impromptu neighborhood party. Jackie drank two glasses of champagne and felt a little better. Matt had several beers. There was spirited discussion about the Buckeye's chances in tomorrow's bowl game. Things felt almost normal, at least for a while.

A well-lubricated Ty Jameson cornered Jackie, alone in the kitchen. "Hey, girl. I was hoping for an encore of our Blakely moment. How 'bout a squeeze?"

She asked, "What Blakely moment?" dredging her memory. She had drunk a little too much, but not enough to forget a Ty Jameson encounter.

He weaved gently in front of her, eyes bleary. "Hey, when I grabbed a little ass after we talked in—"

"I think you're dreaming," she said honestly. As he moved toward her, Jackie spun away, reasonably gracefully she thought. "Find someone else to squeeze, Ty."

Paul Dorsett showed up late, also well into his cups. Neither Jackie nor Matt had seen their attorney since the terrifying day in his office. They mumbled greetings but made it a point to avoid him.

When the big ball dropped at Times Square, there were New Year's kisses all around. Ty got something like a squeeze, though brief. Far more importantly to Jackie, she and Matt kissed deeply for the first time in weeks. She savored the moment.

***

Daniel Berringer had enjoyed the battle. He knew Link Pettigrew was a worthy opponent not yet ready to admit defeat, but the intrigue had ended. He needed a new game; Ted certainly did. The pilot grew more restless every time they spoke. They spent New Year's Eve in Vail where Aldrich skied and studied the taut backsides of young snow-bunnies while Daniel Berringer planned the next activity of the AB gang.

They would change their roles. They would utilize private planes. They would abandon use of the XYZ Farm. It would be a faster, more thrilling game. And it would start soon.

***

Link Pettigrew soul-searched during his post-holiday vacation and decided on full disclosure of his fears. Mac McSoley's expression reflected more shock than eagerness to be involved in this kind of investigation. "Jesus, Link, an agent, maybe two, playing sex games…extortion, murder. Unbelievable!"

"There's some chance of an imposter, but I'm afraid it all rings true."

After half a day of deliberation, McSoley delivered a decision. "It's too speculative, and for the moment it's on our watch. Let's keep pressing. If we find the smoking gun, we'll turn it over."

Link verified that the embezzlement-missing person pattern had not repeated in November or December, information that supported his theory that Jackie Billings had managed to outwit—at least to this point—seasoned killers who had been bright enough, and brutal enough, to elude authorities in Pittsburgh.

***

Jackie did not hear from Link Pettigrew for the entire month of January. She talked weekly with Columbus-based Agent Carmody whose admitted role included checking the possibility she had changed her mind about cooperating in the investigation. At one point she asked Carmody about Link Pettigrew and learned that "another aspect of the case" had caused Link to focus in Washington.

Don Baxter now called weekly, short, indifferent conversations that reflected his increasing confidence that Pettigrew's investigation would end, yielding nothing.

Jackie poured energy into her family and could see signs of the kids' improving spirits, although they continued to spend a lot of time together, and she could easily guess why. Kaye Lassiter showed signs of forgetting past job indiscretions, mostly because Jackie had worked extra hours, unpaid, for years, and had been averaging forty-five hours weekly for the past several weeks. Jackie's employee group had done a wonderful job of keeping things going during the hard times.

Jackie decided to re-enter therapy with Dr. Geiger, although Matt refused to join her. She feared that he was living with her out of duty to his children, and possibly because of concern for her safety. Still, he was there, and that gave her reason for hope.

***

As Jackie entered her office, Laura Geiger stood to welcome her, but failed to deliver a professional greeting. "My God, have you been ill?"

Jackie smiled wanly. "Not exactly. Or maybe I have."

After Jackie recounted her past several weeks, Geiger understood the physical problem, but abruptly ended the session, saying she would need to check her legal status as recipient of news of a probable murder. They went to work after that, but Jackie's earlier issues felt almost trivial compared with her struggle for anything like stability while she battled the plethora of issues that had whirled out of an unspeakably gruesome moment.

For Laura Geiger, the new set of Jackie sessions brought the end of full professional objectivity. She had never encountered such a blend of focused determination coupled with ongoing willingness to reach out for answers and insights. She could barely believe that the same woman could tenderly love her family and find the streetwise toughness to play her side of the remarkable game she had been thrust into.

She tried to help Jackie understand that Matt's reaction was closer to a state of shock than to hatred or indifference; and that recovery remained possible. They explored Jackie's growing fear of being abandoned. Geiger explained that the fear is common for those who lose a parent early, magnified if the other parent isn't close.

Dr. Tollison, head of the clinic, asked to meet with Laura Geiger, "behind closed doors." Of course, Tollison knew first-hand of the tangled legal situation. He had led the meeting with the clinic's attorney that verified their privileged relationship with Jackie. Nonetheless, he said, "I'm not saying we would throw a patient out, but this smacks of harboring a fugitive. I just don't think it's what we're about."

Laura Geiger fully understood his feeling. Their clinic specialized in family counseling and enjoyed close ties with many area churches. Four of their rooms included wall murals featuring cuddly cartoon characters. "Our medical oath is about her care, isn't it?" she asked. "We aren't law enforcement officers."

"I understand that, Laura. I've simply never felt more conflicted." Then, as if to reassure himself, he said, "And it's not about dollars. It's about a vision I've had since youth."

"What are you suggesting that I do, Frank?"

"Encourage her to go to the police. This is a matter for law enforcement."

"Without regard to her well-being?"

Frank Tollison sighed heavily. "Damn it, Laura. Damn it."

"If this clinic can't work with her, I'll work with her privately."

"That violates your contract. You know that."

She nodded her head and met his eyes squarely. "I know that."

The following morning, Dr. Tollison dropped by her office. “I’m sorry about yesterday. Work with your patient, Laura. And God bless both of you.”

***

At Dr. Geiger’s suggestion, Jackie made a determined effort to increase the family’s involvement in their church. “You need to trust God, Jackie, especially now.” But Matt merely showed up, constantly distracted. And Jackie struggled for anything like trust in God. Part of the time she felt overwhelmed by the guilt, unable to pray for God’s help in solving the chaos she had caused. Part of the time she felt like finding a place to hide from life. Much of the time, she felt anger. But she kept trying.

She volunteered to serve on the Outreach Committee, a step that led to bi-weekly family trips to a homeless shelter. Matt participated, if half-heartedly, and that bit of connection helped. Jodi and Sean befriended a man named J.R. Zimmerman who soon convinced them he had once been a pirate. That was fun. And the whole experience was therapeutic, just as Dr. Geiger had promised.

Jackie had an unexpected opportunity for outreach when Sherry Jameson asked to talk. Her marriage was wobbling. She didn’t understand everything, but the sexual side of their relationship wasn’t working. Sherry said, “He isn’t satisfied with anything. He’s gloomy, constantly. He’s drinking more. He’s calling me stupid every time I turn around. I imagine he’ll be wandering soon, if he isn’t already.”

Jackie had no trouble believing that possibility. She did her best to help Sherry, even suggested that she work with Dr. Geiger. But Sherry said therapy felt premature. Besides, she saw no chance at all that Ty would enter counseling.

Chapter Thirty-Two

In early February, Sherry Jameson asked Jackie to join her for coffee. They met in Sherry's breakfast nook, spending a few moments in silence, watching the snow falling gently outside the bay windows. Sherry was clearly troubled, and Jackie assumed their topic would relate to the status of the Jameson marriage.

Sherry met her eyes almost fearfully. "I haven't known whether to tell you this or not, but I think I have to. There's a terrible rumor circulating about you. And about Matt."

Jackie's mind raced. "What rumor?"

Sherry looked almost ill. "I don't believe it. None of us do. But they're saying you killed a man, and Matt covered it up."

Now Jackie felt ill, nauseous. "Who are they?"

"It's just buzzing. You know, like rumors do. Since we heard it, Ty has been checking around to see how it got started."

"And?"

"Paul Dorsett got plastered at the country club the other night and said some stuff. It's not true is it?"

"No, Sherry. It's not true. But I feel really sick right now. I'm going back home."

She shared the news with Matt as soon as he returned from work. He sank into his recliner, eyes closed, face pale. "God, Jackie, this kind of thing could kill our reputations; it could hurt the business, which we sure as hell can't handle. The kids..." He opened his eyes to glare at her angrily. "There's no end, is there? Son of a bitch." And he stormed out of the room.

A day later, Sean approached her, eyes wide, to report hearing the rumor.

Jackie had prepared for the possibility, but the need for deception felt as wrong as it could possibly feel. "Isn't that the craziest thing you ever heard?" They talked for a few minutes. Sean listened with hopeful eyes, because he needed to hope. But his expression remained stricken.

***

Jackie Billings roared back onto Don Baxter's radar screen when his routine phone call included discussion of their attorney's indiscretion. The murder rumor might reactivate law enforcement attention. If arrested, she would likely try to plea bargain with a promise to help prosecutors. The bloodhound named Pettigrew would be sniffing closer.

"The guy can't do that, Jackie," said Baxter, pouring disdain into his voice. "You could own his house if you want it. Here's what you need to do…"

Baxter's advice smoothed the immediate crisis, but the costs included money the Billings could ill afford and indirect exposure in the Dublin *Weekly Tribune*.

Local Attorney Apologizes for Comments

Attorney Paul Dorsett has issued a rare public apology to a Dublin couple for a rumor that emerged from a drunken conversation at a local country club. In a formal statement, Dorsett said, "I deeply regret my reprehensible behavior in making uncontrolled comments harmful to two of my clients. These comments have been taken out of context to create rumors harmful to the good names of good people. I will do everything in my power to undo any damage I have done by my actions.

The Tribune has elected not to reveal the names of Dorsett's clients out of respect for their privacy

William Larimore, the Billings' new attorney, drafted Paul Dorsett's statement. Dorsett issued the statement, word-for-word, hoping for probation rather than disbarment when the Ohio Bar Association reviewed the matter. He again vowed to join Alcoholics Anonymous, although he hadn't yet worked a meeting into his busy schedule.

The bald and heavy-set William Larimore was a thirty-five-year veteran of criminal law, and a man who inspired enough trust that Matt and Jackie tried again for counsel on their dilemma. Larimore absorbed without apparent shock, but said, "If we were certain that Collier was directly involved in a serial murder ring, we might get immunity in return for testimony. But a judge wouldn't grant it if there were any doubt, and there appears to be major doubt. I've never heard of anything like this. I'll look for precedent cases, but I'm not optimistic."

During a follow-up visit, Larimore suggested a bold offensive: Baxter was legally vulnerable for threats to the Billings and for his admitted role in the Pittsburgh extortion plot. Why not try to have him arrested? They asked whether Baxter, if arrested, might take them down with him. They asked whether Baxter might kill them at the first hint of their cooperation with law enforcement. William Larimore pursed his lips and said, "Good questions. I'll keep studying."

***

On the morning after the newspaper apology ran, Matt rushed to his office for a 6:30 a.m. crisis meeting with his project manager and crew.

Minutes before the school bus would arrive, the phone rang. "Jackie, it's Harold. I'm following the emergency vehicle to Riverside Methodist. You'd better get over here."

"What...what happened?"

"We were around the table talking. Matt said he felt strange, faint. But he kept trying to run the meeting. Then he just keeled over. ER got there quickly."

Oh, God. Oh, God. This can't be happening. Not again. "Is he—?"

"I don't know anything, Jackie."

She looked up to see Sean standing in the doorway, concern painted all over his face. "Jeez, Mom, what's wrong?"

"It's your dad. Something's wrong. I've got to go to the hospital."

"We're coming, too."

She replayed a childhood scene she would never wish on her children. "Just go on to school. I'm sure he'll be okay."

"No way, Mom. We're coming with you."

She yielded quickly. "Get your coats."

Harold Manus waited in the ER lobby. He was a grizzled old-timer who had been a Billings Construction employee for nearly thirty years. He liked Matt, although he wished Matt were tougher on the men. Now Matt's toughness felt like a minor matter. Matt's life might be in jeopardy. Harold's future might be in jeopardy. He stood, surprised to be greeting the whole Billings family. "How is he?" Jackie asked. Jodi's search for comprehension showed in wide eyes. Sean looked grim, as if steeled for the worst.

"They're calling it a cardiac event. They're not sure yet what happened."

"But is he—?"

"He's stable now."

"Can we see him?" asked Sean.

Manus said, "I know your mom can go in. You guys wait here and I'll check."

Harold led her toward the automatic entrance door, but turned briefly to check on the Billings kids. The scene behind him was one he would likely never forget. A young wife, face anxious, eyes fearful. A young man sitting beside his sister, arm around her shoulders, trying to be brave enough for both of them.

They ran into the attending physician just inside the door. "This is Mrs. Billings," said Harold.

The doctor was young, heavyset, wearing ER green. "Mrs. Billings, has your husband been under unusual stress?"

"Yes. We're going through a difficult time."

"I'm talking about tremendous stress, Mrs. Billings. Anything like that?"

Harold Manus could see her discomfort, the pain in her eyes. He wondered whether he should leave or stay. She said, "Yes, doctor, he's been under tremendous stress."

"Has his health been good?"

"Yes. He's always healthy. He works hard, and he works out, some."

"I'm hopeful we've had nothing more complicated than an SVT—supra ventricular tachycardia. It's a break in the heart's rhythm often related to stress. Maybe triggered by caffeine. Of course, we'll want a full battery of tests."

"Can I see him?"

"Yes. You can go on in."

"The kids are here; they're thirteen and eight; can they see him?"

"For a few minutes."

Harold said, "You go ahead, Jackie, I'll bring them in."

He wore a light green gown, and sat at forty-five degrees, nose oxygen and IV in place. "Hi, Matt. You scared us."

The corners of his mouth formed a weak try at a smile. "I scared myself. They said I had no measurable blood pressure when they got there."

"That doesn't sound like a good thing."

"No, it's better to have blood pressure."

"The doctor said you might not have had a heart attack. I was scared to death it was a heart attack."

"I didn't feel anything happening in my chest. But I guess you don't always."

"I'm so sorry, Matt. I did this to you."

Before he could answer, Harold, Sean and Jodi came through the cloth enclosure.

Matt said, "Hi, guys."

Sean spoke first. "Are you okay, Dad?"

Matt nodded. "I'll be fine."

Jodi said, "I knew you'd be okay. I just knew it."

***

FBI Agent Carmody in Columbus picked up Dublin newspaper coverage of Paul Dorsett's confession. Straightforward investigation revealed the names Matt and Jackie Billings. Carmody notified Link Pettigrew in Washington, and Pettigrew wrestled with a new level of personal conflict. Truth appeared to be upon him, the truth he had suspected. But what should be done with this kind of truth? Link shook his head. *It's no wonder this woman is struggling to find someone to trust.*

Darren McSoley had accepted the lull in active investigation in Columbus, hoping that the FBI's internal investigation would yield a break in the case. But he had resented from the start Link Pettigrew's baby-soft handling of Jackie Billings; in fact, Mac had noted in his case file the possibility of Pettigrew's romantic interest.

McSoley summoned Pettigrew to his office. "It's time for all-out interrogation of this Billings woman. She looked suspicious to me before. Now it's certain."

"We have nothing that's within gunshot of admissible, Mac."

"Where the hell is your head, Link. I want a straight answer: do you think she committed murder?"

"I'll grant a strong possibility that she has something to hide. But what about fundamental fairness? This woman was being stalked by a serial killer, maybe a team—"

McSoley sighed audibly. "I'm over this shit, Link. Your so-called team theory is highly speculative. The possibility she killed an innocent man is real. You are an investigator. So investigate."

"Every instinct tells me he was part of a serial murder ring."

"Damn it, Link. Even if there is a team, there's a chance she killed the wrong guy, a guy with no intention to harm her."

"Members of a team would be accomplices—"

Mac McSoley rose and glared directly into Link's eyes. "You are not a judge. You are not a jury. I am issuing a direct order. Return to Ohio and conduct a thorough investigation. You will either bring the Billings woman to justice or help break an important case."

Link Pettigrew met the gaze. "Is that what this is about, Mac; sacrificing Jackie Billings for your next big score?"

Now their eyes locked, dueling. "Your sympathy for this woman would be touching, Agent Pettigrew, if you were her priest or her rabbi. Until you are ordained, get off your ass and do your job."

Chapter Thirty-Three

Jackie answered her kitchen phone on a cold Saturday morning. "This is Carolyn Trask, Columbus Police, but just a mom today."

"Yes?"

"My daughter and I are in Dublin; she's seven. Could we buy you and Jodi lunch?"

Jackie frowned, trying to visualize the gathering. Harmless enough, she decided. "Sure, I guess so."

The two women soon sat across a table at Chuckie Cheese, with its inside games, slides, trampoline room, and more. Jodi Billings and Angela Trask had swiftly bonded, now lurching from activity to activity.

They began with light-hearted discussion of Carolyn Trask's challenges as a single mom, But Trask paused in mid-munch of a pizza slice and asked, "Do your kids ever do anything, and be less than honest about it?"

"All kids do, right?"

"I think so. I always try to convince Angela that it's just better to tell the truth."

Jackie studied the woman across from her. Trask's blonde hair was down, longer than Jackie had expected. She wore a scarlet OSU sweatshirt. Her face carried no expression that Jackie could read. She wondered if they taught impassivity at the police academy. Jackie said, "Does she pay attention to you?"

"I don't know for sure, probably not."

Jackie said, "I suppose it depends on how dark her secret is, right?"

"I try to tell her that the darkest secrets are the ones she shouldn't keep. They almost always cause problems later."

"I suppose it's hard for her to decide who to talk to."

"I'm sure it is."

Jackie's stomach churned. She changed the subject, chatting about life as the parent of a teenager. The girls ran by the table multiple times, showing their prizes and asking for money for more tokens. Jackie and Carolyn finished lunch and gathered coats and purses. Carolyn Trask said, "Link Pettigrew impresses me. I think he's a good man."

The lunch with Carolyn Trask became another log on a fire that Laura Geiger had already attempted to light. Laura appeared to be increasingly convinced that Jackie should confess. But Jackie had asked her a direct question: "If it were you, and if you knew your kids would grow up while you were in prison, what would you do?"

Laura Geiger thought for a long moment. "I honestly don't know, but I do know that living a life of fear is like drinking slow poison."

Jackie understood her meaning, too well, but couldn't imagine yielding to the risk of prison.

***

Link Pettigrew had hoped to arrive in Columbus with the kind of breakthrough information that would win Jackie's support. Link read and reread all files and transcripts. He computer-searched. He asked for field assistance in each of the cities from which a woman was missing. "Find husbands, family or friends. Be as sensitive as possible, but find a pattern of sexual involvement before the disappearance. Look for any clue of an extortion plot. Find a breast bite shortly before the disappearance."

Investigators found nothing but a pattern of reluctant, often guilt-filled, discussion of marital difficulties. Link felt grudging admiration for his adversary's tactical skill. He had somehow made it plausible to Jackie that Alicia Radcliff had died accidentally in Pittsburgh. He had sealed all evidence connecting the missing women to Pittsburgh, or to Jackie.

Now scrambling for his breakthrough, Link Pettigrew generated a new shower thought. He had been assuming a two-man team masterminded by a law enforcement veteran, likely FBI. He had assumed that ongoing knowledge of criminal investigations allowed the mastermind to approach a woman vulnerable to exposure of damaging information. He had assumed the mastermind used his case-knowledge to secure or extort his own sexual moments, further setting the woman up for the Cavendish extortion, followed by murder. It made sense, even if an ugly kind of sense.

But today's shower raised an improbability. What were the odds that a law enforcement professional, even one with extensive access to investigative information, could come up with a beautiful woman having the ideal profile, annually, like clockwork? Case files might possibly provide the profiles, but these women would be secondary players in the investigations, not prime suspects. And files rarely include photographs of secondary players.

Once Link saw it, he kicked himself for taking so long. The so-called team included a third conspirator: a scout, a man in ongoing contact with a sizable number of women. And the team generated its own damning, extortion-worthy information. Link continued to believe that the mastermind was a law enforcement veteran. He now doubted that a law enforcement agency's files were being exploited for criminal purpose. He scrambled backward into memory and into his files, recalling that Alicia Radcliff had been involved with a pilot. A possibility.

And slowly, Link's new revelation became a new approach to winning the trust and cooperation of Jackie Billings.

Chapter Thirty-Four

The clock had moved well past midnight. Jackie Billings lay sleepless, back-to-back with her husband, a position that had become common, no doubt easily explained if she ever discussed it with Dr. Geiger.

"Are you awake?" he asked, his voice an odd, anxious whisper.

"Yes, I'm awake."

"I can't do this anymore. I'm drowning. I thought I was going to die yesterday. It did something to me."

She turned toward him, reaching toward him, hoping she could comfort him, knowing another apology would do no good.

"I need some time away from you, Jackie. I'm sorry if I'm weak. I love you. At least I'm trying to. But I can't think. I'm not close to getting over the anger. I'm eating myself up inside."

A different kind of anguish swept through her. "What about the kids?"

"I'll do everything with them that I'm supposed to. I'll get an apartment over at Hartwick. I'll be close. I just need some space, a chance to try to figure out what's going on in my head."

She closed her eyes, as her breathing became short gasps. "Okay, Matt. I can't blame you."

"But, do you think you're safe? I mean from Baxter. If not, I'll—"

"I think so. Things have quieted down. If he wants to hurt me, I doubt you could stop it anyway."

Matt paid another visit to his mother, this time borrowing enough for household items and rent on a one-bedroom furnished apartment, available month-to-month. Hartwick was a standing joke in the neighborhood, known as the place where wayward husbands moved or were kicked. Jackie had not imagined that Matt would ever be a resident, but soon found herself watching her strapping husband, shoulders stooped, carrying two bags toward his truck.

In the days that followed, Matt kept his promise of involvement. But Sean slid toward depression first. Jodi was more buoyant, but nothing like her old self. Jackie dug deep to find the energy to compensate. She studied with them, planned special meals, bought gifts she couldn't afford, and told Jodi stories every night. But she had no good explanation for their father's absence. She and Matt had decided not to sugarcoat the split, meaning no easy promises about the possible outcome. They called it time and space that parents sometimes need to think things through.

A week after Matt left, Sean walked into her bedroom. Although midnight had come and gone, Jackie was wide-awake, reading. She rarely fell asleep before 2:00 a.m. anymore.

"I'm going to help you more, around the house, until Dad comes back."

"That'll be nice, Sean. Thank you."

"He's going to come back, Mom. I know it." He hesitated. She could see his throat working, his chin quivering. "Dad and I had a talk once. About, about…stuff. He'll be back."

"I think so too, Sean."

"I love you, Mom."

"I love you too, Sean."

Sean's visit made that night a poignant experience, but night became Jackie's new enemy. Too often she heard footsteps, although footsteps made no sense. When wind howled through the trees outside, she vividly recalled fearful nights as a little girl in Greenville. Three dreams haunted her: Don Baxter, twice; Ted Aldrich, once; slipping silently into their home.

She thought often about Link Pettigrew and about Carolyn Trask's not-very-veiled advice. Indeed, Link appeared to be a good man, a sincere man, the kind of man she could trust. But so had Aldrich; and so had Baxter; and the nights ran long.

Ten days after Matt moved out, Jackie received a real visit from Ty Jameson. He showed up well into the evening, likely after kids were in bed, likely on a night when Sherry was out with friends. But he stayed only briefly, chatting about a Brett-Sean Scout outing and ending with, "If I can do anything to help you through all this, just let me, or Sherry, know."

Exactly one week later, she heard a soft then gradually more insistent knock on a downstairs door. She glanced toward her bed-side clock: 11:20 p.m. She considered simply pulling a pillow over her head. But too many possibilities came to mind, and ignoring some of them—CPD, the FBI, or Don Baxter—might be unwise. She slipped out of bed, slid into her robe, and followed the knocking to the rear patio door. She noted the twisted grin, considered waving him off, but knew he might simply continue knocking. As the door slid open, Ty said, "Hey, Jackie B., it's time to talk."

His eyes and his voice told her that he had been drinking. She should have escaped gracefully at the door. But she thought that Matt might have been with Ty for drinks, and she wanted to know how Matt was doing. Ty breezed past her, touching her cheek as he walked toward the kitchen. She heard a tab-top pop open. He returned, unsteadily, to the family room and plopped into Matt's TV recliner. She sat on the couch, suddenly sadly aware of the extent to which she craved adult company.

They talked briefly about a barking dog ordinance the home-owners' association was considering, and the conversation went downhill from there. Jackie wanted to talk about Matt and how he was faring. Ty declared Matt a fool who didn't know what a good thing he had—despite Ty's attempts over the years to convince him that he was a lucky man. Jackie listened with something like fascinated disgust. This was Matt's friend since college; her best friend's husband.

He said, "Wanna know when I knew my Jackie was back? Man, you show up at Blakely's in the little bikini, looking good. I mean really good..." He lifted himself out of the chair, walking toward her then behind her while he rambled on. "And there in the kitchen, when I held you for that minute or two..." She felt his hands on her shoulders and she cursed the small part of her that thought his hands felt good. He said, "I could see it in your eyes, Jackie. Just like I could see it when—"

She pulled away and stood. "Time for you to head home, Ty. And don't come back alone, ever."

He walked around the couch, approaching her, his eyes doing their best to undress her, she decided. She pulled the robe together at her throat and crossed her arms, wondering if he needed any further clues. "Goodnight, Ty."

"I'm not buyin' it, Jackie. You wanted me at Blakely's, and you want me now." He reached toward her shoulders with both hands. "And you need it now."

She took one step back, glaring. "If you touch me again, I swear to God I'll scratch both your eyes out." He stopped, making a pathetic effort to focus bleary eyes. The arms dropped to his sides. She said, "Get out, Ty. Right now."

"Don't tell Sherry, okay," he blubbered. "I'm a little drunk. I was just trying to help you."

She felt a wave of nausea. "Just get out of here."

***

On reflection the following morning, Ty Jameson realized he had made a mistake. Booze can make a guy do stupid things. On the other hand, he had probably been within a minute or two of finding the land of milk and honey. Hell, no guts, no glory, right? Hopefully Jackie keeps her mouth shut.

During his drive toward the office, Ty declared Jackie Billings an unappreciative bitch. Hell, she could have simply said she didn't want to screw. He would have been happy to talk to her, or keep massaging away her tension. She had no reason to humiliate him. She sure as hell wasn't some virginal Bible thumper. He knew better. At Blakely's, he had felt her heat. He tried to focus his memory. Jackie shows up in a little bikini, looking damn good after all those years that Matt had dressed her like a nun. She drank her share of Blakely's infamous rum punch, corrupter of women's souls for years. She smiled a cute little smile when he complimented her on the new outfit. But was that Jackie's bikini bottom he had rubbed on—and in—in the kitchen? Was he in the kitchen at all? Sure he was. So what's with the snooty bitch bullshit now?

I've got a little slush left in the expense account. Why don't we deal with snooty bitches while we help our good buddy Matt during his time of need?

***

Matt Billings sat alone in his small apartment, staring indifferently at TV highlights of a golf tournament, picking at a newly microwaved carryout Chinese dinner left over from the night before. Two empty beer cans had joined the clutter of magazines and newspapers on the coffee table in front of him. Several parts of living alone had surprised him, but his indifference about straightening up led the way. He thought of himself as a tidy detail man, but here it hardly mattered.

Separation time had reached three weeks, and all the tries at sorting things out had left him more confused, not less; more like a ship turned upside down, not less. He had been too possessive. No doubt about it. He had assumed Jackie was fine and had snoozed through all kinds of clues that she wasn't. No doubt about it. He had mangled the party dress scene and too many other scenes. No doubt about that, either. He could make a long, long list of things he should have done better. *But son of a bitch, Jackie. Does any of that justify what you did? Could you possibly do anything worse than give me a head full of images of men arousing you and making you beg and taking you and satisfying you? Then there's the video.*

So he had spent three weeks gyrating from anguish to guilt to fury to regret and always returning to anguish. He thought again of his alternatives. He could divorce her. No one could blame him for that. She had put him through hell. He was still in hell. Every waking moment was haunted. But if he divorced her, then what? What about Sean and Jodi? What about Jackie? He had stood before God and these witnesses and took her as his wife, for better or worse. Matt's face twisted into an ironic smile. *Man!* But that day, as he stood there beside her, he felt like the luckiest person in the world. Their life together had been wonderful. Not perfect. But better than he ever thought he would have. He wanted that life back. He wanted to have it back and a chance to make it better.

But I don't know what to do. I love her. I'll always love her. Am I strong enough to forgive her? I don't know. I'm afraid not. My father would never have forgiven this. Not one-tenth of this. Through the blur of mental confusion, Matt Billings finally saw a glimmer of truth. My father tried to keep me away from Jackie while he was alive. He won't be the reason I stay away from her now. But can I ever forgive her?

A glassy-eyed Ty Jameson and his friends showed up at Matt's apartment late that night. "Meet Mindy and Mandy," Ty bellowed, sweeping his arm grandly. "Mandy's mine. Mindy's yours."

Ty had herded the group inside before Matt recovered from his first wave of astonishment. Ty carried two bottles of pre-mixed manhattans into the kitchen and began pouring a round of drinks. He shouted, "Give us some music, maestro." Matt popped an old Van Halen CD into his mini-stereo and returned to his chair. Ty found a kitchen chair and brought it to the party. Mindy and Mandy plopped down on the couch, drinking and laughing. Matt couldn't recall seeing as much cleavage and thigh in one place at one time.

Matt grasped swiftly that Ty had attempted to bring along two clones of Sherry. They were blonde, sunny, and stacked. During a brief meeting in the kitchen, while the men filled a popcorn bowl with ice, Matt said, "If this deal is costing any money, I can't pay my share. I am flat broke."

Ty grinned a crooked grin. "Money is no object, my man. I come with friends because loneliness…" he hoisted his glass, "…and thirst are terrible things."

Mindy apparently knew her assignment. After two rounds of drinks, she rose. "Come with me, Mr. Billings. We have things to discuss in private." She headed for a bedroom hardly ready for entertainment, but she didn't seem to mind. Matt drained his glass as he followed her. *Man, oh, man. What am I doing here?*

She stood by the bed. Matt stood just inside the door, trying to grasp the change in tonight's direction. Solo day-old Chinese had been much simpler to deal with. He tried to decide whether to close the door. Apparently Ty and Mandy wouldn't care. Ty's voice easily snaked its way down the hall and into the bedroom. "You jus' say where, and I'll start nibblin', baby." Matt shut the door.

Mindy put both hands on the hem of her ultra-short white dress, and began lifting slowly. Sultry blue eyes locked on his eyes. Her hands caressed curves as they moved up her body. Her hips swayed gently. The rising dress revealed a tiny pink bra above tiny pink panties. The dress cleared her head. The bra fell to the floor. She said, "Come here, big guy. Let me teach you things you never knew."

Matt walked toward her, vaguely aware that he was simultaneously juggling more emotions than ever in his life: surprised, confused, lonely, horny, angry, and even guilty—although guilt returned him to surprise. If he spent a week with Mindy, he couldn't match a tenth of the pain Jackie had inflicted. Mindy raised her arms, buried her hands in thick blonde hair, and fell backward onto the bed. "Start with my boobs," she cooed. "Kiss me. Suck me." He slid onto the bed on his knees, leaning toward her, kissing her, deciding her breasts were at least twice as big as any he had met personally. She purred deep in her throat and moaned, "Now the other one. Hurry."

Matt's mind hit full race. I don't know what the hell I'm doing. It's way too bright in here. Do I turn off the lights? But then it'd be pitch black. Would she like that? Hate it? Not care? How about a closet light? Is she really turned on, or a professional pretender? Do I care? Will Mr. Big perform when the time comes? Then it happened—possibly the strangest moment of his life. From somewhere in his head, he heard a song that his mother played for him years before. His mom was a huge Elvis Presley fan, and Helen occasionally shared a little Elvis with her son. Matt could hear the song, hear it clearly: the melody, the lilting baritone. *Her hair is soft, and her eyes are oh so blue. She's everything a man could want...but she's not you.*

Matt kissed Mindy on the cheek. "I'm sorry. I've got to go." He adjusted his jeans to minimize embarrassment, walked out of the bedroom, passed the couch where Ty and friend were screwing vigorously, and drove home.

Matt parked at the curb in front of his house, pleased to see light in the bedroom window. The garage door opener hung on his visor, but for reasons he couldn't explain, he knocked on his own front door. After a wait that felt like hours, he saw the shadow of her eye in the door's peephole. The door opened slowly, perhaps tentatively. She was beautiful. Her hair was brown and her eyes were oh so green.

"Hi, Matt."

"Hi, yourself."

"Do you need something?"

"I need you."

"You do?"

"Yes. Now. Always."

Her eyes filled with tears. "I love you."

"I love you, too."

They poured two glasses of wine, sat by the fireplace, and came to the same realization at the same time. They had so much to talk about that it made no sense to begin. She said, "Would you like to go to bed?"

"Jackie, you have no idea."

They hurried up the stairs, sharing light laughter as they realized their rush was far from quiet. "Is Sean asleep," he said softly, as they reached the upstairs hallway.

Jackie whispered, "He'd better be." She opened the bedroom door, grasping his arm to pull him inside. Matt closed the door quietly and turned to face her, finding her eyes in the faint glimmer of a bedside nightlight. They said nothing, but their expressions spoke of separation and pain, loneliness and fear. They stepped into an embrace, at first gentle but soon intense, as if holding a child lost but then found. When they stepped back—their eyes shared a fierceness born of passion, determination, and defiance. At least for this night, for this moment, they would rise above the forces that had attempted to destroy them.

Their lips and bodies came together with a kind of ferocity neither had experienced. She finally broke the kiss, whispering in his ear, "I want us to be naked, Matt." Clothing fell and flew, and they returned to an embrace bordering on savage.

This time, he leaned back just slightly. "Bed," he said hoarsely.

"Bed!" she gasped, taking his hands.

And they were together, on fire, caressing, probing, caring, sharing, protecting, loving. Their bodies made love; their spirits made love; and they exploded together, blissfully, dazzlingly, exhaustingly, triumphantly.

Afterward, while her husband slept peacefully, Jackie stared at the ceiling, aware of an immense weight on her spirit. She and Matt had shared an incredible experience, but she couldn't find complete joy. Tomorrow should be a joyous time with the kids as they welcomed their dad back. But there could not possibly be real joy. She had known it during the time Matt was away. She had poured heart and soul and enormous love into the kids. But there could be no real joy. She wanted to remain free, for her family—a goal that had consumed her mind for months. But she wasn't free. She could never be free.

Chapter Thirty-Five

Link Pettigrew sat alone, staring at the ceiling in a spare office in the FBI's Columbus field office. He hadn't pre-announced this Ohio visit in order to minimize the chances that his adversary could prep Jackie. But even before leaving Washington, he had decided he would rather risk his badge than browbeat Jackie Billings as a murder suspect. Fortunately, his new plan had received McSoley's blessing. Link knew—but might not have fully explained to McSoley—that his play represented another long shot, requiring a break in the steel barriers Jackie and her coach had built.

This whole damn thing was a long shot, he decided, and the most bewildering case he had ever seen. Sometimes the strangeness made him doubt his own analysis, especially about a person as normal as Jackie Billings. Oh, hell, quit BSing yourself, he thought. After you showed her the Radcliff autopsy photograph, you were eighty percent sure she killed a man. When the drunken attorney talked, you were ninety-nine percent sure. McSoley may be an ambitious asshole, but he's right that we should investigate. What's the deal? He's not right about me being emotionally involved is he?

Still, it's an incredibly long leap to meet that woman and visualize a killer. Maybe that's the problem. Maybe I just can't do it. I've done this so long, and seen so much evil, and wanted so badly to crush so much slime, that I can't bring myself to crush a good woman who is trying to keep a life together in Columbus, Ohio. But I'm not ready to retire. I can't go soft every time a case involves an appealing person. So, Link Pettigrew, your boss is right; you need to get off your ass.

If there's a case at all, I've got the pieces put together. He smiled. All I lack is one single shred of physical evidence. Maybe McSoley wasn't so crazy that afternoon when he talked about his interest in Jackie's breast. I wonder if a judge would have granted that subpoena. Well, your honor, we're not erotically interested in her breast, of course, but we'd like to examine it for bite marks, if you please. Probably not. At least I've got a plan. And if my theory is right, and if the plan works, I can track these guys down. Then if there's any justice in the world, we'll find a way to let Jackie Billings live her life. Surely there's a way. Even Mac McSoley can't want that collar.

Until the last thought, Link Pettigrew felt confidence in his analysis. But whether Mac McSoley, or a zealous prosecutor, would leave her alone or pursue her fiercely was another question. Link greatly feared the latter.

Jackie met Link Pettigrew on an unseasonably warm day in early March. They bought Subway-to-go and walked to the same park where she had met Don Baxter months before. Link looked official, blue suit evident under a lightweight tan topcoat. His dark skin contrasted sharply against the coat and a brilliant white shirt. As the March wind whipped at their coats and sandwich bags, Jackie started a discussion about Ohio's changing weather, but Link showed no interest in light banter. Even his initial "Hello, Jackie" had carried a new kind of grim intensity. She wasn't really surprised. Baxter had warned her that Pettigrew would keep coming back and the pressure would continue to build.

He finished salting his sandwich and looked up to focus on her eyes. "They want me to read you your rights."

The words physically jarred her insides. She felt her throat constrict. "What are you talking about?"

"The FBI is sure something happened here. We need to get to the bottom of it."

She felt her heart thudding, but this time blended with an odd weariness. "Why can't this just go away, Link? God, it's been forever."

"It won't go away until it's settled."

She reached into her memory for Baxter advice. The key remained the same. The FBI had no hard evidence. "I have nothing to say."

His expression became a revolving mix of compassion, determination and warning. "I'm going to ask for another kind of help. But first, I'll ask you to consider the danger you're in."

She sighed. "I'm listening."

"Your advisor is extremely dangerous. Say nothing to him about the possibility that we might arrest you, or that we might discuss immunity or a plea bargain. Don't mention any of it, ever."

"I don't know what you're talking about."

His eyes burned into her. For the first time, his tone turned harsh. "Jackie, I like you. You've been through a lot. I may even understand why you lie to me. But I'm asking that it stop. I'm going to bring down two men who are involved in this, and I need your help."

She feared her emotions were showing. She could feel her throat growing even tighter. "I can't help you."

"Because of fear? I can help you if you're afraid of harm."

"Can you guarantee that?"

Link hesitated, analyzing. Her shield had slipped, if only a little—the closest thing to a breakthrough in their multiple sessions. He wished he could seize the moment, but there was only one honest answer. "No. No guarantees. But surely it's safer than what you're doing now."

"I don't think so. I'm safe now. I'm with my family."

"Do you understand my warning about your advisor?"

"Yes." Now she hesitated, obviously analyzing. "If there was an advisor."

Link knew she was slipping back into the forest where she hid. He pressed forward. "There's a way for us to work together."

She waited, watching him warily.

"If your advisor thought you turned on him, you would be killed. If the FBI managed to find him through normal investigative channels, you would not be involved. He would never suspect you helped me."

"I don't see how that could work."

"I'm going to nail the other one first."

"What other one? I don't understand."

Although she had tried again to slip away, he saw a change in her eyes, maybe weariness, maybe awareness that his idea offered some hope. "There are two men. One is your advisor. Is the other one a pilot?"

"Why would I answer that question?"

"Because you want to get this behind you. Because I might be able to help you afterward."

"Might is a weak word, Link."

"I know. It's just a might, but I'll do everything I can."

She deliberated for what seemed like a long time—studying the grass, tracking a gray squirrel as it rocketed up the tree trunk next to them. He waited, sipping from a paper Diet Pepsi cup.

"Yes, he's a pilot."

"Did you meet him while you were flying to Chicago?"

Now he could see fear, plainly visible in her eyes. After another long pause she nodded her head.

"In the terminal?"

Another pause. She shook her head.

"Deadheading?"

She closed her eyes, her breathing becoming labored. She nodded.

"Anything else you can tell me?"

"No. Nothing more, Link. I think I'm going to be sorry about this."

"I'll try to be sure that doesn't happen." He rose and picked up cups, sacks and wrappers. "I'll be in touch."

***

Jodi carried her video game to Sean's special nook in the basement. "Will you play Snow White with me?"

He looked up from his history book. "Do you remember your sacred oath?"

"Yes. Never to tell Brett you play Snow White with me."

"Okay, just for a little while."

They played two games. He let her win both. Jodi said, "Mommy's really worried tonight isn't she?"

"They both are."

"I wonder why. Daddy's home now."

"I don't know, Jodi. I don't know a lot of things."

She shared her greatest fear. "Do you think she's sick?"

"I've thought about that. I hope not."

"Me too. I want us to be all right."

Chapter Thirty-Six

Tracy Washburn drove her ageing Subaru south toward Indianapolis and a rendezvous she could barely believe was happening. She was a second grade teacher at Harrison Elementary in Tipton, Indiana; happily married, more or less, but her destination felt a lot like a date.

They met in New York in a crowded bar in the lower level of the Imperial Plaza Hotel. She had been standing with a group of new friends, all elementary school teachers attending a workshop called *Innovations in 21st Century Education*. He was a businessman in New York to negotiate an import-export deal.

She guessed the dress had caused him to notice her. She had no explanation for wearing it except that the Indiana winter had been dreadfully dreary, and she was alone in New York. The dress was a pretty peach, short and low cut, although she wore a matching jacket until the second or third dance. She had spent some time on her hair, make-up, and accessories. She decided that—for a thirty-five-year-old hick from the sticks—she looked pretty darn good there in New York, New York.

Trey Able was an amazingly friendly guy, but not just to her. She could see him moving among tables and groups standing by the bar, always concentrating on the women. Of course, he had many to choose from. The Imperial Plaza was hosting more than five hundred teachers; at least ninety percent were female. She assumed he was trolling for a companion for the night, so she knew her future with him was not bright.

But he asked her to dance for a second time, and a third. The first two numbers were upbeat, and she felt a bit self-conscious at first, fearful that Tipton-style dancing would look green in New York. But as she looked around the dance floor, she decided that she could twist and turn about as well as most of them, so she began to relax. For an older man, he was amazing. Lithe, limber, smooth as silk. He asked her to dance to a Billy Joel ballad. Unbelievably smooth, and none of the squeeze and thrust or grab-ass that some guys do.

He invited her to walk down Fifth Avenue to a jazz bar he knew. She surprised herself totally by saying yes. Her new friends teased her a bit, but it didn't matter. She had never met them before. She would never see them again.

They had a couple drinks, talked about all kinds of things, listened to some incredible music, and walked back to her hotel. Just inside the lobby, he extended his hand and said, "This has been a wonderful evening. Thanks for sharing it."

Tracy smiled, but processed some real surprise. She nearly joked about expecting something more than a cordial good night at this point. But he appeared sincere, and she was basically relieved. "I liked it, too. Thanks."

"Might we meet for breakfast tomorrow? I really enjoy talking with you."

More surprise, but breakfast sounded just fine. Safe as it could be. Tomorrow was her last day in New York, out at 4:30 from La Guardia.

They shared a great breakfast, and he picked up a tab that would have purchased dinner-for-two and a set of snow tires in Tipton, Indiana. During their last few moments together, he mentioned that his business brought him, by private plane, through the Midwest now and then. Might he call her?

It was crazy, she knew it. But she said yes. She gave him her cell phone number and told him the best time of day to reach her. She really never dreamed he would call.

But now he had contacted her. She would soon be meeting him at the municipal airport two towns south of Tipton. She wasn't proud of that decision, but Tipton is a town too small; adventure is hard to come by; and Hank—all 288 pounds-and-rising of him—probably wouldn't notice as long as she picked her airport carefully.

Chapter Thirty-Seven

At 11:30 p.m., Dr. Laura Geiger remained buried in her home study, listening to Jackie Billings tapes. She wore blue silk, but the outfit included a robe and long-legged pajamas, the unspoken signal to her long-suffering husband, Stan, that it was another work night. The case had become an obsession for Geiger, but tonight involved more than study. Tonight she would reach a difficult decision. She virtually spun in her chair, shifting from tape recorder to computer keyboard to printer to three-ring punch to the binders that now held hundreds of pages. She stopped spinning, grabbed the doodle pad that helped her think, began drawing flower shapes, and tried to decide where experience, conscience, and duty should intersect.

From the beginning, this had been the kind of case you dream about when you start school, and start practicing: A wonderful woman trying desperately to become whole. An incredible array of issues. A colorful supporting cast. And the horrific added ingredient of a shooting.

In ways Laura had never experienced, she had grown to know the characters, and that knowledge had forced tonight's deliberation. Some factors were routine, even if Jackie's case reached the far edge of routine. A mother who qualified as a caricature of herself, so extreme and so distant that damage to Jackie had been somewhat minimized. No such luck for Mia or for the tragic Henry, who soldiered on, loyal physically to Madeline but focusing his spurned love on his elder daughter. Dr. Geiger saw no sign of incest or molestation, but Jackie had received too much of the wrong kind of love for a nine-year-old to handle, and then it was gone. Apparently, before he departed, Henry poured some soldier into Jackie. Max Collier, meet Captain Henry Morris.

Then we have Clancy Billings who almost single-handedly caused the rest of the dominos to begin falling. I truly believe, thought Geiger, that Matt and Jackie would have been fine if Clancy hadn't declared her a slut. But Clancy screwed up his son's head, the Matt-clamp started coming down on Jackie, and eventually, almost inevitably, she rebelled.

I'll say one thing on behalf of Matt Billings. He's the greatest living example I've ever seen of a piece of Dr. Tollison's folk wisdom: *The secret to staying married is staying married.* That guy has been to hell and back, and he somehow hangs in there. So it's a relationship that can survive, if they can weather this crisis. Fortunately they had already done some of the hard work before the big winds blew. If the foundation of improved communication hadn't been built, there would be no chance they'd survive this storm.

Laura Geiger drew a line on her notepad and wrote the word *Survival*. She had reached the key issue in tonight's mental exercise, and she meant survival in its most literal sense.

I know too much about Don Baxter, she thought. I'm guessing this Aldrich is, at the core, a halfway decent guy who has been taken down the wrong road by Baxter. But Baxter is a piece of work: brilliant, a far more gifted con man than Aldrich ever thought of being; cold, calculating, and one hundred percent ruthless. His seduction of Jackie was psychologically manipulative in a way I can't imagine a man could live with. All that comes to mind is a lion tearing apart a crippled gazelle.

Even now, Jackie is conflicted about her feelings toward Baxter. In a way, she understands that she's the conduit for his mind-game with Pettigrew. But she has somehow lost track of the extent of Baxter's manipulation, and the extent of his cruelty. Of course, he is brilliant, and he continues to con. He has constructed a story so solid that Link Pettigrew—another brilliant guy in all this—has failed to punch a hole in it. The so-called survivors that call her are a brilliant stroke, however Baxter is managing that. So Jackie doesn't know who to believe or what to believe and she's terrified of going to prison and probably she should be.

But I know who to believe. I know that Donavon Baxter is a liar, and a ruthless killer. I know it because I feel like the son of a bitch—pardon me, Lord—has been lying on a couch in my office. And I know that he's going to kill her. He'll kill her to keep her quiet. Or he'll kill her for sport. But he's going to kill her.

So what do I do? I'm her therapist, not her bodyguard or private detective. I've already encouraged her to work with the police, and the mini-clue she gave Pettigrew may be a sign of progress. I hope so. But I haven't told her to run to the police. I haven't screamed out loud, *Jackie, he's going to kill you. The guy you think is helping you stay out of prison is going to send you straight to the grave.*

It's not even that simple. If I did scream it, I think she would do exactly the same thing she's doing now. She is so incredibly determined to maintain her family that she'll continue risking her deal with the devil to avoid the risk of prison.

Do I sit quietly with this knowledge and let her die? I suppose it's the professional thing to do. She's an intelligent adult making her own choices. I've let people walk out of my office when I knew they were virtually certain suicides. And they were. And it was a terrible feeling. But isn't this different? This will be a murder that I've allowed to happen. The murder—Review Board, forgive me—of a woman I love.

Her clock said 12:10 a.m., but she called Dr. Tollison anyway. He mumbled his hello. She declared it crucial that they meet early in the morning. She would bring his favorite bagels.

They sat at the small conference table in the corner of his office. Frank Tollison listened to the whole analysis and to Laura Geiger's heartfelt desire to initiate a contact with Link Pettigrew, to tell him everything she knew, and to beg for protection for Jackie, both physically and, as much as possible, in a court of law.

Frank Tollison hurt for her. Emotional involvement is an ongoing occupational hazard. He had rarely seen a more heart-wrenching example. Selfishly, he wished the Billings matter would move on, and Jackie Billings' early arrest would accomplish that. But he said, "You know the right answer, don't you?"

Laura Geiger's eyes filled with tears. "Yes. I know the right answer."

Chapter Thirty-Eight

Tracy Washburn dreaded this drive into the country. Today, she would have her second meeting—off the record, out of the way, thank goodness—with a private investigator named David Belzer who had been hired by Trey Able's very unhappy wife. Belzer didn't know everything; Tracy's brief affair with Able had been torrid beyond anything he would have likely imagined. But he knew enough. And now Elaine Able knew enough to divorce her husband and make life miserable for Tracy.

In a way, David Belzer was helping Tracy. Even he had been surprised, and frightened, by Mrs. Able's fury. Apparently, at its peak, she had threatened to drive to Tipton and do some kind of major violence. Belzer said her threats, screamed with veins bulging in her forehead, included burning down Tracy's house. She had even mentioned owning a gun.

Belzer said he felt real conflict. Elaine Able was paying him; he was just doing his job when he discovered and reported back the affair. But he would feel major guilt if anything happened to Tracy. He offered to try to calm Elaine down, at least enough that all this could quietly fade into the past. Today's meeting, in a way, was Tracy's idea. Belzer admitted he didn't understand enough about the mind of a jealous woman to talk sense into Elaine Able. Tracy said she would be willing to try to explain it to him, although she had to admit that she lacked direct personal experience. Hank didn't inspire much jealousy.

She parked her car behind an abandoned outbuilding on County Road 30A and waited for the very tall, very lean, very striking

David Belzer. He had found the spot; in fact, he had suggested they hike through the nearby woods while they talked.

While she waited, she thought back to their last meeting. Belzer had made it clear that he couldn't help her for long without payment. She said that was a problem, because money was scarce at the Washburn house; the plant had put Hank on limited hours. Belzer had smiled a different kind of smile, and the newly worldly Tracy Washburn knew how she could pay up. But she had decided, firmly, against it. She had made one mistake now causing an incredible set of problems. To make another one in less than a month just didn't make sense. She would tell David Belzer that she would try to save some money each week and pay him a fair price.

Belzer called her on her cell phone and asked her to pick him up. He said he had run out of gas about a mile away. She found him easily, standing by the road, his car parked in a dirt access lane between two cornfields. He explained that he had just enough momentum to get off the road. She thought it odd that a detail-oriented investigator ran out of gas, but she needed his help, so she allowed him to get into her car. They drove back to the original meeting point. He sensed a difference in him, and she felt pangs of fear although she didn't understand why.

He showed her where to park: a spot well off the road beside an abandoned railroad line. She told him about her plan to pay him, and he said that was fine. She joked that she was afraid he wanted some other kind of payment. She said she'd done too much of that, already. He said he understood how she felt; he was okay with it. She felt much better, as if another hurdle had been cleared in putting her life back together.

He said, "I love the countryside here. Let's have an adventure, like we were kids." She said okay. They walked along the old rail lines, sometimes balancing across from each other on the rails, sometimes hopping from crosstie to crosstie. They were actually laughing now, enjoying the gentle breezes of a warm spring day. Wild flowers bloomed purple and white in meadows on both sides of the tracks. The troubles with Trey and Elaine Able felt far away, at least for a while. She decided that it had been silly to feel afraid.

They came to the trestle that crossed the old Williams Creek, mostly dried up now. He said, "I dare you to cross."

She laughed. "I'm a farm girl, David. I've crossed trestles higher than this a hundred times."

So they started across. When they were about a third of the way over, she realized the trestle was higher than she had remembered—or was she just older and more timid? In either case, she couldn't chicken out now. She concentrated harder. A slip would not be a good thing. She turned her head to talk to Belzer about the trestle's height. Her heart skipped several beats as she realized he was only a foot or two away, and reaching toward her.

She had never seen an expression like this one—a twisted grin formed of a strange grimace, almost like he was aroused, or crazy. Hands suddenly grasped both her shoulders. Huge hands. Powerful hands. The hands lifted her, turning her around until she nearly faced him. She looked into crazed gray eyes and shrieked, "What are you doing?" She raised both her hands, trying desperately to clutch his hands or his wrists. "No! Don't!" But he was far too strong.

He whispered eerily, "Goodbye, Tracy."

She felt like a rag doll being tossed aside. The rocks rushed toward her, rapidly transforming from distant pebbles to menacing boulders. The scream stuck in her throat. A horrific jolt. Dark. Still.

Chapter Thirty-Nine

Daniel Berringer sat in his study, making notes, aware that he had successfully surrounded himself with intrigue. The new game—faster, more intense, more opportunities—was well underway, although he battled disappointment in its rush value. Fortunately, Link Pettigrew refused to let the old game die, so Don Baxter continued to face a worthy opponent.

But Pettigrew may have erred, perhaps badly. During his latest Jackie call, Baxter had asked about Pettigrew. She admitted he had recently visited Columbus, but her explanation rose no higher than *he was just in the area*. Pettigrew would not fly to Columbus without a reason. He should have fed her a new tactic, or at least a bone that sounded like a new tactic. Without one, it makes me wonder if she's plotting.

Plotting against me would be a poor choice for Mrs. Billings. But she's been steady as a rock so far. She's been a good student. Hopefully she hasn't done something stupid.

***

In Washington, Link Pettigrew made intense use of computer records, field investigators, and contacts inside the airline industry. He had previously learned Alicia Radcliff's itinerary. Four of his five missing women had flown alone in the first half of the year they disappeared. All had flown on TransSystem Airways. All connected through Chicago.

He notified Jackie Billings that computer work could have plausibly generated the lead she had given him. He asked again for additional information about the pilot or his henchman. Her answer carried decisiveness he knew too well, tinged with fear. "I can't be any more involved than I am."

He made the first of several trips to Chicago, flying commercial on TransSystem Airways, interrogating aggressively.

***

Baxter received an Aldrich call absent the pilot's normal easy humor. "The FBI is snooping, talking to flight attendants and counter people about a pilot who likes the ladies."

Baxter processed the news without surprise. "It's retirement time, Ted. Just get the hell out of Dodge, settle on your sixty acres in Ohio and we'll keep having fun."

Aldrich paused, no doubt processing anger that another career had ended. But Baxter knew he wouldn't risk prison. "Okay, I'll fly today's leg and bail out."

"Just disappear. Now. They're close."

Ted Aldrich cleared his locker, took a taxi to Meigs Field, flew a vintage Beechcraft toward Ohio, and began experimenting with life as a gentleman farmer.

***

Two days later, Link Pettigrew had his man, although the man had vanished. Theodore Hamilton Aldrich was reportedly a charming silver-haired rogue whose ability to meet women was the stuff of legend. Pettigrew had found counter people who helped arrange his meetings, and stewardesses who marveled at his ability to open women up. He found crew-lounge employees who related Aldrich luncheon stories. Whatever Pettigrew's suspicions, he found no one who could imagine Aldrich being involved in violence toward women. One flight attendant said, "He worships women. He treasures time with women, and frankly we treasure time with him."

But Ted Aldrich apparently had something to hide. He vanished without a trace, a disappearance no doubt directed by the team's mastermind.

***

Baxter placed an unscheduled call to Jackie Billings. "We've had a little excitement."

"What would that be, Don?"

"The FBI flushed out Ted, which frankly I find fascinating."

"What do you mean?"

"I would hate to think you had anything to do with it," he said darkly.

"Of course I didn't. I'm not crazy."

"I'd call it an odd coincidence; just a couple weeks after Pettigrew visits you."

"If they found me with a breast bite they could surely find Ted flying around the country. Flight records were probably all they needed."

"You're on thin ice, Jackie. Flight records might find Ted if Pettigrew's serial murder theory was anything but bullshit."

"Don't go there, Don. I'm willing to believe you; I can't do anything about whether Pettigrew believes you."

Baxter shook his head. *This woman is amazing*. "Coincidences usually aren't. Pettigrew talks to you. Ted is flushed out. I don't like the way that looks."

"Good grief. You're the one that keeps threatening me. It would never occur to me to rat out Ted. I haven't even thought about him in weeks."

Her voice carried the right combination of plaintive and confident. Her argument made sense, but he wasn't finished. "I'm in and out of Columbus, Jackie. I'm watching. If I get a whiff of you helping them, there will be a hole in the ground where your house used to be. Do you understand me?"

"Of course. I've understood that for months."

"The video would be fun to release. Don't you think?"

"I understand all that. Damn, give it a rest. I just want this behind me."

Now her voice carried just the right blend of anger and impatience. He clicked off the phone wondering if he had made a monster. If so, she was very, very good.

***

Link Pettigrew called Jackie. "I've got the pilot ID'd. I need a clue to link the second guy. Any clue at all."

Jackie looked for a second burst of courage but found only fear. "Could you connect Aldrich with any of your missing women?"

He paused. "Not directly. But he's easily TransSystem's most notorious lover. It all fits, Jackie. You know it does. The missing women meet Aldrich, just like you did, then something happens to them. Work with me."

"I'm sorry, Link. I'm afraid I've already done way too much."

***

Baxter called Aldrich. "The Jackie Billings game is, hands-down, the most intriguing game I've ever played. She is something else."

"How so?"

"She survived until she became irrelevant. This Pettigrew is major league. He must have fully investigated in Pittsburgh. Learned that Radcliff met a pilot. Learned that a second guy, a so-called FBI agent, laid her. He suspects the same pattern for his missing women, and flight records support it. All Jackie can possibly do is verify what he already suspects."

"Will she?"

"No. From the start, her only goal has been keeping her family together. The video is too damning. It'll keep her shut up. She's smart enough to know she can ride home free now."

"Are we home free?" asked Aldrich.

"Close. Pettigrew is almost out of bullets."

Daniel Berringer awoke with the feeling, a nagging annoyance like an itch just beyond reach in the middle of the back. He took his daily coffee carafe to the lower level study. He gazed into forests now alive with blooming spring, and annoyance became anger, and anger became raw fury.

Time had become his enemy. Death loomed. Not old age. Never old age. But perhaps a law enforcement bullet. Or his own bullet if facing capture. Or his own bullet if facing the slide into insanity that had consumed his mother.

The games had become his life, ABC, AB, and his solo adventures near the beaches of Daytona Beach, Malibu, and Cancun. The games had become his link to his wife, source of useful drug-enslaved contacts, never more brilliantly employed than as Jackie's so-called survivors, proof of my innocence. The games fought the black swirl of depression that had threatened to consume him after the intrigue of his CIA career became the bleak boredom of forced retirement.

So he invented games, and he escalated games when blackness descended. He had found hope in the sweet death of Alicia Radcliff, that mysterious eroticism first discovered when he ended the jealous whining of the beautifully sensual Lieu Thi, his long-ago Vietnamese houseguest.

After he convinced Aldrich that death was good policy, the intrigue trend turned up for two or three years. He lived for the signal from Coffey indicating it was time for D-Phase; the slow, anticipation-filled drive to XYZ; the few hours comforting women terrified by their time with Coffey; seeing life and hope return to their eyes; then taking it away. But then slippage. Less satisfaction than the year before. Flailing tries but failing outcomes—the entire Tracy Washburn affair had afforded no more than six or seven hours of solid intrigue. Fear that black depression lurked, ready to consume his soul.

Yesterday he saw the upside—Jackie Billings' gift of an unexpected new game. Jackie Billings as conduit to the brilliant Agent Pettigrew and the enhanced technical power of the FBI. Incredible. As good as it gets. Pettigrew and I dueling through Jackie—knowing about each other, respecting each other's genius. And I won. I beat Pettigrew, hands down. My wall of evidence held. He never cracked Jackie Billings. I moved Ted at precisely the right moment. Pettigrew never got close to me. I kept a hundred balls in the air, brilliantly.

But shit. I may have beaten Pettigrew and the entire FBI and the Columbus Police Department, but I didn't beat Jackie Billings. She eluded death at XYZ by killing my partner. She eluded death on I-70 with her truck driver. Then she flushes out Aldrich and cons me again. Shit.

Daniel walked to his desk and found a yellow legal pad. He started with rough notes then filled in details. A great game. A game that uses my skill and savvy. A game aimed at a worthy adversary. And best of all, a game with a marvelously symbolic grand finale. Control her. Watch fear rise. Drink in the intoxicating power. And send her plummeting from on high where she dared to fly with me.

He called Ted Aldrich. "Ted, two things: First, we're getting out of the death business. I'm starting to agree with you; the sex is good enough, and safer. Second, I've got an incredible idea for a new game. You'll love this one, pal."

Chapter Forty

On the third Saturday in May, Jackie and Matt drove toward Dublin after a wonderful afternoon at Paramount Kings Island, the massive fun park near Cincinnati. Jackie turned to check the kids. Jodi had fallen asleep in one of the rear seats of their Pathfinder. Sean's head bobbed obliviously as he played roaring music into a Bose headset, a birthday gift from his grandmother.

Jackie said, "Okay, Matt, I need to decide something, once and for all."

"What's that?"

"Whether to confess; you know, turn myself in."

Now Matt swiveled to check the kids. Sean continued to bob. "My God, why would you even think about that now?"

"The old reason, and a new one."

He frowned. "Explain."

"Today, while I was riding the on the roller coaster with Sean, I could tell that he loved it that I was with him. And do you know what I was thinking about while I should have been sharing his wonderful time?"

He exhaled slowly. "Yes I do."

"It's horrible enough to constantly worry about being arrested, and now Laura thinks I should confess, right away, for my own safety."

"What's with that?"

"She says Baxter is more dangerous than…than whatever would happen if I turn myself in."

"It's hard to imagine, after making it this far."

"That's what I told her. Our life is almost normal. I think that, if we survive long enough, the fear won't be as bad. And Baxter's even nice to me when he calls. Just checking in, he says. He even told me a joke last Friday."

"Plus there's some chance that Pettigrew catches the guy, right?"

"There's a chance."

Matt's brow furrowed. "So we have more reasons not to confess, not less. I don't understand what you're thinking."

"Maybe it's just intuition. Maybe it's because I trust Laura. But I have a feeling it's going to get bad."

Matt mulled for a mile or so. "I don't want you to confess, period."

She knew that part of his reasoning involved the possibility he would be arrested as an accessory, but she knew that he was thinking of the kids, not himself. The decision felt complicated beyond all belief. Maybe simple consideration for her husband and for the care of their children was still the most important factor. "Okay, Matt. No confession."

***

Link Pettigrew sat at Mac McSoley's desk, running through a multi-item agenda. The entire Mac crew, and much of the rest of the FBI, had been buffeted by the need to investigate terrorist possibilities. But Mac had not given up on his case in Ohio. When Link successfully flushed out Ted Aldrich, Mac's thirst for a high-profile score reached fever pitch. He had asked for an update.

"We're grinding through the list of Aldrich acquaintances, but it's massive," said Link. "He was a highly social guy through high school, college, Air Force service, and a bundle of high-romance careers including stockcar racing. The long-list has thousands of names; the short-list has hundreds. And we could be looking for a guy he met in a bar somewhere."

Mac McSoley's nodded with something like thoughtful malice. "You're going to have to make your own break, just like with Aldrich."

"Our mastermind did a number on her, Mac. She took an immense risk, and he suspects she took it."

"I want progress, Link. Either your brilliance or your lady friend from Dublin had better give it to me."

Link ground on. He reasoned that his adversary had met Aldrich in college or in the Air Force. But Aldrich attended, spottily, the massive University of Wisconsin, dropping out after three semesters. He had neither pledged a fraternity nor resided in a dorm. Link failed completely to find key Air Force records, possibly left behind after the evacuation of Vietnam. Link agreed, if reluctantly, with Mac McSoley. He needed Jackie Billings.

Chapter Forty-One

Sherry Jameson watched her husband drain his third double manhattan as the family finished dinner. "Brett, Laura, go somewhere," he commanded. "Your mother and I need to talk." The kids scattered immediately. Sherry knew they would go to their rooms and play music, loudly. They had learned to sense when storm clouds were brewing.

Ty mixed a fresh drink, and they moved to their patio. She sat in a lounger, studying trees and flowers, making it a point not to look at him. She knew his agenda, and she didn't want any part of it. He turned a straight-backed metal chair toward her and sat down.

"You embarrassed me last night. I don't appreciate it."

His tone bordered on snarl, but she didn't reply or look at him. She wondered whether a husband had ever delivered a more ridiculous accusation, in the entire history of marriage.

Ty leaned forward, forehead deep red. "What the fuck were you thinking? He's the Denver branch manager, for chrissake."

Ty had invited a guy named Carl Doherty to the house for drinks and dinner the night before. Her job, she thought, was to send the kids elsewhere and to wear a dress that might have embarrassed a French whore. She had gone along with that, but when Doherty cornered her in the kitchen and started mauling her, she shut him down.

Now Sherry looked at her husband. "What did you promise him?"

"I told him you were a very friendly lady, which sure turned out to be horseshit."

"God, Ty, how friendly? He had my dress clear up to my boobs before I got him stopped."

"Quit acting like a goddam goodie-goodie. How many guys in your life have pulled up your—?"

"That doesn't matter. I'm supposed to be your wife now." She didn't like the sound of her own voice. She had decided to stand her ground this time, but she had sounded weak, hurt.

"This guy was not our neighbor," Ty fumed. "You'll never see him again. So what the hell's the problem?"

She had expected that shot. A few weeks ago, in the worst decision of her entire life, she had allowed a re-enactment of Ty's four-hands massage fantasy, this time with their neighbor Bob Bonetti. Mary Ellen and the Bonetti kids were out of town. Everyone drank too much, and she made a horrible decision. But Ty had wanted more. "Let's go all the way," he whispered in her ear while Bob busily manhandled her. She refused; Ty blew up; and now she couldn't look Bob or Mary Ellen Bonetti in the eye at neighborhood events.

"I'm done with all that stuff, Ty."

He took a long swallow of the reddish-brown liquid. "I need certain things, Sherry," he said, his expression practically calling her a disobedient whore. "And you need to make some decisions about our marriage."

Anger swept through her. "That makes all kinds of sense. I should screw a stranger from Denver to save our marriage. Great idea."

"Don't go holy on me, Sherry. That is bullshit."

"This whole thing is bullshit. Where does it ever end? Foursomes? Fivesomes? The Ohio State marching band, what?"

He stood, fury now painted all over his face. "I flat can't believe you would joke about this. You had better think about our marriage, and think about it hard." He stormed out. She doubted he would be back before dawn. She barely cared.

Sherry Jameson walked to the kitchen, poured a glass of wine, and returned to the porch. She had already thought about their marriage, and she didn't like what she was thinking. She understood parts of Ty's frustration. Both kids were struggling in school. Brett had gotten crosswise with the Dublin Police Department after a vandalism prank. Ty had been under all kinds of job pressure, almost from the minute the German company acquired Keller Manufacturing. Higher quotas. All kinds of layoffs.

But she couldn't handle the cycle he was in. Drinking more. Wanting sex as another mind-altering drug, but performing badly. For the first time in their lives, a guy who could go all night in college wasn't going at all sometimes. That made him crazy. Of course, he blamed her. The old stuff just isn't doing it anymore, he said. So he wanted to play new games. When she finally resisted, he drank more, and got meaner. She resisted more. He drank more. She sometimes hated the look and smell of him—nearly unbelievable because she had spent all these years calling him gorgeous.

She hated the spiral, but she hadn't really planned to find a new friend—it just sort of happened. And surely every woman needs a person who treats her like a valued human being, instead of a piece of meat being passed around the table.

She found her purse, pulled her cell phone, and dialed a number she had memorized within days of meeting him.

"Hello, Babes," said the voice. Deep, just a touch of drawl. A nice voice. He told her she was the only one who had his cell phone number. She liked the idea, although he always said "Hello, Babes," rather than "Hello, Sherry."

"Can we talk for a while?" she asked.

"Sure. I was hoping you might call. What's on your mind?"

They just chatted, like they had done several times before. She agreed to meet him again, knowing she would share her body with him again, but knowing he appreciated her mind and soul. She loved the way he made love—gentle sometimes, powerful other times, but never kinky.

She would talk with Jackie soon. Jackie had been a good friend, trying to help her work things out with Ty. And Sherry suspected they might have things in common. Jackie had been glowing for a while a few months ago, although she appeared to be doing more worrying than glowing now. No, Sherry decided, I'll keep him a secret. At least for now.

Chapter Forty-Two

The Billings family spent the weekend at John Bryan State Park where they pitched their tent in a campsite overlooking a wooded ravine. On Saturday, they fished and hiked. On Saturday evening, they grilled bluegill, ate quickly, and rode out a briefly violent storm, huddled together in their tent. Sunday dawned bright and beautiful, a gorgeous day. Sean and Jodi spent an entire weekend without arguing. Matt spent an entire camping trip without major snoring. They laughed together. They loved each other. And Jackie almost dared hope for normalcy.

When they returned home on Sunday evening, their voicemail delivered Sherry Jameson's voice, asking Jackie to call her.

"I'm back, Sherry, what's up?"

"Can you go somewhere with me, to talk?"

Jackie could feel the urgency; she had never heard Sherry like this. "Do you mean yet tonight?"

"Yes, please."

"Sure, I'll pick you up."

She told Matt that Sherry needed help, and drove to the Jameson driveway. She honked twice; Sherry emerged immediately, wearing old jeans and a man's shirt, and slid into Jackie's car. She wore no make-up. The normally perfect hair fell in tangled strands. Her eyes were red-rimmed. "Rough night?" asked Jackie.

"We're fighting for about the thousandth time. But that's not why I need to talk. Hurry, please." Jackie began driving.

***

Paul Dorsett reclined in his hot tub, drinking martini-on-the-rocks from an oversized scarlet and white Buckeye tumbler. He was alone, partly because he enjoyed solitude, mostly because Kate had turned high and mighty again. Still, the night was perfect—warm, but not too warm, lantern lights casting a soft glow on his wooded lot, locusts buzzing, martinis sliding smoothly. Maybe, after he relaxed a bit and the kids headed for their bedrooms, he would go inside, smooth things over, and have a little fun with Kate. He shook his head. Seduction always sounded good about midway through his second tumbler, but the result was usually a disaster. Kate needed to lighten up.

He sat up, startled by a faint sound that might be footsteps and rustling in the trees near the back of the lot. He had been a bit drowsy, worried about dozing off. He was sure as hell wide-awake now, but he couldn't see anything. Kate had damn near grown a jungle along the fencerow at the back of their lot. Then he heard a voice, an odd, unintelligible whispering.

Paul sat forward, frightened now. No one should be inside his fence. Kids maybe? No, that made no sense. And the whisper hadn't been a kid sound. He called out a shaky, "What's going on; who's back there?"

The whisper said, "Goodbye, Paul."

He saw the flash; felt the horrific penetration; felt himself pushed violently backward against the edge of the hot tub. He saw water, bubbling white, from the wrong side. He saw a crimson plume, spiraling upward. He saw nothing.

***

Jackie and Sherry found a huge family steakhouse with a total of three cars in its parking lot. They poured self-serve coffee and found an isolated table. Jackie waited, watching her friend struggle to fight back tears.

Sherry said, “I should have talked to you before. I’ve got big problems.”

“We can talk, Sherry, but I really think you guys need to get into counseling.”

Sherry shook her head. “This is different. This is, well, a lot different. I’m having an affair. Or at least I was.”

Jackie’s eyes narrowed. A Ty affair wouldn’t have surprised her. She hadn’t expected this. “Who? Can you tell me who he is?”

“You don’t know him. It’s a guy named Ted Adams.”

Jackie blinked her eyes, brought her hands to her forehead, and rubbed her temples with her thumbs. *Surely not.* “What does he look like?”

Sherry tilted her head, eyes quizzical. “Older, dark brown hair, a short beard, the bluest blue eyes you’ve ever seen.”

Maybe not. Surely not. “Where did you meet him?”

“At the grocery store. He bumped into me in an aisle, and some stuff I was carrying flew everywhere. He helped me pick things up. Just seemed to be a really nice guy. A week or so later he was there again. He said, ‘If we’re going to keep running into each other, maybe we should get acquainted. How about a coffee?’ I shouldn’t have, but I went, probably because I’ve been so pissed at Ty.”

Sherry fingered torn sugar packets in front of her. Jackie took a deep breath, now convinced that her first fear was unfounded. Aldrich had vanished. Aldrich and Baxter knew the FBI was watching Columbus. Jackie said, “How long has this been going on?”

“About a month I guess. At first, it wasn’t physical. We just found reasons to be together. He’s a pilot. Once he flew me clear to Indiana, just for lunch. And pretty soon…”

Oh, my God. “A caring, super-attentive guy, right?”

Sherry frowned, puzzled. "Well, I guess so. But it was more like I was just fun to be with. He'd tell me I was clever, and funny, and—"

Jackie fought fury. "Why are you telling me this now?"

"I might not have. I had some great times. My life with Ty has been miserable; way more miserable than you know. But now I'm in trouble."

Jackie clenched her teeth. *The two old vultures strike again.* "Why are you in trouble?"

"A guy from the CIA is here, saying Ted's a spy or something. They think I'm helping him somehow. I may go to jail, Jackie."

Unbelievable. "Let me take a wild guess. The CIA guy's name starts with the letter B."

Sherry looked up. "How did you know that?"

"Never mind. Have you slept with…what's B's name?"

"Don Baker. No, of course not."

Jackie stood. "Let's go home. I'll tell you something in the car that you won't believe."

Jackie assured her friend that the CIA agent was a fake. She confessed her own times with the two, then Aldrich and Baxter. She skipped mentioning C. She urged Sherry to avoid any further contact with Baxter, now Baker. "They're playing with us, Sherry. It's got to stop."

As they pulled into the driveway in front of Sherry's house, Jackie said, "You're going to be okay, but we need to be careful. Let me know if Baker contacts you."

"He doesn't need to contact me. I'm supposed to meet him Wednesday at Adam's farm, to help him investigate."

"Don't go. No matter what."

"Okay, Jackie. But you're scaring me."

"Good. Be scared." Jackie paused, trying to decide whether to share the full extent of danger. She decided no, for now. "Mr. B and I stay in touch. I think I can handle this."

Jackie turned the corner onto Duncan Place and saw the two cruisers, lights flashing, one in their driveway, the other at the front curb. She pulled into the drive and saw a uniformed officer standing on their front porch. She approached, nonchalantly stopping to pick up a softball and glove from the front yard.

"Jacqueline Billings?"

"Yes. What's going on?"

"Where have you been, Mrs. Billings?"

"What's this about?"

The officer was young, surely not yet thirty, but his dark brown eyes looked confident, intelligent, alert, and persistent. "Where have you been, Mrs. Billings?"

"At King's Family Steakhouse, for an hour or so."

"Is there someone who can verify that?"

"Yes, Sherry Jameson. A neighbor who lives around the corner."

"Do you own a .38 caliber handgun, Mrs. Billings?"

She analyzed swiftly. The gun was registered. The police knew that, or would know it shortly. An officer was apparently inside with Matt, probably asking questions about the gun. "I won't talk to you unless you tell me what this is about."

"An attorney named Paul Dorsett—your attorney, I believe—was murdered tonight. Shot in the chest with a .38."

Her mind veered violently. *My God. Paul Dorsett is dead. Shot. My God.* She struggled to concentrate, to keep her breathing even. "My husband was at home with our children. I was with Sherry Jameson.

"Your husband is having problems accounting for some of his time. And he can't seem to remember where your handgun is."

She felt new fear swirling, blending chaotically with the dread she had battled for months. "I won't talk to you any more without an attorney."

"That is your right, Mrs. Billings."

The officers conferred in their front yard, apparently talked with higher-ups, and told them to make an interrogation appointment before noon on Monday. Jackie and Matt called a family hot chocolate meeting around the kitchen table. She told wide-eyed kids, "I know this is all hard to believe, but someone killed Mr. Dorsett. The police are talking to us mostly because he's been our lawyer for a long time. Everything will be fine. Be as nice to Angela as you can."

Sean walked into their sleepless bedroom at 11:35. "What were they saying about your gun?" he asked, his eyes searching his father's face.

Matt said, "Paul Dorsett was shot by a .38. We had one once."

"Is that the pistol?"

Matt exhaled audibly. "Yes."

"It was here not very long ago," said Sean, eyes anxious.

"I loaned it to a guy at work," said Matt smoothly. "I'll need to figure out where it is tomorrow. But the world is full of .38s."

Sean studied their faces before turning to the door. "Okay, guys. Night."

After long silence, Matt said, "Do you have any idea how horrible that was?"

With a heart near breaking, Jackie said, "Yes, Matt. I really do."

They left unspoken their shared fear. And the night dragged long.

At 11:30 on Monday morning, Jackie, Matt, attorney William Larimore, and the previous night's two officers met around a Dublin Police Department interrogation table. Larimore confirmed that the officers had verified Jackie's alibi. He verified that they had found no murder weapon. He said, "My clients are happy to help with your investigation, but let's clear up quickly that they are not suspects. Matt Billings did not return from a peaceful weekend camping trip, sneak away from his own children, walk undetected to the rear of the Dorsett property, scale a fence, enjoy the convenience that Paul Dorsett happened to be alone in his hot tub, execute a murder, ditch a murder weapon, and return undetected to his children—all in a ten minute time frame. Are you with me, gentlemen?"

They nodded, and Jackie sensed that they had nothing to fear, at least not today.

Larimore asked, "Did anyone in the neighborhood report a gunshot?"

"No," replied the younger officer.

Larimore turned to Matt. "Does your gun shop sell silencers?"

The older officer chuckled. Matt managed a grin as he shook his head.

"But one more time, Mr. Billings," said the older officer. "Where is your .38?"

"I honestly don't know," said Matt, reasonably calmly. "After Jackie and I decided not to let Sean use guns—and that was years ago— I lost interest in guns and hunting completely."

The older officer scanned their faces. "We're inclined to buy all this, folks. Our guys were all over the property this morning, found footprints in the wooded near the back fence. Appeared to be size thirteen. You're an eleven, right?"

Matt nodded.

"We're guessing the guy stalked Dorsett for at least an hour, waiting for his moment."

Matt and Jackie promised to stay in the country; they promised to provide any information that came to mind; and they headed for their car at just after noon.

As they drove home, Jackie felt enormous relief, but anger was bubbling. She said, "This is all Don Baxter; I'm sure of it."

Matt had been white-faced, almost from the moment they left the interrogation room. "Do you have any idea how close we were to the doors of a prison?"

"Where is the gun?"

"At the bottom of a great big body of water north of here?"

"A lake, or Lake Erie?"

"Erie, last fall. God, if it hadn't been for the shoe size, someone might have given me a lie detector test."

"They're stalking Sherry. The miserable bastards are stalking Sherry."

He looked at her with exhausted eyes, his expression past exasperation. "It's hard to worry about Sherry right now."

"I know. But I need to find a—"

"No more, Jackie. I can't deal with any more today."

Jackie considered making an afternoon appearance at the office. Kaye Lassiter had called this morning's request for personal time "unprofessional," because of the short notice. But new forces were at work, clearly. She needed to think, to understand, to make a plan. But first, she needed a nap, desperately. She put together a quick lunch of grilled cheese and tomato soup. Afterward, she fell into bed, finally finding slumber although her mind battled guilt: Paul Dorsett wouldn't be dead today if… And she couldn't escape the vision of Don Baxter, lurking in the shadows of her town, the son of a bitch.

***

Don Baxter dropped his voice into a deep Spanish-tinted accent—thinly disguised—and spoke to Jackie's office voicemail. "There are any number of ways to bring the police into your life, even without mailing a video, preaddressed to McSoley, FBI."

Chapter Forty-Three

Ted Aldrich, cell-phone at his ear, reclined luxuriously in a hammock overlooking his sixty acres of rolling meadows and forests. Daniel Berringer, newly energized, had called again to update the latest game. Aldrich—now in his third month of B-imposed exile—had found new energy in this game as well, provided by the stunning Mrs. Jameson.

Aldrich said, "How goes it with you and my pretty blonde lady."

"She's a challenge. She fell deeply in love with your ass."

Aldrich chuckled. "I love her ass, too."

"I meet her at XYZ Wednesday. That might do it. If not, one more session and I'll score."

"You're down to seven days, ol' buddy. I'm betting against you this time. This one is mine, all mine."

"I'll score."

Ted's tone turned serious. "I'm glad we're leaving her alone."

"Is it love, Theodore, or are you getting soft?"

"Love has nothing to do with it. She's too damn close to Jackie Billings. I can't believe you dreamed this up."

"Just for the intrigue, Theodore. And maybe a little kiss-my-ass for Mrs. Billings who, by the way, clued the FBI onto you."

"Shit," spat Aldrich, anger rising, "I thought she was under control. "

"The ungrateful bitch betrayed us. Can you believe it? After everything we've done for her." B's chuckle did not suggest mirth. "At this point, I'd like to see her dead."

"Fine with me, my friend. But no jail time."

"Never in jail, Ted. Go down with all guns blazing, remember?"

Aldrich walked outside, continuing to absorb the reality that Jackie Billings had cost him his career. Dead would be fine for her. He headed for his barn and used a pull-rope to roll his biplane into the bright sunlight. He fired up the bird and headed skyward.

Ted thought back to Nam where he and Daniel—the man of a thousand aliases—flew fighters together, began their lifelong search for thrills together, and began hoisting their middle fingers into the face of Death.

He thought again about Sherry Jameson—beautiful, warm, inviting, a kitten, and a tiger. He had given a thought or two to bringing her to the farm with him, as a keeper. Hell, maybe even with her permission. Her husband damn sure didn't deserve her.

He shook his head while pulling the nose back to vertical and starting his five hundred foot climb. Hell, he loved them all. The next one is more important than the last one. And so it will be with Sherry Jameson. He thought about Mr. B taking out Jackie Billings. Couldn't happen to a nicer broad. He was glad that B handled the killing part. Apparently he got a major kick out of that. To each his own.

Of course, Jackie Billings' death will get me a most-wanted poster. Oh, hell, it doesn't matter. I've already earned my most-wanted poster, which is grossly unfair when you think about it. I just love 'em. Really love them. Love them ten times better than their idiot husbands love them, and I'm going to be a most-wanted. Oh, well, what the hell? Beats an oxygen tube and soft food and blue-haired nurses and reading the Bible like a drowning man looking for a life raft.

Ted reached the top of his climb and shut down the engine, playing again his version of Russian roulette.

Chapter Forty-Four

Jackie awoke at 4:15 p.m., refreshed by her nap. For reasons she didn't analyze, she drove to Jodi's elementary school, walked to the deserted playground, and squeezed onto a swing, smiling for a moment at the indication that adult buns are wider than young buns. She swung in a gentle arc, now analyzing as hard as she could, first by running through her alternatives.

She could try to re-establish equilibrium. She had already warned Sherry away from all the craziness. Jackie could admit to Don Baxter that she had inspired Sherry to duck. Maybe the Aldrich-Baxter show will just move on.

She shook her head, worrying that she wasn't yet thinking clearly, aware that hoping for equilibrium was naïve and stupid. Something else is going on here; something major. Don—maybe Ted, too—has intentionally, ferociously, changed my world. I need to face some truth that I've been resisting for a hundred reasons. All of Don Baxter's bull about being a businessman caught up in a seduction game was just that: bull. Link Pettigrew's serial murder theory is correct. And if serial murder is part of their game, Sherry would likely be next.

A voice inside her resisted one more time, as if unwilling to accept that she had brought such horror so close to her family. Is there any chance at all that Pettigrew is wrong? That someone else killed Paul Dorsett. That the women who called me were telling the truth. That Sherry will join the list of the duped and go on with her life. Sure, maybe a two-percent chance. Link told me this kind of analysis is about probabilities.

It would be easy to see that this is aimed at me, even if Paul hadn't been killed with a .38. Sherry may be beautiful, but it isn't coincidence that they picked my friend. Is it anger? Did I mess up their game, so they pull something as blatant as stalking Sherry for revenge? Maybe. That might make sense. But good grief, would they kill her right in front of my eyes? Can they possibly hate me that much? Can they possibly be that arrogant, assuming I'd stand by and do nothing, and remain silent after she's dead?

I can see why they might think that. If I help Sherry, I'd be risking my own life; maybe Matt's life; maybe my freedom. They might think I'd let Sherry solve her own problems; that I'd call her a grown-up who got into this mess on her own. But she really didn't get into this mess on her own. She's my friend, being targeted for no reason other than being my friend. Do they think I could live with myself if I let something happen to her? Could I live with myself?

The answer to that question is *no*, a great big *no*. There is no chance I'd sit idly by and risk Sherry's life. Jackie paused, pushing and pulling the swing's arc higher, letting a powerful truth take hold. Don knows me better than that. He knows I won't sit idly by. Don knew Sherry would talk to me, and he knows that I'll do something about it.

So what does he think I'll do? Wait until he calls on Friday? No. He wouldn't think that. He knows that I've become a lot more aggressive. He thinks I'll come to XYZ, either with Sherry or in place of Sherry. Which? In place of Sherry. He knows I'm suspicious that he's involved in murder. He wouldn't think I'd risk Sherry.

Let's look at it from his viewpoint. Why has he stalked Sherry and killed Paul Dorsett? Paul's death is obvious: another *no law enforcement* warning, as if he hasn't warned me a hundred times already. They stalked Sherry to lure me to XYZ. Why else? It's not to have a chat. Don will talk to me Friday. It's not to learn my opinion about their stalking Sherry. He already knows my opinion: that two old farts should leave my friend alone. There's only one reason for all this. He's going to kill me. I don't know why. I haven't understood their real motives from the start, but he's going to kill me.

Now she could feel her mind clicking at a new level. No, I do understand. It's ego. It's macho pride. It's more than messing up their game. I have managed to mess up Don Baxter's mind, and he can't handle it. This is revenge, all right. But he's avenging his wounded ego.

All of that would mean he respects me. I think he respects me enough to know that I just figured all this out. So what does he think I'll do? He thinks I'll come to XYZ, armed, and try to kill him. He knows I'm terrified of losing my family, but he thinks I'll take my chances with law enforcement if I can kill the murder ring's mastermind in self-defense. So he thinks I'll come to XYZ with a gun, or some other kind of weapon, and he's going to get revenge and a perverse thrill out of tricking me, and trapping me, and killing me. It's lame revenge, in a way. A hotshot con man plots and kills a Dublin mom. But I must be all over that guy's last nerve.

She felt her heart begin to pound, as if it knew the answer even before her head figured it out. She had become stronger over the past few months, but not strong enough to win a shootout at the OK Corral, or at the XYZ Farm. She drove home, prepping for a hard sell to her husband. Matt surprised her with his support, although the support felt born of fearful resignation. "I don't like it, Jackie, but we've made it this far on your intuition."

At 8:00 a.m. Tuesday morning, Jackie's office voicemail delivered Don Baxter's latest threat loud and clear. *There are any number of ways to bring the police into your life, even without mailing a video, preaddressed to McSoley, FBI.*

She found a large envelope on her desk, addressed to Jackie Billings, marked *Personal and Confidential.* Inside she found a folded newspaper page, apparently cut out of the local newspaper from a town called Tipton, Indiana. A page two story had been circled in bold red: Tracy Louise Washburn, age 35 … died in a tragic accident … fell from an abandoned railroad trestle … survivors include her husband Hank Washburn and two children, Hank Jr., age 11, and Tara, age 9 …

Jackie took several deep breaths and sat down to steady herself. She read the obituary again, this time through a light sheen of tears. *Two more warnings about no law enforcement, right, Mr. B? Or are you blinding me with enough anger that I charge directly into your trap?*

She picked up the phone.

***

Although Link Pettigrew had continuously hoped for the call, he was surprised when it came. “How have you been, Jackie?”

“Things were almost bearable until yesterday.”

“What happened yesterday?”

“Do you have enough—what do you call it—*probable* to take Aldrich’s friend?”

He laughed. “That will not be a problem.”

“How soon can you be in Columbus?”

“By nightfall.”

“Can you be ready by tomorrow noon?”

“I’ll be ready,” he said, already visualizing action after long months of frustration. “But I need some information: the name of the police jurisdiction I’ll be visiting.”

“I don’t know. I’ll need to check.”

"Call me back, right away."

Jackie used Mapquest and Google to discover that her XYZ trips had taken her to Ohio's Herndon County. She notified Link Pettigrew. Link reached Sheriff Mel Young and asked for a 10:00 p.m., appointment.

"What's this all about Agent Pettigrew? I don't recall ever havin' a Fibbie visit our neck of the woods, much less a hurry-up meetin'."

"When are you up for election, Sheriff?"

"Next November, why?"

"You help me with this one, and you'll be sheriff for life, my friend."

"That's good enough for a ten o'clock meetin', Pettigrew. See you then."

At Link Pettigrew's suggestions, Jackie began her evening by driving to Jodi's grade school and spending fifteen minutes to confuse a potential tracker. At 7:45, she pulled into the parking lot of an inconspicuous three-story office building on Bellamy Drive in north Columbus. She approached Suite 3-C, her heart hammering in her chest as she tried to remind herself that knocking on this door had to be preferable to death at the hands of Don Baxter.

She knocked. Link opened the door, his expression business-like. "Hello, Jackie."

She said, "Hi, Link," but hung back for just a moment before stepping across the threshold. And she stepped inside.

"The FBI keeps space like this to give agents a place to land, and to investigate," Link explained as he led her through a main roomed crammed with digital equipment, then into a smaller room dominated by a round table stacked high with newspapers and file folders.

"Care for a water?" he asked.

"Yes, please."

He reached into a credenza behind him and extracted two bottles. As he twisted them open, he said, "Agent Carmody filled me in on the Dorsett murder. My mastermind, right?"

She nodded. "Almost for sure. His name is Donavon Baxter, as far as I know."

"Why did you call?"

"He stalked my friend, but only to trap me. He's going to kill me."

"What makes you think so?"

She formed a slight smile. "Remember when you told me about a good gut?"

"I remember."

"I just know he's going to kill me."

"What's the story?"

"I'm going to meet him at an isolated farm tomorrow. I want you to figure out a way to capture him while I talk to him."

Link Pettigrew studied her and shook his head. "Decoy work is extremely dangerous. Let's just surround this farm and—"

"It won't work, Link. He has all kinds of surveillance. He's airborne. He'll be gone before you even get close."

They debated. He reluctantly agreed to allow her to decoy. She sketched the layout of the XYZ Farm. She shared her analysis of Baxter's mindset, and her confidence that he would spend a few minutes playing mind games before finishing his twisted scheme. They worked on the plan and the timing and the backup plans if things went wrong.

At just after 9:00, they walked together into a parking lot barely illuminated by distant porch lights. The night was hot and humid, showing signs of a summer storm. As she turned toward him, leaning against her front fender, still discussing whether the weather might affect their plan, Link Pettigrew conducted a one-man internal affairs investigation. He understood that his feelings were the stuff of combat romance, but in an era when citizens refuse to be involved, this citizen would likely face gunfire tomorrow. On a few occasions during their discussion, fear had flickered in her eyes, especially as he described the maneuver that would get her out of harm's way. But grizzled veterans feel fear when contemplating a shoot-out. Most of the time, her face showed a steely determination. Even now, while Link felt perspiration turning his shirt to damp, she appeared cool, her eyes steady, her voice quiet.

He smiled. "I'm honored to have you as a partner, partner."

"I'm sorry I waited so long. I really am."

"I understand all that, Jackie. That's one of several reasons this has been the damndest case of my life."

"You have no idea how much I want Baxter to go down tomorrow."

"Baxter will go down tomorrow."

She extended her right hand. "Good night, partner."

He took her hand in both his hands. As their eyes met, he thought about embracing her, praising her courage, calling this a great moment in his life. But he simply smiled—at himself as much as at her. "Good night, Jackie. Try to get some rest."

At 9:20 she sat down on Jodi's bedside and launched into girl talk, because Jodi had declared herself too old for Elrod the Bear stories. So they talked, again, about how old Jodi would need to be to get a bra and use real make-up. And Jackie again counseled patience, knowing it would be a recurring theme, hoping she would be there to do the counseling. She said, "Jodi, I want to hold you tight for a while."

"Why, Mommy."

"Because I love you to pieces and I want to squeeze you."

Jodi sat up and held out her arms. Jackie held her until Jodi said, "Mommy, you're poofing all the air out of me."

"Sorry, Sweetie. I just want you to know how much I love you. No matter what. Understand?"

"Okay, Mommy."

At 9:50, she lowered herself into a beanbag chair in Sean's basement retreat, surrounded by video screens, audio speakers, soccer trophies, and two teeny-bikini wall posters she couldn't believe Matt had convinced her were okay. "Sean, I've really been proud of you the last few months. You've been great."

He looked uncomfortable. "Thanks, Mom, I—"

"I've got to do something tomorrow that may be dangerous. I think it'll be okay, but I need to talk to you tonight."

The boy in him looked frightened; the emerging man looked concerned. She knew the two were battling. "What are you talking about?"

"I'm going to help the FBI catch a bad guy."

"Are you kidding me? I mean how?"

She knew he had heard the rumors that she had been involved in a murder. She couldn't imagine how much confusion he felt. But he was a tough kid, just like his dad. "It's too long a story, Sean. But it's true. I just want you to know how much I love you, and how proud I am of you, and—"

"Jeez, Mom, don't cry. "

"Are you too big to give your mother a hug?"

"No, I guess not."

She stood and stepped toward him. This time Jackie felt like the air was being poofed out of her.

***

Mel Young sat at a cluttered desk in a tiny municipal office, still in some awe of a whirlwind visit from FBI Headquarters in Washington. Mel had the kind of clear blue eyes and squared chin that, long ago, was the stuff of TV movies. But the passing years had added another chin or two, and an abundant belly constantly taxing the lower buttons of his shirt. He assessed his new partner as a solid guy absent the arrogance that remained a rap on the FBI in the eyes of local law enforcement. Mel listened, trying to avoid a wide-eyed expression, as Link Pettigrew wrapped up the story of Don Baxter, or whatever his name might really be.

"Man, Pettigrew, last week I personally helped round up four head o' cattle that some kids turned loose as a prank. We're talkin' big time, here."

"That we are. Your collar, my friend. Just be there to back me up."

"How dangerous is this guy?"

"Extremely."

"I'll skip mentionin' this to the misses then. She worried about me roundin' up the cows. 'Damn, Mel', she said. 'If one o' them cows had stepped on your foot, you woulda been out of action for a week'."

Pettigrew laughed. "I think we win by surprise. He doesn't figure she'll bring law enforcement in."

"Why's that?"

"We'll talk about that later. I may need a favor."

***

Late that night, Jackie explained the plan to Matt.

The furrows in his brow deepened as she spoke. "God, Jackie, that sounds dangerous."

"Not long ago, Don Baxter threatened to blow up our house."

"Surely it was a bluff, right?"

"Maybe. But he helped me see something."

Matt waited, puzzled about the educational value of bomb threats.

"I see that love is about living, not hiding. I've wanted so bad for us to be together, and safe, that I've made all our lives miserable and unsafe."

"But we do want to be together, more than anything."

"Not like it's been, Matt. It's no good like it's been."

Chapter Forty-Five

Daniel Berringer surveyed the rural roads that dissected the quilt of greens and browns below him. He enjoyed the knowledge that he likely owned the only twin-engine Cessna in America fitted with a nose-mounted machine gun. Colorful acquaintances could provide valuable assets. He had set three reconnaissance objectives for this morning's patrol: First, to determine whether Sherry Jameson was coming alone. If so, she would be held hostage, killed after Jackie agreed to take her place. Second, to determine whether Jackie would be voluntarily attending the party, either alone or with Sherry. And, third, to determine whether either woman had rallied a police escort.

He had developed a contingency to deal with a police escort. He would roar out of the sky and machine gun the overly clever Mrs. Billings—and Mrs. Jameson, if available—into eternity. He relished the thought; close enough to their windshield to see the terror on their faces as realization hit. Her law enforcement friends would watch, stunned and helpless, while Jackie died. He would turn on them, strafing their cars, no doubt receiving incoming gunfire.

If Jackie approached alone—the likeliest scenario for a dozen good reasons—he would return to XYZ, disarm her, crush her in the head game, and force her into the plane. He could visualize her face as awareness changed to terror. He would simply laugh. And then, grand finale.

He spotted Jackie's Taurus within two miles of her turnoff from Highway 3. He pulled field glasses, dipped his wings, and studied the car. She's alone. He climbed another thousand feet to study miles of surrounding roads. No sign of company. He flew back to XYZ, landed, and positioned the plane beside the barn's rear entrance door, engine running, poised for Jackie's farewell flight.

He sauntered to the farmhouse, figuring it would be at least eight minutes until she arrived. He monitored her arrival via the camera angle atop the barn. He watched through the farmhouse window while she parked her car and walked into the barn. He switched to the internal monitor. She's standing in front of the straw, he thought. I'll bet this is exactly the surveillance scene Collier saw. And she'll be carrying some kind of weapon of mass destruction. Damn, she is a tough one, although undone, as expected, by her own emerging toughness. Let's strap on the shoulder holster and show her how the game is played in my league.

Daniel Berringer entered the barn through the side door, gun drawn. The steady drone of his plane filled the barn. Jackie stood beside the straw, facing the main door, unaware of his arrival. She wore blue jeans, a light blue blouse, and a white cloth jacket. Rookie errors, he decided instantly. The temperature must be eighty-five and the dumb bitch is wearing a jacket. Her right hand is fidgeting like a whore in church inside a jacket pocket. "Jackie," he shouted. "Turn your back. Empty your right hand onto the floor. Now."

She jerked, clearly startled, but turned toward him rather than away as she regained her composure. "Gosh, Don, don't you trust me?"

He fired instantly, almost nonchalantly. Wood splintered between her feet. "Don't fuck with me, Jackie. You have fucked with me all you're going to. Turn around."

Her face went white. All smart-ass cockiness vanished. She turned slowly away from him.

"Drop it."

A small Derringer clattered to the floor. "You're a dumb bitch, Jackie. Playing way over your head. Now let's try the other pocket."

She turned her head, speaking over her right shoulder. "I'm strictly right-handed, Don." Her voice remained stronger than made any sense. She should be terrified. But her comment was another green player's error. He fired at her feet again, kicking a shower of splinters against her legs.

"Drop it, Jackie. Now."

Her left hand reached into the jacket. A second Derringer thudded onto the wood floor.

He walked toward her. "Hands on your head. Now."

She raised her hands. He walked toward her, contemplating a full-body search just for humiliation's sake. And it hit him. *It's a setup. Buying time. Too clever. Too perfect. Her car is a Trojan horse. Son of a bitch. Let's grab her quick.*

In one swift motion, swifter than Link Pettigrew had imagined possible for a man so large, Don Baxter grabbed Jackie's arm, and whirled to a position behind her, his Beretta pressed against her temple, his left arm drawn tightly across her chest, his clenched fist near her throat.

Link Pettigrew advanced, gun drawn, from a position just inside the side door. He had been seconds away from taking Baxter out. But the man's instincts—obviously excellent—had saved him from the deadly error of turning to seek and fire. Even now, he used Jackie's body as shield while he zeroed in on his adversary. Link drew a bead on Baxter's forehead, trying to avoid awareness of the tightly drawn fear in Jackie's face, trying to avoid the distraction of guilt. Mel Young was stationed at the window to Baxter's left. FBI backup was coming, but not soon enough to make a difference.

Pettigrew said, "Drop the gun. Release her."

"Not a chance. Drop the gun and she lives."

"Not a chance."

"Pettigrew, I assume?"

"Correct."

"I had hoped we'd meet."

Link realized that Baxter was focused, at least momentarily on his game, not his task. *Let's play.* "You're good, Mr. B. You are very good."

"Not bad yourself, Pettigrew. But a little too cute."

"Let's do this man to man, Baxter. Let her go."

"Cut the white knight bullshit, friend." Baxter visibly tightened his grip, pressed the gun tighter against her head, and began backing toward the rear door, toward the sound of a plane waiting to fly. Link knew that only seconds remained in a textbook situation. Inaction risked Baxter escaping to kill her later. Action risked a reflex action that squeezes the trigger in a death throe. He knew that Baxter had read the same book. And between them stood a woman who didn't deserve to be here.

"Don't move, Pettigrew. She dies instantly if you move."

"If she dies, you die."

"Won't work. I'm ready to die."

"No one is ready to die."

"Try me."

Baxter had nearly reached the haystack. Another foot or two and he could break line of sight, allowing him to turn his gun on Pettigrew, likely firing blind through the hay, likely effectively. Mel Young would be Jackie's last hope, and that was a frightening thought.

Link risked a quick glance at Jackie's face, wondering if she grasped the crucial nature of the next few seconds. He saw a bit of fear in her eyes, but her mouth was tight, flat, an expression of focused determination. Then her eyes signaled action.

She suddenly kicked her feet backward, and tilted her head sharply right, becoming a plummeting weight in Baxter's left arm. Surprise flickered in his eyes as her weight pulled his head slightly forward. And in the instant that Baxter glanced down, Pettigrew fired. She fell out of his arm, crashing to the wood floor. Pettigrew fired again, then again. B should have been dead. Probably was dead. His eyes were fixed, shock registered eternally on his face. But he didn't go down. And with some kind of reflex, he fired once as he staggered backward. His body fell against the tool bench, and he folded onto the floor.

Chapter Forty-Six

Link Pettigrew sat on the hood of a government-issue sedan, hurting like hell but deciding that this wound—a crease of his left shoulder—was a cream puff compared to the shot through the lung he took in Milwaukee in 1989. The medic had cut off his entire sleeve. The rest of his shirt clung to him, sweat-drenched, partly from the heat, partly from the wound, partly from the intensity of the encounter.

A team of FBI technicians now worked the barn, scouring for evidence related to a set of missing women. Link managed a smile as he watched Mel Young emerge from the main barn door, chatting seriously with a crime scene analyst. Obviously Mel had the good sense to appear busily involved while doing nothing to interfere with people who knew what they were doing. Mel had confessed earlier that he had a clear shot at Baxter through much of the encounter, but had taken into account that he had never shot at a human being in his life, and his hands had been far from steady.

Jackie waited in her car while the medic finished working on Link. She approached him, looking more composed than made sense. She said, "I'm glad you're okay."

"How are you holding up?"

She winced. "It didn't exactly go as planned, huh?"

He shook his head. "I screwed up. The second Derringer tipped him."

"At least it turned out okay, except for your arm."

Link thought of the gunfire that had brought real fear to his gut. When he heard Baxter's first blast, Link had just exited his rear seat hiding place and opened the trunk for Mel Young. "What did you think when he shot at you?"

"I thought I was going to wet my pants."

He laughed, and she managed a tense smile. Grizzled veterans feel the same way, but don't admit it. "You took a huge chance when you dived. He might have killed you. I might have killed you."

"He was going to kill me anyway. Can I go home now?"

"Let's have one of my people drive you home. You're probably more shaken than you realize."

Her eyes went distant for a moment before meeting his. "When I was a little girl, I watched my dad die. I can handle this."

He knew he needed to give her fair warning, although it felt wrong to even mention it. "We'll be digging up every inch of this farm, Jackie."

"I figured that."

"Anything to say?"

"No. Dig away."

Link Pettigrew did not pretend to understand this woman. "Aren't you afraid of what we may find?"

She shook her head, her expression grim, determined. "I'm done being controlled by fear."

"Are you willing to help us bring down Aldrich?"

Without hesitation, she said, "Yes."

"We'll be able to keep this under wraps until at least Friday, so Aldrich won't know what happened to his buddy. I'll get with you by then to work on details."

"Okay, Link." She turned and walked toward her car.

He called after her, "I'll do everything I can for you, Jackie."

She walked without turning toward him, opened the car door, slid inside, and scanned the entire scene. She smiled toward Link, raised her left fist, punched the air, and drove toward the XYZ gate.

In theory, Sheriff Mel Young had become the officer in charge of the crime scene. In practice, he conferred with Link Pettigrew on matters as small as whether to turn off the engines of Baxter's plane. The two men walked around the barn.

"It's okay to turn it off," said Link.

"I'm not current on that model," said Young, who had never been in a cockpit.

Link climbed into the plane and shut down the engines. As he backed toward the door, he noticed a briefcase sitting vertically between the rear passenger seats. He retrieved the briefcase and carried it toward the van that would be his ride back to Columbus.

"Why don't you give me a minute alone with this thing, Mel."

"No problem," said the sheriff, who hitched up his trousers and strode back toward the barn like a man with purpose.

Link climbed into the van and snapped open the briefcase, feeling no surprise that the case was unlocked. Baxter knew, as any veteran knows, that an enemy worth his salt will make short work of locks as puny as briefcase locks. Link found no forms, documents, books, magazines, or even receipts—nothing except a black videocassette carrying a handwritten label: *JB*. Link closed the briefcase, placed it under the rear seat of the van, and rejoined the investigation.

Ten minutes later, a silver BMW 540i pulled into the barnyard. A slight, sandy-haired young man wearing a light blue summer suit emerged and asked for the whereabouts of Sheriff Young. Agents directed the man to the farmhouse, where Young and Link Pettigrew now searched for evidence that might implicate Ted Aldrich. "Hello, Mel," said the young man, his grin tight. "Anyone left to prosecute?"

"The deceased may have had an accomplice. We're lookin' into that." Mel Young gestured to Link. "Meet Agent Pettigrew of the FBI, outa Washington. Link, this is our county prosecutor, Trent Hadley."

Link sized him up. Maybe five-eight, alert blue eyes behind wire-rim glasses, a razor-cut haircut out of place in a rural county. A graduate of a minor Ivy League law school, Link guessed, trying to lever himself into the political big time. Not good.

The two men shook hands. Hadley said, "Who shot the victim?"

Pettigrew eyed him. *Poor choice of words.* "I did."

"Justified, I trust."

Pettigrew's gaze turned to a glare. He simply nodded. Mel Young said, "I'll fill you in later, Trent. I would have killed the bastard myself if Link hadn't handled it."

"That's not what I asked."

Link Pettigrew had never handled this kind of moment well. "Look, Hadley, Sheriff Young and I are working a very difficult case. If you can figure out how professionals behave, hang around. Otherwise, get the hell out of our way."

Hadley met the glare. "FBI intimidation will not work in this county, Pettigrew."

Link snapped, but almost wearily. "Look, junior. I just got shot in your county. I'm doing my job in your county. Now get back in your car, go wherever you go to exercise your overstuffed ego, and wait for our report."

"Be sure your report is complete," growled Trent Hadley.

Mel Young said, "It'll be complete. I'll get with you later."

Hadley turned and walked out the kitchen door, slamming the screen behind him. Mel Young said, "Sorry 'bout that, Link. Young Hadley is what my sweet departed grandma used to call a flaming asshole. His dad's a fancy pants lawyer in Cincinnati. Bought him this job. We'll have to put up with him 'til he gets elected to somethin' in Columbus."

Jackie drove home, replaying the scene over and over in her mind. The terror when he fired at her. The relief that she was not hit; that she was still alive. Baxter grabbing her. The men facing off, jousting verbally. Her decision to drop. Her prayer that Link would be ready when she did. The first blast of gunfire, the horrible sound behind her, and a blaze of gunfire while she clung to the floor. Pettigrew spinning and falling to one knee, grimacing in pain. Don Baxter crumpling onto the barn floor, the gray eyes blank. She clenched her teeth, feeling an odd burst of emotional energy. Those few minutes had been tense, terrifying, gruesome, a lot of things, but also wonderful in a way. A man who had threatened her life—in every sense of the word—would never threaten her again.

She worked in the yard until Jodi came home. She fixed her daughter a snack, and they ventured out on a long bike ride together. When Matt came home, he fired up the patio grill and overcooked the burgers again. Sean had invited Brett Jameson over for dinner and video games, but Jackie could tell that her son was anxious to hear about her day. When they had a moment alone, she said, "Everything went fine."

"Did they get the bad guy?"

"Yes. You'll probably see it on TV. He's dead. An FBI agent shot him."

"Good grief, Mom, were you there?"

"Well, I was there, but we had a plan for me to be safe."

"Good grief, Mom."

Jackie and Matt made love just before midnight, the tender kind of love that had become part of their lives. He went downstairs and returned with Pepsi on ice. They sat silently, propped against their pillows in the soft glow of candles on both end tables.

She said, "I imagine they'll find Collier buried somewhere at XYZ."

"Then what?"

"I don't know."

"I've been trying, but I still don't understand your decision. Everything we feared may happen."

"You've somehow learned to love me, Matt. Better than I deserve. I've been a taker, a sponge; a person willing to risk your safety—and the kids'—for reasons that are pretty darn selfish. This is about learning to love you back." For the first time in a terrifying day, her fierce determination gave way. Her eyes glistened. "You don't deserve the hell I've caused. The kids sure don't."

He slid toward her, putting his hand on her cheek, turning her toward him. "Jackie, I love you; we love you, and we want you here with us."

She nestled into his arms, hoping their embrace would last all night, wishing it could last forever.

***

Link Pettigrew had taken up temporary residence in the Bellamy Drive facility. The clock had ticked to 10:45 p.m. on a very long day. He now sat alone on a hard, straight-back chair, hands locked behind his head, watching the tape for the third time. Every veteran of law enforcement has faced moral dilemmas—what evidence to chase and how hard to chase it; which truth to emphasize while testifying. But Link had never deep-sixed evidence. Now he had a stick of legal dynamite in his video recorder. The scene itself did not surprise a man who had studied Jackie Billings intensely. Even on a grainy video, the expression on her face spoke volumes. Link wondered whether Max Collier had time to know terror as he looked into those determined green eyes.

By long-standing habit, Link tried to avoid difficult decisions when he was tired. And on this night, his mind and body felt as if he'd done fifteen rounds with the heavyweight champion. He placed the video in his own briefcase and headed for the bedroom. Sleep came slowly.

Chapter Forty-Seven

The possibility hit him in the shower on Thursday morning. Link grabbed a quick breakfast and drove to XYZ. He parked in the clearing between barn and farmhouse, chatted briefly with the supervisor of the dig, ducked under yellow tape, and headed into the farmhouse.

He began his search on the upper level, two rooms apparently used as bedrooms. He found clothing, toiletries, bedding, books, and magazines. He dug deep in closets, ruffled through drawers, and poked around in an attic thick with dust. Nothing interesting. The main floor living room had been turned into an electronic command center, mostly surveillance and monitoring equipment. No file cabinets. Desk drawers were oddly empty; no documents at all, not even pens or paperclips. A fully featured Sony videocassette system supported this morning's shower theory.

He entered a small kitchen, obviously never remodeled. Refrigerator and range were ancient, as were a small wood table and two chairs painted pale green. He carefully searched cabinets and a small pantry—all routine supplies except that someone was fond of Jack Daniels; nine bottles stood in precise alignment on a pantry shelf.

The cellar was a clutter of old furniture and assorted boxes. Link guessed that Baxter's crew had moved most of the original main floor furniture into the basement to make room for their electronic equipment. He rummaged through the boxes, finding nothing but small tools, a new-looking hunting jacket, and old newspapers and magazines. He made a mental note to check the newspapers' dates and contents against suspected activity.

He entered a small side room that had likely been a coal bin in the house's early years. A green and white saddle blanket was draped over a shape that Link guessed was a tack box. He lifted the blanket and found an ancient steamer trunk, its top ornately carved, banded with tarnished brass. This lid had been locked.

Link Pettigrew had conducted hundreds of investigations and found thousands of pieces of evidence. He had never been more hopeful or apprehensive. He pulled a not officially sanctioned version of the Swiss Army Knife from his pocket, and made short work of the chest's latch. He opened the lid and found six piles of ornate cream and white doilies. He riffled through the doilies, and hit the bottom of the chest—a bottom not nearly deep enough. He removed the doilies, removed the false bottom, and drew in a sharp breath as he surveyed a long row of videocassettes, each labeled with two initials in handwriting identical to that on the JB tape. Link found a cardboard box, emptied it, refilled it with videos, and climbed the stairs to view his find.

Although the videos carried no date, Link guessed they were in sequential order, based on grime and diminished luster of the black plastic. He inserted the tape that appeared oldest. An attractive young woman entered the barn and waited. Collier—no doubt Cavendish in Pittsburgh, of course—swaggered into the frame. He wore a floppy fishing hat rather than the safari hat that he died in. To Link, his tone and swagger were obnoxious in the extreme. Not surprisingly, he successfully intimidated his prey. Link watched discussion of extortion money, followed by the evolution of the young woman from reluctant role player to a terrified victim of unspeakable sadism. Link felt his breathing go shallow, nausea rising. The grizzled veteran had not seen this kind of cruelty.

He watched for half an hour and realized that hours lay ahead. He fast-forwarded through more of the same horror, finally reaching the woman's release from the bondage equipment. But Collier let her go. He issued a stern warning to never speak of the ordeal. He threatened her and her family. But Collier let her go. And Link witnessed a combination of terror, pain, humiliation, and relief he had never seen on one face.

Link fast-forwarded through five more tapes. The pattern repeated except that the cruelty escalated, as if Collier had spent the year planning new torture. His bondage equipment grew more sophisticated. The terror and pain evident in the women's faces escalated. But Collier let them go, and Link began to fear that his serial murder theory was badly flawed.

Link considered giving up, or at least taking a long break. He felt physically ill, possibly spiritually ill, unable to grasp a man's delight in this kind of barbaric cruelty. But he watched the seventh video, and before his eyes a terrified young woman died. At first Collier laughed—a cruel, disgusting, mocking laugh. Then surprise swept his face, perhaps legitimate alarm. He slapped her face as if hoping she was in some kind of trance. But her eyes were fixed. He walked out of the camera's view, and apparently deactivated the system.

Link ejected the video, dumbstruck that evidence so damning hadn't been destroyed. He examined the video case. Easily the most worn of the set. Apparently someone spent time at this farmhouse watching video. This appeared to be a favorite selection.

In the final set of tapes, the cruelty remained intense, but the video stopped with the woman still bound, still alive. But twice, Collier communicated clearly. "We'll be waiting for a friend of mine." And Link could see it. All of it.

He walked into the bright sunlight of the barnyard, wondering whether, ever in his life, fresh air felt so good or tasted so sweet. He contacted Mel Young and asked him to drop by XYZ.

Link started at the front of the death tape. “This is a man who may have died on this farm.”

Mel Young watched the rape scene begin. “What the hell is he doing?”

“Playing the sickest game you’ve ever seen.”

Ten minutes into the video, Mel Young said, “I can’t watch any more of this. Good Lord, that’s somebody’s wife, or mother.”

“You need to see one more thing, Mel.”

Link forwarded to the point he knew well, and hit *PLAY*.

Mel Young recoiled physically. “My God. He killed her. My God…”

“I wanted you to get to know Mr. Collier, or whatever his name is.”

“My God.”

Chapter Forty-Eight

Link spent most of Thursday and the early part of Friday at XYZ. Teams of FBI and local personnel continued the dig. No bodies had been discovered. Sketchy news coverage broke in Columbus media on Friday. A man suspected of murder had been killed in a shootout with federal and local officers. The man's actual identity was not yet known, as he utilized a variety of aliases.

At 2:00 on Friday afternoon, Link entered Jackie's downtown office. She looked the part of a female banking executive, professionally dressed, well spoken. An interesting contrast, he decided, with the woman who had battled Baxter, and had fired three times into Collier's chest.

They talked possible outcomes. Link communicated his highest probability scenario: that Aldrich would attempt to fade away. The violent members of ABC appeared to be B and C. Based on the airline interviews Link had conducted, Aldrich was a fun-loving guy who treated people like gold, especially women. Jackie concurred, completely.

Because some chance existed that Aldrich would contact Sherry or Jackie. Link prepped Jackie on ways to mine a contact for clues about Aldrich's whereabouts—hopefully an aid to the extensive manhunt likely necessary to round him up.

Link summarized with a promise to protect Jackie in the event Aldrich sought a direct encounter. "We'll set up the damndest reception of his life for Mr. Aldrich. So let me know the instant you hear from him."

***

On Friday evening at 6:00 p.m., Ted Aldrich called Sherry Jameson. Ty was downtown, tied up in a sales training seminar that would run all evening. Their children would spend the evening with friends. Sherry wondered whether a premonition had caused her to encourage their sleepovers.

"Sherry, this is Ted. Have you heard any more from the CIA guy?"

"No. He hasn't been in touch at all."

"I thought you were supposed to see him Wednesday."

"I didn't go."

"Why not?"

"Jackie warned me not to. She told me a lot of things, Ted."

"That woman is becoming a giant pain in the ass?"

"I don't understand any of this. I just don't get it."

"Goodbye, Sherry. Thanks for the memories." His voice had turned cold, harsh.

Sherry called Jackie. "He called me just now. I didn't tell him I knew anything about Baker being dead. But he knows you warned me."

"That's okay. Link and I talked about this happening."

"Can I spend the evening with you guys?" Sherry asked. "Ty and the kids are gone. This whole thing is making me nervous."

"Sure, come on over. Matt can practice on his burgers again."

The burgers were decent. The kids were upstairs in their rooms. Sherry, Jackie and Matt were in the family room re-watching *Butch Cassidy and the Sundance Kid.*

The phone rang at 8:15. Jackie answered.

"Jackie. It's Ted Aldrich, calling from Mexico City. Do you know what happened to Don?"

Jackie hesitated, processing. “We should talk about that, Ted.”

“What’s going on?”

She sensed the change. His expression had gone harsh. But she decided to try to draw him out of hiding. “I’d be willing to meet you—in a nice safe place—and tell you all about it.”

“Talk to me, Jackie. Right fucking now.”

A surge of apprehension raced through her as she heard danger in Aldrich’s voice for the first time—a tone that didn’t fit him at all. But she decided to press on. “I’ll meet you in a public—”

“You dumb bitch. Don’t think you can play with me…ever.” And he was gone. Jackie hung up the phone, replaying the conversation in her mind, studying it for clues.

Matt asked, “What was that about?” concern etched on his face.

“It was Aldrich. Link’s hoping to draw him out, and I think I helped. The FBI will handle the dangerous part.”

She called the cell phone number Link Pettigrew had given her. “Hi, Link. Start getting ready to protect me. Aldrich called. He’s in Mexico City, but I think there’s a fairly good chance he’ll come calling.”

“I don’t like it, Jackie. There’s no plan. It’s important to control the trap.”

“It’s done now, Link.”

At the same moment that Jackie hung up the phone, Ted Aldrich drove past the sign that said *Welcome to Dublin, Ohio*. He would handle Jackie Billings for several reasons. Ted had been out of touch with the news, but he knew, even before she tried to set the trap, that Daniel was dead. Through the years, B had never failed to make a rendezvous or complete a mission. The missed callbacks had only one explanation.

Avenging the other's death had been built into their game, whatever the risk or cost. Ted relished the thought. Jackie Billings had destroyed part of his life. Her destruction of Mark Coffey was acceptable. C had become dangerous. But B was a blood brother, in every sense of the word. Ted drove along the tree-lined streets leading toward White Oak Estates. His jaw was set by fury, but part of him wrestled with amazement, a feeling that he was on the wrong end of a colossal reverse con. Daniel Berringer was the shrewdest man he had ever known, and now B was dead. A year ago, Jackie Billings was an innocent broad, blushing about her *Cosmo* article.

But today, her luck ran out. I wonder how long she figures it takes to get here from Mexico City? The law will try to help her, of course. Likely this Pettigrew. She'll call him, of course. Maybe already has. But not nearly soon enough.

Link Pettigrew had received Jackie's call while he sought a couple hours of stress relief in the Regency Theater at the Dublin Mall. He continued watching the movie for no more than thirty seconds and leapt to his feet. Ted Aldrich isn't in Mexico City. It would make sense to Jackie that he's hiding out there, but there's almost no chance. He knows we're looking for him. Mexican authorities have been alerted. He wouldn't fly commercial. He wouldn't have risked flying a small plane across the border. Damn it. I should have thought of this possibility. Damn it.

Pettigrew forced his way past a row of startled moviegoers, raced out of the theater, found his car, and drove furiously toward the Billings home. He called for backup while he drove.

Sherry Jameson had nearly managed to relax. Good food. Good friends. A fun movie. She heard a loud bang as the front door flew open and slammed shut. She heard thunderous steps in the hallway.

She turned to see the man she knew as Ted Adams entering the family room. She jumped to her feet. Matt rose at the same time from the chair across from her. Jackie had disappeared into the garage, getting a round of soft drinks from the second refrigerator. Then Sherry saw the gun. A huge gun. And she saw his eyes, filled with fury. Then the gun again.

He looked directly at her and snarled, "Well, this is a bonus." He raised the pistol, pointing it at her chest. Sherry raised her hands as if hands could stop a bullet. She tried to scream, but nothing came out. And the whole scene suddenly played in slow motion:

Matt shouting, "No, stop." Lunging past her, toward Adams. Matt suddenly directly between her and the gun. The explosion. The acrid smell. Matt falling at her feet, moaning. Adams stepping forward, pointing the gun at Matt's head. Sean appearing from out of nowhere, throwing himself across Adams' arm. Adams pausing, shaken for an instant, flinging Sean sideways against the patio door. Jackie exploding through the door from the garage, carrying a baseball bat, poised to swing. Her scream, shrill, blood-curdling. "No. No. No, you bastard." Adams turning swiftly toward her. Jackie swinging the bat wildly. Another explosion. The crunch of wood on bone. Jackie gasping, turning toward Sherry, her eyes terrified, her face twisted in pain. Jackie falling across Matt's legs. Adams staggering, trying to remain on his feet, raising the gun toward Sherry, his eyes rolling back, Adams falling across the coffee table.

Sherry knelt beside Jackie. Blood was gushing from her side. "Oh, Jesus, Jesus. Help us," she cried. She found a phone and dialed 911, hands trembling violently. "Hurry. To the Billings residence. 4146 Duncan Place. They've been attacked. They've been shot. Hurry. Oh, dear God, hurry."

Sherry found a kitchen towel and pressed it tightly against her friend's side. She couldn't tell how badly Matt was hurt. Sean had peeled off his shirt to hold it against his dad's chest. He was on his knees beside him, talking to him. "You're going to be okay, Dad. Mom, too. Hang in there." Blood was everywhere.

Jodi was suddenly standing in the entryway. "Mommy. Daddy. Sean. What's wrong?"

Link Pettigrew burst into the room and began directing the rescue effort. With one glance at Matt and Jackie, he called for the Life Line helicopter. Sherry held the soaked towel against her friend's side until paramedics forcibly pulled her away.

Chapter Forty-Nine

The story broke in local, then national news. A vicious serial murder ring had been discovered and broken up with the help of a courageous young woman and her family. But she may have paid the highest of prices. She remained in ICU, hovering between life and death. Her husband, who had stepped between a friend and a killer's gun, had been rushed to the same ICU unit, although less critically wounded.

There were non-stop prayer vigils on the hospital lawn, in area churches and beyond. Strangers in cities across the country overwhelmed a makeshift command center at the hospital, calling about her condition, offering prayers and best wishes, filling an entire room with cards and flowers.

On the fourth day, Matt Billings was moved from ICU to a regular room. Two ribs were shattered. The second blocked the bullet's exit, probably saving Sherry Jameson from being wounded or killed. His left lung was perforated. All wounds would heal.

Jackie clung to life. She would have had no chance except for a kitchen towel and skilled work by Lifeline paramedics and ER personnel. Complex internal injuries required nine hours of intricate surgery followed by long days of anxious vigil. Sherry and Mia and Madeline and Ashley and Helen were among those who waited in around-the-clock shifts. Sean Billings cared for his sister and spent as much time at the hospital as possible.

***

Link Pettigrew had remained in Columbus, active at the dig, a regular visitor at the hospital, although he didn't make his presence known. He called Mac McSoley.

"What's the latest?" asked Mac.

"Touch and go. No new word."

"She's tough," said Mac. "She'll make it."

"I've got the dig report," said Link. "As expected, five women. All kinds of indication of torture. Rough stuff, Mac."

"Anything else?"

"About what we expected. How's the political wind blowing?"

"Mac's Team reigns supreme," said McSoley with genuine satisfaction. "This is a helluva moment for us, Link."

"What's the view from upstairs?"

"We're all praying for Mrs. Billings' full recovery."

"Thanks, Mac."

"Thank you, Link."

Link Pettigrew and Mel Young waited in the farmhouse. Prosecutor Trent Hadley would arrive momentarily.

"Where does the Billings woman fit in? asked Sheriff Young. "I kind of need to know."

"A brave volunteer."

"How'd she get involved with these guys?"

"Baxter—actually Berringer—had tried to kill her before. We knew he'd try again if he had a chance."

"Why'd he try to kill her, Link?"

Link Pettigrew made a decision that he knew might change his life, not to mention his pension. He would not con Mel Taylor. "B thought she might have screwed up their game by taking out Collier."

"You reckon she might've?"

"I reckon she might have."

Mel Young took off his hat and hung it on his right knee. "Was she going to have her video taken? Like them other women, I mean?"

"I'd say that was Collier's plan."

"Well hell, that sure seems like self-defense to me."

"Do you think Trent Hadley will agree with you?"

"Ya know, Link. Guys like that will get it all screwed up, if ya let 'em."

Link smiled. "No argument there, Mel."

"I reckon that briefcase was empty?"

"You're a good man, Mel. Thanks."

Link Pettigrew decided to remain quiet and hope for the best. Trent Hadley remained standing in the kitchen doorway. Mel and Link sat on opposite ends of the kitchen table.

"What's the deal with the man's body among the women?" asked Hadley.

"Musta fallen out with this B guy," said Mel Young.

"There's some speculation the decoy lady might have been involved."

"Did you see the burial site, Trent?"

"Yes. It was grisly."

"I couldn't figger any way a little gal coulda got that guy buried under all that gravel, under an old tractor and wagon, beside all them other bones 'n bodies. I didn't figger she coulda even known where all them other bodies were."

Hadley squinted studiously. "That is hard to figure. But there is one other thing, Mel. She didn't seem to have a video in their collection."

Mel Young's normally mellow expression turned dark. "You surely aren't sayin' you wish there'd been one, are you, Hadley?"

"Well, no. Of course not. Just curious why—"

"I couldn't figger that either, Trent. But I'm surely glad there wasn't one. Be honest, now. Aren't you glad, too?"

Trent Hadley looked at the two men. Link couldn't be sure, but he thought there might be some new wisdom in his eyes. "Yes, Mel, I'm glad."

***

Matt Billings occupied the window bed in Riverside Methodist Hospital's room C-14. On the afternoon of the eighth day, aides delivered Jackie to become his roommate. As soon as they were alone, Matt said, "I don't want to sound like a whiner, but loving you has been pretty hard work lately." It was a line he had worked on, hoping and praying he would have a chance to deliver it.

She gave him a weak smile. "I really am sorry about that, Matt. It won't happen again, I promise."

He told a loving fib that carried its own kind of truth. "I've never seen you looking prettier. Welcome back."

They spent as much time as possible with their children. They visited with friends and well-wishers. Late at night they talked quietly, sharing thoughts and memories, as they read the torrent of cards that continued to flow in, some now coming from overseas.

They learned from Lieutenant Trask that Ted Aldrich was in a coma. He would survive, but had suffered major brain damage. He would spend the rest of his life in a nursing home.

On the morning of the ninth day, Jackie said, "I'm going to confess everything."

"Does that make sense?" said Matt. "After all this? There's surely a chance—"

"I finally see what freedom means, Matt. I won't live under the cloud anymore."

"But, can you live in prison?"

"I've thought a lot about that. I hope it doesn't happen. But if it does, I'm going to find a way to write articles or books or make videos. It'll be a way to touch Sean and Jodi. And I think I have things to say to young people, especially young women."

On the afternoon of the ninth day, they received the visitors they had been dreading. Link Pettigrew strolled into their room, dressed casually, looking surprisingly relaxed. He stood at the foot of their beds. Darren McSoley stood in the doorway, wearing the standard dark suit, but also appearing more friendly than official. The sheriff Jackie had met at XYZ stood just behind McSoley. Matt and Jackie had powered their bed-backs to upright. They were wearing matching hospital blue.

Pettigrew smiled warmly. "We're happy to see both of you."

She tried to find her sense of humor. "We're happy to be here…in a way."

He grinned, but turned quickly serious, "The dig is finished at XYZ. It was disturbing in every possible way, even for hardened veterans. We found the body of a man named Mark Eugene Coffey buried with the remains of five women. For a multitude of reasons, we have decided that he deserved to be there."

"Could you tell who killed the women?" asked Jackie.

"It appears that Coffey and Daniel Andrew Berringer, a CIA agent gone bad, were about equally involved."

Jackie looked toward Matt. She could see pain and fear, but she turned back to Pettigrew. "Read me my rights, Link."

Matt remained silent, staring straight ahead.

Mac McSoley walked from the doorway to stand by Pettigrew. "Jackie, Matt, listen carefully. You are national heroes and you deserve to be. Law enforcement is a very complicated business. There are times when fair and right get tangled up in technicalities. None of us wants that to happen."

Jackie had been braced for the worst for months. She didn't grasp his meaning. "I made terrible mistakes. People got hurt. People died."

"We all regret that," said Mac McSoley. "And we all made mistakes. But we don't want to add you or your family to the list of errors."

Finally it registered. "You mean—?"

Link smiled. "Live your lives, guys, and God bless you."

The floodgates broke. First Jackie, then Matt. Pettigrew found Jackie's nightstand Kleenex box and handed it to her. McSoley helped Matt. And the two men walked toward the doorway, stopped to shake the hand of Sheriff Mel Young, and turned into the hospital corridor.

Chapter Fifty

Jackie Billings sat on the stage just to the left of the podium. Laura Geiger was about five minutes away from ending her portion of the program. Jackie would speak for twenty minutes. After that, there would be ten or twenty thousand questions. The questions never stopped. Jackie checked the audience again, at least three or four hundred, mostly women, of course. They would definitely sign some books tonight.

It was always interesting to study the faces. This will be a hard crowd, in a way. Junior League and guests. Sophisticated. Lots of beautiful hair and jewelry. But underneath, there's a lot of anxiety, questions that can't be answered by glitz and glamour and BMWs. Laura Geiger knew it would be this way. Jackie had learned it quickly enough.

Jackie was not exactly tuned into Laura's part of the talk. She had heard it, what, maybe ninety times. It's like the old joke. Where am I tonight? Oh, yes, it's Saturday. I must be in Atlanta. I guess I'm glad Matt was so supportive of these tours, but this is hard work, and I really miss everyone.

Laura is a great speaker. In fact, Laura's great, period. She made house calls for over a month after we got out of the hospital. Never charged us a dime. She really helped put the kids back together again. It was hard helping them believe life could really return to normal. So now I'm in Atlanta on a Saturday night. Hmm. Is this normal? I need to give that some thought. But they know it's only temporary.

Laura's idea for a partnership on the book was great, too. I might have done one on my own, but it couldn't have been as deep;

the blend of theory and real-life experience is what makes it work. Also gives me someone to travel with. It gets lonely out here.

The publicity from all this has been incredible, definitely more than the fifteen minutes of fame we're all supposed to get. The talk shows have been the most interesting. I'm glad we could start with a couple local things for practice. By the time we hit New York and LA and *Oprah* in Chicago it wasn't quite as scary. No, be honest, it was scary.

The newspaper and magazine stuff is easier. Not as much like a high wire with no net. Being in *Cosmopolitan* was a hoot. Talk about life's circles.

Matt has sure avoided the publicity, at least as much as he can. But the business is doing a lot better. He's running it now like Matt Billings should run it, not like he thinks Clancy Billings would have run it. Dr. Laura's a little worried about whether Matt and I might grow apart. I don't think so. We've come too far, and grown too much. Matt Billings is a good man.

Speaking of good men, it's great that Red Sullivan got in touch. Autographing that book was a true privilege. Maybe Red could give Ty Jameson a few lessons on manhood. Sherry will be all right. Ty's another question.

Things are still a little crazy for the kids. Of course Sean has no trouble getting Tara Essinger to go hiking with him anymore. But he's handling his share of the fame just fine. Something like his dad. Almost, "Aw shucks, 'tweren't nothin'." Jodi's ready to quit feeling like a laboratory mouse. She says people are always reading the book or seeing us on TV and asking her a hundred questions about her part. I'm sure all that will settle down, though.

I think Laura and I are doing some real good. You can tell by looking at the faces and hearing the questions that people are struggling. All kinds of people are struggling. Book sales are incredible. That's surely another clue we're on target. The money's nice, too. I don't know how we could've ever paid the hospital bills if we didn't get a break like this. And we could pay back Matt's mom, and Mia for the family vacation she financed after everyone healed up.

It's really nice of Link Pettigrew to help me work out the details of my women's prison program. Laura got a kick out of analyzing that goal. Makes sense to me. It's only by the grace of God I'm not in a prison, or dead. I'm sitting here partly because of a bunch of heartache, much of which I caused. Payback time, Jackie B.

"And now I'd like to introduce my partner…the real reason all of this has been possible…a woman who knows what it means to take charge of her life…a woman who is making a real difference, every day…a woman I am proud to call friend…Jackie Billings."

Okay, here we go again. They're standing. I still can't believe it when they stand up. I wish my dad could see this. But if he hadn't died, I don't think I'd be here. Maybe he can see this.

"Thank you. You're very kind… Thank you… It's an honor to be here. It really is. Atlanta is a beautiful city. Let me tell you a story about a hurting little girl who became a woman having no clue where happiness was hiding. It's a story about stupidity…and pain…and awareness…and growth…and determination…and, sometimes, more pain…. It's a story about being careful where you look for wisdom…. It's a story about faith lost, and faith found…. But most of all, it's a story about love."

A Note from Bill Corbin

Sincere thanks for reading *The Alphabet Affair*.

I invite your to visit *www.BillCorbin.com* to e-discuss your reaction to the book.

Again, thank you.

Bill Corbin